Bright, Freda, 1929-
Decisions

DECISIONS

DECISIONS

FREDA BRIGHT

ST. MARTIN'S PRESS

NEW YORK

"He Wishes for the Cloths of Heaven," reprinted from *The Poems of W. B. Yeats,*
edited by Richard J. Finneran
(New York: Macmillan Publishing Co., 1983).

Design by Manuela Paul

Library of Congress Cataloging in Publication Data

Bright, Freda, 1929–
Decisions.

I.Title.
PS3552.R4625D4   1984   813′.54   84-11750
ISBN 0-312-19016-6

First Edition
10 9 8 7 6 5 4 3 2 1

to

Helene Jackson Berger

PART ONE

PART ONE

CHAPTER ONE

☐ In the bedroom a dresser drawer snapped shut. Then another. And another.

"Hey, honey"—Jordan's voice drifted in to where she stood before the bathroom mirror putting on eye shadow—"you wouldn't happen to know where my gold cufflinks are, would you?"

No, Dasha Croy responded with an impatient shrug. No, she hadn't the foggiest notion where they were and she was half inclined to answer, "Be reasonable." Honestly, she couldn't be expected to keep track of every single item in his life. But her second reaction was a tweak of conscience.

For Jordan *was* being reasonable, and once upon a time (not so very long ago for that matter) she could have laid her hands on the missing cufflinks without a second's hesitation. Why, when they were first married, when the kids were small, she was the world's greatest living expert on Jordan Croy: the state of his wardrobe, the state of his mind, and what he'd had for Monday's lunch.

But that was before.

Before her life divided so sharply into Then and Now. Into Before and After. Come to think of it, it was rather like those home-conversion features you'd see in the Sunday *Times* magazine section, two-page spreads that showed you on the one side a rambling Victorian cottage, on the other a stunning modern architect's showcase: *Before and After.* And you had to look pretty damn hard to recognize the old house in the new —perhaps a ceiling beam salvaged or a marble window sill—or you'd

3

never imagine the two buildings were one and the same. And the one thing they never showed you was the *During*. The actual process of transformation which, when it came right down to it, was by far the most interesting part of the story.

Not that her own transformation had anything to do with appearance. Indeed, the face that looked back at Dasha from the bathroom mirror had hardly changed in ten years. Sure, the laugh lines were a little deeper, but otherwise? The startling green eyes were just as green, the thick dark hair just as dark, and except for the fact that she'd finally gotten around to having her ears pierced, it was pretty much the same bunch of features as Before.

Before she decided to go back to law school. Before she joined the firm of Slater Blaney. Before she was named by *The American Lawyer* as one of the top ten litigators on Wall Street.

Before she lost all track of where her husband's cufflinks might have gone to.

In the old days, in their Washington Heights apartment, the cufflinks would have been lying in the blue leatherette box atop the maple dresser, along with all her jewelry and a pile of quarters for the laundry machine.

For years, they'd been his only good pieces of jewelry. Dasha had given him those cufflinks the day he first hung out his shingle in New York, an eager and bubbly twenty-four-year-old with a pocketful of nothing but dreams. At the time they'd seemed an enormous extravagance, two engraved slices of gold lying in their little blue Tiffany box, and Dasha had borrowed from her brother to pay them off.

"Oh wow!" She could still remember Jordan's expression. "They're beautiful. But much too fancy," he protested, "at least for now. Maybe later when I hit the big bucks."

Nonetheless he'd been enormously pleased and though he didn't wear them to his office (in a low-income, high-crime area), he would pull them out of the blue leatherette box for special occasions—anniversaries, New Year's, the odd theater party—and wear them with a sense of pride and ritual. "My wife gave me these," he'd say, whether or not anybody asked.

But the blue leatherette box was gone now, along with the maple dresser and the hoard of laundry quarters and that tiny crowded bedroom in Washington Heights. Swept away in a floodtide of success. *Her* success, though she was loath to admit it.

And here in this sprawling apartment overlooking Park Avenue, you could easily misplace an elephant, let alone a pair of cufflinks. The Mausoleum, Jordan had taken to calling the place. He'd had misgivings about the move from the start.

"What do we need an East Side address for?" he'd wondered the first time they'd seen it.

"Why not . . . as long as we can afford it?"

"As long as *you* can afford it," he corrected.

"Oh come on, Jordan. My money . . . your money. What's the difference? Did I gripe all those years when you paid the bills single-handed? *Our* money . . . that's what it is."

"You're right, you're right," he conceded. "I'll stop being a male chauvinist pig."

She giggled. "And I'll stop taking in laundry."

In fact, they'd both been suckers for the high ceilings, the sunlit views through gracious windows. And Dasha was ecstatic at the idea of having an honest-to-God dining room for the first time in all their married life. *Quel* posh.

Yet Jordan had never felt truly at home here. He had a way of drifting from room to room with the tentative air of a visitor at a formal house party, reluctant to put his feet up on the sofa or his drink down on a table for fear of being caught out by an officious maid. And now with both kids away at school much of the year, even Dasha admitted the place was probably too large.

All of which was incidental to the question at hand: (a) the finding of cufflinks and (b) the getting of Mr. and Mrs. Jordan Croy off to the Plaza in time for pre-dinner cocktails.

"Have you looked in my jewelry box?" she called out.

"Why should they be in your jewelry box?"

She dabbed on some perfume, then poked her nose into the bedroom.

"Well, where did you see them last, Jordan?"

"If I knew where I saw them last, then I'd know where to look for them."

"Typical lawyer's reasoning." She laughed.

"Well, I'm a typical lawyer, remember?"

With that, he began groping through his socks drawer with an air of desperation—a tall, loose-limbed man on the brink of forty, looking even lankier than usual in jockey shorts and a white dress shirt from which undone French cuffs dangled limply.

"How about those silver ones we got in Acapulco?" she suggested. "I should think those would do as well."

"Nope. Gotta be the gold."

As a rule, Jordan Croy protested any activity that required his wearing a dinner jacket, even worse if he felt obligated to shave twice a day, and it took all Dasha's wiles to get him to the most routine Bar Association function.

"I wear a shirt and tie all day long," he'd howl, "and I'm damned if I'm going to get dressed up like a headwaiter just to talk shop with guys I see every day anyhow."

But tonight he had laid out his clothes with meticulous care, checking the press of his trousers, the gleam of his shirt, for tonight was special.

The occasion was a charity gala for the Haitian refugees and, indeed, all those political fugitives who had fled for their lives to America only to be greeted with the threat of deportation.

From time to time, Jordan handled immigration problems for private clients, and increasingly the system struck him as unjust. "Especially the Haitians," he explained to Dasha. "You know, if they're sent back, they face the firing squad." He almost never took fees from them. And four months ago, with the flat statement that "I want to do something concrete for these people," he'd formed an action committee, written letters, organized mailings for the fund drive that would culminate tonight at the Plaza.

Yet in a sense, he was doing something concrete for himself. For the first time in years, he was reactivating his life, striving to move out into a world that was larger, more vibrant than the modest law office on Columbus Avenue with the gold-and-black lettering on the window.

And Dasha, knowing how much Jordan had put into the effort, was determined that nothing should spoil his evening. It would be his night, his triumph, and she would keep a low profile. If anyone asked, she'd introduce herself as Mrs. Jordan Croy and nothing more. Jordan could be quite sensitive about that sort of thing.

In any event, it seemed unlikely that they'd be running into people she dealt with professionally, for as Jordan had remarked on numerous occasions, raising money for impoverished Haitians or persecuted Bahais was hardly the number one priority for the corporate honchos down on Wall Street.

She and her husband might share the same bed, the same profession even—but no question, they inhabited different lives.

Leaving him to his quest, she went to her closet and after a brief tour of inspection pulled out a long sinuous shaft of *coupe de velours,* the color of pomegranates.

"What do you think, Jordan?" She held the slither in front of her.

He paused to look at his wife, her dress with a gaze of frank admiration. "You'll look like a duchess. Knock 'em dead, Dasha."

She put down the dress and came over and kissed him. "Come on, darling. Let's look for your cufflinks together."

Within minutes cufflinks were found, zippers zipped, bow ties straightened, sandal straps adjusted, and as she stood before the pier glass mirror for a last quick inventory, he stepped behind her and placed his hands on her bare shoulders.

"Not bad for an old married couple." He grinned at their reflections. Two tall, handsome people, momentarily elegant in evening wear, with the gloss of sleek and healthy thoroughbreds.

She rubbed her cheek against his hand. "Not bad at all!" It was going to be a super evening.

The Plaza was packed by the time they arrived, the turnout even bigger than anticipated. Not the usual society-page glitter either, but *real* people: prominent journalists, artists, leading intellectuals, top academics. You couldn't walk two feet without bumping into a living paragraph from *Who's Who.*

As for Jordan, he was on the threshold of paradise. "That's what I like to see"—he squeezed Dasha's hand—"good people showing up for a good cause. My bet is we'll raise a fortune. Come on, babe, I'll introduce you to . . . "

There was this acquaintance, that one, the men and women who'd been his co-workers on the committee, none of whom Dasha knew. There was champagne to be sipped, canapés to be nibbled, and for a convivial half-hour Jordan basked in well-earned praise while Dasha smiled and shook hands, crooned "very pleased to meet you." She couldn't remember the last time she'd seen her husband so glowing, so utterly confident and in command.

Across the room a large rosy man with a red carnation in his lapel appeared to be beaming at them with the spark of recognition. Jordan nudged her. "You know who that is over there? Senator Mahoney."

Dasha nodded. Who wouldn't recognize the peppery chairman of the Senate Civil Rights Committee, especially when he happened to be your husband's idol? "And what's more," Jordan whispered delightedly, "he's heading our way." Reflexively Jordan reached to straighten his tie.

And sure enough, the great man was wriggling his way through the crowd, belly first, handshake at the ready. In a purposeful stride he swept past well-wishers, past constituents, past Jordan's smiling and expectant face, to grasp Dasha's hand and bury it in a powerful campaigner's grip.

"You!" he wheezed.

"Me?" Dasha blinked with incomprehension. She only knew the man from watching the seven o'clock news.

"Yes, you. You've been pointed out to me as the attorney who argued the Kim case before the Supreme Court. You *are* Dasha Croy, aren't you?"

She flushed with embarrassment. "Yes," she murmured. "But it was just . . ."

"Don't you tell me that it was just . . ." the senator's voice boomed as though through a mike, "because I'll tell *you*. It was just the most significant freedom-of-the-press case since Ellsberg and the Pentagon Papers, and your argument was simply superb. I thought it was about time that you met one of your most enthusiastic admirers."

"How very nice!" She slid her hand out from his grasp. "And it's a mutual admiration society. Both my husband and I are terrific fans of yours, Senator. Jordan darling . . ." She swiveled to effect introductions, but Jordan had vanished and she found herself talking to vacant space. Impossible! How could he have disappeared so suddenly? With an effort, she repressed a ripple of anger. "I'm sorry." She turned back to the senator. "He must have stepped away for a moment. Such a pity. I know he's always wanted to meet you."

She would have gone off in pursuit of Jordan, but the great man continued to hold her captive, plying her with questions. How did it feel to argue a landmark case before the Supreme Court? Did she think there'd be a decision this term? And could she venture a guess as to its outcome? "It's always interesting," the senator pontificated, "when you get two constitutional issues locking horns . . . the right to privacy and the public's right to know."

"Yes yes yes," Dasha murmured. At any other time she would have been flattered, but now she was only aching to get away and find Jordan in hopes of salvaging the rest of the evening. It was another five minutes before the senator released her and she began looking for Jordan in earnest. First the lounge, then the banquet hall. She tipped a waiter ten dollars to page him in the men's room, but by that time she was certain Jordan had gone. Without so much as a by-your-leave, he had abandoned her in a room full of strangers, and all because of a harmless remark by the senator. Why did Jordan do this to her time and again—make her feel guilty for situations beyond her control? As if she had somehow set him up to mow him down?

But that wasn't the case at all. In fact, it was *he* who had humiliated *her* tonight, walking out like that. Well, if Jordan thought she was going to sit around all evening at a banquet table, making small talk to an empty chair . . . no way! It wasn't even as though she'd wanted to come in the first place. She would have been perfectly content staying home for once, maybe watching an old movie or catching up on some work—there was always plenty of *that* around. Okay, then home was where she'd go.

She went to the coatroom feeling half-naked and vulnerable. A woman in a décolleté evening gown shouldn't have to fetch her own coat. Or find her own cab. The whole episode was infuriating. She was halfway out the lobby when she spotted his long familiar legs curled around a bar stool in the Oak Bar. The *fair* thing, really, would be to stalk out without a word as he had done ten minutes earlier. Quid pro quo. But the sight of him sitting at the bar, chin in hand, morosely nursing a scotch, turned her resolution into another round of guilt.

What the hell. It had been his evening and she had robbed him of it. Inadvertently, to be sure, but the end result was just the same. With a sigh, she went in and slid onto the stool beside him.

"I was hunting for you all over, Jordan. How come the vanishing act?"

He didn't look up.

"What'll you have, Dasha? White wine, scotch? Bartender, another Dewar's on the rocks, please."

"You haven't answered my question."

"Well, my dear"—he studied the ice in the glass—"I really wasn't interested in hearing the thousandth instant replay of big bad Kim versus FBC. Can a simple housewife from New York City win the hearts and minds of the Supreme Court? Listen in tomorrow for the next exciting installment of *Dasha Faces Life.* I know the script by heart, remember?"

For a moment she was too stunned to reply.

"In fact we hardly discussed the case, and the senator would have very much liked to meet you."

"Oh yeah . . . sure."

They sipped their drinks in silence, until Dasha finally said, "If you'd rather not be civil, Jordan, then I may as well go on home."

"As you please. I'll get a cab, or would you rather I called for a limousine? That's more your style these days."

"Oh, come off it, will you?" She got up to leave, but he put out a restraining hand. "I'm sorry, honey. I don't know what came over me. Please, sit down and have another drink. As a matter of fact, I've been wanting to talk—about the Kim case, no less. Surprised? I've been giving it a great deal of thought lately. You, me, the case. And what I want to say is"—he swung round to face her, his eyes preternaturally bright— "it's only a lawsuit. That's all, simply another interminable lawsuit. A couple of grubby millionaires in a mud-slinging contest. I know you've been working on it for three years solid but you're losing all perspective, Dasha, letting this thing run our lives."

Was that the whiskey talking, she wondered, or merely sour grapes? But he continued reasonably enough. "You know what they say in law school, you win some, you lose some. And if you lose, it's not the end of the world. Anyhow"—he laughed briskly—"whatever the outcome, you'll get what you want. You'll have earned yourself a place in the law books."

"But what kind of place, Jordan?" She tried to lighten her tone. "As the lawyer who bungled the biggest damages suit in history?"

"Well, you'd leave your mark in the annals of justice. A footnote, anyway." The idea struck Jordan as funny. Ridicule had lately become his defense against her success. "What you lack here, Dasha, is the wide-angle view. Say the Supreme Court mows you down, the worst that'll happen is that you'll get this year's Edsel Award and a job in the company mailroom."

"I'm glad you can joke about it," she said tartly.

"Some joke!" His voice acquired a dangerous tremor. "You think it's a joke that we haven't had one peaceful weekend in the last three years, thanks to this fucking case? That's not my idea of fun and games, and I'm sick of it. Fed up to the teeth with the midnight phone calls, the goddam reporters, you bouncing around the country like some politician on the campaign trail. Okay, you think the worst that can happen is you lose in court—all that work wasted. But what worries me, Dasha, really scares me, is what's going to happen if you win."

"Why, I'll be vindicated, that's what."

"Vindicated!" he snapped. "Oh, you'll be more than vindicated. You'll be a heroine. And where do I fit into this, I ask you. Resident cheerleader? Am I supposed to stay home and watch you on the Phil Donahue Show? Or climb into my monkey suit and eat creamed chicken while you speechify at legal conventions?" And before she could protest, he hurried on: "Because if you win, Dasha, there'll be no stopping you. You can walk away with the firm."

"Now who's exaggerating! As you were saying, it's just a lawsuit, and even if I do come out on top . . . well, Slater Blaney has never had a senior partner under forty, let alone a woman."

"Right. Then you'll be the first. Another first in the Dasha Croy saga. The big corner office, the company Rolls, plus a few million bucks for good measure. Jesus, I won't be able to get past your secretary. 'Sorry' "—he mimicked Frannie Rosen's singsong voice—" 'Mrs. Croy is in conference with God right now, but if you leave your name, I'll see she gets the message.' "

"Oh really, Jordan!" Despite everything, he retained the capacity to make Dasha laugh, above all at herself. "You're being perfectly outrageous, and anyhow, I don't think the opportunity will arise—not for another year anyhow."

"And if it does?"

"If they offer me a senior partnership . . . My God!" She stopped short. It was the kind of thing you dreamed about in law school—if you dared. The kind of thing he had dreamed of, when he was at the height of his dreaming days. "Watch my dust," he had told her then. "Just you watch my dust." Now, reluctant to meet his eyes, she turned away. "I don't know. I would have to do some long hard thinking. It's all too iffy . . . "

"But *I* know, Dasha, because I know you. Sooner or later they'll make the offer and you'll accept it. You will indeed. You've never once turned down a chance for advancement, and you sure as hell wouldn't turn down this one. That much I know. The only thing I don't know" —he sucked in his breath—"is if I can cope with being married to the First Lady of the blue-chip bar. Let's hope it never comes to that."

She stared at him in wild disbelief. "Do you realize what you're saying, Jordan? That you actually want me to lose? I find that incredible. Dammit, I've invested three years of my life in this case . . . "

"And I've invested over fifteen in our marriage."

"So have I," she shot back, but his words had a chastening effect. "And most of 'em were pretty good by any standard. I grant you we've been going through a bad patch lately, but there's nothing that can't be worked out."

He considered, shook his head, then raised his eyes to her. He was pale as death.

"You're killing me, Dasha."

"What!"

"You're killing me. You're eating me alive. You don't mean to, and sometimes I don't think you're even aware of it, but that's what it all comes down to. No. No, I won't go back upstairs with you. I don't think I can even go on living with you much longer." He slipped a twenty-dollar bill under his half-empty glass. "Very well. Let's talk it out. Let's go back to the Mausoleum and talk it through once and for all."

She followed him out of the bar without a word. Ten minutes later they were home.

To call it a talk would have been an injustice.

It was a marathon—spilling through the night into the dawn and on into the daylight hours of Sunday.

Yet it began simply enough with Jordan, arms folded, sitting on a straight-back chair in the living room, saying: "In the first place, I love you very much."

It was a simple statement, uttered without fuss or drama—and Dasha's heart turned over at the words.

He's going to leave me. My husband is going to leave me.

It was too formal a declaration, too clearly a setting of the scene. If you were happily married, you didn't need that "In the first place" at all. There would be no conditions, no sequences to be ticked off in numerical order. The mere words "I love you" would have sufficed.

Dasha held her breath and waited for the second shoe to drop. But Jordan didn't continue. Instead, he fell to an intent study of the pattern in the carpet. And when he spoke next, his tone was thoughtful.

"I guess," he said, "by any reasonable yardstick, I'd be considered a successful man. I imagine a lot of people envy me. Why not? I'm in the prime of life, enjoy excellent health. I've been privileged with a superior education. I've got a lovely wife, two terrific kids whom I miss like crazy, but that's beside the point. Last year, I earned forty-seven thousand two hundred dollars, all of which I duly reported to the IRS. Not a fortune these days, mind you, but still substantial. Enough, I should think, to place me up there in . . . what? Let's say the top ten percent income bracket in America. I earn more than most tenured professors or research chemists or members of the New York Philharmonic, all of whom are considered distinguished and successful people. Not bad for a guy who started out with beans. Okay, okay"—he held up a hand to fend off interruption, but Dasha had no intention of breaking in. It was a summing up, she realized, a basic self-inventory, as if he felt compelled to justify himself. But to whom?

Jordan cleared his throat. "As you would be the first to say, Dasha, money is not the proper measure of success. Mozart died broke, after all. Rembrandt, too, I believe. But you could hardly call them failures. On the other hand, who would want to live and die like Howard Hughes? So let's leave money out of it for the time being and look at other aspects. Professionally. Well, I don't want to blow my own horn, but I would say I'm a fairly successful guy. I have a good reputation among my clients. In fact, most of 'em think I'm pretty hot stuff. It's Mr. Croy this, and Mr. Croy that. Granted, they're not the most sophisticated people in the world, my clients, not bankers or international tycoons. But the point is I've earned their trust and their respect legitimately. And it is goddam nice to be looked up to now and then, as you well know. So"—he drew a deep breath—"I think we're agreed that, by any normal standard, I've enjoyed both financial and professional success. How about the domestic front? How am I doing as a husband and a father?"

It was a rhetorical question, and Dasha made no attempt to reply.

"Yeah. . . ." He nodded slowly. "I would say on the whole I've been a successful family man. I've worked hard. I've provided. My family always came first. I've never screwed around, although I've been tempted as often as the next guy. But to me it was never worth the risk, because the only thing that ever mattered"—suddenly his voice broke—"was that my family should be happy. *That,* to me, was real success. And when my wife decides, at age thirty, she wants to go back and finish law school —Jesus, I was proud of her."

Dasha's throat tensed. Here it was after all. *In the second place.*

"So proud."

He raised his eyes to hers, and now his words were no longer rhetorical, but a merciless laying bare of his inmost feelings. "Yes, I was, Dasha. It meant a great deal to me that you were pulling out of your shell, that you decided to venture out and do something with your gifts. You think I don't know how much courage it took? And the day you got the offer to join Slater Blaney, I was over the moon. I couldn't wait to tell everybody that my wife, the Dasha everyone knew and took for granted, was asked to join the best goddam law firm in New York. Other guys' wives taught school or did bookkeeping, but mine was going to be an associate at Slater Blaney."

Jordan remembered the day well. He'd had to go up to White Plains to handle a mortgage, and when the formalities were over, he and the other lawyer had gone out for lunch.

"What do you think, Frank?" Jordan poured out the story of Dasha's coup. "You know, they hired only four associates out of maybe five hundred applicants, and my wife was the first one they picked. That's something, isn't it?"

"If it were my wife," Frank Shea had replied, "Jesus . . . I'd be jealous as hell!"

"Come on, Frank. That's infantile."

"So sue me. I'm infantile. Look, I'm not telling you how I *should* feel in those circumstances. I'm telling you how I *would* feel. I got to hand it to you"—and he gave a good-natured shrug—"you're a bigger man than I am, Jordan Croy."

And in his heart of hearts, Jordan had believed that he was.

"You know, Dasha"—he scrutinized the memory a bit longer, before putting it aside—"I sometimes wonder if that wasn't the basis of my pride in you. Maybe I was even prouder of myself. Because every time you accomplished something big, I was proving what a great guy I was, how generous, unselfish. None of the run-of-the-mill chauvinist hang-ups for yours truly. Because I had done it too, you see. And yet . . . " He paused in his self-examination. "And yet it strikes me now that maybe I was patronizing you. It was always at the back of my mind that the situation would remain: me, the established, experienced lawyer, and you, the bushy-tailed novice. You'd look up to me, ask me for advice. I guess that's what I expected. And even when our careers were fifty-fifty, it was okay between us, Dasha. But the truth is—I never expected you to go so far so fast."

"But what difference does it make?" Dasha pleaded. "It's not as if we're in competition. Oh God, darling, only minutes ago you were saying that by all reasonable criteria, you're a successful man."

"Oh yes," he burst out, "I can tell myself that story day in, day out and almost come to believe it. But the fact is when I'm with you, Dasha" —his eyes were bright with despair—"I feel like a goddam fucking failure!"

"Don't say that!" She ran to put her arms around him. "It's not true. You know it's not true."

"Don't tell me what's true or not true, Dasha"—he pulled away from her grip. "I'm not talking about logic, I'm talking about feelings. I *hate* it when people ask me, 'Are you her husband?' and that becomes my only identity. I feel like a pimp, an adjunct. I hate the people you deal with, your hotshot new friends, the driving competitive world you live in. I hate the way they look down their noses at me as if I'm not quite sharp enough, not quite tough enough to play their brand of Big League hardball.

"I feel their contempt, Dasha. And sometimes I feel yours. I even feel it from the children. Every now and then I see that look in their eyes that says, 'Mom's the one with the power, the clout.' It never used to be that way."

15

"Oh, Jordan." She burst into tears. "What is it you want? We can't turn back the clock."

"I want you to remember what we had."

But she was afraid to give herself over to memory, for one false step would plunge her back into those blank, mindless years—pleasant enough in their way but unrepeatable in light of who she was now.

"We're lawyers." She mustered a painful smile. "We're supposed to be able to negotiate anything. Let's hear your terms and go on from there."

"There's only one, Dasha. If you've ever loved me . . . "

"I've always loved you . . . "

"Then Monday morning you'll go to the office and hand in your notice."

She turned ashen. "You promised you'd never ask that of me."

"Promises. We've made a lot of solemn promises over the years. We promised to love and honor. We promised for better or worse, till death us do part. Forsaking all others—that was part of it, too. Well, I've done my damnedest to live up to those promises, but there's a limit." He sucked in his breath, his voice dropping to a whisper. "Not everything in life is negotiable."

They talked. For nearly twenty-four hours they talked. It was a compendium of feelings—now rational, now tearful; now angry, now honest. A balance sheet of old hurts and new grievances. A journey full of promising detours and abrupt dead ends. And ultimately, it was a draw.

For despite all evidence of good intentions—the empty coffee cups and overflowing ashtrays, the crumpled tissues strewn through the place —nothing had been resolved. Toward evening on Sunday, Jordan threw in the sponge.

"That's it. *Fini.* I've said my piece. The next move is up to you." He rubbed his hand gingerly against his cheek. "Boy, do I need a shave. And you know something else? I'm starved. Shit, honey, we haven't eaten in twenty-four hours. What do you say I send out for Chinese?" He loped to the phone and began calling in the order. "The beef with black bean sauce, a double order of spareribs . . . "

Some butterfly shrimp, she said mentally.

"Some of your butterfly shrimp, the usual rice and stuff and, oh yeah, go easy on the MSG!"

Dasha blew her nose and laughed. They knew each other's tastes so thoroughly, and who but Jordan would think to remember that monosodium glutomate made her sneeze? For that matter, who but Dasha would know that boysenberries made him break out in hives. No question, they knew pretty much everything about each other—allergies, ticklish spots, favorite shades of red, sizes in belts and gloves and underwear. Two people who had spent their adult lives gathering bits of information that could be of no possible interest to anyone else in the world.

"What's so funny?" Jordan hung up the phone. "I know, don't tell me. I ordered enough for an army, right?"

"I guess I always say that, don't I?"

"Yup. And we always eat it, don't we?"

She found a peculiar comfort in the utter banality of the exchange, familiar words that fitted like old sneakers. "Truce?" She smiled, and he nodded.

They ate in the kitchen on a bare wooden table, spooning food out of cardboard cartons in half-conscious repetition of the time when they were first married, and takeout Chinese had been their Sunday night treat. The one day of the week without dishes.

"Yessir . . . that was just what I needed." Dasha licked her fingers, then began rooting about in the brown paper bag. There was extra soy sauce, another packet of noodles, but "You know what? They forgot to put in the fortune cookies. Think we ought to ask for our money back?"

He didn't respond, merely sat there building a log cabin out of sparerib bones with an increasingly bemused expression.

"Tomorrow," he said finally. "Tomorrow you tell me my fortune."

"But I . . . "

"Yes or no, Dasha. A simple yes or no."

When she entered her office on Monday morning, she was no closer to a decision.

And the ultimate irony was that she had never set out to be a lawyer. The only thing she had ever wanted to be was a perfect wife for Jordan Croy.

CHAPTER TWO

☐ "We can't all be chiefs," her mother used to say. "There have to be Indians, too."

Theirs was a household equally divided between chiefs and Indians (or—to put it otherwise—between male and female), with the chiefest unquestionably Maxim Oborin.

Dasha's father had been born in what he would always think of, Russian Revolution or no, as St. Petersburg. For generations, his family had been court musicians to the czar, and as a child he too had shown prodigious talent on the violin. But with the fall of the Romanovs and the ensuing civil wars, his hopes of making a career in his native land were dashed and instead he fled, hardly more than a boy, to the more hospitable shores of America. He arrived at Ellis Island bearing nothing but a single suitcase and his Guadagnini, confident nonetheless that a brilliant future awaited him. The streets, he had heard, were paved with gold. To his chagrin, however, he discovered that they were more densely paved with scores of other Russian émigrés, fiddles in hand, all sharing the same improbable dream.

For more than ten heroic years, he pounded on managers' doors, did battle with boardinghouse landladies, scrounged recording dates and students wherever he could, before settling down—a chastened and greatly disappointed man—as assistant concert master to the Boston Symphony Orchestra. In his own mind, he had suffered a monstrous defeat; yet as orchestras go, the post was decidedly a plum. For it enjoyed a unique status among the Brahmins as a prestigious institution, as much a part of the local establishment as Harvard or the State Street banks. Before long, Max, with his striking presence, his Nijinsky face and melodious Russian accent, was cutting a dramatic figure in the musical salons of Beacon Hill. It was in one such parlor that he kissed the hand and promptly won the heart of Miss Harriet Whittaker.

She was a slight, shy woman, overly well bred, with a distinct talent for self-abnegation. At twenty-five, she already felt the dead hand of spinsterhood upon her, had resigned herself with secret sighs to a life of afternoon teas with the other "ladies" and long empty evenings over crewelwork. And then came Max—Max with his broad cheekbones and white silk scarf and black Sobranie cigarettes. More than a man, an artist, for whom it would be a privilege to suffer and sacrifice! In her eyes, he epitomized all that was brave and hot-blooded, a romantic alternative to the pallid future that otherwise loomed ahead.

Her parents were horrified. Inviting musicians to dinner was one thing, having them marry into the family quite another. But Harriet, looking from her boiled-fish father to her cold-potato mother to the dry and sexless ancestors on the wall, knew better. She married Max without further ado. "I gave up everything for my husband," she would say repeatedly. It was a boast, not a complaint. From the day they married to the day she died, she devoted herself utterly to the furtherance of her husband's comforts—sorting his socks, emptying his ashtrays, learning to cook borscht and pelmeny—and feeling grateful for the privilege. Max, too, was content. In the land of the free, he had found himself a slave.

It was an unlikely union but a happy one, made happier still within a year of their marriage by the birth of a son, Alexander. By all rights, Max should have been the most satisfied of men. His colleagues respected him, his students feared him, his wife worshipped him. He had a comfortable home in one of Boston's prettiest suburbs, a charming cottage in Tanglewood. Yet he continued to be haunted by a sense of loss.

When the great violinists came to solo with the orchestra, he would watch them lynx-eyed from behind his music stand, and in his mouth there was the taste of bile.

There they stood in the limelight—Heifetz, Elman, Millstein, Stern —all Russians like himself. All products of the same schools, the same masters. On those occasions he would come home moody and black-browed, and Harriet, who recognized his anguish without truly comprehending its provenance, would offer comfort by saying: "I thought Heifetz sounded a bit scratchy this evening." Max appreciated her loyalty; at the same time he would dismiss her judgment contemptuously. "My dear, you know nothing about music." He was honest enough as an artist to concede that Heifetz had played superbly, far better than Max himself ever could or would. And that hurt even more.

Nonetheless Max had one great consolation. Let the Heifetzes of this world enjoy their fame. Was there even one among them who could boast a son like Alex? Surely not.

Almost from birth it was apparent the boy was a genius. By the time he was one, he was talking fluently; by five, he was chattering in Russian and French as well. At the age when other boys were grappling with their multiplication tables, Alex could figure square roots in his head, name not merely the capitals, but the official flowers and birds and mottoes of every state in the union, reel off great dates in history or Red Sox batting averages with equal aplomb, recreate move by move the tournament chess games of Alekhine and Capablanca. He had a memory like blotting paper, capable of absorbing trivia or philosophical niceties with undifferentiated ease.

He dazzled his teachers. "Another Einstein," they would burble. "A walking encyclopedia." Or, "President—that boy could grow up to be President." All of which, to Max's ears, was music far sweeter than Mozart. Handling Alex, grooming him for greatness became the principal goal in family life. Max charted a prestigious path for his son: Choate, Harvard naturally, then Oxford or the Sorbonne—after which Alex would be loosed upon the world. The name Oborin would leave its imprint on America yet.

"Alexander the Great," his awestruck mother called him, while his classmates referred to him, with a good deal less affection, as "The Little Czar."

Alex was ten when, almost as an afterthought, a second child was born to the Oborins. "Only a girl," as Max put it, "but a pretty little thing." She was christened Darya, after her paternal grandmother, called Dasha from the start, and casually scouted to see if she too bore those gifts so abundantly bestowed upon her brother.

She did not.

"Why, the child isn't even particularly musical," Max conceded with a puzzled air. "Not that it matters. She'll grow up and get married. Those big green eyes . . . who could resist?"

In fact, he was enchanted with her, quite satisfied that his daughter, for whom he had an endless litany of pet names and diminutives, was neither more nor less than what she appeared. Women, Max firmly believed, were put on earth to please men, and Dasha pleased him very much.

She was indeed a pretty thing, having inherited her father's high coloring, his Slavic cheekbones, and also a good deal of his passionate temperament. The last, however, was a mixed blessing, something to be curbed rather than encouraged, and she learned early on where she stood in the family firmament. Power was a male prerogative; it was the natural order of things. As for mental prowess, it was clearly an encumbrance that would hamper her progress toward the altar and eventual happiness.

In this matter, as in everything else, Max was an effective teacher. With the exception of sopranos and ballerinas, her father saw no purpose served by women entering the professions or flexing their intellect. They would succeed only in making themselves and the men in their lives miserable. Suppleness, pliancy: Those were the qualities to be treasured in a woman, ideally combined with a measure of elegance. For although a reasonably faithful husband, he nonetheless considered himself a connoisseur of beauty, quick to beam his approval whenever a pretty woman caught his notice.

In this area, Dasha felt she could pass muster. There were the large green eyes, the artless smile, above all, the heavy dark hair that hung waist-length, uncut from one year to another.

"Such hair!" Her father would take a thickness of it in his hands and rub the strands between his fingertips. "Such beautiful hair. Like the finest Russian crown sable."

Then Dasha would smile and purr, and quietly recognize the time was ripe to wheedle an extra helping of ice cream or lay the groundwork for a new bicycle. For if Alex could achieve his aims through intellectual glitter and the winning of scholarships, Dasha, too, was possessed of indigenous weapons. And she was quite clever enough to realize their value.

In Max's eyes, the family was now ideal. He had fathered a brilliant son and a pretty daughter; the one to be admired, the other to be adored.

Should an outsider comment on occasion that Dasha gave evidence of being a bright and spirited girl as well, he would shrug and remark, "She's as bright as she has to be."

Harriet was equally satisfied. "One prodigy in the family is quite enough." By Dasha's reckoning, it was one too many, for it was the nature of Alex's brilliance that he would eclipse all lesser light, and Dasha never felt at ease in his presence.

When Alex entered Harvard still shy of fifteen, she was making mudpies in kindergarten. When he sailed off to Oxford to take up his Rhodes scholarship, her sigh of relief was mixed with envy and resentment. And when in his early twenties he electrified the diplomatic community with his prophetic *Post Stalinism and the Politics of Cold War,* a text that was to lay the cornerstone of American foreign policy for some years to come, Dasha was struggling with the throes of adolescence.

At fourteen, she had fallen in love madly and vicariously with everything and everyone French. The unwitting instrument of this infatuation was a postcard Alex had sent her from Paris. "This is it, kiddo. *La vie de bohème,"* ran the message. The picture was a street scene in Montmartre—cafés, cobblestones, mansard roofs—that spoke of a particularly Gallic *joie de vivre.*

Dasha papered over her room with photos of Belmondo and Gérard Philippe, and giant posters of Yves Montand. She made a point of mastering the intricacies of past and present subjunctives, the only person in her class to do so. All of which won her a resounding A in sophomore French, but did little more than elicit raised eyebrows from her parents.

It was a phase, they recognized, and if left uncatered to, would surely pass.

Thus when Alex came to spend a weekend in Boston, Dasha found herself actually looking forward to the reunion. She would ask endless questions about Parisian high society, astound him with her grasp of the language, and provide herself with more fuel for her fantasies.

That night at dinnertime, Alex did indeed bring up the subject of his sojourn in France, although his discourse was more in the nature of a lecture than a casual give-and-take. For twenty minutes he indulged in a detailed analysis of the French political system, while Dasha was aching to hear about movies and music and clothes. When he mentioned the name De Gaulle, she felt empowered to join the conversation. The French general had always struck her as a grand and imposing figure, and there was Alex poking sly fun at him.

"In my opinion," Dasha broke in, but she never got to finish her sentence.

"Your opinion!" Max burst out laughing. "We're talking politics, Dashenka, not hair ribbons. Young girls don't have 'opinions.' As you were saying, Alex," and he turned to her brother.

She sat there stunned for a minute, then excusing herself in a low voice slipped out of the room barely noticed. In her mother's sewing box lay a pair of jagged-edged pinking shears, strong enough to cut through the heaviest wool. Dasha took them, stepped into the bathroom half-dazed. *In my opinion*—the words kept running through her mind; then with a few swift strokes she hacked off her hair at the ear-line. Ten years of Max's beloved "Russian crown sable" wafted to the floor, dark and feathery against the cold white tiles. In the mirror, a hideous and mutilated stranger gazed at Dasha. Dreamlike she shook her head and returned to the dining room. Her mother was pouring coffee into little gold-lipped Wedgwood cups. Max was the first to see her.

"My God!" He jumped to his feet amid the clatter of overturned china. "My God, Dasha, what have you done?"

She wet her lips.

"In my opinion . . . " she began, desperate to complete the thought, but the words refused to come. For indeed, what was there she *could* say, about De Gaulle, about French politics, about anything in the world that could conceivably be of interest to others? "What have you done, Dashenka?"

Her father's words shocked her into awareness, and now she could only see his horrified expression, her mother's anguished disbelief. Her hands flew to her hair. It felt coarse and prickly as steel wool. What *had* she done? She had destroyed her beauty, and to what end? So that she might have her father's ear? Catch her brother's eye?

And to Max's agonized "Why, Dasha—why?" she could only weep, "I don't know."

She lay awake all that night distraught and confused. Had she committed this outrage merely to get attention or to wound her father? Only long after did she come to see in that gesture a futile, but nonetheless profound desire to prove that she was in charge of her life, in control of—at the very least—that most negligible aspect of her person, her hair.

The incident was never again referred to in the family, threatening, as it did, to lead them all into dangerous waters. The following morning her mother took Dasha, head swathed in a kerchief, to Best's, where an elderly hairdresser managed to repair the worst of the damage. "Very nice." He fluffed out the boyish new cut as best he could. "Very . . . you know, *gamine*. Kind of like Jean Seberg in that French picture, *Breathless.*"

Thus ended Dasha's outbreak of adolescent revolt, and a few months later she was absorbed in matters closer to home than her Parisian fantasies. Boys liked her. They were always flirting, calling up, buzzing around the house. And she discovered that with the right balance of smiles and deference, learned from her mother, she could have her pick and it would be but a matter of time until she settled upon one nice young man and got married. That life offered alternative courses, that a girl could remain single and still hold her head up in a crowd, was beyond her comprehension. Marriage was freedom, independence, success. Every house on the street taught the same lesson.

By the time she was a senior in high school, she had the particulars all mapped out: the Gorham silver, the bridesmaids' dresses, the French Provincial furniture culled from the pages of *Better Homes.* Her father had once promised her a wedding reception at the Ritz Carlton and now, with some of her girlfriends already engaged, she began to build upon the image. In her mind's eye, she envisioned the rounds of surprise parties, linen showers and luncheons, the invitations on creamy white bond and that magnificent moment when she entered the grand ballroom on her father's arm trailing yards of white satin. The big decision was where to throw the bouquet. For once in her life, everybody's eyes would be upon her—admiring, approving. Her picture would appear in the Sunday *Globe,* "photograph by Bachrach," and her name—her new name—in print. And no one would ever ask again, "Are you related to Alexander Oborin?"

Yet in this as in everything else, her brother managed to steal her thunder.

In 1961, Alex Oborin had been summoned to Washington at the President's bequest, the youngest and the brashest of the Harvard Mafia surrounding John F. Kennedy. Within a year, he consolidated his establishment status by marrying the daughter of a distinguished Southern senator. The wedding was a gala affair—flashbulbs popping, reporters gathered all around. Half of official Washington had turned out—"the half that counts," Alex noted smugly—and the President himself was best man. Max was in heaven. He had been photographed clinking champagne glasses with Jackie Kennedy, shaking hands with the President: souvenirs that would decorate his studio wall for years to come. Had ever a son so amply repaid a father with happiness?

"Well, Dasha, it will be your turn one of these days"—he patted his daughter's hand on the return trip to Boston—"although there's no rush about it, absolutely no rush at all." And Dasha had brooded all the way home.

Clearly there were events and EVENTS, and suddenly her Ritz Carlton fantasy paled into insignificance. The mere act of marriage was not enough, she realized. It was who you married that conferred importance. She too had been struck by her brief exposure to Mrs. Kennedy, and that night studied herself closely in her bedroom mirror. There was, she fancied, a resemblance to the President's wife: the dark hair, the wide-spaced eyes, the vivid coloring. But far more striking than any surface similarity was one profound difference.

When Mrs. Kennedy talked, everyone listened. Even if she said nothing more earth-shaking than "Please pass the salt," she was accorded respect and attention. She was a somebody, Dasha concluded, because she had married a somebody. A woman wrapped in her husband's power, endowed with his charismatic glow.

Very well then. Dasha too would marry a somebody. She would capture the heart of some future ambassador, some potential captain of industry, someone to whom even Alex would have to kowtow. It was essentially a question of spotting talent.

Certainly none of the boys she dated came anywhere near the mark, and in any event her father had a way of scrutinizing each young man who came to the house that made Dasha writhe.

For all his talk about Dasha's eventual role in life, he remained adamantly possessive. Protective. In Max's eyes, she would always remain the family pet, would never be a grown woman. And as for finding a husband, she didn't believe there was a boy alive who could withstand her father's inquisitions. If only she could go away to college—Chicago, California, anywhere well beyond the parental reach. But Max was firmly opposed. There were plenty of excellent schools in Boston.

It was only after great tears and protestations that she was finally permitted to go away—and then no further away than Smith. Smith, Max reluctantly conceded, would be acceptable. Harriet had gone there. Harriet was a "lady." Ergo, it was a school to which Dasha might safely be entrusted.

The Class of '66 had the misfortune of being precariously poised between generations, bound by "I Love Lucy" at one end and the topless bathing suit at the other, equidistant between *McCall*'s fading dream of "Togetherness" and the very different "togetherness" that would later be symbolized by Woodstock.

Nice girls didn't. Certainly not nice girls like Dasha, and when she arrived at Smith in the autumn of '62 with a trunkful of cashmere sweaters and Peck & Peck skirts, it was to find herself in the company of like-minded girls. Even the brightest among them largely shared Dasha's sense of priorities. The goals were clear, the road was straight, the outcome never in doubt. Four pleasant, convivial years on campus, followed (unless you were lucky enough to be engaged by graduation) by a brief stint in New York or Boston as a secretary, a researcher, a publisher's assistant. You were marking time until the main event, and the most coveted degree you could earn was your MRS. The term "career girl" was essentially a euphemism for old maid.

Dasha was seventeen, one of the youngest in her class, naive and utterly without direction. Routinely she signed up for the liberal arts courses, a little French, a little history, but the bulk of her energy was reserved for serious business: exploring the social opportunities with which the area abounded. There were "mixers" with the boys from Amherst, square dancing at U. Mass, coffee shops, bookstores, movie houses, basketball games where a college girl might go in tingling expectation of encountering some equally nice boy from a neighboring campus.

On average, she fell in love twice a month. "He's so intelligent," she'd come back floating after the first date, or "so sensitive"; yet on better acquaintance, Prince Charming always proved to have feet of clay and hands like flypaper. Once body contact was established, the boys tended to drop the scrim of manners and disillusion set in quickly on both sides.

Flirting was one thing—what did you live for if not male adulation?—but being pawed and probed and treated like merchandise, that was quite another.

"You won't respect me," she would plead.

"I'll respect you, Dasha. Believe me, I'll respect you all the more."

But she didn't respect *them*— the boys with their sweaty fingers and thrusting tongues—and the prospect of losing her virginity to some hot-handed jock who was interested in "just one thing" was repugnant. Where was love in all this? Where was admiration? Surely John Fitzgerald Kennedy had not courted Jacqueline Bouvier in such a crass and unchivalric manner.

To add to her distress, the boys often made her feel guilty, as though she had led them on with false expectations. "Is it my fault you have such fantastic boobs?" one eager young man taunted her. Clearly, her anatomy was her own worst enemy, and she responded by withdrawing into buttoned-up necklines and bulky sweaters, dresses that seemed impervious to assault.

"There are no Galahads," she grieved to her roommates one night, after a back-seat struggle that had almost ended in rape. "No Galahads anywhere!" Yet improbably she clung to her dream of finding one.

The night she met Jordan Croy would later assume all the aspects of legend.

"That awful espresso."

"Those terrible murals of the Bay of Naples."

"You were wearing little heart earrings, I remember."

"And you had on a tweed jacket with leather patches. I thought that was terrifically intellectual looking."

"My campus-poet pose. Actually that jacket had been out at the elbow for years."

"You were pretty arrogant, you know."

"Not really. I was just trying to impress you. My God, you were sexy!"

"Was I?"

"Fantastic knockers."

"Honestly, Jordan. Well, it's a good thing you kept your thoughts to yourself. I would have clobbered you with my handbag. I was very prim and proper in those days."

"And I was so goddam pompous. 'Champion of the people.' Did I really say that?"

"So help me, you did. Oh Jordan . . . we were such babies."

She was, in fact, just eighteen. She had returned for her sophomore year with a vague anxiety that she had exhausted the resources of the district, that "Mr. Right" was not to be found here, at least not in the Amherst fraternity houses.

The Caffe Barbetta was a coffeehouse just outside of Northampton, a dank crowded barn with murky lights and undrinkable espresso that nonetheless did a booming business among local undergraduates. Ostensibly the attraction was hearing live folk singers; actually it was one of those choice places where, for the price of a coffee and pastry, a co-ed could mingle and socialize without losing face.

"I almost didn't go," Dasha would reflect years later. She had been dragged there by a couple of her roommates, with a feeling that it would be another evening wasted.

The place was crowded by the time they arrived, the air thick with the scent of smoke. It was the first crisp evening of the year. On the dais a tall, rangy fellow in faded chinos and a jacket that was a trifle too short at the wrists was tuning his guitar. Then without further ado, he hoisted himself atop a high wooden stool and thrummed across the strings for attention. The face was grave, the eyes brown and mournful behind horn-rimmed glasses, and he looked as if he were up to something very serious indeed. Tragic, conceivably, and Dasha geared herself for yet another pained rendition of "Sixteen Tons" or "Water Boy."

"Ladies and gentlemen," *thrummm*, "I was going to offer you an authentic folk ballad deep from the coalmines of Appalachia. But . . . " *thrummmm*, "I've gotta admit, the furthest underground I've ever been is the sportswear department of Big Jim's Bargain Basement!"

Dasha tittered, and for a moment she caught his eye. He was wonderfully attractive.

"And so . . . " The young man swept his hand across the strings once more. And so he was going to leave the folk songs for the genuine folks, and instead address himself to the truly vital issues of the day. With that, he strummed a few quiet bars of intro, then began singing in a pleasant baritone.

If we can put a man into outer space,
Why can't we cure the common cold?
If we can lick the Russkies in the armament race,
How come my sweat socks have green mold? . . .

It was nonsense, pure and simple, but witty nonsense, spoofing college athletics, Amherst profs, the purported virginity of Smithies, current TV commercials, ROTC, all topics guaranteed to please a college crowd, and the audience ate it up. From time to time he would plunk a chord, stop and invite his listeners to add their own punch lines. "If we can put a man into space . . . " He singled out Dasha with a forefinger. She paused, scrambled for thought. "Why can't we invent non-run pantyhose?" she shot back, a line that got grateful laughter from the girls in the room and a convivial wink from the guitarist.

It was a clever routine, and Dasha wondered if the singer would table-hop when his turn was over, but instead he ceded the mike to a Joan Baez lookalike, retreated to a table in the far corner of the room, and proceeded to bury his nose in a pile of books.

An hour later she'd forgotten him completely, and it was only on her way back from the ladies' room that she noticed him still at his table, still deep in books. She hesitated for a moment, not wishing to intrude, but long experience with musicians had taught her that they all relished compliments. Besides, she hadn't spoken to one man tonight.

"I liked your act very much." She leaned over the table. "Very clever. Do you write your own material?"

He glanced up briefly, then muttered, "Lightweight."

"Lightweight?" Dasha echoed. Had she misunderstood?

"Lightweight . . . lightweight," he reiterated. "Lightweight fluff for limp-brained undergraduates."

Dasha went scarlet. "I'm sorry. I was only trying to be polite." She turned to stalk off when he sprang to his feet.

"Please, I'm the one who should be sorry. I didn't mean to sound so boorish. It's just that . . . well, I was all involved in a book and . . . " He smiled unexpectedly and there was something very sweet and vulnerable in his face. "I guess I'm not used to getting compliments from pretty girls. Can I make amends by getting you a cup of coffee? Please say yes, or I'll feel like a total swine for the rest of the week." He swept the books to one side and shepherded her into a chair with a show of formality. "You're a Smithie, aren't you? I can tell by the Fair Isle sweater."

He too was a sophomore, at Amherst, and when Dasha commented that she hadn't seen him at any of the mixers, he shook his head and frowned.

"No. I don't have time for that sort of stuff." Not that he had anything against social life in general, but it really was pretty trivial when you put it into perspective. He couldn't speak for other people, of course, but he for one had no intention of frittering away the most important years of his life hanging around dance floors looking for girls. Only reason he was here at Barbetta's tonight was to earn a few extra bucks. It paid better than waiting tables. He'd done that all last year and he didn't think he could ever look another pizza in the face.

"I gather you're working your way through college?"

"'Fraid so."

"Well, perhaps I shouldn't keep you from your studies." He made no motion to detain her, yet she was reluctant to leave. He seemed such a refreshing change, so intense. So studious. "That's quite a stack of books you've got here. You planning to read them all tonight?" She picked up the top volume.

"*Post Stalinism and the Politics of Cold War.*" She read out the title with a smile. "Are you enjoying it?"

"Enjoying it!" That struck him as funny. "Well, if you haven't read it, all I can say is that book is a masterpiece . . . an absolute masterpiece" —Dasha sucked in her breath—"of the most pompous turgid prose I've ever had the misfortune to read. What's more . . . " He went on for several minutes, knocking the logic, the style, the whole premise, and concluding with "Would you believe this Oborin guy is one of Kennedy's top advisers? Jesus, no wonder we had the Bay of Pigs fiasco."

Dasha was speechless. There was no way, on the heels of such a diatribe, that she could admit to being the culprit's sister. She herself had found the book totally unreadable, but that was beside the point. Here was someone, this arrogant young man with no credentials, suddenly proclaiming that the emperor had no clothes. The presumption was breathtaking.

"I suppose," she gasped, "I suppose you think you could do a better job of it—advising presidents and all."

"When and if the time comes, I sincerely hope so. Although I haven't yet decided whether or not to go into national politics." He spoke as though it were an imminent possibility. "I think I'd prefer working behind the scenes."

"Doing what?"

"Practicing law."

"Another Perry Mason?"

"No, I mean a proper lawyer, a top man in a top firm. New York or maybe Washington."

To Dasha, that evoked an image of black-suited zombies in starched white shirts quibbling interminably about "parties of the first part, parties of the second part." She rolled her eyes.

"Isn't that . . . um, kind of stuffy?"

"Stuffy!" Good God, how could she possibly think the law was stuffy? Didn't she realize it touched on every single aspect of people's lives? Did she have the faintest idea of how many lawyers have become presidents, diplomats, senators, chief executives of the nation's greatest corporations? Why, there wasn't another profession that could hold a candle to the law. No. Not even medicine, not when it came to shaping the world we lived in. Wherever you looked in government, big business, big labor, lawyers were the driving force. Just think of it! A single lawyer, one solitary champion of the people arguing before the Supreme Court—well, that man could change the course of history!

The words came spilling out. His eyes glittered; his cheeks were flushed. There was a New York rhythm to his speech, a vibrancy that conjured up busy streets and rushing subways, a real and dynamic world beyond the campus. And Dasha, touched by his enthusiasm, could only conclude that if the law was dull, this ardent young man before her certainly was not. She wanted to learn more, wondered what place he envisioned for himself in the grand scheme of things, but he stopped short, apologetic.

"Just listen to me, I sound like a broken record. But you. Tell me something about yourself, other than the fact that you're a sensational listener." His eyes scoured her face. "What are you planning to be when you get out?"

For the first time since entering Smith, Dasha was embarrassed by her lack of vocation. Here was this wonderful guy knocking himself out, working his way through college, and there was she . . . drifting, simply having a good time on her father's money. She dithered for a moment.

"I haven't quite decided yet, maybe something in the arts, or writing. Anyhow, I'd much rather hear about you."

But she didn't get to hear more, for in the corner of her eye she could see her girlfriends waving furiously that it was time to leave. "Maybe some other time . . . "

"You're not going so soon!" His face fell. "I *do* talk too much and now I'm driving you away. Can I see you again some time? I don't even know your name"—it struck him—"and you don't know mine. I'm Jordan Croy. And you're . . . ?"

At that moment she could have kicked herself. Why hadn't she said right off she was Alex's sister, instead of letting him go into that tirade? But it was too late now. Instead, she scribbled "Dasha" on a cocktail napkin and added her phone number. "I'm at the dorm. Call me when you get a chance."

"Dasha?" He inspected the napkin. "Just Dasha? No last name? Sounds as if you're hiding from the cops."

She paused. Considered. Mumbled something.

"I'm sorry. How do you spell that . . . as in Merle Oberon? As in"—his eye fell on the book—"as in— Oh *wow!* I really put my foot into it, didn't I? Is he a relative of yours?"

"My brother." Dasha managed a nervous laugh. "But please . . . please don't think you've offended me. I'd feel awful if you did and I'd really like to see you again." She took the napkin, stuffed it in his breast pocket, and fled before he had a chance to reply.

That night she went to bed with her thoughts full of Jordan, his voice, his presence. The way the dark hair fell across his forehead. The long sensitive fingers. The wrists emerging from shabby sleeves. He had outgrown his jacket, she realized with a near maternal surge of warmth. That was moving, romantic. All the boys she knew came from prosperous homes like hers. But Jordan . . . even the name intrigued her. She could hardly wait to see him again, woke up early next morning geared for his call. But he didn't call, then or the next day or the days after that; and when weeks passed without a word, her confidence slowly turned to dismay.

He had liked her. She was certain of it, and the only thing that could put him off must have been the stupid business about Alex. True to pattern, her brother had fouled up her life. If she never heard from Jordan Croy again, it was Alex's fault. Goddam Alex.

She saw him next in the dead of winter, a chance encounter on a Northampton street. She had turned a corner and there he was, thumbing through second-hand books at an outdoor stall, totally absorbed. It took all Dasha's courage to tap him on the shoulder.

"You don't remember me, do you?"

But he did. "Why, Dasha!" He pumped her hand with the delight of a man who'd just won the sweepstakes. It was so good seeing her again. How was she? How was school? Yeah . . . it was awful about the Kennedy assassination. He hoped her brother had landed on his feet. An Undersecretary of State now? Wow, terrific! Did she have time for a cup of coffee and a doughnut?

She did indeed, but it wasn't until the second cup of coffee and after a good deal of small talk that she took the plunge and asked: "How come you never called me, Jordan? Did you lose my phone number?"

He flushed guiltily, murmured something about being very busy, lots of exams, and Dasha presumed he had been involved with another girl. But now he seemed eager for a closer acquaintance.

"If you're free next Wednesday, well, I'm the captain of the Jefferson Debating Team and I'm doing my number next Wednesday night. Come hear me speak, and after we could go out for a bite."

Dasha flushed with pleasure. "I'd like that very much. What are you debating, by the way?"

"Capital punishment. Should the Supreme Court abolish the death penalty?"

"And are you for or against?"

"Me personally, I'm dead set against it, if you'll excuse the pun. To my way of thinking, it's nothing more than legalized murder. But as it happens, I'm assigned to argue the other side. The luck of the draw, I suppose."

"Still," Dasha reasoned, "lawyers have to do that all the time, don't they? Argue cases they don't believe in."

Some did, he agreed, although that wasn't the sort of advocate he'd choose to be. One day he would be able to pick his cases on merit, fight the good fight. Nonetheless the upcoming debate would be an invaluable experience, particularly since everyone he knew and respected opposed the death sentence. There was a challenge in arguing the unpopular side of an issue.

"Well, I'll be rooting for you anyhow," Dasha promised.

"Because you believe in the death penalty?"

"Because I believe in *you.*"

"Resolved!" Jordan's voice rang out across the auditorium, strong and clear above the scraping of chairs, the fidgeting of feet. "Resolved that justice demands an eye for an eye, a life for a life."

A hush fell across the room and in that moment Dasha knew, felt it in her bones, that tonight Jordan would sweep all before him. No matter that he'd begun with the chips stacked against him. Already he commanded the audience with his height, his authority, the rich timbre of his voice. She was transfixed. Everything about him bespoke the titan. His arguments so forcefully reasoned, his speech, his wit, above all his romantic bearing—the tall spare figure, the striking planes of his face, the mouth at once mobile and manly. Incredible to think that he was not yet twenty! What would he be at thirty, forty? She had but to shut her eyes and envision him a few years hence in a great hall with marble columns addressing the highest court in the land on some matter upon which the very fate of the nation depended. And he would captivate them—those nine old men who had seen everything, heard everything. And on that glorious day she would be sitting amid the onlookers, proud and happy, and at the height of his triumph they would exchange secret glances. Why even tonight, despite youth and inexperience, he radiated what her father called "star quality."

Jordan finished his speech to a burst of applause and descended the rostrum—face flushed and dewy with sweat.

"Was I okay, Dasha?"

"You were wonderful, Jordan! Absolutely wonderful!" He took her hand to lead her through the throng of admiring students and for the first time in her life Dasha felt herself a goddess on the arm of a god.

"How could I help falling in love with you," he would later recall. "You made me think I was Superman."

He didn't say it at the time, however. He was too unsure of his feelings, of hers. He had also, by the time he brought her home, begun to have second thoughts about his victory.

"It's an eerie feeling," he told her, "this business of advocating causes you don't believe in, and I wish to hell I could have argued the other side. Frankly, it's the one qualm I have about becoming a lawyer. You have to defend the guilty as well as the innocent. Of course, ideally, once I'm established . . . " He pulled the car up in front of her dorm and switched off the motor. She turned her face half-expecting to be kissed, but he seemed troubled and faintly brooding.

"Words are funny things, Dasha," he said finally. "You can pick and choose among them, squeeze 'em, stretch 'em, manipulate them to fit any cause or conclusion."

"You have a gift, Jordan. You're marvelous with words," she acknowledged. "But maybe if you have ethical doubts about becoming a lawyer, you should be a writer instead. That way you can pick your issues."

He shook his head. "Writers have no real power, even the best of them." He sat for several minutes, eyebrows furrowed. Then: "My father was a writer. A very successful one. He's dead now, but in his day he was just about the hottest playwright in television. Martin Croy. Does the name mean anything to you? No, I can see it doesn't." He reeled off a list of program credits, and though they sounded impressive, none rang a bell with Dasha.

"I guess they were before my time."

"They were, and in a way that's my point. Fifteen years ago his name was on everyone's lips. Today he's totally forgotten. So much, you see, for the immortality of the written word."

"I gather you were very young when he died?"

"I was seven. Old enough to remember him. He was a great writer and a great man—at least in *my* eyes. You may never have heard of Martin Croy, but tell me, Dasha, did you ever hear of the Red Network?"

And that *did* ring a bell.

His father was—Jordan began softly—a pioneer. In the days when television was a new and bumbling medium, he was the first to recognize its potential for serious drama, to see it as an instrument of social change. "Before my dad came along, TV was nothing but dancing legs and Charlie Chan movies. After him, it was . . . well, Paddy Chayefsky, Rod Serling, *Playhouse 90*. You name it, Martin Croy paved the way for it."

The rewards for a man scarcely thirty were enormous, and Jordan's earliest memories were of a huge, sunny apartment, overflowing with guests and laughter. The phone was always ringing, the Steinway playing. "And the kitchen . . . boy, it was something! You could open the refrigerator at any hour and it was always full of whatever you wanted. Hothouse peaches and chocolate eclairs and bags full of wonderful deli from Zabar's. I had the feeling all of life was going to be like that—a nonstop feast."

His father must have thought so, too, for during those brief years of glory he lived as he wrote—boldly, extravagantly, leaving caution for lesser souls. His home was a hospitality suite for everyone in the business and, ironically, it was this very hospitality that brought about his downfall.

The early fifties marked the onset of a witch hunt that tore the entertainment industry in half. In the wake of the cold war, committees were springing up from New York to Hollywood. Vigilantes of the cultural world. There was, they claimed, a conspiracy afoot, a so-called Red Network of actors, writers, and producers devoted to the insidious spread of Communist propaganda. Among those suspected of subversion were numerous visitors to the Croy household. Inevitably, the accusatory finger pointed to Martin himself, and soon he was being hauled up to testify, his every teleplay scrutinized for coded messages, his social life pried into and picked apart.

Was he now or had he ever been a member of the Communist Party? Absolutely not, Martin swore under oath. Was not his home a gathering place for Soviet sympathizers and fellow travelers? Maybe Martin had his suspicions, but he was not the sort of man to betray his friends. He refused to "name names" and this refusal was seen as evidence of guilt.

"At the time, of course, I didn't understand any of the issues involved." Jordan sighed. "What did I know about politics? I was a kid. All I knew was that my dad was on the 'blacklist.' Truth is, I wasn't too sure what a blacklist was, but in our house, it was like Gestapo was to Jewish kids in Germany. You didn't have to know what it meant to know it was bad."

Suddenly, Martin Croy was a non-person. Friends no longer visited, phones didn't ring. The network chiefs who only months earlier had courted and cosseted him no longer returned his calls. He had gone from fame to invisibility, from prosperity to near poverty in less than a year.

For Jordan the change was traumatic. In mid-term, he was plucked out of prep school and the family moved to a drab working-class quarter of the Bronx.

"My first day at P.S. 188"—he gave a self-deprecatory laugh, but with an edge that made Dasha's bones ache—"I turn up all togged out in my blue prep school blazer with the Trinity crest, neat little white shirt, school tie. Jesus! I damn near caused a riot. I went in there looking like Little Lord Fauntleroy. I must have come out looking like I'd gone ten rounds with Rocky Marciano. That was the end of *that* blazer."

"Oh, Jordan. How awful for you!"

Her sympathy stopped him short.

"I don't know why I'm telling you all this." He shook his head. "It sounds like I'm blaming my father for what happened. I'm not. He was a terrific guy—the best. Just I guess he wasn't much of a manager. And anyhow, what happened was a lot worse for him than it was for me."

Jordan retained an enduring memory of his father sitting in a bathrobe, haggard and unshaven, in front of the TV set hour after hour. Just sitting there, watching the works of writers who had gone along with the prevailing tide.

"What agony that must have been for him. And yet he never sold out, Dasha. Never named names. They broke his heart but they couldn't break his will."

Six months later, Martin Croy was dead. He had been driving home from an interview in Manhattan and was caught in a thundershower. The car skidded. The brakes failed. And in full view of horrified onlookers, both car and driver plunged through the barriers of the Triborough Bridge into the East River. It had wanted only that for the tragedy to be complete.

"And your mother?" Dasha wanted to know. "Didn't he leave any insurance?"

Jordan shook his head. "Apparently not. He was a young man, after all, and I guess he thought he would live forever."

Thus Charlotte, widowed at thirty, found herself virtually destitute with a child to raise. Nothing in life had prepared her for such an eventuality. She had no skills, no experience, no assets other than a sweet manner and a certain modest chic. She took the only job she could find, selling sportswear in a Madison Avenue boutique. The hours were long, the pay miserable. But, she'd promised Jordan, it was only a stopgap. Now, a dozen years later she was still in the same place, the same routine. Perhaps her life might have taken a happier turn had she remarried, but Martin's death had left her shattered. She had neither the heart nor confidence to venture out into the great world again. "Such a waste, such a waste," Jordan sighed, and Dasha was unclear whether he was referring to his father's death or his mother's life. She only knew that it had cost him a great deal to tell her this much, and now she took his hand. "Terrible." Her voice trembled with tears. "What a terrible story."

"That it is," he said. "But I didn't tell you about it to win your sympathy, much as I value it. What I've been trying to explain is . . ."

"Yes?"

That he was on his own. She had to understand that. There could be no question of his mother paying for college, let alone law school. He'd have to make his way as best he could. So far he'd been lucky. He was at Amherst on scholarship, and managed to make ends meet by playing club dates four, sometimes five, nights a week. Even so, he had a long hard road to travel, many spartan years ahead before he could even begin to enjoy the pleasures most of his classmates already took for granted.

"You, for instance. You wondered why I never asked you out. I guess you thought I was pretty cool and boorish but . . . Oh hell, Dasha!" he blurted out, "I'm just in no position to get involved, let alone with someone like you. Yeah, I thought about you a lot these past few months, I couldn't put you out of my mind. No, I didn't lose your phone number. I could repeat it in my sleep. I went to dial it about one hundred times. But what would be the point? Believe me, I would have given my eye teeth to be able to call you up, invite you out to dinner, take you dancing somewhere nice. But even if I did, even if I could afford it, what right do I have to take up your time? Let's face it, Dasha, you're way out of my league."

"Don't say that!" Dasha began crying. "Why, you talk as if I were some kind of silly debutante only interested in Greek letter boys and dumb parties, as if I have to be wined and dined every waking moment. I don't judge my dates by how much money they have."

"It's not just the money"—Jordan stumbled for words. "It's every-thing . . . you, your family . . . "

"My brother!" She seized upon it. "That's it. Just because Alex is a 'Big Deal' in Washington, is that what makes me out of your league? Well, let me tell you, Jordan Croy, you're every bit the man he is. Better. All I could think of tonight while you were up there on the platform was how dynamic you were, how brilliant. You had everyone eating out of your hand—me included. And now that I know what you've been through . . . " She flung her arms around him and laid her head against his chest. "Oh Jordan, you're simply the finest person I've ever met. Don't ever ever walk out of my life again!"

From that night on, the word "we" would stand for Jordan-and-Dasha. They were inseparable, or as nearly so as his schedule allowed. For Jordan was a goer, a doer, an all-A student, captain of the debating team, vice-president of the English Honors Club, an activist in campus politics, shuttling continually between classrooms and meetings and his after-school jobs. Dasha's one complaint was their lack of time together. Some days she would only see him for a snatched cup of coffee, some days not at all and her sole contact would be a long whispered late-night conversation over the hall phone, frustrating and unsubstantial.

Sundays, however, they had all to themselves. Punctually at eight he would roll up in a battered Volkswagen and honk the opening bars of Beethoven's Fifth, at which signal Dasha would come flying down the stairs, afraid of forfeiting one precious moment. But even the hours from then until midnight hardly sufficed for everything they had to say to each other. "Tell me about your day, what you did, what you ate . . . " He was infinitely curious about her—her tastes, her opinions, her friends, family; forever plying her with questions, pressing books upon her, volumes of poetry, criticism, current events, always with the injunction: "You have to read this and then we'll talk about it." Or, "Who are your favorite composers? Your favorite presidents? What do you think are the ten best movies of all time?" And once when she parroted an opinion of his, he took offense. "Really, Dasha, you're much too bright to let other people do your thinking for you."

"Even you?"

"Especially me." He laughed.

It came as a jolt to discover that her perceptions actually mattered. She began to develop a sense of "self," which in her life had hitherto been lacking. She told him as much one day and he made the comment "Well, that's not so surprising. Your father sounds like a terrific chauvinist."   .

"Race you to the Dean's List," he challenged, when the mid-term exams were upon them and she, eager to please, accepted the dare. For the first time since entering Smith, she turned to her studies with a vengeance. Unconsciously she began remolding her life, not from any newborn sense of vocation but out of the desire to be worthy of Jordan, to stand high in his esteem. In fact, she was in training to become his wife —the kind of wife a public man might be proud of.

But at the heart of everything—beneath the talk of books and ideas and politics—their relationship was founded on a violent sexual attraction. They could hardly keep their hands off each other.

After they were married, Jordan would make light of it. "My God, we were a couple of horny kids. I felt like one of those early Christian martyrs—all hot talk and cold showers." At the time, however, it was no laughing matter.

Each Sunday was a test of fortitude, an inching forward to the act of love. The daylight hours passed harmlessly enough, but when it grew dark, Jordan would scout out some lonely country road "where we can talk in privacy." And soon there was no pretense of talking.

It was heaven, it was torture, there in the cramped seat of the Volkswagen—feverish sweated hours, all mouths, all hands, frantic gropings, half-unbuttoned caresses. The first time he touched her thighs, her body went thick with desire. "Please," she would say. Not "Please don't"; simply, "Please," but whether she meant stop or go, she herself hardly knew. All she knew was that she loved the warmth of his hands, the scent of his skin, the feeling of her flesh against his. "Oh God, Dasha"—he would bury his head in her naked breasts—"you're driving me crazy!"

But the road was never lonely very long, and suddenly there would be a brutal glare of headlights, a quick springing apart, a rapid rebuttoning of buttons. Then Jordan would start up the car without a word and drive grimly back to Smith.

"Goodnight, Jordan."

"Goodnight. I'll call you tomorrow." A last swift brush of the lips and Dasha would slink up to her room, disheveled, blood still pulsing in her ears, to spend a restless night.

The curfew, the strict rules about men in the rooms, now seemed infantile, a monstrous invasion of her private life.

Six more years, she would think, before Jordan was done with school and passed the bar. But she couldn't wait six years. Sometimes it seemed she couldn't wait another night. "If I don't marry Jordan Croy, I shall die."

And could *he* wait? she wondered. His frustration was even more apparent than her own. Once on that long and tense drive home, he suggested that it might be better if they stopped seeing so much of each other. Better for both of them. But the prospect of breaking off with Jordan was unendurable, even greater than her fear of her father's anger. For Max was *there,* far away in Boston—and Jordan was here and now. She began to feel persecuted, subject to foolish restrictions, outmoded morality. Other Smithies were having affairs, albeit discreetly, girls who weren't half as much in love as she was. Yet she couldn't bring herself to suggest a motel. The whole idea was so sordid. It was unworthy of everything they felt about each other. If only there were some haven as beautiful as their love. And then she remembered with a shock—there was.

Her family owned a cottage in the Berkshires, convenient to Tanglewood, where Max taught each summer. When the season was over, Harriet would drain the pipes, cut off the power, roll up the rugs, and tape the key under the front-door lintel where it would remain undisturbed through the winter. "And it's only an hour's drive away," Dasha told Jordan, her eyes glittering at the prospect. "There's an enormous fireplace, we could bring a picnic, a bottle of wine . . . "

"But that's housebreaking, Dasha."

"Who would ever know? Anyhow, it's my place as much as theirs. Come on, honey, where's your sense of adventure?"

Truth to tell, he needed very little coaxing.

She had never before seen the house in the snow, and it looked virginal as a bride, white against white on the silent mountainside. The key was where her mother had left it. She opened the door and took a deep breath. "Just like in *Doctor Zhivago*." Everything was covered with rime.

For the next hour they bustled furiously, building a roaring blaze in the living-room fireplace. The bedrooms were bitter cold, uninhabitable, but at last they staked out a circle of warmth before the grate—a cozy island in a frozen sea.

"We should have brought bedrolls," Jordan mused. "This is going to be like camping out."

"I'll go fetch a blanket."

She returned a minute later with an armful of colors. "Woven by Navajos for my little girl," Max had said years ago when he gave it to her: a bright Indian blanket in a geometric pattern of brilliant reds and yellows and greens. The wool felt nubby and sensual against her skin, the colors had never seemed so dazzling. In the silence she could almost hear her heart.

"My God you look so beautiful"—Jordan's eyes caressed her— "Exotic . . . like a firebird." He took the blanket from her hands and held it. " 'Had I the heavens' embroidered cloths . . . ' Do you know Yeats' poem?"

She shook her head, and Jordan's voice grew soft with an intimacy she had never heard before:

> *"Had I the heavens' embroidered cloths,*
> *Enwrought with golden and silver light,*
> *The blue and the dim and the dark cloths*
> *Of night and light and the half-light,*
> *I would spread the cloths under your feet:"*

He knelt before the fire and smoothed out the folds of the blanket with tender fingers, then rose to face her.

> *"But I, being poor, have only my dreams;*
> *I have spread my dreams under your feet;*
> *Tread softly because you tread on my dreams."*

The poem finished in a whisper. For a long time they stood motionless, hands clasped, wrapped by the fireglow, isolated from the cold and lifeless world beyond. Merely stood there, aching with the fullness of the moment, until he broke the silence.

"I love you, Dasha. No one will ever love you more."

That day too became part of their legend. The open fire. The Navajo blanket. The knowledge that "we belonged to each other from the start."

Slowly, wordlessly, they undressed with the heightened awareness of new lovers, with the fierce pride of young and beautiful bodies. She placed her fingertips on his naked shoulder, then slid her hands down his body. Flesh had never felt so sumptuous—his flesh, her own. And as she stood there, her palms on his hips, her nipples brushing lightly against his chest, she stopped to savor the moment and fix it in her mind forever. "For as long as I have memory," she thought, "this time will always be the first time, this man my first love. And nothing will ever be the same again."

Afterward, they lay in each other's arms replete and happy, while the fire burned down to embers until the encroaching cold reclaimed the room.

"Was it the first time for you too, my darling?" she asked. He answered with a kiss and she was certain it was. Then he said, "We belong together, you and I."

"Forever"—the word hung unspoken in the air. They would belong to each other forever.

That was twenty years ago, and now "forever" seemed to be coming to an end.

CHAPTER THREE

☐ She entered her office Monday morning with an absurd sense of expectation. As though—to be perfectly illogical about it—she might find there, among the familiar briefs and books and furniture, some answer to her own inner chaos.

And why not? That was her job, after all, untangling other people's problems, cleaning up their messes, arriving at the most ingenious solutions.

"Yes or no," Jordan had said. "All I want is a simple answer." But who was there to counsel the counselor?

Years ago, when they were first married, they'd had a next-door neighbor who solved thorny questions by opening the Book of Proverbs at random. A crazy system, but who could say it was worse than any other? And Dasha herself knew of a corporate honcho who refused to travel over water without a go-ahead from his astrologer. Not to mention the local judge who decided a case by flipping a coin.

God! If it were only that easy. *Heads I stay married, tails I don't.* All the agony of choice taken right out of your hands.

But of course it wasn't simple. The sun streaked its customary path across the rosewood desk. The little black and onyx clock (Jordan had given it to her only last year with an engraved inscription: *To my favorite jet setter*) marked the time on both East Coast and West. The ashtrays were emptied, the carpet freshly vacuumed, and the paperwork on the Selby merger lay piled high where she had left it Friday afternoon. Not a trace of magic anywhere, simply the cool and ordered ambience one might expect to find in the office of a Wall Street lawyer. Except for a crude, childish drawing that hung on the wall facing the desk. It was a picture of a horse done in Crayola—orange mane, purple tail—cheerfully munching daisies in a meadow. The artist had signed his name with gusto: "Geoff Croy Age 8." The paper was beginning to yellow.

Dasha had hung that drawing on the wall of her cubicle the day she first reported to work at Slater Blaney, a pointed reminder of priorities. And it had followed her over the next half dozen years, from that tiny airless warren through a series of promotions to rest now in these far more luxurious surroundings.

Come in, come in, the room beckoned discreetly. Your secrets will be safe here, your dilemmas will be resolved. Everything from the porcelain lamps to the manicured plantings to the polish on the silver desk set intimated "the best of the best."

An insider, however, someone with a practiced eye and a thorough knowledge of the firm's pecking order, might arrive at a more exact calculation. He would tot up the number of windows, count the buttons on the phone, measure the thickness of the rug, the width of the desk, determine whether the view was south to the harbor or north to the Empire State, pace off the distance from the partners' dining room. He would add all these factors, divide by square footage, and thus determine precisely how many rungs of the ladder the occupant had already climbed. And how many—or how few—were still to go.

Near the top, such an observer would conclude. Wrenchingly, tantalizingly near. Dasha too had made such inventories on occasion. Yet she could never do it without misgivings. What difference, after all, did an extra window or another couple of buttons on the phone really make? Symbols, that's all they were. They didn't make you a better lawyer, a nicer person. Any more than a wedding ring made you a happy wife.

Still, they were symbols of money and power and achievement. Symbols that you had triumphed in the toughest arena of all. In the best of all law firms, Slater Blaney.

But this morning she made no such inventory, simply stood in the doorway for an uncertain moment, shrugged, then strode over to the desk to check the messages. As always the bright pink slips were stacked high. URGENT. PLEASE CALL. URGENT. Nearly two dozen URGENTS. But there was only one truly urgent matter this morning: what she planned to do with the rest of her life.

She restacked the messages—they could sit for a while. If Jordan had his way, they would sit undisturbed forever. She wandered over to the window. Before her stretched all of Manhattan. The perfect fix for a skyline junkie. Even on those days when she was too busy to raise her nose from her desk, there had been a thrill in knowing that the view was on call at every moment. She would miss that view like crazy. Well, maybe when this was all over, if it didn't hurt too much, she could come down here and pay the few dollars for the guided tour, then take the visitors' elevator up to the Observation Tower. For auld lang syne, so to speak. Strange to think her everyday view was a classic treat for out-of-towners. Already she could feel withdrawal symptoms. Routinely she lowered her eyes to the concrete expanse of Nassau Plaza, and then she saw them. The Kimfolk.

Even from this vantage point, high above street level, there was no mistaking them: the crimson blazers, the white trousers, the boys with their dapper straw boaters, the girls with flowers in their hair. A pretty sight they were, a lively splash of color against the gray flannel and dour pinstripes of the passersby. She counted heads briefly—more than a dozen in today's vigil. The nice weather brought them out. For the thousandth time she wondered if her nephew was among them, but there was no way of telling. She couldn't make out faces from this distance, nor hear the chanting, nor read the placards they carried. No matter. She knew the message by heart:

FATHER KIM LOVES YOU.

Not me he doesn't. Not yours truly, Dasha Croy. Yet it was hard not to feel a certain complicity with the demonstrators. They had, after all, waited with her for three arduous years. They, too, had suffered through countless rulings and motions and appeals and reversals, with still no idea as to the outcome. You couldn't hustle the Supreme Court into making hasty decisions, least of all in the lawsuit that some journalists had dubbed "The TV Trial of the Decade" and others—more flamboyantly if less factually—"The Battle of the Billionaires." To Dasha, it was simply "The Case." The Case that could either kill off a promising career or launch a great one. Whichever, she wished it were over. Every Monday she would arrive at the office in a flutter of hope that today would be the day, for the Supreme Court liked to keep its secrets right up to the last possible moment, and their timing usually came as a surprise. But six months of Mondays had come and gone and now there was every likelihood that there would be no decision this term.

How bizarre, then, to think that she might not even be practicing when the judgment was delivered. That she might just pick up a newspaper one morning or switch on the radio to discover it was finally settled. Three years of bitter litigation, three years of her life, her best efforts, condensed in a news bulletin.

Go home, she wanted to shout to the kids below. *Stop this nonsense and go back to your families. Your parents love you. Miss you.*

Sometimes they frightened her with their blind belief, their anger. She must, she supposed, represent the epitome of the American establishment when she appeared in the courtroom: cool and efficient in gray flannel or crisp black gabardine. Yet watching them now as they milled in the Plaza, peddling their pamphlets and albums, they merely looked pathetic. *Kim vs. FBC* was neither a blood feud nor a witch hunt. It was a lawsuit.

Not "just a lawsuit," as Jordan had said, but a great one. A landmark step toward the clarification of a grave constitutional issue. *Which takes precedence: A man's right to control the story of his life? Or the public's right to know the truth?*

Had the cards been dealt differently, Dasha could well have represented the Reverend Elijah Kim instead of the FBC network. Moreover, as a top-flight professional, she would have fought just as tenaciously on the other side.

Still, she was glad the cards had fallen as they had, proud to be arguing for a legal cause that in her heart of hearts she knew to be right.

If only she could be so certain in evaluating her private life. So very sure her choice would be the best one.

"Yes or no," Jordan's words echoed in the silent room. "A simple yes or no."

Yes.

Yes, she would do it. She would march into Blagden Geere's office pronto and explain "a crisis in my personal life." Only you didn't march in on the great man just like that. The prospect was too daunting. Instead, maybe, she ought to circulate a memo among the partners, and sneak out like a thief. *Due to unforeseen circumstances . . . I deeply regret . . . Much as I have enjoyed working here . . .* Of course, she would never be able to look any of them in the face again. And what a ghastly, unprofessional thing to do.

No.

No, she couldn't She could not just walk away leaving reams of unfinished business behind. How could Jordan imagine that she would? It was grossly unfair. Say what you will about a new era having dawned, a new equity between the sexes, it always came down to the same thing. Women were expected to make the sacrifices. And even were she to do so, cut the cord with one clean swipe, what then?

"I can't go on being nothing but Mr. Dasha Croy," he had said, and she sympathized with that. But could she, after all the struggle, after everything she had made out of herself, ever go back to being nothing more than Mrs. Jordan Croy?

She shot a last glance at the gathering in the Plaza, then went to her desk with a sigh.

"Frannie?" she buzzed the intercom. "Are you there? Do me a favor, will you, sweetie? Hold my phone calls and cancel my appointments for today. Tell them that I'm tied up in court. Then, I want you to bring me an enormous pot of coffee, the largest you can find. I've got a full day's hard thinking to do."

CHAPTER FOUR

☐ From that first rhapsodic day in the Berkshires, they considered themselves engaged. The matter was never in question. Lover, mistress, paramour, bedmate: Those were tawdry words—words that threatened to reduce their love to the level of a cheap affair. They were engaged, and as soon as Jordan got his law degree, they would join the ranks of respectably married couples. To Dasha, particularly, nothing less than the worthiest of intentions could justify the fact that she had betrayed her father's trust. Yet for the time being, it was clearly better that their parents be left in the dark. Jordan felt his mother wasn't yet ready for such news, and as for Max—given the faintest inkling about what was going on, he'd simply yank Dasha out of college. That is, unless Smith expelled her first.

In fact, the Sunday at Tanglewood hadn't eased the pressures as Dasha had hoped, merely intensified them. All she could think about was the years and years of waiting. For Jordan, it was even less tolerable. His first full taste of sexuality, the admission that he was utterly in love, relegated everything else to second rank.

"I hate it!" He clenched his fists with rage. "I despise all this hole-in-the-corner stuff. I can't eat, I can't study for thinking of you. It's like I'm living part time. I want to go to bed with you every night. I want to wake up to you every morning." Maybe he wouldn't go on to law school after all. Maybe just finish his degree, find a job, and get married. In fact, why should they even have to wait that long? He'd be twenty-one the end of next year, and what the hell—there were plenty of other careers.

"You don't mean that, Jordan!" Yet she too was tempted.

In fact he did and he didn't. He was confused, unhappy, trying to

49

balance goals that seemed at war with each other. In the end it was Dasha, guilty and tearful, who settled the question.

"If you quit school for me, Jordan, I think you'd wind up hating me some day. You'd probably never forgive me and I'd never forgive myself. I'll wait for you just as long as it takes. Meanwhile"—she wiped her eyes—"we still have our Sundays."

For the remainder of that year and the first half of the next, the summer cottage was their sanctuary. Sometimes they would open the door and immediately fall upon each other like animals, coupling as though their very lives depended on it. But in time their visits began to assume a more reasonable, domestic air. The fierce white heat of discovery had gradually banked into a warm steady glow. They would arrive with Sunday papers, books, a transistor radio, and settle in for a leisurely day. When the weather was mild, Jordan liked to rent horses from a nearby stable and they'd spend easy hours exploring the trails. But mostly they "played house," as he called it—talking, reading, relaxing, making love in what was clearly a preview of marriage.

The following summer their idyll came to a close. No sooner was the house opened for the season than Max begin sniffing through the rooms, kicking the unexplained ashes in the fireplace. "We've had intruders over the winter. Tramps, I imagine." At summer's end, he had the locks changed, pocketed the spare key, and asked the Lenox police to keep an eye on the place.

"Like the grinch who stole Christmas," Dasha informed Jordan when he returned to school. "I guess it's motel rooms from now on." The thought depressed them both, but it mattered less than she had feared, for by then they were thoroughly grafted onto each other's lives.

It was her ardent hope that he would go to Harvard Law. She could live at home and still be near him; moreover, she was certain that the prospect of having a Harvard lawyer as a son-in-law would predispose Max in his favor.

Jordan, however, was doubtful. "Just getting in is such a rat race. Anyhow, I could never scrape up the tuition."

"On scholarship maybe?"

But that was unlikely, for Jordan's performance had slipped during the previous year. He was no longer the Amherst *wunderkind;* the zeal that had once gone into campus dazzle had been rechanneled into the love affair that continued to engross them both. And for Jordan, time was a finite commodity. Shortly after they became lovers, he dropped out of the debating society, much to her dismay. "Look," he explained, "I *have* to work nights. I *have* to see you. Those are the constants. And until they invent the thirty-hour day, something's gotta give." Now, at the start of his senior year, it was no longer certain he would graduate with honors. Inevitably, Dasha felt herself to blame.

"About Harvard . . . " she persisted.

"Honey, I'm not going to apply simply so they can turn me down."

"Well, maybe my brother could pull some strings up there. Alex knows everybody who's anybody."

With that, Jordan exploded. "For Chrissakes, Dasha, you couldn't conceivably ask him to do such a thing! One, it's highly unethical. Two, I can't see Alex doing me any favors. Three, I wouldn't accept if he did."

He and her brother had met the year before. Alex had come to deliver a lecture and afterwards the three of them had gone to dinner at a French restaurant. "My treat, Dasha. I know how broke you students always are."

The restaurant was hideously expensive and Jordan's eyes boggled over the menu. "I'll just have the chicken salad," he murmured, adding that he wasn't terribly hungry.

"Nonsense!" Alex called over the waiter. "We'll have the *escargots bourguignon* to begin with; then . . . " He went on to order copiously —tournedos Rossini, wild mushrooms, a Nuits St. Georges 1952. Playing Moses to a couple of hundred worshipful undergraduates that day had done little to modify his ego or his appetite. He felt very much the *grand savant.*

"Well well, young man, so you're going to be a lawyer . . . " He then launched into a series of anecdotes, some of them scandalous, about "Abe" (Fortas) and "Bill" (Justice Douglas) and "good old Ramsey" (U.S. Attorney General Clark), while poor Jordan struggled manfully with his first dish of snails and all its attendant paraphernalia, unable to return anything other than "Oh really? How interesting."

Dinner over, Alex dropped Jordan off, then drove his sister back to Smith in a fat black Lincoln. "He seems a nice enough kid, that Croy fellow, although someone should teach him how to eat snails. Tell me, are you sleeping with him?"

"Alex, don't be crude!"

"I'm not crude, just curious."

"We hope to be married," she said with some dignity, and Alex burst out laughing. "Then you *are* sleeping with him."

"For God's sakes." Dasha panicked. "Don't say anything to Daddy. He'd kill me."

"Stop being an utter asshole, Dasha. Don't you think it's time you got out from under the old man's thumb?"

"Promise me, Alex—promise me you won't say anything." She felt increasingly desperate.

"Relax, will you? If I can keep Lyndon Johnson's state secrets, I think I can manage to keep yours too. Enjoy. Enjoy."

The incident troubled her for weeks. Not just Alex's lord-of-the-manor manner, but her own response and above all Jordan's patent unease throughout the dinner. He had been fidgety, tongue-tied, wary of putting either a foot or a fork wrong in the presence of so august a figure of authority. Yet his behavior hadn't come as a total surprise, for by now she knew Jordan intimately, his weaknesses as well as his strengths. For all his intellectual gifts, he was prone to sudden bouts of panic. What had initially impressed her as an almost divine arrogance proved, on closer scrutiny, to be in large part a defense, a smoke screen designed to obscure a deep and painful insecurity. Every now and again she had seen some trivial incident—a brush with a traffic cop, a bad exam result, a check that bounced—throw him from his moorings into a sea of doubt. She understood. It was the legacy of his blitzed-out childhood, and her heart bled for him. But the subject was too sensitive for discussion and she felt she could best help him by a show of unswerving loyalty and affection. If Jordan lacked confidence in certain areas, it would be her job to supply it. To believe in him even more than he believed in herself, yet to do so with subtlety and tact. That was a woman's highest role.

Accordingly, she now dropped all mention of Harvard. But when Jordan did tell her, a few weeks later, that he had made an application to Seneca, she was thunderstruck.

"Seneca! My God, that's the boondocks . . . a million miles from nowhere."

"It's one of the best small law schools in the country, Dasha, and I stand a good chance of getting a scholarship."

"And what about me, Jordan? About us?"

"Don't worry, puss. We'll figure something out. Maybe you could get a job up there."

"Doing what . . . picking apples?"

The more she thought about it, the more impossible the situation became. Had it been Boston, New York, even Chicago, she would have joined him, found some sort of interesting work, made a new circle of friends. But Seneca! What on earth could she do there? And what reason could she possibly give her parents for moving to a remote part of upstate New York? True, some of her classmates were cutting family ties, starting to live openly with their boyfriends. But they didn't have Max Oborin for a father.

Yet the alternative, a three-year separation from Jordan, was un-thinkable. The solution, when it came to her, was simplicity itself.

"I'll apply there too, that's what. Why not, Jordan? I'm pretty sure to be accepted. I've got the grades. Just think, we'd be together full time, go to class together, study together, live together . . . "

"Why, Dasha"—Jordan was as puzzled as he was pleased—"you always gave me the impression you thought law was boring."

"It won't be boring if I'm with you."

"And if I'd been planning to become a doctor instead . . . ?"

"Then I'd apply to med school! Seriously, honey, once I'm involved I'm sure I'll find it interesting, and who knows? Maybe we could even practice together after we're married."

She'd said it half-kiddingly, but Jordan was intrigued. "Croy and Croy, Attorneys at Law," he mused. "It would be a whole new ball-game."

Dasha was correct in presuming she'd be accepted at Seneca. The real hurdle lay in getting her father to foot the bill. She planned to work on him over Easter vacation.

"A lawyer!" Max's jaw dropped. "This is the first I ever heard about your wanting to be a lawyer. What is this, Daryushka, a joke? A passing fancy? Or"—the idea dawned on him—"am I supposed to plunk down all that money so you can go husband-hunting? There are plenty of eligible young men right here in Boston."

"Really, Daddy!" He had hit so close to home that she was genuinely outraged. "The way your mind works! Believe me, I've never been more serious about anything in my life." But Max simply refused to discuss it. "Not a word, Dasha. Not one word more about this nonsense." Her mother, predictably, refused to intervene.

Dasha's response was to give him the silent treatment. Yet Max was finding the impasse equally painful. He had always had an affectionate relationship with Dasha, and now the sight of his daughter—angry, taciturn, sulking about the house, cold and withdrawn—was more than his self-esteem could tolerate.

"I'll buy you a car, Dashenka," he said over dinner one night. "A snappy little convertible. Any color you like, red, even. Come home and I'll buy you a car."

"I don't want a car. I want to go to law school."

He rose from the table and slammed out of the room. For the next few days they waged unremitting psychological warfare, with Dasha progressively thin-lipped and Max growing gloomier and gloomier. "This is the thanks you get for sending girls to college," he would mutter to no one in particular. But two days before she was due back at Smith, he came to her room. She didn't invite him in.

"Very well." He stood on the threshold glowering. "You say you want to become a lawyer, then convince me. Be a lawyer on your own behalf and we'll see what kind of advocate you are."

The following evening, between the hours of eight and nine, he would be available at his studio on Huntington Avenue. During that time she could plead her case, if she chose. He considered that eminently fair.

"With you the sole judge and jury?" Dasha retorted. "Is that your idea of being fair? In other words, I'm supposed to audition, like one of your students."

"He who pays the piper calls the tune, Dasha. Take it or leave it."

She spent the next twenty-four hours closeted in her room, preparing arguments, numbering points 1 through 10 on lined paper. The majesty of the law. Her academic record. The importance these days of women having a profession to fall back on. But when it came to the night, watching Max sit stonily on the piano bench, his shoulders set, arms squarely folded, she knew there was only one argument that might obtain. She had not wanted to use it, hated the thought, but in love and war . . .

"Finally, point number ten. You owe it to me."

"Owe it?" The saturnine eyebrows shot up.

"Yes. You owe it to me by way of proof that you care as much for me as you do for Alex. You subsidized him through—my God, *two* doctorates—to say nothing of Oxford and that year in Paris, the trip to China. Well, I'm not asking that. All I'm asking is three more years."

"But Dasha, be reasonable. How can you com—"

"Compare?" she burst in. "How can I compare myself with Alex? Is that what you want to know? Because we're both your children. Because you love us both the same. Because"—her voice broke, but she forced herself on—"because you're a fair and just man. I want to believe that, Daddy. I want to believe that more than anything in the world. And if you deny me this chance, that's tantamount to saying, 'You are nothing, Dasha. You're not a real person. Just something pleasant to have around.' You'll have put a price tag on me, on your love, your affection. You'll be saying, 'The girl is worth this much, the boy so much more.' "

"This is blackmail!" Max was livid with anger. "Pure emotional blackmail. How dare you speak to me like that!"

It was no good. She had known from the start it would be no good, and now her eyes filled with the quiet tears of defeat. Her voice dropped to a whisper. "I'm talking about something much more basic than law school, and you know that." No sooner were the words out than she recognized their truth. Law school was incidental. Even Jordan was incidental. The issue lay elsewhere. And now that there was nothing more to lose, she was able to articulate, for the first time in her life, an emotion she had never before even dared to admit.

"From the day I was born, I've felt like a nonentity. Second fiddle. That's a term you can understand, isn't it? You know, the same way you feel when Heifetz is playing with the orchestra—he's up there, you're down here. He's Heifetz and you're a nobody. No, don't bother to deny it, I guessed that long ago. You may have scared me sometimes, Daddy, but you've never fooled me. And I'm not criticizing, I'm sympathizing. I know what you're going through because I've felt that way all my life. With you it's Heifetz or whoever, with me it's Alex. But at least you had your chance, all those years when you were young, those years in New York when you were trying to make it on the concert stage. You had your fair chance, now give me mine. That's all I'm asking. Don't tell me I'm a nothing, without the right to think or dream"—she raised her head—"simply because I'm a woman."

He didn't answer. Merely sat at the piano, his face a landscape of pain; then slowly he began picking out notes with one finger—a fragment of Bach, lorn and fugitive.

"All A's," he murmured over the music.

"What?"

He struck a major chord and folded his hands in his lap. "You can go to law school for as long as you get all A's."

"You mean it?" She leaped from her chair and was on him with a lunge that nearly overturned the piano bench. To her astonishment, his cheek was wet with tears. "Oh Daddy, I'm going to be the best goddam student that ever hit the place."

For years she would look back upon that confrontation as the toughest, most important case she'd ever argued.

But that, of course, was before *Kim vs. FBC.*

CHAPTER FIVE

☐ The buzz of the intercom shattered her reverie. Jordan! Who else would Fran put through in defiance of a strict injunction to hold all calls? It would be Jordan, his old reasonable self, phoning in the spirit of compromise.

She picked up the phone. "I've got Mr. Miller from our Washington branch waiting," her secretary burst out, and before Dasha had a chance to protest, a man's voice came over the wire, urgent and rapid. "Dasha? Walt Miller here. We met at Greenbriar last year. Listen, I just had a call from a guy I know, clerks at the Supreme Court and . . . " Dasha looked at the clock. Two minutes past ten.

"Today!" She managed a whisper. "They're going to rule on the Kim case today!"

"Yup. It's on the docket this morning. You should be getting the word by mid-afternoon at the latest. I just thought you'd like a little advance warning. Meanwhile, I'm sending one of the kids over to stand by, and he'll give you a ring as soon as he hears what's happening."

She paused for a moment to let it sink in. Today. Today of all days. "Jesus, Walt, I can hardly believe it's almost over. Well, thanks for letting me know. We'll be in touch."

She had scarcely hung up when Fran appeared in the doorway, flushed and expectant.

"I had to put the call through," she apologized.

"I can't believe it," was all Dasha could say. "I guess you heard, we'll have the decision on the Kim case today. I don't know whether to laugh or cry."

"I was wondering, Mrs. Croy, in light of all this, if I should be making any special preparations. It might be a good idea to get some champagne in, and is there anything you want me to do about the press?"

"No no no." Dasha shook her head vehemently. The imminence of the decision had taken her by storm, pushing everything else out of her head. "Not a word to anyone about this yet, and as for champagne—well, for all we know, we could wind up drinking hemlock instead. Three years." She shook her head in wonder. "Three years I've waited for today, would you believe it? Three years in the making." She gave a self-conscious laugh. "Sounds like a Hollywood epic."

"Cast of thousands, cost of millions. That's what they say down in the cafeteria. You know how the associates kid around."

"Don't I just. Any other messages this morning?"

Her secretary ran down a list of names—clients, associates, one of the senior partners wanted to see her, and, "Oh yes, a Professor Morton. 'Nipsy' Morton? Do I have that right?"

"Really!" Dasha was intrigued. "Did he say what about?"

"He'd like you to conduct a seminar on First Amendment next year. At your convenience, they'll work around your schedule."

"Well, isn't that nice!" Imagine. Nipsy Morton of all people. "Tell him I'll get back to him later this week."

Yet the moment Fran left her office, Dasha burst into a yard-wide grin.

"Me lecturing at Seneca," she marveled. "How's them apples!"

Apples.

In Paris, Danny the Red was ripping up cobblestones outside the Sorbonne. On Broadway, theater-goers were flocking to see a show proudly billed as "The First Nude Rock Musical." In California, Dr. Timothy Leary was preaching the merits of LSD to the converted. In Washington, Alex Oborin had quit the administration in protest to Vietnam and launched his widely syndicated column, "One Man's Mind."

In Seneca, the autumn of '68 was primarily distinguished by a bumper apple crop, for the village prided itself on being the Apple Capital of the Northeast. Other than groaning orchards and the cider press, the town's chief ornament was the venerable Seneca School of Law.

The school itself was an architectural jewel, with elegant Greek porticoes, oak-paneled lecture halls, and a reputation for producing worthy, though not always world-beating, graduates. Yale might be more prestigious, Harvard more ancient, but none offered such a serene environment in which to prepare for the bar.

Jordan and Dasha had settled down into their second year. Almost halfway through, Dasha approached the milestone with mixed feelings.

What they had wasn't marriage, but certainly the next best thing. And if living together was what her presence there was all about, then it had been a wise decision. To share—not just homework, but rooms and meals and pillow space and towels—was a continuing source of pleasure. He was easy to live with, pliant and sweet-tempered, and she prided herself on the knowledge that they were more than just another pair of college lovers: they were best of friends, closest of confidants. "My other self," Jordan sometimes called her.

Economy dictated that they live in the dorms. They occupied two tiny boxlike rooms, white and spare, big enough only to accommodate a single bed, a small desk, and a couple of chairs. They studied in his, slept in hers, an arrangement which the proctors at Seneca cheerfully ignored. It was a relief to be treated like responsible men and women preparing for the noblest of professions. As long as bedroom etiquette remained reasonably discreet, the authorities turned a blind eye.

But the new liberalism that was sweeping the country seemed to have left the Oborin household untouched. The first time her parents announced they were coming to visit, Dasha succumbed to a bout of panic.

"Your razor . . . your shaving cream . . . " She began tearing through the medicine chest for bits of incriminating evidence. "And would you check under the bed for socks?"

Jordan shook his head, perplexed. "Jesus, you're really terrified of them, aren't you?"

"I just don't want to hurt their sensibilities."

"Well, am I finally going to meet them, at least?"

"You'll meet them, I promise."

In fact, Dasha preferred to contrive a seemingly chance encounter in the corridors: "Oh, hi there, Jordan. Mother, Daddy, I'd like you to meet a fellow student and a very good friend." Yet despite her artlessness,

Max was quick to sense vibrations. Within seconds he had Jordan backed to the wall and was bombarding him with questions. Where was he from? Who were his people? What were his plans after passing the bar?—a routine Dasha remembered clearly and painfully from her high-school dating days.

Forewarned, however, Jordan rose to the occasion and the inquisition passed off amiably.

"A nice fellow," Max remarked later. "I like his ambition. That's a delightful quality in a young man," and Dasha turned beet red with pleasure.

"He really liked you," she told Jordan the moment her parents left.

"And if he hadn't, Dasha, what then?"

"It wouldn't have mattered." She kissed him full on the lips. "I'm a big girl now. Anyhow, that's a theoretical question, *thank God.*" But if she was satisfied with the results of the encounter, Jordan was not.

"I felt like an idiot, coming in the back door like that, You'd like them to meet a good friend. They're going to be my in-laws, after all. I think you might have told them we're engaged."

"But I couldn't, Jordan."

"Why not? There's nothing immoral about two people wanting to get married."

"Well, for one thing . . . I don't have a ring," and before Jordan could interject, she raced on. "I know you'll think it's silly, I think so too. Personally I couldn't care less, but you don't know my parents. They're very conventional and little symbols like that mean a lot to them." One look at Jordan's face, pale with shock, made her regret her words. "Please, forget it. I'm sorry I even mentioned it."

He said nothing, but the following Monday he came to her room bearing a tiny white leather box. "Here, darling!" He slipped the ring on her finger, a modest chip of a diamond in a nest of seed pearls. "Now it's official."

"You shouldn't have," she burst out. In fact she was overjoyed. There it was on her finger—visible proof of their love. "But how? Oh, honey"—her euphoria was short-lived—"I hope you haven't gone into hock for this."

He laughed. "Who'd be crazy enough to give me credit?"

No, he hadn't gone into hock. He had sold the Volkswagen. "It was just an old heap anyhow. I was lucky to get as much as I did for it. And what do I need a car up here for?" He lied with a semblance of gaiety. "Dinky town like this. Gonna get myself a bike instead."

"You shouldn't have!" Dasha repeated, this time heartfelt. That car had meant a great deal to him—his freedom, his sole indulgence. "I didn't mean for you to do anything rash."

"It was only a jalopy, Dasha." He put his arms around her. "But a diamond is forever. And at least we can stop prevaricating. God!" he groaned. "How I hate telling lies."

"You're funny." Dasha laughed through incipient tears. "For a man who's in love with total truth, you sure picked one helluva profession."

That night, they both wrote home about their intentions.

To her astonishment, Max took the engagement in his stride. Even with relief, she suspected. In his mind, it marked the end of this "law school nonsense."

Jordan's mother responded by taking a Trailways bus up to Seneca her first free day.

"I'm very happy Jordan's found someone so nice," Charlotte Croy said, folding her hand about Dasha's. She was a slight, immaculate woman, compulsively neat and younger than Dasha had envisioned, with the remnants of a fragile beauty. She had the same dark liquid eyes as her son; and as she sat across the table in the Copper Lantern Tearoom, those eyes were wide with fear.

My God—Dasha watched her aligning the silver, refolding the linen napkin with military precision—*she's even more nervous than I am.*

"Of course Jordie couldn't marry until he's able to support a family, and that will be years and years yet," Charlotte said in a voice full of hope. "Anyhow, I think it's a terrible mistake marrying too young . . ."

"Mrs. Croy . . ."

"Please, call me Charlotte."

Dasha swallowed. "Charlotte. Jordan and I are both of age, and I'm perfectly capable of working too. We don't want to put it off forever."

The brown eyes scrutinized her more closely. "Do you really intend to be a lawyer? Imagine that."

"I'll be honest with you," Dasha confessed. "I came here to be with

Jordan. All I really want is to marry him." *As soon as possible,* she almost added, but seeing the poor woman's expression of dismay, knowing how harshly life had already treated Charlotte, she amended her sentence. "Once he's passed the bar, of course."

"He has to watch his pennies, you know. Young people don't live on love alone."

Dasha groaned inwardly at the cliché. The woman was so frightened, so cautious, so fearful that Jordan might aim too high and fall too low. Her husband's bankruptcy and death had left an abundance of scars.

"I understand." Dasha bowed her head to the inevitable. "And I'm prepared to wait."

Yet she found waiting difficult. She had the sensation of biding her life away "playing house." And sometimes when the trees were in blossom and the air sweet as honey, she felt a willingness to forgo the larger dreams. She could picture herself and Jordan spending the rest of their lives in Apple Capple; in one of those white frame houses at the edge of town, with a couple of kids, a dog or maybe a pony. Or if not Apple Capple, some place very like it. There could be worse lives than that of a country lawyer, and Jordan, too, admitted it had its appeal. But whenever he went to New York, he came back restless, feeling, as he said, like a pilgrim to another planet.

"The world's going to hell in a handbasket," he said, snapping a textbook shut one night. "Vietnam, civil rights, the ecological revolution. Big things happening left and right, and here we sit wasting our time on boring boring contracts."

"Contracts aren't boring, honey," she replied. "Once you think of them in human terms, they're kind of fascinating."

"Eat-Rite Restaurants versus Kowetsky Exterminators on the riveting question of whether their agreement requires bi-weekly or twice-monthly service calls." He snickered. "That's your idea of fascinating human drama?"

Curiously it was, in a way.

Their first year had raced by swiftly and successfully. Dasha, mindful of her father's injunction that she get all A's, had rolled up her sleeves and plunged in. She had come prepared to work hard. What she had not been prepared for was that she would fall in love with the law. Yes, even with "boring boring contracts."

Each case was loaded with incipient drama. *You* promised. *He* cheated. *She* lied. *They* defaulted. You sloughed away the verbiage and each case was about people. Men and women in conflict. Angry. Grasping. Foolish. Proud. Were the guys at Kowetsky Exterminators trying to screw Eat-Rite out of four extra service calls a year? Or was Eat-Rite aiming to pull a fast one on the bug killers? Eat-Rite. Jesus, the place sounded like a cockroach paradise. And what about Kowetsky? Was that a Polish name? Russian? Maybe the man was a foreigner, a guy who couldn't grasp the wording of the contract. Could he even read English, she wondered. In which case, he'd entered the agreement in good faith. Still, as the old joke went, "Ignorance of the law is no excuse, ma'am. The fact remains you shot and killed your husband."

Yes, Dasha loved poking around in these waters. She had inherited some of her father's perfectionism, she supposed. "Nit-picking," Jordan called it, and he was always groaning about getting mired down in trivia. She saw it instead as groundwork that enabled one to take the imaginative leap into an infinity of speculations.

For Jordan, the transition from college to law school was proving more difficult. Even for a student with no other calls on his time, the volume of work was crushing; and to Jordan, playing four nights a week at a roadhouse, it sometimes verged on the unmanageable. He would come home at one in the morning, eyes red from weariness, then study till he fell asleep over his books.

"Give up the crummy job," Dasha pleaded. "It's beneath your dignity. It takes up too much time."

"I wish I could, but I got this terrible habit. It's called eating."

The first time she suggested he share her allowance from home— they might manage if they cut expenses way down—his answer had been to pucker up and whistle "Just a Gigolo." The second time, he had taken umbrage. "I am not yet reduced to living off money from my fiancée's father." He had firm views about responsibility, and Dasha, knowing how sensitive he could be on matters touching his pride, never raised the question again.

Moreover, he was doing quite well. Given the time, he was a meticulous workman, and his first-year grades had been above average.

Hers had been better. Outstanding, in fact, and she almost felt called upon to apologize.

"My father would have my scalp if I goofed off." Her progress delighted and mystified Jordan. "You have a real flair for the stuff," he'd say. Or, "Who knows, we may make a lawyer out of you yet," to which Dasha would answer with a noncommittal shrug. She was wary of taking the business too seriously; it was only a time-filler until marriage. Because she deemed herself essentially a dilettante, she felt she might treat herself to the luxury of taking risks in class. Nothing suited her better than to quit the beaten path and go for the long shot. Once or twice she fell flat on her face, but more often her approach paid off and she would be rewarded with an intoxicating sensation of being in full control and a delight in her own ingenuity.

"You sure are lucky, Dasha—or was that woman's intuition?" Jordan teased her about playing hunches. But they weren't hunches, they were insights, although it was a term she was reluctant to use. It sounded so pretentious.

During the course of that first year, she began to form the disturbing notion that she might be better suited to the law than Jordan. She was quicker to perceive relationships, root out inconsistencies, to cut through the verbiage and zero in on the core of a complex situation. And sometimes, when she and Jordan were studying together, she would leave him several paces behind.

The villain, she was convinced, was the financial pressure Jordan labored under. "That damn job of yours. I'd almost rather it was another woman." Of course student performance was not the acid test of ability. It was the world beyond that would take your measure, evaluate your clout. And there, undoubtedly, Jordan would shine. He had the presence, the commitment, the command of language. Above all he had—his favored term—"the fire in the belly."

Nonetheless when she was asked to join the *Law Review* at the end of that year, her response was troubled.

"I'm flattered, of course," she told Professor Morton, "but I'm not sure I should accept."

He was a short, stocky, disputatious man, with the wiry hair and darting movements of a terrier. The students called him "Nipsy" behind his back.

"How can you hesitate, Miss Oborin?" He rubbed his eyes as if to see her better. "You must be aware that this is a very significant opportunity, quite an achievement for a first-year student. It's just about the first thing prospective employers will look for on your résumé. No serious student would think of turning it down. And, I may add, that I went out of my way to recommend you to the editors." Without further ado, he set about outlining the work, discussing deadlines, suggestions for articles of interest. Then he paused and looked at her with a quizzical expression. "If you don't mind a personal question, I've often wondered . . . your name. Tell me, are you any relation to the Washington columnist?" And when she said she was, he nodded vigorously. "Like brother, like sister."

"What do you mean, Dr. Morton?"

"I mean that talent obviously runs in your family. You know, of course, that you have enormous potential. If you go about it judiciously, you could have a very big career ahead of you."

Her heart thudded, her throat grew tight.

"For a woman, you mean."

"For anyone!" He glared at her. "And you should begin planning for it now. Where have you been, Oborin? Don't you read the papers? It's a whole new world out there, and if you've got the right stuff, the opportunities are unlimited. So don't give me any sexist alibis. I have, I repeat, great expectations of you, both as a student and as a lawyer."

She asked for two days to think it over, hoping that in the interim Jordan too would be asked to join the staff. Only when it became clear that he would not did she finally mention it in an offhand manner.

"*Law Review!* Good God, Dasha." For a moment he was taken aback, then he pulled her to him in a bear hug. "Congratulations! That is simply marvelous. I suppose I was hoping I'd be asked too, but it's probably just as well. *Law Review* is almost a full-time job in itself, I understand." He didn't harp on his disappointment; nonetheless he was all over her for every detail. What would she be working on? Who else had been selected? What did Nipsy Morton have to say?

"He said . . . he said . . . " Dasha stumbled. She had no desire to rub it in. "Well, actually, he didn't say much, and I got the impression that I was picked because they felt they needed a woman's name on the masthead. Keeping up with the times and all that jazz."

It was the smallest, the whitest of lies, but she went to bed that night with an impure conscience. For the first time she had deceived him. "And the last time," she promised herself under cover of darkness. "Absolutely the last."

Thus their first year ended. Jordan spent the vacation as a summer associate with a New York law firm. Dasha went to Tanglewood as usual, and when she returned, it was with a vow that there would be no repeat of the *Law Review* episode. It was not a question of her doing worse. Jordan would simply have to do better. She would see to it.

The Harlan Fiske Stone Club was an organization run by students, for students. Strictly speaking it was an extracurricular activity, but in the pecking order of campus life it was an activity of consummate importance. More than any course in the official syllabus, the club offered budding lawyers a chance to gain practical experience in the art of litigation through a series of mock trials. The surroundings were simulated, the cases were not: they were real and vital cases drawn from the dockets of the appellate courts.

Club members were divided into two- and three-student teams. A pair of teams would then be assigned to argue opposite sides of a given case before a panel of third-year students.

From the outset, Jordan and Dasha had functioned as a unit with considerable success. Jordan particularly shone in these circumstances. He was quick-witted, fast on his feet, and the situation was tailor-made for his gifts. Now he was looking forward to the Moot Court Finals.

Each year, those club members with the best track record were chosen to compete for substantial cash prizes. The finals were more than an honor, for on that day the bench would be peopled not by fellow students but by leaders of the bar: outstanding professors, nationally known attorneys, judges from state and federal court. Brilliant careers had been launched by students who had distinguished themselves in the process.

Jordan breathed a sigh of relief when he was selected. Dasha, too, had been asked. And, by what struck them both as a capricious quirk of fate, they were assigned adversarial roles.

She was convinced there had been some mistake. She and Jordan had worked together so long and so effectively, it seemed unlikely they would

be pitted against each other. The next day, she collared the club president
to sort the matter out.

"Look, Bernie," she asked him outright, "could you juggle around
the assignments and put me on the same team with Jordan? We operate
very well together."

"Sorry. Everything's been organized."

"Then at least put me on a different case."

"I *said* it's all organized. Too late to change."

"Oh come on," she wheedled. "You talk as if it's all been written
in stone and handed down from Mount Sinai. Jordan and I have always
been a team."

"Tweedledum and Tweedledee."

"What's that supposed to mean?" Her blood began to boil. "I get
the impression that you split us up deliberately."

"Well, let's say I wanted to spread the talent around. Croy and
Marshall Loomis against you and Al Schwartz. I think it'll be to everyone's benefit." And when Dasha pressed him further, he grew prickly.
"Goddam women! Okay, so you and Croy have the hots for each other.
That's your business, but this is law school, dammit, not a Saturday night
social. What do you think . . . that when you get out into the real world,
you're gonna have any say about who you're up against? Don't be
ridiculous. The guy who was your colleague one week could be your
adversary the next. There's nothing personal about it. And if you don't
have the balls to go the distance, then you should get the hell out of law
school and find yourself a more ladylike profession."

"But—"

"No buts, Oborin. We've offered you a place in the finals. Take it
or leave it."

"*You're a shit, Bernie Farrell,*" she wanted to say, "*nothing but a
chauvinist shit.*" Yet at heart she knew logic was on his side and to back
down would make her appear contemptible.

"I'll take it."

He grinned. "See you in court, counselor."

She had done the right thing, Jordan was swift to assure her. "You
have to play the cards you're dealt. Now I don't want to see any slacking
off on your part. Play hardball. What Bernie said was true, you know,
so promise me you'll give it everything you've got."

"Yeah ... well." She sighed. "One thing, though. You know there's a thousand-dollar prize for the winning team? Whoever wins, you or I, we're guaranteed five hundred."

The case was a tortuous one, a complicated litigation against a public utilities company touching upon half a dozen points of law, too much for any one person to research. She and Al Schwartz broke it down into compartments and then began to prepare their briefs in utmost secrecy. When she encountered Jordan in the library, she would merely smile and nod. He would invariably wink back.

"Like one of those old Tracy and Hepburn movies," he said the night before the ordeal. They were sitting in her room in bathrobes, eating peanut butter sandwiches, both bleary from overwork.

"Only Hepburn and Tracy didn't eat peanut butter sandwiches, I betcha."

"Mmmmm." He munched a while in silence. "You know I was thinking, when this is over, what say we blow a hundred dollars off the top of the prize money and treat ourselves to a bang-up weekend?"

There was a lovely inn overlooking Lake Cayuga, the 1812 House, where they had splurged one Sunday on a lavish lunch. Dasha had taken the brochure, and now they pored over it. Horseback riding, French cuisine, four-poster beds. "Fireplaces in every room." Jordan laughed. "Sweet shades of Tanglewood. I'll make reservations."

Topekian Industries vs. Texas Light and Power.
"We're ready for the plaintiff."

Jordan squared his shoulders and strode up to the bar. He had bought a new suit for the occasion, and now decked out in gray flannel with a striped rep tie he looked very self-possessed, very businesslike. In a few sentences he outlined the case swiftly and clearly, then began laying the groundwork of his argument with a wealth of citations. Quite where he was headed Dasha couldn't as yet say, but he obviously had a definite direction in mind. By her side at the wooden table, Al Schwartz was making notes. He leaned over to whisper, "Jordan's in good form today," and she nodded back.

Yes indeed. He was in top form, primed like a racehorse, full of energy and conviction. She hadn't heard him speak so forcefully since Amherst. Then, almost imperceptibly, his voice wavered, a faintest note of hesitation crept in, not distinct enough to be noticeable to the assembly but Dasha felt the first prick of alarm. It passed, and Jordan began to reveal his strategy.

"The fundamental issue here is the liability for pipeline maintenance . . ."

"MacFarlane." Unconsciously Dasha's lips moved, her mouth formed the syllables *"MacFarlane."* Why, this whole business Jordan was raising had been settled once and for all in *MacFarlane.* By the Supreme Court, no less. She had the case number scribbled down somewhere in her notes, and there was no doubt—not a shred, not a shadow—that the *MacFarlane* decision invalidated Jordan's entire line of attack.

"MacFarlane!" She screamed the word in her mind, trying to psyche Jordan, warn him, half-believing he would pick up her vibes. *Go back, please, before it's too late, or else I'll clobber you with MacFarlane.* But on Jordan plowed, oblivious, and having pegged his direction and apparently resolved his doubts, proceeded with the inexorable drive of a lemming headed toward a cliff. She listened on in horror, then turned to Al, wondering if he too had caught the gaffe, but Al was merely pulling at his ear. No, why should he have? It had been her area of research exclusively. Anyhow, it wasn't as if *MacFarlane* was one of your great sexy landmark decisions, but still . . . She had dug it up routinely weeks ago, made a note of the number, and put it aside. It never occurred to her that the opposition would pursue such a patently erroneous line. Or was she the only one familiar with the ruling? In a few minutes the floor would be Dasha's, and what in God's name should she say? *"MacFarlane?"* Could she do it? Could she annihilate Jordan with a single word? And yet . . .

And yet, she could barely repress a shudder of pride, a kind of self-congratulation that she alone of everyone here—even the visiting members of the bar—yes, she alone had dug down to the solidest core of the matter. It was one beautiful piece of research, if she said so herself.

But why did it have to be Jordan up there? If only it had been someone else. Anyone else. Marshall Loomis, for instance. Or better yet, that prick Bernie Farrell. What joy it would be to get up and send him flying.

She had never considered herself a competitive person, but for once in her life Dasha was smitten by the will to win. "Fire in the belly," Jordan called it, and she had presumed it was merely poetic imagery. But suddenly the image crystallized, took life. As if some alien creature had lodged inside her, burning, furious to get out and take on the world. She could see the moment, taste it—vivid and dramatic—when she would rise to her feet and utter the word *"MacFarlane."* First a look of surprise, puzzlement, then a respectful awe would sweep across the faces of the men on the bench. There would be a raising of eyebrows, a sage nodding of heads, and that federal judge, the fat one with the mustache—he'd bathe her in a huge smile of approval. Yes, she could see it. Hear it, too—the ringing praise, the congratulations from friends, colleagues, teachers. "Terrific! Great! You really socked it to 'em, Dasha." Then the announcement that "This year the Harlan Fiske Stone Prize goes to . . ."

Talk of Eve and the apple, was there anything in God's earth to compare with that kind of temptation? To be a somebody in this distinguished crowd, a name to be conjured with and remembered.

Ten feet away, yet it might have been across the Atlantic, Jordan was winding up. He looked different, unfamiliar in the three-piece suit and white shirt. A stranger. An adversary. His forehead was damp with a fine band of sweat, his dark eyes ringed behind the horn-rimmed glasses.

He finished speaking, took off his glasses. And in the hush that followed, he turned not to the bench, not to the audience, but to Dasha, craning his neck to seek her out with a sweet and expectant smile. *Did I do all right?* She could read his mind. He wanted to confirm that she was still there, to remind them both that in all the crush of people—judges, classmates, visitors—theirs was the profoundest tie, the most intimate bond. Hers, the approval that mattered most. And at the sight of his smile, Dasha froze.

Crazy! She had been crazy to believe for a single instant that she could do such a thing to Jordan. Jordan to whom the proceedings today meant so much. Jordan with his doubts, his insecurities. What the hell was wrong with her? Where was her sense of priorities? This was *moot* court, for Chrissakes. By definition that meant academic, hypothetical. How could she have mistaken it for real life? But that smile of Jordan's, that quest for her love and approval—*that* was real.

"Is counsel ready for the defendant?"

"Hey, Dasha." Al Schwartz poked her in the ribs. "You're on." She stared at him in terror, afraid he might come out of nowhere to say, "Hit 'em with *MacFarlane.*" But all Al said was "Good luck."

Zombie-like, Dasha forced herself to her feet and crossed over to the bench. All she could think of was that she would open her mouth and the forbidden word would come vomiting out—*MacFarlane.* She clenched her lips. Must not, must not utter it. Think of anything. A stone. What she had for breakfast. Think of other aspects of the case. Anything —as long as it didn't begin with an M.

She tried to shape an opening sentence. Something simple like "On behalf of Texas Light and Power," or, "I suppose you're wondering why I've asked you here today." No, that was silly. Come on, girl, pull yourself together. How about just trying "Gentlemen." Good, she would try that.

She opened her mouth to speak. Nothing came. Her arms were rigid by her sides, her vocal cords paralyzed. Even the slightest movement seemed beyond her. In the heavy atmosphere of the room she could make out shuffling, mumbling, before her see the questioning faces on the bench. Yet she was as though stricken dumb, and might have remained rooted to the spot indefinitely had not Jordan sprung up behind her and pushed a glass of water in her hand.

"Take your time, love, and don't be nervous," he whispered in her ear. "You're going to be fine."

She swallowed some water, returned the squeeze of his hand and managed a barely discernible mutter. "Ready for Texas Light and Power . . ."

It was not, Jordan would later assure her, a total fiasco. He'd heard a lot worse. And in fact she did get through her appearance somehow, almost by rote, making a few points now and again. But it was a limp and disaffected performance, for only the smallest part of her mind was engaged in the argument. The larger part was still bent on suppressing that terrible word: *MacFarlane.* She never spoke it, battled it down a thousand times, and as soon as she finished slunk, exhausted, back to her chair, not daring to look Al Schwartz in the eye.

Jordan's partner got up for rebuttal, Al, too, would have his turn, but essentially the fight was over. At the first opportunity she fled toward the ladies' room.

Halfway down the hall, an angry voice rasped out "Oborin!"

It was Nipsy Morton.

"What the hell got into you back there, I want to know? I saw you. You had *MacFarlane* on the tip of your tongue. Why didn't you cite it?" He was white-lipped with rage, as if her failure had been his own. "You could have demolished Croy's whole contention," he hammered away at her. "Why, for God's sakes . . . why?" Until Dasha, wretched and trembling, blurted out: "I couldn't. I couldn't bring myself to do it. Don't you see—don't you understand? We're engaged. We're going to be married."

"Married?" Morton gave a contemptuous snort. "What has that got to do with anything? Married, my ass! You know until today I had you figured for someone really out of the ordinary, but what you did in there was despicable. You were thinking like a woman, not a lawyer. It was worse than bad law, it was bad ethics. Your only duty is to fight for your client. That's where your loyalty belongs. Lawyers have been disbarred for less. And as for Croy, if your young man isn't capable of handling defeat, then he doesn't deserve to practice law either!" He turned on his heels and stomped off, growling "Married!" as though it were an obscenity. Dasha ran to the ladies' room and threw up.

A few hours later she was curled up under a comforter in a huge four-poster bed while Jordan uncorked champagne by firelight. The room was as charming as the brochure had promised: period furniture, dormer windows framed in chintz. The wallpaper sported a pattern of rosebuds and ivy that reminded Dasha of her bedroom in Boston.

"Aaah, this is the life." Jordan watched the bubbles rising, then handed her a glass. "Here's to, darling."

They clinked glasses. He took a few sips, then rotated the glass thoughtfully between his palms.

"What happened to you tonight, Dasha, a case of stage fright?"

"I don't want to talk about it."

"I appreciate that. Still, you know, it's always productive to examine what went wrong. How else do we learn from our mistakes?" In the firelight he couldn't see the set of her jaw, and continued on a drift of his own. "I learned something, too. You weren't the only one with the jitters, if that's any consolation. I . . . well of course you couldn't have known about it, but I had a moment of total panic up there tonight. That pipeline liability tack. I only got the idea coming home from work on Tuesday and at the time it struck me as pure dynamite, like one of your famous hunches. Yeah, it was risky, but I figured I had a good chance. About halfway through I almost got cold feet. You know, I hadn't researched it all that thoroughly. The truth is . . . " He paused, and for one wild moment she wondered if he had actually guessed the truth. But in the rosy light of the wood fire, he appeared content, fully at peace with himself. "The truth is I was never absolutely certain if you or Schwartz were going to pull the rug out from under. Suppose there'd been a precedent, a high court ruling . . . I would have been up shit creek. Thank God there wasn't." He laughed softly. "The important thing is, my hunch paid off."

In that instant she felt his senior by about one hundred years, infinitely wiser, infinitely sad. Jordan wasn't made for the long shot, the high-risk gamble. His hunch had been nothing more than a wild stab. Yet in a way it was her fault; she had dared him to the precipice.

She put down her glass on the night table.

"I *said* I don't want to talk about it any more. You had the stuff, I didn't. Let's leave it at that. You know, here we are"—she leaned back and clasped her hands behind her head—"in this beautiful room. You . . . me, the fire, the four-poster. My God, when was the last time we shared a double bed? In some crummy motel in Massachusetts? And wallpaper. I don't think we've ever made love in a room with wallpaper. It should be real, Jordan. You and I in our own home, our own bedroom . . . flowers in a vase, pretty wallpaper."

"It'll come, Dasha." He sat down beside her and stroked her hair. "Not so far off now. Another year or so."

"Another year." She sighed. "Sometimes it seems like another lifetime. Oh darling, it's been such a long hard day. Let's put it all behind us and make love."

Someone kept shaking her—gently, persistently.

"Wake up, Dasha. Come on, sweetie, wake up."

"Wha . . . ?" she mumbled. "What's wrong?"

"Wake up. You've been having a bad dream. Grinding your teeth, muttering something over and over."

She sat up with a start. "Muttering? What did I say?"

"I don't know. It sounded troubled, sort of like . . . like *I'm falling I'm falling*."

MacFarlane. MacFarlane.

"You're right, Jordan." She burrowed into his arms for comfort. "It was a very bad dream. A nightmare."

The next morning over breakfast in the dining room, she told him she had decided to quit law school. No, there was no point in discussing it. Her decision was final. It had nothing to do with yesterday's events. She had been mulling it over all year long. Last night had merely confirmed her resolve.

"I never wanted to be a lawyer, honey. You knew that from the start. And anyhow, I don't believe in doing things by halves."

She wanted to get married. Not a year from now, not six months from now. She wanted to get married right away.

"But, Dasha, be reasonable."

"I've spent nearly five years being reasonable. I'm twenty-three, for God's sake, Jordan, and I'm . . . well, I'm pissing my life away."

Most of her friends from Smith were married, starting families even. But she had spent some of the most important years of her life living in dormitories, eating cafeteria food, waiting for Jordan. She could wait no longer. She wanted her own home—even if it was nothing but a cold-water walk-up in Seneca, even if they had to furnish it with orange crates. At least it would be theirs.

Jordan was stunned. "But to throw it all away, Dasha, because of one bad experience!" He was convinced it was the moot court "defeat" that was making her so intractable. If she would stick it out at least until the end of the year . . .

"No, Jordan, not even another semester. Now hear me out. I've always gone along with you in everything, but this once it's my turn."

They would marry, find a place to live, and Jordan must quit his job immediately. Couldn't he see he was jeopardizing his career, both their futures? Why, only last night he admitted that he had come unprepared. The hours that should have been spent in the library had been squandered instead singing foolish songs for foolish people in a tavern. Okay, he'd been lucky last night. But he might not be so lucky again. And it was crazy to trust to that kind of luck once you were out in the real world. He'd have to really knuckle down, because she wasn't about to sit back and watch him risk everything he'd dreamed about for years for a few measly dollars. Anyhow, he had some prize money now, and that would tide them over until Dasha found a job of sorts—coaching students, typing, picking apples if it came to that. Whatever, she would support them both until Jordan passed the bar. This was the sixties, after all, not the Dark Ages. Plenty of women were seeing their husbands through school and if her parents didn't approve—well, tough.

"And if I don't approve, Dasha? What if I can't repay you?"

Well, that was tough too. She loved him too much to stand by and do nothing while Jordan made hash of his opportunities out of some antiquated notion of male pride.

"I'm laying down the law, Jordan. I'm not going to while away my life treading water. If we don't get married now, then frankly, I'd just as soon pack up and go back to Boston. Darling"—she gripped his hand and pleaded—"please don't say no out of false pride. You know I'd do anything in the world for you. The only thing I can't do is let you spoil your chances."

"I've never been faced with an ultimatum before." Jordan's voice cracked. "And I can't believe you really want to give up law school. I know how much you like it."

"I love it," she said honestly. "But I love you more . . . more than you will ever know."

He agreed to her terms on one condition. "If ever, Dasha, once I'm established, if ever you want to go back and pick up where you left off . . ."

"I doubt that I will."

"But if ever you do, you know you can count on me. That's the least I can do to repay you."

Four days later they were married in Seneca Town Hall. Jordan wore his new three-piece suit and Dasha looked very pretty in a silk print dress, clutching a sprig of apple blossoms. Seneca apple blossoms full of spring and new life.

CHAPTER SIX

☐ "May I offer you some coffee, Blagden?" She reached for the pot.

"No, thank you, my dear. I'll settle instead for a few minutes of your time."

The old gentleman lowered himself into a chair with movements so fragile one could almost hear the clatter of his bones.

For Dasha it was always an effort to address Blagden Geere familiarly, rather like roller skating in Arlington National Cemetery or chewing gum in the Oval Office. For in his way he, too, was a national monument, a former Attorney General of the United States, a hero of the Nuremberg Trials. However, it was an unspoken law of Slater Blaney that partners address each other on a first-name basis, the pretext being that they were all—from the most senior to the youngest—on equal footing and that the firm was essentially one big happy family.

All pretense of democracy aside, it was a singular honor to be called on in her office by the firm's oldest member, the lone survivor of its founding fathers. She crossed her hands respectfully and waited.

"I understand we're to have a ruling on the Kim case today." He exhaled softly. "At last . . . at last. You must be nervous as a cat. I remember the first time I waited out a Supreme Court decision. Every minute seemed like a century. It was the spring of thirty-three, I recall. *Winterbotham versus Manero,*" and he was off on one of his rambling excursions into the past. Forgivable, surely, when one had such a distinguished past in which to ramble, but the old man's recollections often proved a test of his listener's patience. Dasha heard with half an ear, trying to keep her eyes from glazing over as he recounted details half a century old in an increasingly circuitous narrative. *When he's done,* she resolved, *I'll tell him that I'm leaving the firm.* She felt very sad.

"But of course"—at last he showed signs of winding down— "that was 1933 and this is 1983." *1984, Blagden,* she corrected mentally. "And," he concluded, "after all that I lost the case. What a blow! I wanted to crawl into a hole and disappear. Yet here I am fifty years later, still lawyering." There was a note of triumph in his voice, and Dasha realized that there had indeed been a point to the long discursive anecdote: to raise her spirits in the face of possible defeat.

"However"—the old man rubbed his parchment hands together— "I haven't come here to talk about the past but about the future—the future of Slater Blaney. We are, I like to think, the finest law firm in the country. Not the oldest, not the largest, merely the best. And from where I sit, it looks as if we are about to enter an era of expansion." He began outlining some of the matters looming on the horizon—mergers of industrial giants, takeover battles, company reorganizations. "And who's going to see all this through, I ask you? The senior partners? The Management Committee?" He smiled wanly. "I may be hard of hearing, my dear, but not as yet totally deaf, and I understand we're referred to as the Geriatric Ward. Unflattering, but on the whole not inaccurate. The time has come, I'm afraid, to entrust the management of the firm to younger men. And women," he added almost as an afterthought.

Dasha listened to him dry-mouthed and dazed. She had not expected the conversation to take such a turn. Was it yet another example of an old man's rambling? Or had Jordan been correct and they were going to offer her a senior partnership? If so, perhaps she should speak out now, cut off the speculation at the root. *My husband and I have decided . . .*

No, that sounded weak. Uncertain. *I have decided in light of my family obligations . . .* She wet her lips, when Geere broke in on her resolution.

"Thank you, my dear. I will have some coffee after all."

Grateful for the reprieve, she poured them each a cup.

At the first sip, his eyebrows furrowed. "That's very strong," he said, "and very, very rich."

"It's Kenyan," she replied. "A special blend, but once you've developed a taste for it, all the other kinds of coffee are blah."

"Like power." He smiled and took a second tentative sip. "That's what they say about power. It's addictive, you know, and everything else is bland and dull in comparison. That's how come no one ever retires around here—not even us ancients."

"Oh, I don't know"—there it was, the perfect opening. Dasha ventured a toe in the water. "I could leave, certainly, and become a private person again."

"Could you?" He peered at her above the top of his glasses. "Oh, I think not. You're one of us, Dasha, a born competitor. No, don't shake your head, my dear—not until I've finished what I have to say. We've decided, you see, to expand the committee by the addition of two, perhaps three senior partners. You won't be surprised to learn that your name is at the top of the list."

Her heart skidded to a halt.

"Surely," she said, "that would depend on the outcome of the Kim case. If I lose . . . "

"If you lose, it may, perhaps, delay the offer by a few months. Whatever the Supreme Court thinks, we've been more than satisfied with your performance. That's why I came here today—to assure you that whatever happens, you have a great future here at the firm. You're the next wave, Dasha, the new generation. And one day your hands will be on the helm."

He rose to leave, a tall stooped man who had seen his life become a legend. He took her hand with an unaccustomed formality. "And good luck today. I trust you won't find the wait too tiresome."

Her first instinct the moment he left was to tear to the phone and share the news with Jordan. But that would only complicate issues. For the hundredth time that morning she checked her watch. Only eleven-seventeen. Unbelievable. The old man was right. Every minute like a century, he had said. She checked her watch against the desk clock. They were only seconds apart.

Funny, but there had been years—she smiled at the thought—years when she hardly bothered to wear a watch, let alone a Patek Philippe. When time had slid through her hands unnoticed and was gone before she had a chance to look around. When she counted in seasons, not minutes. When her alarm clock had been the cry of a waking baby. When her husband's footsteps in the hall marked the end of the work day. A time when it sufficed to be Dasha Oborin Croy and nothing more. Or DOC as it said on the towels her mother had sent her after the wedding.

"Doc," Jordan used to call her on occasion. "What's up, Doc?" he'd holler first thing when he came home from the office. Even before he reached the door she would hear him bounding up the staircase, buoyant, youthful, too impatient to wait for the elevator. And she would dash out into the dark of the hall to greet him. "What's up, Doc?" he'd sing out. They'd kiss, and within minutes pour out to one another the highlights and the low spots of their day in a great gush of confidences.

Just as now, intuitively, she wanted to share Blagden's news with him, a reflex action from so many years of marriage. For a moment her fingers danced above the buttons on the intercom. But when she did call, it was from a private phone hidden away in a drawer of her desk, a phone with no number on its face.

She dialed. It rang just once and a voice came on the line—a voice rich in the accents of Groton and Harvard.

"Dasha? Is that you, darling?"

"Yes," she breathed. "You were right. Today's the day."

Crestview Village boasted neither a crest nor a view, although it could stake some claim to being a village. It was a vast middle-income housing project in the upper reaches of Manhattan, a dozen high-rise apartments in businesslike brick facing each other across treeless malls. Inside, the corridors were of poured concrete, the walls of plasterboard, the ceilings so low Jordan could brush them by standing on tiptoe. The emphasis throughout was on the cheap and functional.

Yet for the young couples who lived there, Crestview offered reasonable space at reasonable rents, a commodity hard to come by in New York. And you could raise children without ever leaving the premises. There were supermarkets, playgrounds, discount stores, a McDonald's, even a movie house all within the confines, to say nothing of a ready-made social life. For most of the residents—young teachers, social workers, newly minted dentists and CPA's—Crestview was destined to be a stopping-off point en route to the eventual home in the suburbs. For the less ambitious, it was a way of life.

The other Manhattan—the Manhattan of theaters and concert halls, of elegant shops and corporate headquarters and uniformed doormen—began a hundred city blocks to the south. By subway it was only half an hour distant, but psychologically it was another world.

"Only temporary," Jordan muttered when he signed the lease. "Just until I get established."

Dasha was six months pregnant when they moved into Crestview with the ink barely dry on Jordan's degree. And now settled at last in "Fat City," as he liked to call it, the job hunt began in earnest.

Well before graduation, he had drawn up detailed lists of New York's blue-chip law firms and shot off a flood of résumés, requests for interviews, applications, letters. "The buckshot approach," he told Dasha. "Sooner or later I'm bound to score." Now, having moved to the city, he began following up his leads with a vengeance. Each morning he would spring out of bed bursting with energy, shower, shave, check the freshness of his breath and the polish of his shoes while Dasha pressed out his good flannel suit. Then off he'd go, her kiss still fresh on his cheek, for another grueling day of interviews on Wall Street or Park Avenue.

The hiring partners at the giant law firms were invariably patient and polite. Just as invariably, their answers were a muted no. "No, we're not hiring at the moment," or, "Call us next year," or simply, "Thank you for your time."

One recruiter, more candid than his brothers, put it on the line. "Frankly, Mr. Croy, we hire exclusively from Harvard, Yale, and Columbia—and then only the top ten percent. I think you'll find the same holds true of most of the other blue-chip firms."

"Are you telling me I should forget it?" Jordan asked.

"There are other kinds of law than 'big law,' you know. You're a personable fellow and I've no doubt you'll have a good career once you've found your niche, but I wouldn't hold out much hope for a top firm."

He returned home that night profoundly discouraged. "This firm asks me if I'm in the Social Register, that firm only takes *Law Review*. The guy today . . . if you're not Ivy League, go crawl under a rock. Christ, Dasha, I can't even get a toehold." He picked disconsolately at the tuna casserole. "Well, maybe it just wasn't meant to be."

"It's *their* loss," Dasha offered quick comfort. "But you know something, I could never really see you as a hired gun for the big corporations. Anyhow, I understand the associates in those places work eighty, ninety hours a week, so when would I"—she patted her swollen stomach—"correction, when would *we* ever see you? Money isn't everything, and maybe you'd be happier in some kind of government job . . . public service, Legal Aid maybe."

"Those jobs don't pay beans," he groaned. "And what kind of life is that anyway, plea-bargaining for muggers and junkies? I won't kid you. I wanted that job today so bad I could taste it. And the salary! My God, we could have been in clover. With all due respect to your cooking, Dasha, I can't see us eating tuna fish the rest of our lives. Tuna fish, spaghetti, meat loaf, Salvation Army furniture, and a neighborhood movie once a month. Here we are with less than a hundred bucks in the bank, a baby due in September . . . My God, darling, what have I let you in for?"

She wanted to say, "Don't be frightened. Everthing will work out," but the words stuck in her throat. This was *not* what she had bargained for. Her pregnancy had been an accident, the result of one careless if delightful lapse, and it was only made feasible by Dasha's quiet confidence that Jordan would go directly into a law firm. That, and her perpetual impatience to get on with "real life." Now, in the face of his despair, the best she could offer was "If worst comes to worst, darling, and you want to sweat it out, I'll borrow some money from Daddy to tide us over." In truth, she had already borrowed a thousand dollars from Alex without mentioning it to Jordan, and she was reluctant to tap the same source twice.

"I am not about to borrow." Her husband was adamant. "No way anyone's ever going to say Jordan Croy didn't meet his family obligations. I married you, I'll support you—and that's final."

It was a sore point with him, this business of responsibility, and Dasha was aware of its genesis. For despite the lip service Jordan paid his father's memory, his feelings were confused and ambivalent. "You can't eat Emmy Awards," he once made the tart comment. "You can't even hock 'em. I should know." And while for public consumption he spoke about his father as a gifted writer and uncompromising idealist, Jordan at heart harbored a smoldering resentment. Even after all these years, it rankled that Martin Croy had chosen personal pride over family welfare, that he had spent and squandered and danced his day in the sun, only to leave his wife destitute and abandon his boy to the vagaries of fate.

"Nope." He simmered down now and patted Dasha's hand. "I'm not in the market for handouts. I'll just have to face the realities that maybe it'll take me a little longer to get where I'm going. Above all, I don't want you to worry. I'll hit the placement agencies tomorrow morning and take the first honest job I can get."

And that too—ran the presumption—would be just a temporary measure, like Crestview.

Ryan, Rubinoff, Torres & (now) Croy occupied a narrow storefront on Columbus Avenue. A few weeks before the baby was due, Dasha trotted down with an armful of houseplants, arriving just in time to see the sign painter put the final flourish to the newest name on the plate-glass window.

"Well, what do you think?" Jordan greeted her at the door.

"Just great!" The gold leaf glittered freshly in the sun. "Your name up in lights."

"Yeah, well," he mocked, "not exactly Cravath Swaine or Slater Blaney. But when it comes to 'ethnic,' we've got it all over those guys. I think they took me on to be the token WASP. Come on in, I'll show you around."

Inside were four small offices, serviceable if unadorned, and a cluttered reception room with barkcloth walls and fluorescent lighting. Three people, Dasha noted with satisfaction, were waiting, seated in bright green plastic chairs.

Not imposing, she decided, but lively. The same could be said for Jordan's new colleagues. At thirty-six, Tom Ryan was the office's grand old man. A freckled energetic Brooklynite in a polyester suit.

"We get some business in off the street," he explained to Dasha, "but mostly it's what we hustle up ourselves. Personal contact, that's what counts. Family, neighbors, friends, friends of friends. It would help if Jordan's a 'joiner' . . . you too. Church groups, school committees, that kind of stuff—and let 'em know that you're a lawyer's wife."

"Do you do much criminal law?" Dasha asked. She had a nervous vision of Jordan being harassed by midnight calls from robbers and junkies.

"Not much. Bob Rubinoff handles that end of things. But mostly we get civil stuff—matrimonial, immigration, landlord-tenant disputes, P.I. That's legal shorthand for personal injury," he clarified. "Like say someone has an accident . . . "

"You don't have to explain anything to Dasha," Jordan said. "My wife was a law student herself."

"But not any more." She smiled and patted her stomach contentedly. "I'm into bigger things."

"A career alternative," Ryan laughed, then turned serious. "You understand what the situation is here, I hope. I can't offer your husband any guarantees, although he will be getting some of our overflow. We give him the space and he gives us a certain amount of service in return. The rest is up to him. Still, I think there's enough opportunity here for a man to earn a decent living. Not the Ritz, mind you. But not the pits either. Something in between. I think of it as shirtsleeves law."

"In that case," Jordan said, glancing down at his wrists. He was wearing the cufflinks Dasha had given him the night before. "In that case, I'd better roll up my sleeves and plunge in."

Robin was born three weeks later in Columbia Presbyterian—a lusty, squalling eight-pounder with a shock of black hair.

"She looks a little like Max," Jordan commented as Dasha was being wheeled out of the delivery room. He had been by her side throughout.

"Sounds like him too," Dasha murmured, still groggy from the ordeal. Where was she? What day was this? Wednesday? Thursday? Thursday. A faint bell rang.

"Gee, honey, weren't you supposed to be in court all day today?"

"Don't worry about it. I got a postponement. The judge understood —at least I hope he did. First things first, I always say." He squeezed her hand.

Barely a year later, the Croys had their second child, Geoffrey— a delicate beautiful boy with Jordan's olive skin and soulful eyes. And this time the pregnancy was welcomed, for Dasha had found what she believed to be her destiny.

She could not pinpoint the moment when she recognized her husband would never blaze trails or make history.

The germ of that perception had been planted back in law school on the night of moot court, taking root in his mind as well as hers. And although he would always look back upon that evening as a victory—indeed, the high point of his Seneca years—nonetheless the brief brush with danger had had a sobering effect. Little by little he began trimming his sails. If he couldn't be a great lawyer, he could be a good one. The early vision of himself that had so captivated Dasha he now saw as an outpouring of adolescent fantasy, the pipe dream of a lonely boy.

"What a hot-air artist I was at eighteen," he would recall with embarrassment. "It's a wonder you ever put up with me."

For Dasha, the acceptance of this newer, narrower horizon came more slowly, and occasionally she would chide him for setting his sights too low. To which Jordan replied, "If I make a mistake, it's my client who gets punished." But she too was pragmatic. You don't shoot the moon when you've got two small children to support, as Jordan reminded her; and by the time she had taken the measure of his limitations, she realized they didn't matter one whit.

He was an able attorney, prudent and conscientious, on his way to building a comfortable practice. He was also (and to her mind far more important) a loving husband and doting father.

The anxieties of those first months gradually dissipated. Before long Jordan was earning a modest living. Piece by piece the Salvation Army furniture found its way back to the Salvation Army, replaced by sensibly priced items from Macy's and an occasional splurge from Sloane's. It was a good, if not spectacular life, and on those rare moments when Dasha thought back to law school, it was without regrets. Indeed, there was a dreamlike quality to those forgotten days, as though they had happened to somebody else. The past paled when contrasted with the present reality of coping with two small children.

"It's amazing," Dasha often remarked, "that two kids could be so different—in looks, temperament, everything. You'd hardly think they were brother and sister." The contrast was inescapable. Robin, so bright and lively; musical, too, with a true Oborin love of the limelight. And Geoff with his long silky lashes, his smile at once timorous and hopeful. Dasha adored them both, but although she would never admit it, cherished a particular soft spot for the little boy. There was something intensely vulnerable about him, a sensitivity that called out to Dasha's protective instincts. He lacked his sister's easy confidence. The bark of a dog, an imagined rebuke from a stranger would send him scurrying to the comfort of Dasha's lap. She felt mild guilt about the attachment, wondering if she wasn't, perhaps, encouraging his timidity, and yet there was something gratifying about his need for her. It complemented her own need to feel that she was vital. Wanted. No question but that one kiss from her could set Geoff's world to rights.

"What power we have over our children," she told her next-door neighbor. "Doesn't it ever scare you, Deena?"

And Deena Lewis laughed her sensible laugh. "Just you wait till they're teenagers, honey, and then you'll see who wields the power around here. Me, I can hardly wait until my kids grow up and fly away."

"I suppose . . . " Dasha murmured, although she found that distant future impossible to envision. Children were not merely her own, but Crestview's raison d'être. They dug in the sandboxes, rode their tricycles into flowerbeds, and on rainy days strewed the floor with Lego while their mothers chatted over endless cups of instant coffee.

But if, by day, Crestview was a world composed of women and children, by night it was a society geared to married couples. In this circle, the Croys—young, good-natured, and attractive—found themselves with more friends than they had free evenings.

Jordan in particular enjoyed status by virtue of his law degree. He was brighter, wittier, better educated than most of his counterparts, and they tended to treat him with deference.

"Counselor" was a frequent mode of address. "What do you think, counselor?"—and Jordan would be plumbed for his opinion on all manner of things from politics and the economy to personal and legal problems. It happened with such frequency that Dasha finally felt compelled to step in. "Jordan has a law office, you know," she suggested to Billy Ashburn over a bridge table one night. "Perhaps you should consult him professionally."

"Now, now, Dasha"—Jordan flushed with embarrassment as much for Billy as for himself. "We're all friends here. I wasn't giving away any secrets."

Later, when the company had gone, Dasha brought the matter up again. "It's a competitive world out there, so why should you give away what other people charge for? I don't want to spend the rest of my life in a four-room apartment."

"You won't," he promised. "Just another couple of years."

In fact, their friends and neighbors did, gradually, form the bulk of his clientele; their social life became a felicitous mixing of business with pleasure.

So the evenings passed in nickel-dime card games and pot-luck dinners, with blue-jeaned informality the prevailing style. And sometimes when the beer was flowing freely and the hour running late, Jordan would pull his guitar out of the closet. "If We Can Put a Man Into Space" had long since been updated, courtesy of Apollo XI; Jordan now sang of "A Man on the Moon."

Their weeks fell into a pattern: bridge, Tenants Association, Couples Club, socials. On Sunday mornings, Charlotte Croy would come to baby-sit. She lived only a few minutes away.

"You really shouldn't," Dasha protested. "You're on your feet all week, so why not take it easy on your day off?" But Charlotte couldn't be argued down.

"What do I have in life if not for the babies?" she liked to say. "Granny's little darlings, they are," and she wore their pictures in a locket around her neck.

It troubled Dasha that Charlotte had no visible life of her own.

"You ought to get out more, Charlotte," she suggested. "Go to some nice resort or take a Caribbean cruise. They're quite reasonable, you know, and if it's a question of money, Jordan could . . . "

"We used to go to the Riviera, Martin and I, aboard the *Liberté*. First class, I might add. The service was so beautiful on the French Line. Martin used to order Piper-Heidsieck for breakfast."

Her abiding passion, other than her grandchildren, was for the opera, and one Christmas Dasha and Jordan surprised her with a pair of subscription tickets for six evenings at the Met.

"How very sweet of you," Charlotte said. "Of course Martin and I used to have a box at the Met, an entire box for ourselves every Monday night."

"Well." Dasha was hurt. The tickets had seemed such an ideal gift. "I understand the acoustics are just as good in the balcony, and anyhow it's the music that counts."

"Yes, indeed," Charlotte said mournfully. "I'm really going to enjoy it. Although who I'll go with, I can't imagine."

"You've got to understand," Jordan said later that night, "she didn't mean to offend you. It's just that my mother is one of the walking wounded." And in time Dasha came to see that her mother-in-law's harping on the past was not a pulling of rank but rather a defense: her way of placing herself *hors de combat* and withdrawing from the competition of everyday life.

So now when she insisted on being Sunday morning babysitter, Dasha acquiesced without complaint. Dasha and Jordan would start the morning with a lazy brunch at a neighborhood restaurant complete with Bloody Marys, then take in a movie or museum, or go appliance-shopping at the Cross County Mall. On the way home, they'd stop for takeout Chinese, and finish the evening around the kitchen table with Charlotte and the kids, all feasting greedily out of cardboard cartons. Then almost as a ritual they would wind up the night making love.

The next morning a new week, one just like the last, would begin.

"Well," Jordan sometimes would say of his neighbors, "they may not be the greatest intellects since Einstein. But *good* people. Salt of the earth." Occasionally he would mumble something about moving to the suburbs one day soon; more rarely talk about renting an office downtown in pursuit of a more challenging practice. But truth be told, he had found his niche just as the Wall Street recruiter had foreseen.

And if she thought about it, which she rarely did, Dasha admitted that she too was happy and fulfilled.

On their sixth anniversary, Jordan took her to the Rainbow Room high atop Rockefeller Plaza for dinner and dancing, a gala treat.

"This is how it should always be." He looked out over the lights of Manhattan. Then his face grew grave. "I had wanted more for you, Dasha. I wanted you to have some of life's candy."

"No." She blinked back the tears. "I wouldn't change anything . . . not a day, not a minute. And I don't want anything ever to change."

But nothing in life, she soon discovered, remains static for any length of time.

That September, Robin entered kindergarten. The following year, Geoff too started school.

The first morning Dasha escorted him to the door of P.S. 115, it was with a sense of foreboding. Geoff had been nervous as a colt the evening before, had wept over the breakfast table a half-hour earlier. Now Dasha went inside with him and introduced herself to the kindergarten teacher. "He's quite frightened about starting school," she whispered. "You see, he's never been left with strangers before." She wanted to go on, to explain that Geoff was sensitive and easily intimidated, to plead his case, so to speak; but the brisk young woman in the polka-dot dress would have none of it.

"He'll be perfectly fine, Mrs. Croy, I can assure you." She gave a quick smile. "Don't think of it as losing a son. Think of it as gaining thirty hours of freedom a week."

"She's right," Dasha thought. "I'll go home and clean the closets." By God, she had an infinity of hours in which she might do exactly as she pleased. Peace. Privacy. Freedom. She cast a last look at Geoff with his stricken eyes, kissed him goodbye, and headed for home.

By quarter of twelve, she had completely reorganized the bedroom closets; by half past she had rearranged the dresser drawers. As she worked, the thought persisted that the phone would ring at any moment and she would be asked to take a tearful Geoff home. Poor baby!

But the phone didn't ring, so instead she whipped up some brownies, lovely nut brownies, a special treat for that first traumatic day. True, Robin had taken to it right away, but Geoff was different. So much more dependent.

Well before school broke for the day, she was at the gate ready to dole out instant comfort at the moment of release. But when the doors opened and the children spewed out, it took her a long moment to find him in the crush. There was Robin, but Geoff? Ah . . . there he was, deep in a conversation with another kindergarten kid. She darted over, encircled him with a hug, and to her anxious query, "How was school?" he answered, "Oh, Mommy, it was such a good time."

All the way home he babbled on about Ken and Marcia and Scotty who kept gerbils and Miss Goldman. "She's the prettiest lady in the whole world." Dasha wavered between relief and jealousy. *Why he didn't even miss me!* She could scarcely believe it.

The next morning she cleaned the children's toy box and washed windows. In the afternoon she made chocolate chip cookies, then since the oven was on anyway tried her hand at whole wheat bread. It was a disaster, but she wouldn't give up. It took the next few weeks to get the hang of bread-making, but no question there was something deeply satisfying about the process.

"Hey, Dasha," Jordan said one evening over dinner. "What's with all this bread-making?"

"You're always saying package bread tastes like Styrofoam, I thought you might like something home-baked for a change. That's a Yukon sourdough, by the way. What do you think?"

He chewed thoughtfully on the heel, then beetled his brows.

"Is this how you spend your days, Dasha—baking?"

"I enjoy it." There was a hint of defensiveness in her voice. "The kids like it, you enjoy it. What's wrong with baking?"

"Nothing I suppose." But he looked troubled.

A week later he brought the matter up again in the warm afterglow of lovemaking.

"I think you ought to get out more, darling. A little less kitchen, a little more social life. Why don't you do something with your girl-friends?"

"What girlfriends?"

"What do you mean, what girlfriends!" There was something in her tone, a sense of injury, that Jordan found alarming. "Deena Lewis, for instance."

"Deena's working part time at the library."

"Shari?"

"She's gone back to college . . . studying anthropology of all things. I thought I told you that."

He named a few of the other local mothers, but this one was working or that one had moved to Long Island or "I never cared for her, not really. We were only friendly because of the kids. That's true of most of the women around here."

That revelation must have shocked him, for he said nothing for a good few minutes. Then, very gently: "How about you, Dasha? Would you like to go back to school? You could finish up, maybe take the bar exam summer after next."

"You must be kidding, Jordan." The idea was so absurd she had to laugh aloud. "I could never hack it anymore—that discipline, that volume of work. I think my brains have turned to mush. Besides which, I've probably forgotten everything I ever knew."

"Stop knocking yourself, Dasha. You were terrific in law school."

"Was I? That was a million years ago."

"Okay, if not law, then look around and see if you'd like to take up something else. Philosophy, drama—whatever interests you. How about costume design, something like that?"

"There is something I'd like, Jordan." She placed her hand on his thigh.

"Anything, darling. Just tell me and if it's within my power . . . "

"I think I'd like to have another baby."

"Jesus God!" Jordan sat up abruptly and switched on the lamp. "You're not serious, I hope."

She blinked in the light, her eyes bright with tears. "Yes, I really think I would."

He shook his head despairingly. "Be reasonable. As it is, I don't know how I'm going to see two children through college, let alone three. And we don't have the space. I . . . we . . . " He stumbled for words. "Look, sweetie, you're bored and lonely—I see that—and you think you can fill the void by having another baby. It's something to do, someone to look after. But say we have another baby, then what? Sooner or later they're gonna grow up and you'll be right back where you are tonight, wondering what to do with the rest of your life."

But Dasha was in no mood to hear home truths. "You said I could have whatever I want, and now you're going back on your word." She switched out the light and slept with her back turned toward him at the very edge of the bed.

The next day he came home from the office early, his face drawn and gray. He carried a bunch of chrysanthemums as a peace offering.

"I couldn't get any work done today, thinking about our discussion last night. If that's what you want, Dasha, if that'll make you happy, okay, let's have another baby."

But she shook her head. "No, you were right, Jordan. Absolutely right. It was an idiotic idea."

"Well, I want you to do something for yourself. Maybe go out and buy yourself something sensational. I can't bear to see you so depressed."

"I'm not depressed." She burst into tears. *"I am not depressed!"*

She continued with her baking and a few weeks later expanded her repertory by exploring *The Wonderful World of French Pâtés and Charcut-*

erie. You could spend an entire day, she discovered, just assembling a perfect *galantine de veau,* no matter that Robin insisted on calling it meatloaf.

Most of her experiments turned out well; when one didn't, she would immediately throw it in the garbage, slam down the lid, and begin again with all new ingredients.

By Christmastime, she had gained more than twenty pounds.

Not long after, Harriet Oborin died of a massive coronary. It was a sudden death, completely unforeseen. She had never been sick a day in her life.

The funeral was held in the very church where she had been baptized sixty-five years earlier. Before the service, several of Max's colleagues from Symphony gathered around the altar to mark her passing with the Adagio from Schubert's String Quintet in C Major. Dasha remembered the work from her childhood as being her father's favorite piece of chamber music. Had it been Harriet's as well? Who could say?

No matter. Funerals were for the living, not the dead. She looked over to Max. He had appeared so drained, almost shrunken this morning, but now his breath rose and fell softly in time with the aspiration of the strings. He seemed to take on color. Vitality. Extraordinary, Dasha realized. He was drawing sustenance from the music.

When the last chord faded, the minister rose to deliver the eulogy.

" 'But many that are first shall be last; and the last shall be first,' " he began. "Matthew, nineteen. We are gathered here today in memory of Harriet Whittaker Oborin, beloved wife of Maxim, devoted mother of Alexander and Darya"—Dasha and her brother exchanged moist glances—"beloved grandmother of David, Jacqueline, Mark, Robin, and Geoffrey. Hers was a life spent in the unselfish service of those whom she loved . . . " Dasha bit her lips to keep from crying. God, that was true, so true.

It was a dignified ceremony, mercifully brief, and afterwards most of the mourners repaired to the house in Brookline for sandwiches, cake, and Schnapps. At the height of the crush, Alex pulled her into the little downstairs den.

"How are you, Dasha? I haven't really seen you in, must be, over a year. You're looking . . . " He started, she was sure, to say "You're looking good," but it was too blatant a lie. "You're looking well," he said finally. "Put on a little weight, have you?"

"You too, Alex. You're developing a bit of a corporation yourself."

"So Caroline keeps telling me. It's the goddam banquet circuit. Nesselrode pie till it's coming out of your ears. You should be thankful you're in private life. How's everything at home? The kids?"

"Just fine. Yours?"

They spent the next few minutes catching up on family news. Alex found it difficult to keep a note of fatherly boastfulness out of his voice. Mark was in fourth grade, smartest kid in his class. Jackie was taking ballet lessons, "simply loaded with talent. And David! He is some 'boychick,' as Dad would say. You know he starts high school next year, but already he's an academic hotshot, a born leader, and just a natural all-round athlete. We're trying to decide between Choate and Phillips Exeter. My own preference is for Choate—old school tie and all that jazz—but Caro feels that Exeter offers greater scope, more social opportunities. What do you think?"

"Why ask me, Alex? I'm no authority on prep schools. Our family happens to patronize P.S. 115."

"Nothing wrong with that," Alex jumped in. "Personally, I'm a great believer in the public school system. A profound believer. It's the cornerstone of democracy, and I'm sure your kids are getting a fine education. Frankly, if it were up to me, our kids would go to school in Georgetown. But you know Caroline. She still hangs on to a lot of those old Southern values." He switched the subject. "Actually what I wanted to talk to you about was . . . "

Max. Someone should really stick around after the funeral and talk some sense into their father. It was crazy, his staying on in this big barn alone. Wouldn't it be better if he bought one of those neat little condos on Beacon Street? A helluva lot more practical. "I'd talk to him myself, Dasha, but I've got to catch the shuttle back to Washington tonight. Got a meeting first thing tomorrow with Pat Moynihan."

"Well, we're planning to go back tonight, too, Alex. It's a five-hour drive."

"Couldn't you stay for a couple of days, Dasha? Just you? Maybe help Dad sort things out. I would if I could, you know that. But . . . " He shrugged.

But you're a busy man and I'm the one who's expendable. "I'll have to check it out with Jordan," she said.

"I already have"—Alex squeezed her hand gratefully—"and he agrees it's a good idea."

"So the two of you just put your heads together and disposed of my time." Her eyes welled and she blinked back the tears. It had been a day already full of strong and disturbing emotions.

"It's not like that," Alex protested. "It's simply that Dad will take it better from you. You always were his favorite, Dashenka."

"Don't butter me up." She broke from his grip. "I'll stay. I'll talk to him. I'll be the dutiful daughter just like Mom was the dutiful wife."

That night when the company had gone, she sat with her father in the kitchen, served him tea in a glass, and broached the subject of his future. She went, in fact, far beyond Alex's suggestion.

"Maybe you should cut down on your teaching load a bit, Daddy." He looked at her blankly and she mistook his silence for endorsement. "Cut down on your teaching and maybe even think about retiring from the orchestra. I imagine after all these years it would be lovely to get away from these fierce Boston winters, maybe live down south for a while. Enjoy a little golf, some fishing. After all," she said gently, "you *are* seventy."

"I know how old I am, Dasha. I don't need you to remind me. Florida . . . fishing . . . " He shook his head. "What nonsense you talk. What are you trying to do, turn me into a living mummy?" He pulled his cardigan tight about him, as though to ward off the cold of the grave. "Undoubtedly you mean well, but you fail to understand. I play the violin. That is what I do. I've done it every day of my life since I was four years old and I intend to keep on doing it for just as long as I have the strength. And now more than ever. With you and Alex living so far away . . . your mother gone, what else is there in my life but music? I thank God for it. And when I die—which I expect won't be for many years to come—I hope it will be with my fiddle tucked under my chin and my right hand holding the bow. Don't you see? Can't you understand?" He folded his hands on his lap and smiled sadly. "No, Daryushka, but then there's no reason why you should. You've never had any real knowledge, any real sense of . . . "

"Of what, Daddy? No sense of what?"

He paused. "Vocation. Calling." He dropped the matter. "I appreciate your staying on here, Dasha, and tomorrow—if you would—I'd like you to go through your mother's room. Take anything you want for yourself and Robin and give the rest to the Morgan Memorial. Would you do that for me, darling?" He reached into his pocket for a handkerchief and honked his nose furiously. "Now if you'll excuse me, I'll turn in. It's been a long hard day."

He went upstairs but not to bed, and long into the night she could hear the distant sound of Bach sonatas on the violin.

The next two days were spent clearing out her mother's room. The job proved less onerous than anticipated, for Harriet had been a neat and well-organized housewife; nonetheless it was painful, this handling of her mother's lingerie and shopping lists and lipstick stubs. In a drawer of the rosewood desk, Dasha found, neatly tied, all the letters she had written home, prudently edited, from Smith. She sat down for a nostalgic hour to read them through.

There they were, a recounting of half-forgotten exams and events and people. *I went skating with a friend Sunday over at Hadley and we nearly died of the cold,* she read. *Do you think I could get a new parka?*

The friend, unmentioned, was Jordan; and they had wound up that same afternoon making love in a crummy hotel off the Mass Turnpike. No mention of that, either. Lying lying letters—yet her mother had kept them all, lovingly tied with a blue ribbon.

She set the correspondence aside, something to share with Jordan when she got home, and went on with her task. Finally, she attacked the closets. She picked up a worn alligator pump and ran her hand across the grain, as though by touching it she might conjure up her mother's presence. But in death as in life, Harriet remained retiring, elusive; and with a start, Dasha realized there was something missing in the room.

True, there were memories abounding here—of Dasha's childhood, of Alex's triumphal progress, countless bits and pieces from Max's life. But of Harriet herself—her will, her spirit—there was nothing. It was eerie. Eerie and frightening. As if the room were haunted by the very *absence* of a ghost. How could Harriet die if she had never lived?

With a growing sense of anguish, Dasha began rooting through the ample closets looking for some sign—a diary, a pressed corsage, a love letter—anything that would bear the distinctive imprint of her mother's hopes and dreams, the mark of her personality, her life. There was nothing to be found but old clothes.

Then in the depths of a linen cupboard her outspread fingers fumbled against something bulky and unfamiliar. She pulled it out. It was a large unbound portfolio of Moroccan leather lined with watered silk and held together with a fading black ribbon. Dasha had never seen it before.

She sat on the floor and opened it carefully. Inside were perhaps two dozen—certainly no more—large, meticulous pen-and-ink drawings of a Boston that had since disappeared. *Huntington Avenue,* the first sketch was entitled. Why, Boston had wooden streetcars then, she marveled, and looked at the bottom corner for a date. There it was—1932, with the initials beneath, H.W. Dasha turned the pages carefully.

They were amazing, the drawings. Not professional quality perhaps, but beautiful and sensitively rendered, with a fine eye for the telling detail. Dasha turned each page with wonder and reverence until she came to the last, the only drawing in the collection that was not a street scene. It was a portrait of Max—just a head and shoulders with a soft scarf loose about the throat, but the artist had caught him perfectly, the wavy jet hair, the glowing smile, the eyes bright and full of mischief. He was devastatingly handsome, a true heart-breaker. Dasha looked at the date —1935. The year her parents married. And beneath her initials Harriet had drawn a tiny character: Ω Omega. The last letter in the Greek alphabet. The end.

Dasha shut the portfolio gently; then sitting down on her mother's bed began to weep. She wept for the woman that might have been; she wept for the talent wasted, the spark extinguished, the years of self-denial.

"A life spent in the service of those she loved," the minister had said. But had it been any life at all? Or had she died without ever having lived? "Beloved wife of . . . mother of . . . grandmother of . . ." A person to be defined only in terms of other people.

And Dasha herself? Could she expect a different fate? She peered across the room at her reflection in the dresser mirror and saw a listless woman of thirty, decidedly overweight, with the shadow of resignation in her eyes. Would she, too, be like her mother—one of those women who clung too tightly, feared too much, living only through her husband's accomplishments, feeling life through the triumphs and failures of her children? And when she died, would they say of her, Here lies Dasha Croy, the daughter of, the sister of, the wife of, the mother of . . . But of herself? Nothing. A cipher. A being that had only existed in reflection, invisible until illuminated by the light of others.

The room, hot and airless, suddenly seemed to close in on her.

She leaped to the window, flung it open. A bitter January wind whipped into the room, strewing papers, carrying snowflakes in its wake, as Dasha stood there gasping, swallowing great gulps of Arctic air into starving lungs.

No! I don't want to live like that, die like that. I want to do. To dare. To climb. To soar. And when I'm old, I want to be able to look back and say that I've engaged with life to my limits, grasped it with both hands. That I've known, thought, felt, traveled. That I've met interesting people, done significant things. That I've made a difference in the world at large. And when I'm dead, they will say of me: Here lies Dasha Croy—a somebody in her own right.

The knowledge came to her with the force of revelation. She looked out of the window at the frozen landscape. Beyond, out of sight, there was a vast and brilliant world. Beyond was Alex, walking the corridors of power, exchanging ideas with the great and the gifted. Her father— incredible man—even now in rehearsal at Symphony Hall, a vital part of a magnificent entity.

She had chosen to live in a world that grew narrower and narrower each day until the moment—and that moment must come—when she would have entombed herself alive.

Jordan had sensed it. A dozen times in these last few months he had urged her to reach out, trying desperately to warn her against this crazy self-immolation. But she had been unable to hear him until now. Now in this room his words came back: "I want you to do something for yourself, Dasha."

She shut the windows with a healthy slam, finished her cleaning, then went downstairs to await her father's return.

"I've decided to fly home tonight," she told him as he came in, "if that's okay with you. I've finished upstairs. Everything's in cartons, all labeled."

"Thank you, darling." He handed her his coat. "That was very sweet of you." He followed her into the kitchen while she made tea, and for one of the rare moments in his life felt obliged to explain himself. "I imagine it looks odd to you, Dasha, my going back to work so soon after your mother's death, but . . . "

"Please!" she interrupted. "You know what the unwritten motto of international royalty is supposed to be? 'Never apologize, never explain.' " Max looked at her, puzzled. She poured tea into his favorite mug, then put down the samovar and hugged him. "Keep practicing, Daddy. You keep right on practicing."

Jordan met her at the airport. "How was it, sweetheart?" he asked, after kisses were exchanged. "Was it very hard?"

"You know," she replied, "I did a lot of thinking in my father's house. An awful lot . . . "

"And . . . ?"

"And I've come home with three resolutions. One, I'm going to lose twenty pounds. Two, I'm going to catch up on my reading this winter. And three"—she grinned—"you better get used to eating packaged bread all over again, my love. I've decided to go back to law school."

Jordan's answer was to sweep her up in a bone-crushing hug.

"Just tell me what I can do to help."

For some years after he would say it was the wisest decision she had ever made, and she would invariably tease him, "Except for marrying you, my darling."

CHAPTER SEVEN

☐ Shortly after twelve, her office door swung open and Fran Rosen popped her head in. "All quiet on the Washington front," she reported. "The Court's broken for lunch and if you don't mind, I'll run out and do the same."

"What? Oh sure." Dasha started from her reverie. "Sure . . . run along. I think I'll go out myself and get some air into my lungs." She suddenly ached for physical activity.

Outside, the midday sun had burned off the chill and the weather had turned glorious. She headed away from the Plaza where the Kimfolk held sway and into a crazy-quilt of narrow streets that had been laid out long before the Revolution. Once they had been footpaths and sailboat slips, but progress had turned these modest byways into sunless canyons, towering phalanxes of banks and brokerages, high-rise strongholds of corporate wealth. The most expensive real estate in the world.

But at street level on a balmy day, the sidewalks were noisy and bustling. Messengers darted through the crowds, secretaries chattered on hurried lunch hours. Noontime browsers nibbled at oversized pretzels and kept an eye out for the unrepeatable bargain. Wherever you looked the streets were lined with peddlers, with makeshift stalls, with vendors who —for lack of other opportunities—had spread out their wares on the ground, blanketing every available inch of concrete.

Dasha picked her way through the crowds, alert and exhilarated. It was another world, these streets behind the office, with bargains being hawked on every corner in every accent. The melting pot; she smiled to herself. Or more accurately, the frying pan, for you couldn't go two feet without being assaulted by the aroma of wonderful cheap food that wouldn't be granted table space in the Slater Blaney dining rooms: pizzas, kebabs, falafel, Chinese dumplings, Italian sausage.

At the corner of Battery Park she bought a hero sandwich at an umbrella'd stand. "With sauce or without, lady?"

"Oh, *with!*" Then she walked off bearing a dripping meatball sandwich in a square of wax paper, thinking, "The Supreme Court should see me now!"

She found herself a bench overlooking the harbor and tackled the sandwich before it fell apart. The view was the same as the one from the executive dining room and the air more invigorating. She hadn't lunched like this since she'd been finishing up at Columbia. On nice days, as soon as there was a break in classes, she'd zip out to Morningside Park and curl up with a sandwich and a law book. In retrospect, she couldn't guess which she wolfed down faster. In those days, she had felt as if the devil were at her heels and a single moment's idleness would be time lost forever.

She learned a lot during the final year at law school, not all of it from books. She learned that it was possible to live on four hours sleep a night. That competition wasn't a dirty word. That work could be more fun than fun.

And that she was one very smart cookie.

One Saturday in the middle of term, she and Jordan had gone to Greenwich Village for a festival of silent comedies. It had taken considerable coaxing on Jordan's part and a good deal of guilt on hers, but she would have felt guiltier still by not going. They hadn't had a night out in months. So for two glorious hours they laughed themselves weary over the antics of Buster Keaton and Harold Lloyd, then afterwards went to a little basement restaurant on MacDougal Street. Jordan was still chuckling when the Chianti came.

"That movie tonight kind of reminded me of you."

Why, Dasha asked.

"Well," Jordan went on, "you know that funny quality old movies have of movement being speeded up, life clipping along maybe twenty or thirty percent faster than it actually does—so even when someone's walking, it looks like they're running?"

"And that's me?"

"That's my Dasha."

She laughed appreciatively. Trust Jordan to find the apt analogy, although she suspected he was only half-joking.

From that moment she had stepped off the plane from Boston to greet him with her plans, life had scudded by at breakneck speed.

Some of the pressure was external. Columbia was tougher than Seneca, the competition was fierce, and it had been no easy matter to get back into the rhythm of study after such a long fallow period. But largely the pressure was self-imposed. She had to be first in her class, the best of the brightest. Nothing less, she felt, would justify the unmade beds at home, the TV dinners, the dust collecting on top of the refrigerator. And the expense! They might have had a down payment for a house in the suburbs for the price of tuition, to say nothing of the cost of books and sitters. It struck her that everybody was making sacrifices—Jordan, the children, her mother-in-law—and she felt honor-bound to prove, not least of all to herself, that her return to college wasn't the dilettantism of a bored housewife but a serious investment in a career. The greatest stimulus, however, was the matter of age.

> But at my back I always hear
> Time's wingèd chariot hurrying near

Marvell's couplet haunted her. She could not rid herself of the notion that she was late, perhaps too late, that she was entering the race a half-dozen years behind the front runners and the only way to catch up was by scrambling twice as fast.

To Jordan, this near-demonic burst of energy was puzzling. He was delighted, as he told her repeatedly, that she was tackling the work with such determination, and had begun resuscitating that old-time dream of Croy & Croy. "We could have an awfully good practice, you know. You'd be a whiz at the matrimonial stuff." Yet he couldn't share her sense of urgency.

"Why do you have this compulsion to get it all over in one big swallow? You're so hard on yourself, honey. So what if it takes the extra year or two."

"Oh God, Jordan. Now or never. Otherwise I'll be dead of old age by the time I take the bar exams."

"Better old age than exhaustion."

"Better exhaustion than boredom."

"I guess it depends on your scale of values," he said mildly.

They had, indeed, spent some long evenings on that very matter—the relative value of things—and come to revised conclusions.

Children were important, spotless closets were not. Passing exams took precedence over gourmet cooking. Wash-and-wear hair was the greatest invention since heated rollers. Gristede's delivers. So does the dry cleaners for another buck or two. In a pinch, you traded off money for time.

It took a while to realize she didn't have to do everything herself. That domestic chores could be divvied up or paid for or—in a crunch —neglected. That even first graders were capable of bed-making and table-setting, that by and large they felt flattered when asked to join in. But theory was one thing, acceptance another, and Dasha often felt like an embezzler, stealing time, sneaking off to indulge herself in homework while Jordan loaded the dishwasher or took the children shopping.

"I feel like a shit," she apologized every so often, until he finally replied, "Don't worry, Dasha. I'll get my pound of flesh back when you're working for me at Croy & Croy."

He was thoroughly supportive, taking inconvenience in his stride. The one change he balked at was the curtailment of their social life.

"I can't," she said early in her final year, "I just can't fritter away a whole evening at the Espositos'. I've got exams coming up. Will you make my apologies for me?"

"I can't do that." He was perplexed. "You have to come. We've gone there every Columbus Day for the last six years and Nina would be terribly hurt if we don't show."

"You go, sweetie. I'll call her and explain."

Unaccountably, Jordan exploded. "Goddammit, Dasha! What'll it look like if you don't turn up? As it is, Nina thinks you're high-hatting them . . ."

"Oh, come off it!"

"No, you come off it. Is it too much to ask you to spare one evening now and then? Poke your nose in, even if it's just for an hour or so."

But there was no way, Dasha knew, she could escape the Espositos' annual bash with simply a handshake and a hit-and-run drink. She had a clear image of parties past—fifty people squeezed into four small rooms, tons of food and wine. She wouldn't even be missed, except by Jordan, who right now was looking daggers.

"Okay, okay," she conceded. "But let's try to get home before midnight."

The party was precisely as anticipated—hot, loud, friendly, crowded, boring. And everyone was so terribly nice to her, so curious about her progress, almost as though she were a visitor from an alien planet. "Hello stranger" was the greeting, followed by "I just think you're so *brave* going back to law school," or a jocular "I wish I could get *my* wife to get off her duff and do something," and most often, "How come we never *see* you any more?" The amenities over, Dasha found she had less and less to say to her old acquaintances. Their lives were already diverging.

She did get into an animated discussion with Herky Fischer, who asked her with what appeared to be genuine interest what she thought of the Patty Hearst trial. Dasha, who had followed the case closely, began an enthusiastic analysis of some of the finer points of the defense. Indeed, she was just warming up when she noticed Herky's eyes dulling over. With a shock she realized she'd been boring the pants off the poor guy, so who was she to criticize the other guests?

For the next few hours she socialized, small-talked, did justice to the Chianti, the chicken cacciatore, fought off a third helping of cannoli, and promised herself a solid week of melba toast and cottage cheese. By midnight the heat of the room had gotten to her and she could barely keep her eyes open. She staked out a corner of the sofa and was nodding off when Jordan came to fetch her with a "Wakey wakey, Dasha. Time to go home." Then a final round of noisy goodbyes and kisses and promises extracted that it wouldn't be so long before she saw Nina, Hank, Tim, Rusty, Sonya, et al. again.

"Well now," Jordan said as they were crossing the quad. "That wasn't so terrible, was it?"

"Very pleasant," she murmured, "but I was dead on my feet. God, it was hot in there." The night air was bracing, however, and by the time they reached their building, she felt fully alert. "If you don't mind, sweetie, I think I'll put in an hour or two studying. I seem to have got my second wind."

Jordan stopped short and stared at her. "You amaze me, Dasha. You couldn't keep your eyes open at the Espositos' and now you're ready to stay up till three."

"It was hot in there," she began to apologize. Then, "Let's face it, honey. It's not the most stimulating household."

"In other words, you have selective fatigue." He studied her face in the harsh light of the hallway. "Don't move too far away, Dasha."

"I'm not sure I follow you."

Instinctively he lowered his voice. "You go to a very elitist school, I appreciate that. Fun and intellectual games down on Morningside Heights. You spend your days with very bright and privileged people, so maybe folks like the Espositos look pretty pale by comparison. But they're real people too, remember. They're your friends, your neighbors, and one of these days, they'll most likely be your clients. Or if not them, then people very much like them. All I'm saying is, try not to distance yourself too much."

"Honestly, Jordan," she bristled. "You make it sound like I was grinding my heel into the faces of the proletariat simply because I dozed off at a party."

"Enough said." He shrugged and unlocked the door. "I'll take the sitter home and you go study."

She went into the kitchen, brewed coffee, opened Cowett on Blue Sky Law, then spent the next five minutes reading the same sentence over and over. Impossible to concentrate, with Jordan's complaint fresh in her mind! He had such an air of gentle injury, one would have thought her falling asleep at a party somehow constituted a criticism of him.

Yet she was struck with the sense of being poised between two worlds: one as soft and easy as old sneakers, *his* world, the other tense and fiercely competitive. Go compare the exuberant give-and-take of a classroom controversy with the drone of a Crestview kaffeeklatsch. Compare the clatter of ideas with the clatter of Tupperware parties. Compare big dreams to small talk, genuine wit to tired Polish jokes.

May as well compare day and night.

She had joined a study group, composed of top third-year students —lively, contentious, irreverent—who took nothing for granted. Their avowed purpose was to walk off with every major honor the school had to offer and let the bodies fall where they may. They styled themselves the "Morningside Mafia."

Jordan found the sobriquet offensive. "It sounds like you're training to be assassins, not officers of the court."

"Oh come on, Jordan. Where's your sense of humor? They're a bunch of bright terrific guys." She believed he was being a trifle pompous.

But now, working at the kitchen table while he walked the sitter home, she wondered if he was, in an odd way, jealous. Not sexually jealous—that would have been absurd. But jealous nonetheless, secretly resentful that she was sharing laughs and gossip and the occasional beer with a group of outsiders. That a new circle of people—perhaps *too* bright and terrific—was providing her with a more exciting life than he had offered thus far.

Was she shifting her loyalties? Cutting him out? She didn't believe so.

And yet here she was at one in the morning hunched over a text on interstate securities law for Chrissakes instead of making love with her husband. Which was how their party nights usually ended.

Small wonder Jordan was resentful.

With a guilty twinge she shut the book, dug out her shortest sexiest nightgown, splashed a dollop of Calèche on the inside of her thighs, had second thoughts about the nightgown, and got into bed. When Jordan did return she was under the covers naked and fragrant. "Poor baby." She wrapped her legs around him. "I've been neglecting you something awful."

It was a given that as soon as she graduated, she would join him in a husband-wife practice. Yet inadvertently it was Jordan himself who launched her on a separate path.

One of the glories of the third-year curriculum was Blagden Geere's course on Constitutional Law. Jordan suggested she take it, even though the content was, as he said, "a little high-flown for our kind of practice. Still, honey, how can you turn down a chance to see a living legend face to face? Should be very inspiring. He was my idol in college, you know."

She knew, indeed, and Jordan's much-thumbed copy of the great man's autobiography had long held pride of place on their bookshelves. Truly, Geere had been a giant of the bar, a noble relic of a classic era. "I'm dying to know what he's like in real life," Jordan kept saying, until finally, for her husband's enlightenment as much as her own, she enrolled in his class.

The first day she turned up with a vague expectation of a John Houseman lookalike, autocratic and rotund, ready to reduce the boldest student to mush. In the flesh, however, he proved to be a scrawny old man with the gentlest of smiles, dressed in a faded blue pullover and baggy slacks. Was this the legal lion whose oratory had saved the Millsboro Boys from a lynch mob? The guiding spirit of Roosevelt's Brain Trust? The fiery prosecutor of the Nuremberg Trials? The former U.S. Attorney General? Why, his voice hardly carried ten feet.

"Your lion," she declared to Jordan, "turns out to be a pussycat." But if the flesh was frail and ancient, the brain remained remarkably able, and his classes had a way of catching fire, illuminating not just the letter of the law but the great moral issues that lay behind it. Dasha adored the sessions, and prided herself on the classroom interplay, giving as good as she got. The old man singled her out on numerous occasions. "My dear young lady," he would address her, "may we hear from you on this matter?" Young indeed! Dasha was ever conscious of being older than most of her classmates, but clearly age was a relative thing.

She enjoyed the course not just for itself but for the pleasure of sharing it with Jordan. She would bring home the highlights, rehash the details so he might live it vicariously. One night with particular glee she mentioned that she had "bearded the lion in his lair."

"What's that supposed to mean?" Jordan asked.

"It means," she gloated, "that I caught Geere with his pants down on a point of law. He was explaining the doctrine of irrebuttable presumptions, and . . . " She went on to detail the gist of the old man's argument, concluding, "But he was dead wrong, you know. *Weinberger versus Salfi* . . . it's all in there. Justice Rehnquist wrote the decision. Well, when I told him . . . "

"When you *what?*"

"Well, when I pointed out his error . . . Oh, don't look at me like that, Jordan. I did it very nicely. 'With all due respect, sir,' and that kind of jazz."

"You mean to tell me"—Jordan folded his arms—"that you pretend to know more law than the former Attorney General of the United States? Jesus, why even bother to go to law school?"

"For heaven's sakes, Jordan. I'm not claiming to know more than Blagden Geere. I'm just saying on this one particular point I happened to be right and he was wrong. I appreciate how much you admire him, but he's not a god, after all. He puts on his pants one leg at a time just like the rest of mankind. Anyhow, whose side are you on?"

"What a question! I'm on your side, naturally, but the point is— Okay, let's say for the sake of argument that you actually were correct . . . "

"For the sake of argument!" She could scarcely hide her distress. "I *know* I was right."

"Even so," Jordan went on, "even if you were, do you think it's a wise thing for you to have done, cut down a guy's legs like that in public? A man who's a national monument. How do you think Geere felt, being made to look like a meathead in public?"

"Pretty awful, I suppose." Already she regretted her lapse.

"You bet awful. The thing is, it doesn't pay to buck authority that way, Dasha. The big guys always win."

"I guess I should apologize to him. Still, you know, you didn't used to talk like that, honey. Ten years ago you were such a fire-eater. Gonna fight for truth and beauty single-handed. And now . . . "

"And now I'm a grown-up. Please, sweetie"—his was the voice of calm reason—"don't take offense if I tell you you've led a pretty sheltered life so far. Smith, Crestview . . . and let's face it, even law school is just another dose of make-believe. Nine-tenths of the stuff you're learning won't have any practical application. It gets you past the bar exams, that's all. But the world? Take it from me, toots, the real world has damn little to do with lofty Supreme Court decisions or—what did you call it?— the doctrine of irrebuttable presumptions. The real world is sitting down with another attorney and closing a mortgage or maybe negotiating a few hundred bucks more in an insurance claim. It's winning the respect and confidence of the people around you, and you don't do that by rocking the boat. Okay, I'm not the firebrand I was when I was twenty and maybe something was lost in the transition. But people like you and me, we have to tailor our dreams to fit the circumstances."

"What do you mean, 'people like you and me'?"

"I should only speak for myself, I suppose, but . . . Do you know what *hubris* is, darling? In ancient Greece it was when mortals dared to defy the gods, a kind of insolence on the cosmic scale. *Hubris.* That was my father's number, and look where it got him. As for me, I know my strengths, Dasha, and my limitations. I've built a pretty good career, so why should I eat my heart out chasing after the impossible? There's too much else in life that's important."

He was right, of course. Career wasn't everything. Still . . .

"You sell yourself short, Jordan. I've always felt that."

"No." He smiled and shook his head. "I just admit I'm mortal like the rest of us. Like you too, honey. Think about it."

She brooded about Jordan's comments all weekend long. It was the first time he had openly admitted—not defeat, certainly, for he had seemed content in himself—but that he had finally given up the quest for the brass ring. There was to be no more talk of "It's only temporary," or "When my big break comes." The years spent as a working attorney had rid him of illusions. He had indeed grown up, and perhaps it was time she did too. Looking through Jordan's eyes, she could see that her behavior in Geere's class had been sophomoric, swiping at a decent old man who deserved better. A cheap shot.

She was not surprised on Monday to find a note requesting a meeting in Geere's office that afternoon and spent the interim composing a tactful apology.

Punctually at three, she found him behind his desk, looking preoccupied and dour.

"Well, young lady," he began, "you had me up all night Friday over my law books."

"I'm sorry, sir. I . . . "

"Sorry? What do you have to be sorry about?" He peered at her over the steel rims of his glasses. "I'm the one who's sorry, being caught out in a sloppy bit of thinking. You, on the other hand, must be quite pleased."

She stood there, tense, not certain if she was being complimented or entrapped, until he finally motioned her to a seat and poured some sherry.

He nattered on for some moments about *Salfi* and irrebuttable presumptions, then smiled. "Have you ever wondered why I teach here, Mrs. Croy, an old party like me, who ought by rights to be soaking up the sun at Palm Beach? It's certainly not the money, nor is it missionary zeal. I do it for exercise. It's the best way I can think of to keep my brain from getting as stiff and arthritic as my fingers. And at my age, it's the only organ that can still function properly. So when someone like you comes into my class, full of piss and vinegar, ready to throw down the intellectual gauntlet, it quite makes my day. You're very good, you know. Exceedingly sharp."

Dasha fidgeted with her drink. She had not reckoned with this turn of conversation and found it embarrassing.

"Yes, very good indeed," he continued. "You have a first-class mind and a real grasp of issues, all the makings of an exceptional lawyer. May I ask what you plan to do with your gifts?"

"Do? Why, I'm going into practice with my husband."

"And what kind of practice would that be?"

"Mortgages, marriages, and misdemeanors." She gave a self-conscious laugh, then described Jordan's clientele briefly. "No grave constitutional matters at stake, I'm afraid. Just a cozy neighborhood practice."

"I see. Well, of course if you're totally committed . . . " He leaned across the desk and pinioned her with his eyes. "You'll be selling yourself short. You realize that, don't you?" His words landed with the force of a boomerang, for she herself had lobbed that very phrase at Jordan but a few nights earlier.

"I . . . we . . . " she stumbled. "I believe it will be a very comfortable living."

"Comfortable, yes, if comfort is indeed the criterion, rather than challenge. One wouldn't think it commensurate with your skills."

He waited for her comment, but Dasha could say nothing that wouldn't sound either self-serving or self-deprecating.

"I expect you know," he resumed, "that I am still an active partner at Slater Blaney. I was there when the firm was founded fifty years ago and I still keep my hand in its affairs. By all counts we're acknowledged to be one of the half-dozen most influential law firms in New York. In fact, although I must admit to personal bias, I truly believe we're the very best, bar none."

Jordan had said as much, too, she recalled.

"We're therefore able to offer young lawyers enormous vistas, a chance to practice at the highest level, in the most sophisticated areas. International law, antitrust, labor mediation, mergers and acquisitions . . . " He went on to outline the range of the firm's activities. No mortgages and marriages here, thank you very much. Nothing less than the daily storming of legal Mount Everests.

Dasha listened quietly, like a child being read a fairy tale, a fable full of enchanted towers, white stallions, bold Prince Charmings swooping to the rescue. Wonderful stuff, to be sure, but it had nothing to do with her. Nothing to do with real life.

A figure was mentioned. A storybook figure that merely heightened her sense of unreality. It was substantially more than Jordan had earned all last year.

"Of course that's an entry-level salary, you understand. For those who make partner . . . "

More golden embroidery followed thereupon. Murmurings of the Washington office, the Paris branch. Legends of partners who had become federal judges, corporate chiefs. Partners who had virtually sat at the right hand of God. And God was the one who was taking advice.

"True, we work our recruits very hard at first, sixty hours a week on average. I won't deceive you on that score. Yet I believe I'm justified in saying that the first couple of years with us are a learning experience at least the equivalent of a doctoral program. No, superior, because you're dealing with real problems in the real world."

The real world. His phrase made her nervous. According to Jordan, the real world was to be found behind lettered glass windows on Columbus Avenue. She wished the old man would stop spinning out fantasies.

"Well, Mrs. Croy? What do you say?"

"To what?" Her mouth was bone dry. Must have been the sherry.

"You needn't wait till you pass the bar exam, if that's what's worrying you. You can begin the day after graduation."

She balled her hands together to contain their trembling. There must be no misinterpreting his words.

"Am I to understand, sir, that you're offering me a position at Slater Blaney?"

"Dear girl! I don't usually speak at such length to no purpose." But he must have sensed her distress, for his voice softened. "No, Mrs. Croy. I'm offering you much more than a position. I'm offering you the opportunity of a lifetime."

"Oh, I couldn't"—the words burst forth unbidden. "It's out of the question. I'm terribly flattered, terribly *moved* by your faith in my abilities, but I'm already committed. It wouldn't be right . . . it wouldn't be honorable . . . "

"Now, my dear, I won't take no for an answer. Not yet at least. Not until you've had a chance to think it through. You should discuss it with your family, your friends, your colleagues. Then come down and look over the firm . . . "

Please . . . please don't do this to me!

"It's no good." She shook her head vehemently. "I just can't. There are personal factors involved, obligations."

"I appreciate that, and loyalty is a most estimable quality. But remember, you also have an obligation to yourself. Think it over in the fullest sense, then come back and see me next week."

She stumbled from his office blind with anxiety, only to walk, literally, into a friend from her study group.

"Whoa there!" Jeannie Leventhal put out a steadying hand. "You could be arrested for lurching without a license. What's up, Dasha? You look thunderstruck."

"Oh Jeannie," Dasha cried. "Can you keep a secret? I have to talk to someone before I explode."

They sat for an hour over Heinekens and pretzels in a Broadway bar.

"Frankly," her friend said, "I don't see this as a real dilemma. If Jordan's half the man you say he is, he wouldn't hold you back. Hell, I should think he'd welcome your getting a break like this."

"He would," Dasha said. "At least in theory. But in fact? I think it would be a terrific blow to his ego. I've half a mind not even to tell him."

"I thought you two were so close."

"We are," came the reply. "But there's close and close, and some things are better left unspoken." Like the *MacFarlane* case that night in Seneca. Like the money borrowed from Alex. "You know, the more I think of it, the less inclined I am to say anything." She already regretted having confided this much. "Anyhow, I've nine-tenths decided to turn it down, so why spoil his peace of mind? I don't want him to feel I'm making a sacrifice."

"And aren't you?"

"In a way," Dasha sighed. "It's so goddam ironic, really. If it were any other firm but Slater Blaney! He applied for a job there years ago and they dumped on him because he wasn't Ivy League. It damn near broke his heart, because in his opinion they're the greatest. Anyhow, it's a moot question. Jordan's counting on me to join him and that's that."

"You're funny, Dasha." Jeannie chewed on a pretzel absent-mindedly. "On the one hand you say you want to vanquish tigers; on the other, you're reluctant to get out from behind your husband's shadow. I should think it would bother you, playing second fiddle."

The phrase stung. "It's not a question of second fiddle, Jeannie. Don't make me out to be some dumb-bunny Nora in *A Doll's House*. I think I could have a pretty good career with Jordan. I've got plans, believe me, to turn that practice into something really substantial. I want to expand, bring in new clients, maybe get into other areas of law."

"In other words, you want to add class to the act."

"I wouldn't have put it so crudely but that's the general idea."

"And Jordan? How's he gonna feel about playing second fiddle?"

"Why does there have to be a second fiddle, I'd like to know? There *are* such things as fifty-fifty relationships. And I like to think ours is one of them."

"You're the judge." Jeannie shrugged. "But—did you ever meet the guy I'm living with, Dmitri?"

Dasha had a vague recollection of a stocky young Greek with marvelous teeth and minimal English.

"He's an artist, you know, and I presume a competent one. His specialty is something called neo-symbolist collage. The point is, I know zilch about art, modern or otherwise, and my abysmal ignorance in that area can only be surpassed by his colossal ignorance of anything that has to do with law and lawyers. All told, it works out fine and we hardly ever rub up against each other. Professionally, that is," and she grinned.

Dasha considered this. "It doesn't sound like there's an awful lot of communication."

"No, but no real competition either. And no conflict about who's going to get to the finish line first. You want my advice?"

"Short of leaving Jordan and moving in with a Greek neo-symbolist, yes, I do."

"Take the Slater Blaney job. You'd be crazy not to. Conceivably you could spend the rest of your life kicking yourself . . . or worse yet, kicking your husband. There's no road more attractive than the road not taken. And if you really are nutsy enough to turn it down"—she patted Dasha's hand—"how about putting in a good word for me?"

Riding home on the bus, Dasha pondered Jeannie's advice.

The interview with Geere had shaken her profoundly: not only the fact of the offer, but the realization that she had let slip her true feelings about Jordan's career.

"Mortgages and marriages," she had described his practice, and in retrospect the words sounded snide, demeaning. She had belittled her husband's work before an outsider. It was a shabby act, petty and disloyal. Yet the fact was, she believed he was wasting his talents as she would be wasting hers. More than ever the thought of burying herself in a second-rate practice made her restless. If only Geere hadn't dangled bigger prospects before her! But he had, and it was not an opportunity likely to recur, least of all once she had joined Jordan in his business.

Among the lessons learned this past year was the realization that she possessed greater drive than her husband. She wasn't so impertinent as to presume herself the better lawyer, but she was, essentially, tougher. More resilient. And those were the qualities that made for big careers.

Did Jordan see this too, she wondered. It was doubtful, for he tended to think of himself as the experienced pro, while viewing her as the housewife who had traded in her apron for a bookbag. True, he was always assuring her they would be equal partners, but the presumption was that she—the novice—would constantly refer to him for guidance.

Well, maybe. At least in the short run. But what if she sprinted past him within a year or so? What if her expertise became the greater?

She was a fast learner, enterprising and adaptable, and it took no great leap of the imagination to perceive that she might be the stronger lawyer. What, then, if clients came to prefer her services? To pass him over while seeking her out? She could hear it now: the ring of the office phone, the voice at the other end explaining, "No, I wanted Mrs. Croy, not Mr." God forbid it should come to that.

Long experience had taught her how vulnerable he was, how delicate a creation his self-esteem. The memory of earlier defeats—especially his rejection by the leading law firms—was still fresh enough to make her wince. Jordan wanted to be admired and respected.

The more she thought about it, the more perilous the idea of a Croy

& Croy partnership appeared. *Croy versus Croy* was more likely. Inevitable, in fact. If there was anything she despised, it was domineering women. "Iron butterflies," Jordan called them, and she had no intention of joining their ranks.

Yet how was she to behave as his partner? Would she be expected to stifle her impulses, live in perpetual fear of showing her clout? Consciously, Jordan never encouraged her to kowtow; subconsciously, he craved her uncritical support.

Sooner or later they were bound to have a clash of professional judgment. What then? Would it be her wifely duty to defer to him? If so, it would have to be done with subtlety and guile, for her husband must never see through the imposture. She would be playing a role, as her mother had done. The very idea made her nauseous. No. She couldn't go through life dissembling. She would end up losing all respect both for herself and for Jordan. No marriage could survive such a strain.

The alternative was clear: Accept Geere's offer.

What had but one hour earlier seemed an impossibility now loomed as an absolute imperative. Jeannie was right. She must take the job. It was better to compete with total strangers. Then she wouldn't have to hold back for fear of wounding him, fear of surpassing. She could go all out, breathe freely, with no qualms about unleashing her gifts to the fullest.

By the time the bus arrived in Crestview, she was convinced that the Slater Blaney offer was a blessing, a solution worthy of the wisest marriage counselor. And surely Jordan would see it too.

At home there was the usual after-school mob scene: the kids, their friends, the scramble getting dinner on the table. Charlotte dropped by, then a neighbor who stayed and stayed and stayed.

It was bedtime before Dasha found herself alone with Jordan, and by then her confidence had begun to dissipate.

"You'll never guess what"—she faked a casual tone, then proceeded to sketch in Blagden Geere's proposal. Perhaps her approach was too casual, for Jordan's response was a mystified smile.

"He thinks you should apply for a job at Slater Blaney? If you ask me, it's a waste of time. They're Social Register only, I believe."

"Not apply, exactly. In fact, he made me—well, a firm offer." She swallowed. "Forty-five thousand to start."

"You're kidding!" The smile vanished instantly. "You . . . he really asked *you?* Wow! That's really wild. You must have charmed the pants off the old boy. Very flattering and all that, but I suppose you told him you've got a job lined up already."

"I told him I'd think about it and discuss it with you."

"Jesus!" Jordan sat down heavily on the bed, eyebrows furrowed. "That was the last thing in the world I expected to hear, but okay—let's discuss it. Unless, of course, you've already made up your mind."

"No no . . . " she lied. "I think it should be a joint decision. However . . . "

There were so many considerations, she began. First of all was it wise, she couldn't help wondering, for the two of them to be in business together? "We'd be cheek by jowl twenty-four hours a day, seven days a week. In the living room, the kitchen, in bed. And at the office too?" Maybe it was too much of a good thing.

Then, realistically, there was the money. She didn't have enough fingers to enumerate everything this household wanted. *Needed.* To begin with, a proper piano so the kids could have music lessons. Robin had been after her for months. The Chevy was definitely on its last legs. Jordan's office could use some redecorating. And now, for the first time since they were married, they could seriously think about looking for a proper house.

"I'd feel guilty passing up that kind of money. You've been scrambling so long and so hard."

"Would it bother you, Dasha, that you'd be earning more than I would?"

She tried to fathom his expression without success. "Why, sweetie?" She parried the question. "Do you think it would bother you?"

"I asked you first, although it seems to me that money is a peripheral issue." He busied himself with his shoelaces refusing to look up. "You realize that if you go there, you'll be one of maybe two hundred lawyers? They don't call those places law factories for nothing. Whereas, if you come in with me, you're a major piece of the action." He peeled off his socks and hurled them across the room in the general direction of the laundry hamper. "However, it's your career, your decision."

"You're not being much help, Jordan."

"Help! You've already made your mind up, so why do we have to go through the motions? You don't want my advice, Dasha. You want a rubber stamp. Obviously, Geere filled your head with visions of sugar plums. Well, if you think you'll be happier as a small fish in a big pond, that's your privilege. More importantly, you want to use the bathroom first or should I?" He rose without waiting for her answer and was gone an unconscionable time.

By the time he returned, she was sitting up in bed shaking with barely subdued anger. That kind of pettiness was the last thing she'd anticipated from Jordan, so utterly out of character. He must have felt so too, for he sat down beside her meekly, his eyes sad and contrite.

"Sorry about tying up the john so long, but it's where I do my clearest thinking. Dasha, I'm sorry. I don't know what got into me just now. The whole business just took me by storm and . . . what can I say? I guess I was a little bit jealous. Take the job," he urged. "I absolutely insist on it. I'd never forgive myself if you turned it down for no other reason than that I'm such a churlish bastard. I think it was all that talk about salary threw me off. To my ears, it sounded like you were rational-izing, trying to find excuses. You don't need any. You want to go to Slater Blaney because you want to go to Slater Blaney. And that's reason enough for me. So go with all my blessings, darling, and knock 'em dead down in Wall Street. However it works out, I'm with you all the way. Never doubt it. Still"—he gave a heart-catching grin—"you've got to admit you sure were lucky catching the eye of Blagden Geere like that."

"Lucky." The word made her wince.

"Luck has nothing to do with it," she was tempted to quote Mae West, but the snappish retort died in her throat.

Tonight had been very rough on his ego. And if he chose to see Geere's offer as a lucky break, she wouldn't quibble. Perhaps he needed that rationale to make the whole business more palatable, to account for her having passed so easily through a door that had been locked against him. Let him call it luck; she could hardly begrudge him this modest consolation. And in return for that petty illusion, Jordan was offering something immense: his unstinting support in her new career. No holds barred. It couldn't have been easy—for him, for any man.

"I'm lucky," she echoed, and her soft smile finished the sentence. Yes, indeed. She was lucky in her husband.

"But tell me," he teased. "Will you still love me when you're rich and famous?"

She giggled, and her newly chastened mood communicated. Jordan slid into bed with a happy sigh, nestling up against her with the easy familiarity of thousands of nights spent together, their bodies a seamless confluence of hips and thighs and arms and lips.

"Mmmm, you smell wonderful!" He nuzzled against the hollow of her breast, and the last tiny grain of rancor vanished at his touch.

"And you feel wonderful." She slithered into his arms, entwined her legs around his own like a caduceus, and for a long time they lay motionless, flesh touching, lips brushing, sharing the same breath, the same heartbeat.

It was late, the world was silent. The muted glow of the bedside lamp suffused their bodies with a rosy flush. *Like firelight,* Dasha thought. *Like the enchanted firelight of a snow-bound cottage in the Berkshires.* And in that enchanted light, the harshness and friction of the day evanesced. Against the flat of her belly she could feel Jordan grow hard and strong, throbbing against her with the urgency of youth. Her nipples tautened.

How extraordinary! How extraordinary that after all this time, all the countless caresses, the intimacies without number, they still had the power to arouse each other, to explore each other. She reached down to hold him, warm and thick, to guide his thrusting flesh into her body that now opened like a flower beneath him. For a moment he paused. Searched out her eyes. And then he entered her in an assertion of love that brooked no denial, moving rhythmically, powerfully within her, as fresh and unabashed as Adam in the delight of his first coupling with Eve. Snake-like, she locked her legs around his buttocks, pulling him to her with all her force until she could no longer say what was she, what was he. And as he drove his flesh joyously into hers, the years fell away. They were young and beautiful and discovering passion together. They were once again what they had been, what they would always be: first lovers.

Over breakfast next morning, Jordan announced to the children, "Your mother has just landed one of the most terrific jobs in New York, which is not surprising"—he winked at Dasha—"because your mother is one of the most terrific women in New York."

Geoff mumbled his acknowledgment through a mouthful of toast, while Robin asked, "Will your picture be in the papers?" and upon being told that it wouldn't, turned her attention back to the Giant Jump-Rope Giveaway offered on the cereal box.

"Such is fame." Dasha laughed good-naturedly. "Trying to compete with a box of Crunchy Munchies. Okay, you guys. Eat up and I'll walk you to school."

The school was only ten minutes away, but with the passage of time, every step of the journey had become encrusted with bits of time-consuming ritual.

First you stopped for hot rolls at the corner bakery, then you said good morning to the Crossing Lady in her plastic orange poncho. Then hand-in-hand down Fort Washington Avenue, where Geoff was allotted two minutes time for conversation with the newsboy's ancient German Shepherd. All the while, of course, Robin was taking scrupulous care not to step on the cracks in the sidewalk. That was an almost magic ingredient of the morning routine.

"What would happen if you stepped on a crack?" Dasha inquired as they arrived at the schoolyard. "Would the world come to an end?"

"I don't know." Her daughter was puzzled by the question. "I just always never step on the cracks."

Dasha kissed them goodbye and watched until they were safely inside the grounds. At the gate, Geoff turned around and gave her two tiny waves. Just two—no more. That was part of the ritual too.

Dasha waved back, then headed for the bus to take her downtown.

What traditionalists kids that age were! She sighed half-aloud. The most dyed-in-the-wool conservatives—about food, about clothes, even about the route they took to school.

And here she was, by contrast, on the brink of a new career, aching for nothing so much as change and challenge. Of course youngsters need structure and security—she recognized that—yet as the bus pulled away from the school, it struck her that for the first time in their lives she and the children were subtly heading in different directions.

If her returning to law school had been a minor upheaval in their lives, her joining Slater Blaney would undoubtedly prove a major one. Inevitably, it would disrupt the familiar pattern of their days.

How many more mornings would she be walking the children to school, she wondered. Not too many—not with the long commute to Wall Street in the offing. And how many other traditions would go by the boards? She shifted uneasily in her seat, instinctively turning for a last glimpse of the playground.

Blagden Geere had warned her the job would be demanding, calling for immense reserves of time and energy. Energy she had, an almost bottomless supply, but time was different. Time was a finite commodity, incapable of being stretched, and every minute spent in one place had to taken out of someplace else. Stolen, if necessary. She only hoped there would be enough to go around, enough to maintain the comfortable rhythm of her children's daily life.

Still, she told herself, other women worked and raised kids and found a successful balance. She would, too. It was largely a matter of moving cautiously like Robin—and making sure you didn't step on the cracks.

PART TWO

CHAPTER EIGHT

☐ There was an anecdote Max Oborin liked to tell about the golden age of violin-making.

In the late 1600s, the finest instruments originated from three rival families whose workshops were side by side in the Italian village of Cremona.

First were the Amatis, and outside their shop hung a sign: "The best violins in all Italy." Not to be outdone, their next-door neighbors, the family Guarnerius, hung a bolder sign proclaiming: THE BEST VIOLINS IN ALL THE WORLD!

At the end of the street was the workshop of Anton Stradivarius, and on its front door was a simple notice which read: "The best violins on the block."

Max's story came to mind the day Dasha first reported to work. Slater Blaney was housed—along with many of its closest competitors —in a glass-and-chrome tower near Wall Street. In the vaulting marble lobby, a wall of water perpetually cascaded over abstract sculptures while overhead a flight of angular metal mobiles threatened to transport the visitor into the next century.

Fifty floors above, the entry to Slater Blaney was a study in contrast: a simple oaken door with the firm's name written neatly in a black Spencerian script. We may be large—the elegant lettering seemed to say —we may be rich and powerful, but we are not gaudy.

Despite its aristocratic frontage, however, Slater Blaney was a relative newcomer in the Valhalla of downtown corporate law. The firm was founded in the 1920s by a trio of young firebrands who were viewed in their day as vulgar gate-crashers. In the thirties, the firm made legal history by winning a series of notable victories for the liberal cause, and contributing a partner to Roosevelt's Brain Trust. It expanded furiously during the war and, in an effort to win corporate clients, managed to rid itself gradually of the liberal taint that had marked its freewheeling youth. By the time Dasha arrived, it had long since settled down comfortably in the top echelon of the blue-chip bar.

Thus though its clientele and philosophy had varied over the years, its reputation for excellence remained unchallenged.

From its ranks, Slater Blaney had furnished the nation with judges, a senator, three ambassadors, and even on one occasion a presidential candidate. He lost by a landslide, but in so doing managed to put his firm's name on the nation's lips.

"We're not the biggest firm in town," Andy McCabe informed Dasha, "but we sure are the toughest. I've been working here two years and I'm still impressed."

He was a bustling young fellow, assigned to show Dasha around on that first morning, a prospect he clearly relished. For despite the sobriety of his pinstripe suit and the polish on his black wing-tip shoes, he was bubbly as a kid at a circus. Dasha took to him at once. He reminded her of Jordan in his college days.

"Oh, I'm impressed already." She smiled. "Just walking into the reception room knocked me out. I thought I'd stumbled into the Museum of Modern Art by mistake."

"We got them beat by a mile." Andy shepherded her down a long corridor lined with seascapes. "Right now, you're passing the biggest collection of Winslow Homers in existence. Plus"—he swung open a double door, peered into an empty conference room, then ushered her in—"plus this is a genuine Van Dyke. We outbid the Met for this picture, and the interesting thing about it, the reason why the firm was so hot to own the painting is that it's supposed to be a representation of St. Ives. According to the legend, he was a lawyer—the only one who ever achieved sainthood. A martyr for his client, no doubt."

"Rather gives you something to strive for, Andy."

"I'll keep that in mind." He grinned. "Meanwhile enough of the art tour. Let me show you the heart and soul of the joint."

First, the library—nearly a hundred thousand volumes staffed by librarians working round the clock. Then the typing pool. It too operated on a twenty-four-hour basis, as did the copying facilities and the messenger service. There were file clerks, proofreaders, paralegals, translators, every service one could conceivably use. He showed her the conference rooms, one larger and more elegant than the next. Then . . .

"This is the dining room." He ushered Dasha into a cheerful, spacious hall with fresh daffodils brightening every table. The luncheon special, the bulletin board said, was fresh salmon and *émincé de veau zurichoise*. Dasha sniffed appreciatively. The partners had their own dining room, Andy explained, which was strictly Spode and Waterford. "However, even the peasants around here get to eat pretty well. I'd say the equivalent of a Mimi Sheraton two star, minus the booze, of course. But what can you expect for free?"

"Free?" Dasha echoed. "That seems awfully generous."

"Not really. Look . . . say you're just going down the street to the Chock Full O'Nuts, it's going to take you ten minutes each way. That's twenty minutes in all, plus add in the time it takes to get your check, pay the bill, leave some change for the tip. Before you know it, you've pissed away nearly a half-hour, excluding eating time. And that's a half-hour when you could have been working at your desk, putting in maybe fifty dollars' worth of billable time. Believe me, it's cheaper for the firm to give you a filet mignon than have you pay for your own burger in a hash house. We've got a fully equipped gym one floor up. The same reasoning."

He steered her down a long corridor toward an oaken door, massive and faintly forbidding. "After you." Andy swung it open noiselessly, plunging Dasha ankle deep in pale Gulistan carpet. Instinctively her guide lowered his voice, for here the halls were quiet with the hush of power.

"This is it—the sanctum sanctorum, where the senior partners hole up." *(Someday,* she sensed the yearning in his voice, *someday me too.)* "It's the heart of the mechanism, so to speak. The real clout behind Slater Blaney."

Dasha looked about her respectfully but there was nothing to be seen except secretaries, stationed like ferocious watchdogs, before a solid phalanx of closed doors.

Then they turned a corner and a shaft of daylight poured in.

Through an open door, Dasha managed a glimpse of a magnificent corner office. "Office!" she thought ruefully. It looked bigger than the entire Croy apartment. And furnished—dear God, but it was splendid—with a sultan's pile of Oriental rugs, English cherrywood polished to a fare-thee-well, and what looked suspiciously like a Renoir perched over the Sheraton desk. Even from the threshold, the room was redolent of beeswax and fresh roses. Beyond the confines stretched a panoramic view of the harbor, while in the further distance the Statue of Liberty thrust high a torch bright with promise.

Dasha drank it in speechlessly—the space, the light, the art—then turned to Andy for enlightenment.

"How do you get an office like that?" She hoped her tone sounded sufficiently light. And Andy answered in the same vein. "Same way you get to Carnegie Hall. Practice, man, practice. Had enough? Come on, let's have lunch."

Over salad and grilled sole at a Fulton Street fishhouse, Andy told her what to expect.

"Be prepared to work your ass off. You're going to find the next couple of years will make law school look like a Sunday outing. Geere told you sixty hours a week, did he? Well, the old boy always did have a gift for understatement. A hundred would be more like it."

The firm, he explained, made big money off the sweated backs of the young associates, billing clients handsomely for each hour they racked up. Thus, the longer the hours, the more the firm had to gain, the better you looked in their books. No, he answered Dasha's question, the associates never ganged up to put a stop to the practice. "Oh, sure we grouse, but we just keep on trucking. And you know why? Because we all have a vision of that big corner office you saw this morning."

The competition was rigorous, unremitting, to see which of the associates could work the hardest, claim the longest hours, score the biggest number of Brownie points.

A story was told of a very ambitious young man who actually managed to clock up twenty-four working hours in a single day, only to be one-upped by a rival who flew to California, working every moment on the plane. "What with the three-hour time difference," Andy laughed, "he squeezed twenty-seven billable hours out of the day. Can you top that?"

"I'm not sure I want to," Dasha said.

"Oh you will, once you get caught up in the essential madness. Everybody wants to play the game. And in a way, there's no choice, really. You either ride the wave or you get drowned by it."

To make partner! That was the dream, the driving force behind the feverish competition. And chances were three to one against making it. "Right now, there are one hundred fifty associates more or less, and only forty-three partners. You can figure out the odds for yourself." So it wasn't enough simply to lead the pack in the number of billable hours put in. Along the way you had to give evidence of guts and talent and enterprise. "Plus, it never hurts to have a rabbi—a partner who'll take you under his wing." Every step of the way, she would be monitored as closely as a Russian missile, her work subject to constant reappraisal. And during those first couple of years, she would be working in different departments, under different supervisors, before she settled down to a specialty.

The firm handled only civil law, dealing almost exclusively with corporate clients. "So you won't be defending any Mafia honchos or neighborhood ax murderers. Just your normal thieving cheating conniving big businessman." She should expect a lot of client contact. "The idea is, you eventually get to know their business even better than they do, so how can they live without you?" The client list ranged from giant industrials to Wall Street banks to the behemoth First Broadcasting Corporation.

"And all the while you'll be treated like minor royalty. First-class this, first-class that. The firm's fabulous when it comes to perks. But don't kid yourself. We associates are basically coolies, doing the research, working the night shifts, putting in our six years hard labor."

"Six years!" Dasha groaned. "That's forever."

"Be grateful. In most firms it's seven. Anyhow, that's the point where the decision is made about who gets anointed to partner."

There was an organized progression. Junior associates, "That's you and me." Senior associates, "Us a couple of years from now." Junior partner, "If Allah is merciful." And senior partner. This last he punctuated with a sigh.

Now and again, he continued, some hotshot might shave a year or two off the ritual. But the hard truth was, most associates never made it at all. And once passed over, they'd either leave to try their luck elsewhere or stay on as senior associates locked into some narrow specialty—the professional equivalent of the dead letter office. The firm never fired except for egregious misconduct, but neither did it offer second chances.

"But you're a smart girl," Andy went on. "So let's say you make partner—junior partner, anyway. Now you're entitled to a piece of the pie. At the end of the year you get a chunk of the profits and in a way that's your compensation for all the shit you took earlier on. You can stop right there, if you don't mind settling for a measly couple of hundred thou per annum. But if you're ambitious . . . "

In theory, all partners were created equal. In fact, some were a lot more equal than others. For at the top of the heap were the dozen men —no women as yet—of the Management Committee, and they were truly the powers that be.

At senior partner level, he explained, you were not operating so much as a lawyer but as a seer, a diplomat, a maker of deals, an architect of industry. Andy laughed. "When I was a kid there was this character in *Li'l Abner* who was supposed to be the World's Biggest Expert. On everything! He charged a hundred bucks a word for his advice, so just a how-do-you-do? could set you back a fortune. God forbid he told jokes at those prices. That's our Senior Management Committee—eleven of the World's Greatest Experts on Everything plus one resident rainmaker."

"Rainmaker?"

"A rainmaker is a guy who brings in the big bucks. He makes sure the clients stay put and stay happy. In other words, he goes out on the golf course and makes rain. If not for him, we'd probably all starve. It's anybody's guess what the senior partners pull down. Half a million, a million a year?" He shrugged. "It gets to a point where money is meaningless . . . just a way of keeping score. Because *then* you're hobnobbing with presidents."

"And after you've made senior partner," Dasha teased, "what do you do for an encore?"

"Ah then"—he gave a mock salute—"you divvy up the universe with Darth Vader."

"Very interesting, though I can't imagine sacrificing my life to climb the ladder. Besides, Darth Vader's not my type. Can I ask you a personal question? What brought you into the firm? Is your father a lawyer?"

"My father runs a camera shop in Queens. I'm here because I was recruited, same as you. They made me an offer I couldn't refuse. Why do you ask?"

"Well, I had heard"—Jordan's experience came to mind—"I've heard that it's very WASP here and if you're not in the Social Register, it could affect your advancement."

"Bullshit!" His eyes flashed with anger. "That is absolute bullshit. Who told you that, a recruiter from a rival firm?" When she shook her head, he continued, "Then I bet it was someone who didn't make the grade. If this firm weren't a meritocracy, I would never have come. I had plenty of other offers. As far as background goes, my dog has a better pedigree than I, and he's a mutt. No, Dasha. Truth is, this place is less cliquey than most. Naturally they assume you know better than to drink out of a fingerbowl, but all they really care about is performance. What I said about us being coolies, that's not really true. We're the aristocracy, you and I, just by virtue of having made it into the firm. As a Slater Blaney lawyer, you can pull rank on nine-tenths of the attorneys in New York. We're the elite, Dasha. The super achievers. And for all my griping, I wouldn't be anywhere else. I bet your husband's awfully proud of you."

"Oh, he is." Dasha flushed. "He thinks it's terrific. I'm dying to bring my kids down one day and show them the place. How about you, Andy? You married?"

Not yet, came the reply, but soon. Just as soon as he could haul his girlfriend off to the altar. "I'm still old-fashioned enough to believe in marriage, and so's Melanie."

"You're not postponing it to see if you make partner, are you?"

"Good lord, no. I'd get married tomorrow—well, not tomorrow because I'm tied up in meetings all day. But one of these days . . . Stick around and I'll invite you to the wedding."

After the glories of the morning and the luxurious lunch, Dasha's office was a distinct anticlimax: a tiny box with a glass compartment in the door, spartanly furnished with a desk and a banged-up metal file cabinet. No window either, worse luck.

Within an hour of settling in, she met the partner who'd be supervising her for the next few weeks. A redoubtable Southerner well in his fifties, Porter Collins appeared to take it for granted that Dasha—novice though she was—was perfectly capable of helping to frame a multi-million-dollar contract. It seemed incredible, this being laden with major responsibility her very first day at work, but it was a day full of remarkable happenings, not the least of which was Collins dropping into her office late that afternoon. "Call me Porter, by the way," he said, handing her a long white envelope. "All the lawyers are on a first-name basis here." She opened the envelope. It was a check for one thousand dollars.

"I don't understand."

"Just our way of saying welcome aboard."

She came home bubbling—and late!—with enough superlatives to start an avalanche. Slater Blaney was the greatest. Her colleagues the best. The whole experience not to be believed. Some of Andy's ebullience found its way into her voice. "Goddam," she thought. "He's right. The enthusiasm is contagious."

And to top it off, there was that thousand dollars sitting in her pocketbook. She turned to Robin, feeling like Santa Claus. "Well, princess, what say we go shopping for a piano on Saturday?"

"Oh Mommy!" Robin was on top of her with a killer hug, and Dasha winked to her husband. "Who says you can't buy love!"

Jordan heard it all out with a good-natured smile.

"Well, we don't have any Renoirs on our modest premises, I'm afraid. But my aspidistra is coming along nicely."

"You're a darling for being so patient." She kissed him. "I'm turning in early, I'm bushed."

But lying in bed that night, sleep refused to come. The events of the day, the people, the myriad impressions all crowded each other for space in her mind's eye. And that Harrington contract they'd put her on. God! It was a thing of beauty, intricate and elegant as clockwork.

Now, stretched out in the darkness, with Jordan sleeping heavily by her side, she began to figure out ways of making it even more beautiful. Tightening up the tax deferral clause, for instance. Yes, she was pretty sure she could improve on it. Damn sure. In fact, she could hardly wait until morning to attack the thing afresh.

She'd get up early tomorrow. Sixish . . . be at the office by seven.

When sleep finally claimed her, the last vision imprinted on her eyelids was a gracious Renoir smiling down from the wall.

CHAPTER NINE

☐ She walked down the corridor of the Palmer House teetering on high strappy sandals. Where the hell had her room gone to? Damn, it was right here just a few hours earlier. Ah, *there* it was. Never should have had that second brandy, to say nothing of the Nuits St. Georges or those dry martinis on the rocks. The perils of the road, Alex called it, and he was pretty accurate on that score.

Should call Jordan. Meant to earlier. What time was it in New York anyhow? One-thirty in the morning . . . way too late. She'd give him a ring first thing tomorrow.

The road, depending on how you looked at it, was either the greatest boon or curse of the job. Everybody bitched about it, but Dasha had the sneaky feeling that most of the gripers, the men in particular, enjoyed it at heart. There was a certain mystique about the road, a kind of macho boasting of missed connections, jet lag, and what some dumb hotel in Dallas had done to their laundry. Or maybe they just enjoyed getting away from their wives and kids. Slater Blaney was certainly a graveyard for marriages. Not hers, thank God, but the divorce rate up there must be at least double the national average, though whether that was the cause or effect of so much time on the road, who could tell?

For her, thus far, the road had consisted chiefly of shuttle flights to Washington a couple of times a month, usually returning the same day. If she stayed overnight, she'd put up with Alex and use the trips as an excuse for a family reunion.

Funny how Alex had changed in his appraisal of her. It was no longer "my kid sister from New York." Lately he'd taken to introducing her to his dinner guests: "My sister is a lawyer with Slater Blaney." It was as though for the first time in her life he actually saw her as a human being with a history and a character. As a person who might actually have something interesting to contribute to a conversation. She didn't like Alex any better for this new attitude, but she liked herself better, and that was sufficient.

Now the firm had sent her to Chicago to attend a week-long seminar, and the trip was managed in typical Slater Blaney fashion—first class all the way. Although why they had to book a bedroom the size of a dance hall for one lone woman was beyond her. The Palmer House was elegant, the seminar a real eye opener, and it had been enormous fun meeting lawyers from all over the country.

During the course of the week she'd become particularly friendly with a brisk young lawyer from Denver. His name was Burt Stapes. He had fire-engine hair complete with matching mustache, and despite his drawl, he was possessed of a quick and irreverent sense of humor. They lunched together most days, talking shop and taking full advantage of their respective expense accounts in a search to find Chicago's greatest steak house.

The seminar finished on Friday and the next morning she was scheduled to fly back home. It was Burt's suggestion they spend the last night in town pursuing the quest for the perfect steak and seeing a bit of Chicago into the bargain.

The evening began with a couple of dry martinis in the Pump Room, continued with a châteaubriand at Enrico's, and midnight found them in a piano bar atop the John Hancock nursing Napoleon brandy in oversized snifters. He had just called for a second round when she noticed the time.

"Ouch!" She grimaced. "I've got a plane to catch tomorrow, so I think I'll call it a night. It's been fun."

"It still could be fun." He caught her hand before she had a chance to get up and brought it to his cheek. "The night's not over for hours yet." He brushed his lips against her fingers in a gesture so light she wondered if she could have imagined it. Suddenly, she was fiercely conscious of his physical presence—the texture of his sports jacket, the heat of his body, so close to her on the banquette.

For a moment she sat frozen, then burst out laughing. "You're not coming on to me, are you, Burt?"

He was nonplussed. "My God, you New Yorkers don't mince words, do you? I had thought of it as something a bit more romantic, but . . . yeah. You could say I was coming on to you, although I never thought it would be a source of such amusement."

"I'm sorry." Dasha gave him a friendly pat on the shoulder. "I didn't mean to sound so crude. It's just . . . for heaven's sakes, Burt, I'm an old married woman."

"Don't 'there there' me, Dasha. If you don't want to go to bed with me, that's one thing. But old? What are you, thirty, thirty-one?"

"Thereabouts."

"Well, you make it sound like you're ready for the boneyard. You've been doing this all week, you know?"

"Doing what?"

"Talking about yourself is if you were a matron in a Midwest sorority house and therefore no male could conceivably make a pass at you. You're a very sexy lady, I'll have you know. No . . . don't interrupt. You've get sensational legs, a terrific figure, and an absolutely delicious mouth, even when you're chewing on your lipstick like right now. So why do you find it incredible that someone is just aching to go to bed with you?"

The conversation was becoming absurd. She couldn't help wondering if he were teasing her. If so, it would be idiotic to overreact. If not, she should stop all such talk here and now. Without, of course, wounding his ego. The whole business was terribly embarrassing.

"That's very flattering, Burt"—she decided to steer a middle course —"and you've made me feel a whole lot younger, but not, I'm afraid, any less married. So let's just keep it friends and colleagues, shall we?"

He seemed to accept his defeat with good grace, and she was glad she had not made a whole to-do. Friends and colleagues it would be. She put out her hand for a goodbye shake, when suddenly he pulled her to him and kissed her full and hard on the lips. For one surprising moment she felt his tongue streak inside her mouth. She was too stunned to do anything. But he released her with an enigmatic smile.

"Well, so long, Dasha Croy. Have a good trip home. Maybe we'll meet again some other time."

She didn't even say goodbye—simply fled, as though the devil were at her heels. The whole business was totally outrageous. Or so it seemed at the time.

But half an hour later, reviewing it from the safety of her hotel room, her reaction struck her as ludicrous.

A man had kissed her—that was all. She could still feel his lips on her own, warm and moist. Still smell his aftershave lotion, a scent she didn't recognize. A simple kiss, and she had behaved as though raped. Odd, when she came to think of it, but she didn't recollect ever having kissed a man with a mustache before. "Another first for Dasha Croy," she thought as she began packing for tomorrow's journey. Jordan would probably find the whole business a hoot when she told him. He'd been kidding her about her "virgin" trip for the last couple of weeks, teasing that she'd find a demon lover in a strange hotel room and never come back to old Crestview. Well, Burt hardly qualified for demon lover, and the kiss was just a kiss after all. Just a kiss—unexpected and unexpectedly pleasant—from a man she'd never see again. Big deal.

She washed her face, brushed her teeth and slid into bed, yet a bit of Burt's scent seemed to cling to her. Unaccountably, she found it disturbing. Surely men made passes at women every day in the week, so there was nothing to get uptight about.

Except that the men in their circle, the husbands at Crestview Village, spectacularly did not make passes. Oh, the New Year's Eve buss and maybe a playful pinch at a party, with a broad wink and a "Don't tell my wife"; but they were a conservative lot, her neighbors. The sexual revolution seemed to have passed them by. Crestview was a time capsule of pre-Woodstock morality.

Which was just about how far back she'd have to go for a memory of being kissed that way by any man other than Jordan.

The room was silent with that special quiet of grand hotels. The bed was enormous, biggest bed she'd ever slept in. Dasha slithered under the covers and stretched out an arm, half expecting to encounter Jordan. Then it hit her.

She had never in her life been on her own before. Not really. Not like this, alone in a strange hotel, a strange city, accountable to no one in the world. Until this week, every night of her life had been spent either in college dorms or within the family circle.

Imagine! She was thirty-three years old and this was the first time in her life when she had been accorded total freedom to do . . . whatever. Get blind drunk. Fall asleep with her clothes on. Or take a total stranger into her bed.

Not that she would do such a thing—not that she would dream of abusing her freedom and Jordan's trust—but the point was she *could*. She could, this very moment, be lying in bed with Burt Stapes, naked, making love, and no one would ever be the wiser. For one sensuous moment, she half-welcomed the idea, then vehemently tried to scoff the notion away.

Still, how ridiculous she must have appeared this evening, how full of moral outrage. Somewhere over the years she had lost all sense of herself as seductive, as overtly sexual. She hardly ever thought of herself these days as a woman who might excite desire in any man but her husband.

Yet when she was young, in college, there had been no greater thrill than seeing herself reflected in men's eyes. She had lived for boys, for dates, for male adulation. Flirting had been her principal business in life. But all that, of course, was before Jordan. The sexual revolution had passed *her* by as well.

Briefly, shamefacedly, she gave herself over to a hitherto unknown speculation. What if she had accepted Burt's overtures? What would he have been like as a lover? Better than Jordan? Worse?

Physically, he was a completely different type, broad-shouldered and square where Jordan was lean, almost bony. What would Burt's arms have felt like around her, his hands on her flesh, his body pressed against hers? She couldn't imagine. It was as though all those years of faithful marriage had robbed her of the erotic wherewithal for creating un-bounded fantasies. She had no basis for comparison, no memory of different caresses. All she knew was Jordan's lovemaking.

She had a colleague at the office, a woman a couple of years younger than Dasha but vastly older in sexual experience, who took on and discarded lovers with a speed that was truly breathtaking. Miranda spoke of them prosaically enough, yet occasionally she would remark that she had met a man who was "fantastic in the sack" or "a really innovative guy, you know?"

Dasha didn't know. And since Miranda never amplified, the subject remained clothed in mystery.

Was Jordan innovative, fantastic in bed? What were the yardsticks? All Dasha could vouch for was that they had a lively sex life, that they had made each other happy for a dozen years now, and that he was still the most attractive man she knew.

So here she was, in that most traditionally erotic setting of all, a distant hotel room, finding herself very poorly equipped indeed for conjuring up a truly juicy fantasy concerning a red-headed lawyer from Denver. In truth, she hardly knew where to begin.

Look at me. She smiled into the dresser mirror. A lone woman occupying one small portion of an enormous bed. The left side, as it happened. Of course. She had always slept on the left side, Jordan on the right. It was a frozen fact of their life together. Like who got which shelf in the medicine chest. Or towels. His. Hers. Pure habit, yet it had assumed the force of immutable law.

Ergo: Here she was in this vast bed in this strange town with all the space in the world to stretch out on, and still she huddled on the old familiar side. So much for speculation about sex with a total stranger. She had yet to learn what it was like sleeping on the far side of the bed, for Chrissakes!

Well, tonight she would. She might not be up to taking on demon lovers and carousing in the singles bars, but at least she could explore the other side of the bed. She stretched, sighed, turned out the lights, and unthinkingly reached out for Jordan's hand.

Too bad he wasn't there. She really did feel rather—romantic. *Oh what the hell, be frank,* she told herself. *What you really feel is horny.* No matter. Tomorrow she'd be sleeping in her own bed once again. With Jordan by her side, be it right or left.

She rose early next morning with the incident pushed well to the back of her mind. Or so she thought as she went about her business briskly.

Yet some of the mood must have insinuated itself, for subconsciously she dressed for the day with greater care than usual, applied a trifle more eye shadow, an extra dollop of perfume, and left the hotel with a jaunty spring to her step. At the airport she ran into another Slater Blaney lawyer and they sat together on the flight home.

He was a balding paunchy partner well into middle age, and Dasha certainly had no intention of flirting with him. Yet he seemed unusually playful, as if he sensed something different about her. "Have you had your hair cut recently? It looks very nice."

"Thank you." She reached to fluff it out instinctively. "But no, I haven't." Harry Biggs shrugged. "It sure does look nice."

The trip home was uneventful. They got off at Kennedy and were heading for the cab ranks when their progress was stopped by a cluster of teenagers, arms full of books and carnations. They looked as if they had just stepped out of a turn-of-the-century photograph, in straw boaters and candy-stripe blazers. Dasha's first impression was of a school outing, but one of the boys—fresh-faced kid with clean blond hair—thrust a carnation into her hands. "Would you buy a flower, ma'am? It's in a good cause . . . to help . . . "

She didn't catch the end of his sentence, routinely reaching for her pocketbook, when Biggs shoved the boy aside unceremoniously. "Piss off, will you? You're bothering the lady. Sorry about the language, but those cult kids give me a pain in the ass."

Harry's dour mood failed to dampen her spirits, and she was whistling when she strode through the door.

"You're looking very pleased with yourself," Jordan commented. "It must have been a good trip."

"Terrific. But it's great to be home. And you know what, the first thing I want to do is . . . ?"

"Make love, by any chance?"

"Jordan, you're a goddam mind reader."

"I missed you too, darling," he confessed.

And if she never did mention being kissed by a redhead in a Chicago piano bar, it was because the incident was too trivial to recall. Yet that night in Chicago had left its legacy. It had endowed her with a fresh awareness, a heightened sense of her own femininity. From that date on, although she never thought of it as cause and effect, she began to dress with more care, more flair. Even a good dark suit, she realized, masterfully cut, handsomely fitted, emboldened with a smashing piece of jewelry, could elicit that admiring look in men's eyes. That was pleasing. And there was no law demanding that attorneys be downright dowdy. A little less Macy's and a little more Bendel's could do wonderful things for the ego. So why not? As she found herself saying more and more frequently these days—"I can afford it."

The year that marked this subtle change in her appearance wrought far more dramatic changes in the Croys' domestic life.

From the start it was clear that she would have neither time nor energy for running the house, and they were going to need substantial help. "Hire somebody," Jordan urged her, but she was reluctant to turn her home, above all her children, over to an outsider. In the end, it was Charlotte—or more accurately Charlotte's varicose veins—that suggested the solution.

Twenty-five years as a saleswoman had taken a heavy toll. "My feet are killing me," she voiced the oldest complaint in the lexicon of women. "I'm going to have to find another job." But what else was she capable of? She decided to look for work as a paid companion. From there it was but a logical step, and both women hit upon the idea simultaneously. She would look after the children, run the house, and slap together the odd meal or two.

The arrangement proved a godsend. The children were in good hands. Jordan, too. She'd no longer have to subject them to the daily inquisition. Did you practice your scales? Finish your milk? Remember to take your hay-fever pills? With Charlotte in charge, all was right with the world. At last, *at last,* she could concentrate on the work at hand.

Her first year at Slater Blaney, Dasha poured herself into the job with an abandon that bordered on the reckless. She loved the place with a sweeping irrational affection. "It's only a law firm," Jordan sometimes reminded her. But to Dasha it was something more.

Working there—she once tried to articulate the fascination she felt —was like belonging to the best, most exclusive club in the world. Automatically, you became an insider. A factor. A vital part of a powerful whole. And everyone else in the club was just as bright and terrific as you were. It was a heady sensation.

Which was not to say that the firm was free from in-fighting or that the competition didn't get pretty hairy at times. You lived by your wits each waking moment, kept your eye out for the strategic opportunity.

But above and beyond the occasional drawing of blood, there was a profound sense of union. A camaraderie of the battlefield. After all, who but your colleagues shared the same running gags, the same peeves, the same slang even? And who but your colleagues shared the same enemies?

Crisis was the order of the day. You learned to live with it, to relish it. A day in which all had gone too smoothly was a day that was lacking in zest. And often, when the going got rough, when you felt truly beleaguered, there was that delicious sense of shared danger. You were under siege from the hostile outside world, flung together like French Legionnaires in a desert fort. It was "us" and "them," nothing else existed, with "us" always being the good guys.

It was a sensation new to Dasha, this *esprit de corps,* this sense of loyalty to something other than family, larger than family. What made it doubly satisfying was the knowledge that she was succeeding on a different set of terms.

The first months she moved from department to department, getting the feel of the firm, making friends, working for a range of partners and senior associates. Almost invariably, each partner tried to hang on to her services. "You can't have her," old Jack Willis grumbled to another senior. "You had her all last month. Now it's my turn."

To make her mark in these exalted circles was legitimate cause for pride.

But best of all was Jordan. He had been as good as his word—better! —encouraging her every step of the way. Their marriage had moved to higher ground, she believed, now that they were equals. They could offer each other not just love but professional respect as well, enjoy a truer intimacy, an intellectual balance. They were no longer simply husband and wife, but two people with lively ideas and a wealth of mutual interests. Her joining the firm had enriched their lives beyond measure, probably the best thing to happen to Mr. and Mrs. Jordan Croy in years.

It was a fresh start (for only now did they dare admit it) for a marriage that had begun to grow a trifle stale.

Thus as Dasha moved up to become a second-year associate, she could survey her realm with satisfaction. Life was thrilling. Marriage was wonderful. The kids were terrific. Success seemed assured.

Had she been possessed of a superstitious nature, she might have knocked on wood.

CHAPTER TEN

☐ "Hey, Dasha." Andy McCabe handed her a file of papers. "You like wrapping your jaws around chewy problems. Try this one on for size. But first, read the memo."

It was a beaut—from Franklin Hunicutt, no less, reputedly one of the firm's biggest honchos. Dasha scanned it rapidly, then shook her head. "The irresistible force and the immovable object. An absolutely classic case."

"Yeah . . . Hunicutt doesn't think it can be resolved at all. Hence the memo. You're welcome to take a crack at it. This one's open season and anyone who can figure out a happy ending is going to be hot shit around this place from now on. That is, if you don't go certifiably whacko en route."

"Thanks a lot, buddy."

Yet she took the memo because the question it raised was a particularly intriguing one. Besides, who could resist the opportunity of playing Gangbusters now and then?

First Broadcasting Corporation was not only the oldest of Slater Blaney clients, but the most lucrative as well. The two firms were founded in the same year when a fresh-out-of-law-school attorney befriended an equally youthful entrepreneur. Emmerich Furst was the proprietor of a small upstate radio station when broadcasting was still in its infancy. Money was hard to come by for a young immigrant, yet already he nursed a dream that would eventually make him one of America's most powerful men.

In those days broadcasting was seen to be a novelty, and programs ran largely to sermonizing or readings from Shakespeare or lectures on the art of bird watching. What it needed was the showman's flair, the thrill of melodrama, the laughter of low comedy, the raw energy that would make it a true competitor to the thriving film industry.

What radio needed was Emmerich Furst.

He had a vision of gathering other stations into his fold, providing uniform programming for all, then garnering huge profits from the economies of scale. In short, creating a national network.

Accordingly, he changed the "u" in his name to an "i." Emmerich Furst had become Amory First, and First Broadcasting Corporation was born.

Eventually the network grew to achieve if not preeminence, then equal footing with NBC, CBS, and ABC. And in one area particularly, that of profits, it perennially outstripped its competitors. "No one ever went broke," First liked to quote Mencken, "underestimating the intelligence of the American people." The key to FBC's success was soundly based on its creator's unfailing genius in catering to the crassest, most vulgar of tastes.

He it was who developed the first quiz show, who pioneered the most mindless of comedies, the most mawkish of soap operas. He it was who broke with tradition, becoming the first broadcaster willing to accept commercials for laxatives and corn plasters.

"Everybody hates our product but the slobs," he would chortle. "The slobs—and the stockholders."

The advent of television merely confirmed the wisdom of his judgment.

Within the trade, NBC came to be known by its Rockefeller Plaza address. People called it "30 Rock." CBS, with its austere Eero Saarinen architecture, was called familiarly "Black Rock." ABC, in deference to its music programming, was known as "Hard Rock." And FBC inevitably was designated by its detractors (which included the entire cultural establishment) as "Schlock Rock." As for First himself, he had earned the epithet "King of Crap."

He laughed all the way to the bank.

But in the 1930s, success and untold millions were yet to come. The Depression squeezed him hard. There were weeks when it was all First could do to meet the rent. That the fledgling network did survive was in large part due to very hard lawyering and considerable financial aid from Ralph Slater. When First couldn't pay his legal fees, Slater let it ride, accepting stock in lieu of money. It was the best investment a lawyer ever made.

In the ensuing years, the network and firm grew up in tandem, ultimately achieving one of the closest, most enviable relationships in the history of corporate law.

By the time Dasha joined the firm, Ralph Slater was long dead. But Amory First remained as vigorous, as driving and driven as he had been half a century past. In some ways, even more so. At an age when his erstwhile competitors were moldering in their graves or reduced to a diet of milk-toast and Geritol or basking amid a lifetime's accumulated honors, First embarked on a new course entirely.

He was determined to amass, before death could catch him, the largest conglomerate in America. Like a desperate Don Juan, fearful of losing his virility, he wanted everything he saw. No company was safe from his embrace.

Some of his acquisitions were shotgun marriages. Some were eager brides. More than a few were palpable rapes. But they were all consummated in one fashion or another. First was not a man to shy from a fight.

Within a short period, FBC had swallowed up half a hundred lesser companies. And now, according to the memo in Dasha's hand, he had set his heart an acquiring a venerable Boston insurance company, Pendleton Life.

First popped the question. Pendleton blushed and accepted. And another happy marriage seemed under way. Indeed, the two were practically at the altar when a voice from the background came forth to declare that the impending nuptials could not take place.

There had been, in the company's original charter, an obscure clause that stipulated Pendleton could never be sold without the consent of all its stockholders. The proviso had made sense when the firm was the exclusive property of the Pendleton family, but it had gone public years ago and now the stockholders numbered in the thousands. There was no way of obtaining unanimous consent.

Yet Amory First refused to take no for an answer. It was up to his lawyers to find a way out.

Dasha puzzled over the problem throughout the afternoon with growing frustration. There had to be a twist, an out. Or did there? Every lawyer in the firm had failed in the attempt.

It was past six before she looked up from her desk. Working late was nothing new, but from the start she had set a cardinal rule: She went home each evening and had dinner with the kids. No matter that most nights, she'd whip back to the office and keep on slugging until midnight. At least there had been that private break in the day. At least she'd met her personal obligations.

But tonight, everything was running too late. She called home. "Why don't you all come downtown," she asked Jordan, "and we can eat near the office?" He didn't want to. She wheedled. He groaned. She won.

"Well, okay, Dasha," he dragged out reluctantly, "if the mountain won't come to Mohammed, I guess Mohammed'll have to go to the mountain."

"You're an angel. See you in an hour."

She took them to dinner at Fraunces Tavern, consoling herself that if it wasn't home cooking, at least it was a history lesson. "Washington ate here," she informed the children. "This is where he said farewell to his troops." Geoff was unimpressed, more concerned with studying his food with a suspicious air. He looked as though someone were trying to poison him.

"I'm not going to eat this gunky stuff," he announced.

"What do you mean, gunky? It's cauliflower."

"I don't like it. It looks funny."

"You haven't tasted it," Dasha said. "You'll like it."

"*Won't!*" he challenged.

"Then don't!" she snapped, and Geoff sulked throughout the rest of the meal.

"I think he'd rather eat at McDonald's," Robin explained. "When Daddy said we were eating out, I guess he just assumed it would be McDonald's."

"Well, this is better than McDonald's." She had a sneaky feeling she was being put on the defensive, though what crime she was guilty of, God only knew. Children were such born conservatives. "In any event, Geoff can speak for himself. What are you?"—she made a feeble joke—

"his mouthpiece? And what about you, Robin? Would you rather eat at McDonald's?"

"I don't care."

"Well, that's just dandy." Dasha called for the check. "So much for our big night out."

Dinner over, she darted back to the office. It had been a sour start to the evening, leaving her in a gloomy mood. As for the solution to the Pendleton dilemma, it remained elusive as ever. After four more sweated hours, Dasha called it a day. Here it was midnight and she had arrived at the grand total of zero. Out of habit she threw the papers in her briefcase, but in fact she was ready to write off the evening as a total waste. For all the work she'd accomplished, she might as well have spared her family the long haul downtown. And spared Geoff the cauliflower.

"If the mountain won't come to Mohammed . . . "—Jordan's remark came back to her. Funny expression, that. She paused. What was the rest of the cliché? Oh yes, then Mohammed must go to the mountain.

Like the goddam problem she'd been working on. Only with Amory First as Mohammed.

She laughed aloud and tried to push the analogy from her mind. Talk about ridiculous!

If the mountain won't . . . indeed!

If Pendleton won't . . .

She sat down again slowly, abstractedly, reaching out of habit for a yellow legal pad.

It was all wrong. Inside out and ass backwards. Yet she couldn't dismiss it out of hand. Just because something hasn't been done before . . .

With an audible whoop, she unlocked her briefcase and tore her way through the memo once more.

Long after, she would say that Jordan had given her the inspiration. All she had done was execute the deed.

"Jordan, honey!" She gave his sleeping body the gentlest of shakes. Shitty thing to do but she couldn't sit on it a moment longer. She'd just go through the ceiling from euphoria.

"Honey, wake up. I've got to talk to you or I'll die!"

"Whaaa . . . is there a fire? The kids?" Jordan jerked up with alarm. "What's the matter?"

"Nothing. I mean nothing's wrong. In fact everything's right. I figured it out—I figured out the Pendleton deal!"

"Hey, Dasha . . . " He turned on the light and rubbed his eyes. "It's three-thirty in the morning." He blinked again, wide awake now. "You really did? You really solved it?"

"No," she gloated. "*You* did actually." She spilled it out—the mountain, Mohammed, Pendleton—then sat back breathless, waiting for congratulations.

Jordan shook his head. "I don't understand."

"What's not to understand? Like I said, it's simple. Instead of Pendleton merging into FBC, we do it the other way around. FBC merges into Pendleton, then we gobble 'em up from inside!" She gave a few details, but only a few, for the whole thing was absurdly simple.

Jordan didn't like it any better second time around. In fact, his response was emphatic. "It's not simple, Dasha. It's simplistic. You know, for a bright lady you sure come up with some screwball ideas. If you'd thought it through, you'd see you're talking about a physical impossibility. Ants don't swallow elephants, least of all in business. Believe me, I've had ten years more experience than you and I know a lead balloon when I see one. I worry now and then that maybe the pressure is getting to you. You're putting in too many late hours at that place, starting to lose your perspective. Well, anyhow no harm's done. At least you haven't shown it to anybody."

But she already had. At least she had got it down in memo form and placed it in her Out basket. Barring earthquakes, it would arrive on the desk of Franklin R. Hunicutt first thing in the morning. And she didn't even know the man. Some introduction!

Jordan was so certain, so assured, that in the face of his attitude her exuberance began to fade. Not that he was an expert on corporate law, but he did have a large fund of common sense. Probably right about those late hours, too.

Still. "You're absolutely sure it won't fly, Orville?" She tried him one more time.

"Absolutely positively. Sorry, love."

"Yeah, well, me too. Ah what the hell"—she sighed and switched off the light. "Maybe tomorrow I'll go invent the wheel. Goodnight, darling."

"Goodnight, Dasha, or what's left of it."

She slept late the next morning, reluctant to face the day. It was after ten when she got into the office. There was a note on her desk, bright pink, marked URGENT. "Please see Frank Hunicutt," ran the message. *"Pronto."*

It was *the* office. With the Renoir. The Orientals. The fine English furniture. The view you could die for.

From behind a Victorian partners desk, a man in a nubbly tweed jacket sprang up and bounded across the room to greet her, engulfing her hand in his own.

He had the bluest eyes she'd ever seen. Blue as sapphires. As the sky at noon. That was her first impression. Her second was of sheer animal vitality. This has got to be the wrong person, she had a crazy idea. He didn't even look like a lawyer; more like somebody who just happened to be passing through the city on a brief stopover between Nantucket and Aspen. Sunburned, ruddy, with a thatch of crisp ginger hair, he had the radiant glow, the physical presence of an athlete in the peak of condition. He should be squinting in the sun from the prow of a catamaran or smashing out serves at Forest Hills. In any event, clearly a man who should never be indoors at all, let alone trapped in an office on a rainy February morning.

And if he didn't look like a lawyer, he looked even less like a senior partner. She'd always figured the executive suite as a miniature Home for the Aged, the "Truss Brigade" as Andy McCabe called them. Blagden Geere, Porter Collins, "Young" Harrison Cobb—a mere stripling of sixty. Theoretically, you could get there in less than ten years. Historically, it took the best part of a lifetime.

But the man before her didn't belong to that generation at all. He belonged more to hers. Forty, forty-five? Hard to tell. Hard to say whether the hair was streaked with sunshine or with gray.

"Hello. I'm Frank Hunicutt"—the blue eyes fixed on her face with a bright intensity. "And you, of course, are the author of that extraordinary memorandum. You like to take risks, don't you?"

"Well . . ." Should she explain it away as a bit of midnight madness or try to recapture the confidence she had originally felt? She took a deep breath. "I realize my solution sounds rather simplistic, but the way I envisioned it working . . ."

144

He stopped her with a roar of laughter. "Good God, woman, never defend yourself! Not until you're attacked. Otherwise you'll have talked yourself into a corner for no reason at all. As for your memo, there's nothing to explain. It's the sort of thing one either grasps intuitively or not at all. *Of course* it will work. Why shouldn't it? Although I expect you'll particularize the details. And as for simplicity . . . ah, that's the genius of the thing. I can't believe no one thought of it before. But come, come"—he led her to a small suede sofa the color of butterscotch. "We'll have some coffee and get acquainted. I want nothing less than the story of your life. But first, you'll have to satisfy my curiosity. What on earth gave you the idea?"

"You're going to find this ridiculous," she said, "but in a way that *is* the story of my life." And she gave him a precis of her dinner arrangements the preceding night, and her husband's chance remark about the mountain and Mohammed. "That's where the idea came from," Dasha concluded, expecting a laugh that never materialized. Instead, Hunicutt clasped his hands behind his head and shot her a look of sheer wonder.

"You know, you've just proved a pet theory of mine."

"Oh?"

"About the natural superiority of women."

It was Dasha's turn to laugh. "You don't mean that."

"I do indeed. I've been riding herd on this board for the last ten years to get out and recruit more women. Not just to comply with the letter of the law, but go out to the schools. Recruit. Bring 'em back alive. This firm has been a male bastion for too long. Women see things from a different stance, they have different insights. I'm not talking about intuition, mind you, but judgment. Perception. I truly believe that women are more pragmatic, better equipped at getting down to basics, and it's an utter absurdity for any firm that wants to be on top to rule out fifty percent of the available brain power. When Blagden told me he'd recruited you last year, I was delighted. I'm only sorry I didn't have a chance to meet you before. But"—he shrugged—"you know how it is, too many calls on one's time."

Such as skiing, sailing? Getting a sunburned nose in midwinter? Lucky man! The coffee arrived, fragrant and steaming, in gold-lipped Limoges cups. It was the best coffee she'd ever tasted.

"It's Kenyan," he said. "We discovered it on safari a couple of years ago and both went crazy about it. It's a blend that used to be exclusive to Treetops, but now my wife has it imported regularly. I'll have some sent around to your house tomorrow, then there'll be three places in the world where you can get it. And now"—he settled back—"tell me all about yourself."

She tried to escape with a quick run-down, the usual potted bio, but he wouldn't let her get off lightly. "No no no. I want the real you, not a résumé. What your hopes are, your long-range goals." But in fact he seemed more interested in her personality than her professional qualifications.

She had gone to Smith, had she? His wife had gone there, too. Class of '59. Just a little before Dasha's time. Had she caught the Picasso show yet? Oh she must, she must. An opportunity not to be missed. And yes, in answer to her question, that was indeed an early Renoir, painted the year he met Monet. What did she think of the new Broadway season? Of Bjorn Borg? So her father was with the BSO! He understood it was the best orchestra in the country, although he himself could hardly tell one piece of music from another. All he knew was he fell asleep at Wagner and tapped his feet at Verdi. What grades were her kids in? Did they like school? Had she considered sending them to prep school?

He had a marvelous voice, cello-rich and Harvard-accented, deep in the center, warm at the edges. Dasha wavered between delight and confusion, scarcely knowing what to make of the barrage.

Only you, his eyes spoke to her. *Only you* have my undivided attention. Tell me what you think about everything, for *only you* exist at this moment.

It was an intoxicating experience. No one had ever treated her like this before, as if she were a head of state or—at the least—a Hollywood star, whose every little word was of moment.

"And now that we've got the vital stuff out of the way—art, life, and the universe—let's get down to trivia. How is the firm treating you? Are we keeping you happy?" His questions became more specific. He wanted to know which areas of work she enjoyed most, where she felt most at home. What were her goals, he asked. "Outside of making partner, of course."

"Oh no no no," he interrupted her recitation. "You don't want to get bogged down in the Trust Department, writing wills and holding old ladies' hands. All that boring crap. We want you in on the action. What do you know about television?"

"How to turn on the set." Dasha set down her coffee cup. "But I'd like to learn more."

"Good." He beamed. "Because from now on you're going to be up to your ears in FBC." She would be reporting to him directly, and the first order of the day was to familiarize herself with the structure of the network. "Ideally," he said, "you'll get to know more about their business than they do. And that means covering the whole legal waterfront, so to speak. But I think you'll find it fun. The people, too. They're bright and hustling. The thing to remember is, you're essentially dealing with modern-day pirates. It's not a business for sensitive souls. You know"— he smiled fondly at the thought—"you could inscribe the entire ethical code of the TV industry on the left buttock of a fly and still have room left over for the phone book. Whenever those boys come here to lunch, I count the silver, metaphorically speaking. Do I scare you?"

"Nope," Dasha said. "You just make it sound exciting."

That was it for now, he said as he showed her out. She should go back to her office and begin drafting the opinion on the Pendleton merger. "Where is your office, by the way?" She told him.

"The black hole of Calcutta." He shook his head disapprovingly. "I'm sure we can do something better for Dasha Croy. You're going to be around here for a long long time, so we'll just have to treat you right."

She floated off in a state of unremitting rapture.

To be proven right in spite of Jordan's dour warnings. That was beautiful.

To be praised, promoted, *rewarded* for being right! That was heaven on earth.

Ah, there was Andy McCabe—poor fellow—slaving over a hot desk with a grim expression as if today weren't the greatest day since the dawn of time.

"Grab your coat!"—she swept his papers aside with a peremptory gesture—"because I'm about to buy you the biggest, fattest, non-expense-account lunch in town."

"What have I done to deserve this?" Andy asked.

"That memo last night, remember? The immovable object? I moved it!" She told him about the meeting with Hunicutt. "He practically gave me the medal of honor. Jesus, I don't know how to thank you."

"Yeah, well, some of us are born great and some of us have it thrust upon us. And some of us just keep on truckin'. Buy me a pair of dry martinis and I'll try to forgive you."

"I'm sorry, Andy." She came down to earth long enough to see he really looked dejected. "I hope you didn't think I was trying to steal your thunder? You *did* ask me to give the Pendleton thing a whirl."

"No, it's not that. I'm happy for you, Dasha, I truly am. It's just that . . . ah, fuck Pendleton, fuck the firm. Fuck women. Fuck everything!" He crumpled a paper full of angry doodles and threw it in the wastebasket. "I'm being blackmailed."

"Really blackmailed?" Dasha was incredulous.

"Emotionally blackmailed, and believe me, Dasha, that's a helluva lot worse."

Over lunch he poured out his woes.

Did Dasha remember Melanie, the girl he'd been engaged to? She'd gone and married somebody else. "Would you believe an accountant?" Okay, that was last year and he'd had time to lick his wounds. Nobody ever died of a broken heart, right?

Then he met somebody else and fell crazy in love. Her name was Josie, she taught grade school, and they'd been living together since Christmas. The thing was, he explained to Dasha, being a lawyer's daughter, Josie could be expected to understand the pressures he was subjected to. She'd understand about the broken dinner dates, the all-night sessions, the road, the heartburn, the occasional weekend spent behind the desk. Hell, her father was one of the country's top litigators, so it wasn't as if she were a civilian!

"The trouble is she understands too well. Anyhow, Josie says she doesn't see much point in cohabiting with a traveling suitcase. If I want to live with her—which I do, if I want to marry her—which I do, if I want to have children—which I do, it's gotta be on a completely different basis. Last night she handed me an ultimatum. She's moving to Vermont in a couple of months and she won't be coming back. She wants me to go with her."

"And leave the firm?"

"That's the size of it. Honestly, Dasha, can you see me as a country lawyer?"

"Why not, Andy, if that's what'll make you happy? I used to think being a country lawyer, or a country lawyer's wife for that matter, would be just about the pleasantest life on earth. And a marvelous way to bring up kids. Of course it's not how *I* see you that matters, Andy. It's what *you* believe that's important. You just have to follow your heart."

"My heart's giving me mixed signals, Dasha."

She nodded. That was something she understood.

"The thing is," he continued, "I want it all. Is that so unreasonable? Yeah, probably. But suppose I turn Josie down, keep sweating it out here, and after all that I don't make partner. Christ! It'll all have been for nothing. Oh well . . . enough of my problems. How about you? Will you deign to know me when you're rich and famous? And what did you think of Frank Hunicutt? The proverbial man who has everything. He's something else, isn't he?"

"Merely colossal." Dasha was delighted the conversation had gotten round to that extraordinary man. "What do you know about him? And how does somebody that young ever get to be senior partner?"

"Well, first of all you gotta be smart."

"That much I can figure out for myself."

"Second of all, you gotta marry smart. His wife, you should know, is Ralph Slater's only child, with more millions than a dog has fleas. Which puts Frank in the enviable position of having the whole of FBC right in his pocket. Plus he brings in a lot of new business . . . the golf course or whatever. Wherever people are rich together. I don't know what kind of lawyer he is, pretty good, I imagine, but apparently he's world class in the charm department. He's managed to keep Amory First securely in the fold since Slater died and that—by all reports—is no mean trick. My guess would be that Hunicutt probably accounts for more hard profit than any other man in the firm."

Which would make him, Dasha thought, *the most powerful of all the seniors.*

"He really seemed to like me," she mused.

"Let me guess. Hand on your knee and 'What's a nice girl like you . . . ' "

"Oh come on, Andy. You're so jaundiced today. I mean he seemed to like me as a lawyer and a person."

"In which case you're in luck. I'll tell you one thing, if I had Frank

149

Hunicutt for a rabbi, my problems would be solved. At least I'd know that I was going someplace in this firm."

The man who had everything, Andy had said. And every source confirmed that Frank Hunicutt was indeed the favorite of the gods.

Martindale-Hubbell, the lawyers' bible, gave him their highest rating. The Harvard year book identified him as Phi Beta, *summa cum,* Porcellian, *Lampoon,* topping off with a substantial list of athletic honors. *Who's Who* made a note of his clubs (Metropolitan, Century), his homes (Sutton Place, Southampton, and Hobe Sound), his hobbies (lawn tennis and sailing), and his children (Chadwick, Amory, Laura).

But what the reference books failed to capture—at least to Dasha's satisfaction—was the man's essential quality, the boundless enthusiasm, the radiant warmth. He had done wonderful things to her ego, she realized. She had left his office feeling as if she were quite the most remarkable person in the world, awash in a wave of confidence, and even though she knew this technically not to be true, nonetheless some of the glow followed her home that evening.

"Now hear this." She triumphantly announced her news over dinner, then couldn't resist following it up. "Well, Jordan, I was right after all. An ant can swallow an elephant, if I've remembered your analogy correctly."

"Okay, so it worked; a lucky guess. Congratulations. You wouldn't by any chance happen to know if my topcoat's still at the cleaners? I brought it in last Wednesday. Geoff, we do not use our fingers to eat French fries. Not if you want to watch 'Mork and Mindy.'"

She stared at him in disbelief. Didn't he hear himself? Didn't he see how he was cutting the ground out from under her? There was no point in saying anything, certainly not until after the children were in bed, but by then her resentment had reached the breaking point.

"My theory was not a guess, Jordan, and I find it insulting for you to imply that it was. You know"—she made an effort to control the tremor in her voice—"you have a way of belittling me, of knocking me down professionally that is beginning to wear a bit thin."

"*Me!*" He was genuinely astonished. "How can you say such a thing? I'm your biggest booster."

"Are you? All I know is, at the office everybody thinks I'm terrific.

My opinion is solicited left and right. No, I'm not talking solely about what happened today, but consistently. When I'm there, I feel good about myself. Confident. Assured. But the moment I get home, I begin to question my judgment. No . . . that's not entirely accurate. *You* question my judgment. You act as if everything that happens to me is just dumb luck, 'catching the eye of Blagden Geere,' charming my way into Slater Blaney. As if I hadn't worked my butt off to get there. That bothered me at the time but I let it slip. And now you're doing it all over again. You seem to operate on the assumption that simply because you've been practicing law longer than I have, you know more than I do. Well, you may be the expert in handling two-bit insurance claims or doing house closings, but when it comes to corporate law, Jordan, the sort of thing I spend my work day doing, I regret to say you don't know beans. And goddammit, I will *not* be patronized."

She had said more than she meant to say, and was, perhaps, even more startled than Jordan at the depth of anger revealed.

"I don't think I deserved that, Dasha," he said quietly. "I don't know what constitutes being patronized. I gather by that you mean the slightest word of criticism. I *do* know that when you come home at night—that is, those nights when you come home before three—the only talk in this house is about you. Your triumphs, your deals, your clients. You are so goddam wrapped up in yourself. Tonight, for example—okay, you had a big day at the office. But did you even think to ask me what kind of day *I* had? Whether I won that eviction case for Mrs. Gonzalez? I did, by the way, and that was pretty important—if not to you, then certainly to the Gonzalez family, who would have otherwise wound up in the street. I'm not making myself out to be a saint or a public service hero. We're both doing jobs. All I'm saying is, don't be a prima donna, Dasha. That's not like you."

He paused to let his words sink in, then murmured softly, "You know, this is ridiculous. We're both talking as if we were adversaries. As if nothing in life mattered but careers. You and I never used to argue, Dasha, not like this. And I hate it, I despise it . . . this picking at each other. I'm sorry you feel that I've been patronizing or hypercritical. That certainly was not my intention, but you feel what you feel and that's what counts. Perhaps in the future you shouldn't ask my professional opinion, just go your own way. Because it seems to me if work is going to be a continuing source of friction between us, we both ought to make an effort not to talk shop so much. We've got enough other things in life to think about." He raised his hands in the classic gesture of surrender. "Truce?"

"Truce. You're a bigger man than I am, Jordan Croy." She gave him a conciliatory kiss, relieved that he had defused the situation, and the subject was dropped for the evening. But it troubled her for weeks after, with the dull throbbing of a low-level toothache, how very close they had come to the precipice. From that night on, their lives subtly began to assume separate patterns.

The Pendleton merger went through without a hitch. When the final draft was sent to FBC, Frank Hunicutt broke with the convention that associates do the work and seniors get the credit. He went out of his way to see that Dasha's name led the list of signatory lawyers. It was a singular honor, a public affirmation that her star was in the ascendant.

She decided not to mention it to Jordan, although she certainly would tell him if he asked. But he never did, which was just as well. It would rankle him to know how quickly she was moving up in the firm. She herself found it almost embarrassing, and had no desire to rub it in. In any event, he appeared incurious.

Besides, it wasn't as if they didn't have a wealth of other things to share. The kids. Family life.

Robin was doing them proud with her piano, practicing like mad to Dasha's if not the neighbors' gratification.

In fact, Robin was doing them proud in all departments from her glowing report card to the number of merit badges on her Girl Scout uniform to a feature role in the school Christmas play.

In a way, Dasha's going off to work had had a briskly therapeutic effect upon her daughter. Independence agreed with her. A self-starter by nature, Robin lived in a state of permanent bubble.

"An exceptional child." The school principal was effusive. "A truly gifted young lady and very highly motivated." Dasha blushed red as though the compliment were meant for herself.

"And Geoff?"

"Ah yes," he added as an afterthought. "Your boy is doing quite nicely too, as I recall."

The disparity in her children's achievements was not lost upon Dasha. And though she made a point of trying to bolster her son's self-image, she was certain it was not lost upon him either. He had grown hypersensitive of late.

The situation troubled her. She felt for both her children. Indeed, she had only to reach back in memory to find the parallel: the brilliant older child, the quiet younger one obscured by a dazzling sibling.

Perhaps, Dasha thought, if they didn't live in such cramped quarters, it would be easier for Geoff to emerge from his sister's shadow. This cheek-by-jowl existence, the lack of privacy, the piano going all the time: They were irritants that would exact their toll on any household. Surely the time had come to find another place to live.

The more she thought of it, the more convinced she was that given breathing space, the pressure would be off all of them. Jordan, too. In pleasanter surroundings, he'd be more likely to take her career in his stride. At least she could get out of his hair when he got grumpy.

In the meanwhile, she avoided talking shop at all costs, either with him or the children. It was the sensible thing to do.

Yet as the mood at home darkened, the office grew more attractive. And the fact remained that Hunicutt's compliments had her in rhapsodies. In a world full of carpers and quibblers, it was wonderful to know that there was one person who thought she could do no wrong.

CHAPTER ELEVEN

☐ There were few things on earth capable of shaking Alex Oborin's equanimity. World War III, conceivably. A flying saucer invasion of Georgetown. And . . .

"David!" he howled to his sister over the telephone. "I don't know what's got into the boy, Dasha. Here he is at the crossroads of his life. He's got to choose between Harvard and Princeton, some tough choice, let me tell you. And you know what that crazy kid wants to do?"

"Chase girls?"

"Even worse. Chase flyballs."

"You're not making sense, Alex."

Alex sighed. "What I mean is, he wants to be a baseball player. A professional baseball player. Can you imagine?"

And he was off for another ten minutes expanding on the infantility, the idiocy, the sheer impossibility of the notion that any son of his— "with his advantages, his privileges, with *me* to set an example"—should fritter away his manhood trying to wallop a spherical bit of leather with an elongated wooden stick. "If it were chess at least, but *baseball!*" Clearly a purely physical enterprise was no fit occupation for the eldest son of Washington's most respected pundit.

"Well, Alex," Dasha said, "maybe you're taking it too seriously. It might do the boy good to get away from the academic grind for a year or two. Give him a chance to find himself. It's not as if he were embarking on a life of crime, for heaven's sakes."

"Don't give me that crap, Dasha. If he were your kid, you'd be

154

climbing the walls. What do we do it all for, if not for our children? Anyhow, with your permission I'd like to ship him off to New York this weekend. Try to talk some sense into him. You're his favorite aunt. Maybe he'll listen."

David duly arrived on the Friday afternoon shuttle and despite Dasha's distaste for playing family monitor, she secretly had to agree with Alex. It *did* seem inconceivable that this sweet gangly uncompetitive seventeen-year-old could ever break into—let alone survive—the notoriously tough pro-sport circuit.

For the son of a celebrity he was very much a "gosh gee-whiz" boy; naive, painfully ill at ease in New York, allowing himself to be shepherded to and fro like a lamb. Dasha took him to the Met for culture, to Bloomingdale's for sweaters, and ultimately to Peppermint Park for comforts of a yet higher order.

It wasn't until David had plunged into a butterscotch caramel sundae dripping with chocolate that she tackled her mission. Her nephew listened like the dear sweet boy he was, finished his sundae, and swallowed a large glass of ice water by way of Dutch courage. But if David had seemed uncertain about the streets of New York, he was emphatic about the geography of his emotions.

"I won't go, Aunt Dasha, so please don't try to work on me. You can't say anything Dad hasn't said a million times." His eyes suddenly welled. "You don't know what it's like having him for a father . . . always having to prove I'm the best of the best of the best. What I think, what I want—that means zilch to him. I don't need him to tell me I'm probably never going to be a great ball player. I think I said that just to frost him. I'll probably never be a great *anything."* He swiped his eyes with the back of his sleeve. "But one thing I promise you I'll never be, and that's a junior edition of him! He's so . . . so . . . " David fumbled for the words, "he's so damn smart, so successful, there's no way I'm ever going to catch up."

No, Dasha thought sadly, Alex is so damn stupid. But aloud she said: "Okay, I understand why you don't want to go to an Ivy League school. You feel people will be making comparisons. What about some other college, David, maybe even a different part of the country?"

"Dad wouldn't allow it. If Harvard was good enough for him, it should be good enough for me, right?"

"If I convinced him?"

"If you can get my father to change his mind about anything, then you're the greatest lawyer in the world."

It took a lot of arguing, blandishments, and a couple of hundred dollars' worth of phone calls to Washington, but the following autumn with everyone's blessing David left for California to join the freshman class at U.C.L.A.

Thus the incident had been resolved satisfactorily, but it left Dasha with a bad taste. "Just wait till your children are teenagers," Alex had said at one point, and his warning had led her to reexamine her own situation.

It was one thing to have basic confidence in the children, quite another to think that they would, uniquely, miraculously, manage to be impervious to the terrors of childhood, to withstand the temptations and blandishments of New York.

They were good kids, certainly, in the sense that they didn't lie or steal. They were conscientious about their school work and could be relied upon not to disgrace her or Jordan in public.

Yet increasingly she felt she was losing control, that with each passing year they were moving beyond her grasp.

At ten, Robin was personable rather than pretty, with tangly black hair, generous features, and a pudginess that still hinted of baby fat. Yet she knew, as many people thrice her age did not, precisely what she intended to do with her life. She was going to be a pianist, no buts about it, and that knowledge had given her the confidence to stare down a king.

From the day Dasha first picked out a battered though thoroughly usable upright piano from a dusty showroom on Twenty-third Street, Robin had seized upon music with the force of revelation. She had her grandfather's passion, his commitment, and—it quickly became apparent —his talent as well. She tore through the beginner books as if they were so much popcorn, and within a remarkably short time was tackling meatier works—Bach, Haydn, Mozart—to the astonishment of the local teacher. "The problem," Jordan laughed, "isn't getting Robin to practice. It's getting her to stop."

When Max descended on New York for Christmas, he was thrilled with his grandchild's progress, and before returning home he had wrung from Dasha the promise that Robin should be put in the hands of a master pedagogue.

"Grusinsky. Nikita Grusinsky. I'll call him tomorrow and see if he'll take her on."

"Oh, Dad, really! Robin's only ten."

"Yes yes, I admit that's a bit late, but let's hope she can make up for lost time. And then of course you'll have to get her a Steinway."

"A Steinway." Dasha laughed. "We could hardly fit another jam jar in this house, let alone a grand piano. Besides, I'm not sure I want to turn a child that age into a workaholic."

"When I was her age, Dashenka, I was practicing six hours a day and I can't say it did me any harm. And as for the piano, it's time you moved to a proper apartment anyhow. You people don't have room to breathe. Isn't that so, Jordan?"

And Jordan, being the least disputatious of men, had smiled politely.

"Don't mind my father," Dasha said after the paternal siege was over. "You know how he likes to run things. Still, it really is time we moved out of here. We've outgrown Crestview, we truly have, honey. And the kids have, too. I think they'd have better opportunities in . . . in more of a"—she hesitated—"in a less provincial neighborhood."

"Mmmm." Jordan chewed on his glasses. "I'll have to think about it."

In the end, Dasha took her father's advice, and sent Robin to the great Grusinsky. The old Russian charged a fortune, nearly as much per hour as a Wall Street lawyer, but what was money for if not for the children? Yet it was a decision Dasha had been reluctant to make. There was a strangely self-sufficient quality to Robin's life, as if she had deliberately chosen to foreshorten her childhood, to forgo the usual sports and casual fun. Sometimes, when Robin was practicing, Dasha would stand in the hallway listening, watching that small determined figure, hunched intently over a Schirmer edition in its bright yellow cover, rapt in a private world that admitted of no intruders. And in those moments, Dasha felt a sense of awe. It had taken Dasha so many years, so many turnings, before she stumbled on her own vocation, and yet here was this ten-year-old, with no confusion, no air of doubt about her. Robin not only knew where she was going; she seemed to know how to get there.

Geoff was another matter entirely.

He had retained that "forlorn puppy" quality of early childhood, a fact that Dasha alternately found endearing and infuriating. But what had been soulful in a toddler now translated into a kind of sullenness, an ominous preview of adolescence. Subtly, almost subconsciously, he seemed intent on turning even the mildest of Dasha's directives into a silent contest of wills. All she need say was "Why don't you wear your green sweater today?" for him to wear the blue. Which was a matter of no particular moment, except that he contrived to look injured into the bargain. She tried reverse psychology, but that didn't work any better. If she said, "Wear the blue" when she meant, "Wear the green," he would still wear the blue, with a look of sweet compliance. He had a great core of stubbornness, and when pushed into a corner, chose the path of passive resistance.

Dasha was certain she knew the reason why.

"He resents my going out to work," she told Jordan. "It's as simple as that. For some reason, Geoff still expects me to be there with milk and cookies when he gets home from school."

"Do you want me to talk to him?"

"Let me try first."

She sat down with him patiently on half a dozen different occasions, explaining that "Sandy's mommy works, and Linda's mom. And poor Scottie! His mother works nights."

"You work nights too."

"Touché," she said mentally. Aloud she countered, "Only when I have to, darling. I'm not happy about it."

"That's all right," Geoff answered coolly. "I don't mind."

There was nothing more she could say. No open rebellion, no actual defiance. On the surface, he went through the motions of acquiescence.

It wasn't as though he were a troubled child, she consoled herself. He did well at school, had sufficient friends, and for every step he pulled away from Dasha, he pulled that much closer to Jordan. That's okay, she thought, it's good for a boy to look up to his father. But his aloofness rankled, coming back to haunt her at odd moments in the office.

"What's the matter, Dasha? You look down in the dumps."

"Do I, Andy? Sorry."

They were in the library checking citations, but she couldn't concentrate on the matter at hand.

"Come on. You can tell old Uncle Andy."

By contrast, he was exceptionally buoyant this morning. So buoyant she didn't have the heart to dampen his mood.

"Kids!" She sighed. "Just having a little trouble with the kids. Geoff mostly, but . . . it'll pass, I'm sure."

"Don't knock 'em," he returned. "Kids are wonderful. Life is wonderful. Ah screw it!"—he slammed a book shut gleefully. "Screw it, I repeat. Down with *stare decisis* and *nolo contendere*. And up with *Amor vincit omnia*."

"What on earth . . . " She stared at him.

"Where's your Latin, Dasha? That means, 'Love conquers all.' Bet that's one phrase they didn't teach you back in law school."

She leaned across the cubicle and planted an exuberant kiss on his cheek. "You're getting married! How wonderful. I can't tell you how delighted I am."

"Yeah, me too. Actually, talk about kids, we managed to put the cart before the horse. Josie's two months pregnant and well . . . we decided to take the plunge. What do you think? Can you picture me as a paterfamilias, changing diapers and all that jazz?"

"I sure can, and listen . . . don't buy a thing! I've got a ton of baby clothes—pink, blue, take your pick—all stashed away in my father's attic in Boston. A crib, bassinette, the usual, plus a very good English carriage. It was a gift from my brother. Those things cost a fortune, you know."

"Well, I'll have to check with Josie. She may want to buy her own." He looked at her with curiosity. "But thanks for the offer. How come you kept that stuff all these years?"

"Oh, I don't know. My dad has the space and"—to her own surprise, her eyes brimmed over—"and I guess I thought we'd have another baby someday. It just kept hanging round in the back of my mind. But . . . it seems it was not to be. No matter." She shrugged and changed the subject. "Now tell me all about the wedding. Who, what, when, where? And above all, are we invited?"

"You bet your ass. Two weeks from Sunday at the UN Chapel, with a reception after at the Mandarin Palace. So don't tell me you guys can't make it."

"Wouldn't miss it for the world. So Josie finally came around to your point of view! Well, of course the baby makes an enormous difference."

"Nope," Andy said. "I'm the one who came around. Dasha, my sweet, you're looking at the next leader of the bar in Rutland, Vermont, which is how come we picked the Mandarin for a fond farewell. Probably my last chance to get decent Chinese food."

"Maybe you can get the Mandarin to deliver." Dasha smiled almost enviously. "Anyhow, congratulations. I think it's absolutely marvelous."

"Yeah." Andy sighed happily. "Me too."

The reception was a great big loud wonderful goodbye.

At one point in the afternoon, Dasha noticed Andy's father sitting alone, looking lost in such a youthful crowd. She went over and chatted with him for a bit. He seemed grateful for her company.

"We're all going to miss Andy," she said.

"Not as much as I will," came the answer. Ben McCabe was a widower, Dasha knew, and Andy his only child. His son's impending departure had cast a pall. "However"—he made an effort to stop the spread of gloom—"I'll manage to keep busy, I suppose. I have my shop, my record collection . . ."

"Oh?" She remembered Andy once having mentioned it. "You're an opera buff, aren't you?"

"An opera maniac is more like it."

With that the tumblers started clicking, and before she left, Dasha had finagled Ben into having dinner with them the following Sunday.

"Dasha the matchmaker," Jordan laughed as they were driving home. "Do you really think he and Charlotte will hit it off?"

"Why not? He struck me as awfully pleasant. He's lonely, she's lonely. Anyhow, there's no harm in trying. Just don't tell your mother that the fix is on. You know how she clams up when she's nervous. What did you think of my friends, Jordan?" There had been a number of people from her office at the wedding, and she was curious what Jordan had made of them.

"They seem like lively enough people," he remarked, "although you guys sure do talk shop a lot. It was a social occasion, after all."

He turned off the West Side Highway with an expression of distate. "Damn potholes! They're absolutely ruining the undercarriage. That road should be condemned. In fact, the whole city is falling apart. You know, Andy has the right idea, getting out of New York before it collapses completely."

"Why, would you rather live in Vermont?" She looked at him curiously. "Come on, you're a born New Yorker!"

"I may be a New Yorker but that doesn't mean I have to be a masochist." He drove for a while in silence. "You know Geoff was mugged at school on Friday?"

"He wasn't exactly mugged, as I understand it. I gather there's some kind of protection game going on there, where the older kids hustle the younger ones for their lunch money."

"The point is, the boy's afraid to go to school in the morning."

"Then let's send him to private school. Let's send both of them to private school. I've said that repeatedly, Jordan."

"That's a stopgap, not an answer. I think the time has come for us to get out of the city. We're in pretty good financial shape these days, so what say we start looking for a home in the suburbs? Westchester would be convenient. Up around Mount Vernon, or maybe a little bit north of there."

They were driving through Harlem now—angry streets, crumbling buildings, gutters overflowing with garbage. Jordan's rhapsodies were the more pointed by contrast.

"The fresh air . . . the good schools . . . grass, trees . . . " he crooned.

"The commuting!" Dasha broke in. "My Lord, Jordan, that would be about seventy minutes each way for me. I'd *never* get home in the evenings."

"Then maybe you wouldn't put in so many hours. Besides, you can work on the train, lots of people do."

"They don't have a law library on the train."

"Or you can work less hard. That's a thought, too. Plus we'd have the time together on the train. I don't know why you're so resistant to the idea of the suburbs. When we first came to New York, all you talked about was escaping."

Jordan's notion that they move to suburbia couldn't have come at a more inopportune time. Big assignments were coming at her left and right. The last thing she needed was to sit on a train for two boring hours every day. It seemed to Dasha completely insensitive of him to propose such a thing. Could it be that he still didn't take her career seriously?

Or was it that he took it *too* seriously? So seriously that he was threatened by it and hoped to divorce her from the office. Because one thing was certain: once she was "buried" out in the suburbs, there'd be no more popping back to the office after dinner. No more late-night bull sessions. No more drinks with the guys. Above all, no more of those good-natured rehashes and licking of wounds which often constituted the best part of the day.

It was raining when they pulled into Crestview, and the housing project loomed shabby and sodden in the afternoon gloom, with its leaching bricks and rusting ironwork. The playground where she had spent so many hours when the children were young was a sea of mud and empty candy wrappers.

"I hate this place!" Dasha shook her head vehemently. "I hate it and I've hated it for years. It's like living in a filing cabinet. I hate the smell of cooking in the hallways. I hate listening to our neighbors' bedroom arguments. We have no space . . . no privacy. You're right, Jordan. We can't go on living here another six months, but there has to be a better alternative than the suburbs. Let me see what I can figure out."

A few days later, she phoned him from the office in a state of high excitement.

"Drop everything and meet me at noon on the corner of Sixty-fifth and Park."

"What's up?"

"You'll see."

What they saw was a spacious apartment, built in the days when families were large and help was cheap, when kitchens were kitchens, living rooms had parqueted floors, and builders didn't skimp on details. The Croys tramped through the rooms in an awed silence, then headed for the street.

"Thank you." Dasha returned the keys to the doorman with a smile. She slipped her arm through Jordan's.

"Isn't it gorgeous, darling? Absolutely sumptuous." She answered her own question. "How many bathrooms did you make that out to be? Three and a half, I guess, if you count the little shower off the maid's room. We could always use that one for a laundry."

"Have you lost your mind, Dasha? You shouldn't even be *looking* at places like that." Jordan pursed his lips disapprovingly. "Christ, you've got to be talking half a million dollars!"

"A quarter of a million. Jordan, it's a steal. Besides which, what do you think a house in a good suburb costs these days?"

"A helluva lot less than Park Avenue."

"The thing is, we'd be getting an insider's price. Ellie Woods in our Trust Department put me onto it. The apartment belonged to one of her clients. He died last week and now the widow wants to liquidate everything pronto and move to Palm Beach. Jordie, it's a fire sale, practically. And my God, what an investment!"

"Even granted it's a bargain, Dasha, and I've done enough real estate to know that, still it's way out of our league. The mortgage you're talking about—if we could get one—and the down payment. We don't have that kind of dough."

"Can we at least discuss it over lunch?"

First—she explained when Jordan had settled into his scotch and water —Commercial Trust of New York was a Slater Blaney client. She'd already spoken to a friend over there, a top loan officer. He'd give them a mortgage well below the going rate.

Second, Frank had told her she'd be getting a whopping bonus for the Pendleton deal. Plus her annual raise was due next month. Third . . .

"Third"—Jordan broke in—"is the same as second and first. Why don't you just come out and say it, Dasha? You earn the bigger bucks so you get the bigger say."

She was too shocked to do anything but give an outraged howl.

"I'm sorry." He reached across the table and took her hand. "I didn't mean that to sound the way it did. Come on, honey, let's not argue about *money*, of all things. But don't you see the way you sprung this one on me? For ten years we think and plan for a place in the suburbs and now, all of a sudden, you're talking about a Park Avenue penthouse. That's pretty rich for my blood."

"It's not a penthouse," she said, "just a nice apartment, and you're making me feel like I've committed a crime."

"It's not a crime, darling. It's just that I wish you'd be—well, a little more realistic."

"You're the one who's not being realistic, Jordan. You seem to think we should go on living the way we always have, on the same petty scale, with the same measly economies. That was tolerable ten years ago, but we're not kids out of school any more. It's a whole new ball game, and if you truly want to be realistic, this apartment is well within our means. We've got two good careers going here. So what is all this nonsense about *my* money and *your* money, as if they were two separate currencies? When people love each other, what difference does it make whose money gets spent? We're partners in a marriage, not a pair of nit-picking accountants. All that really matters is, it's *our* money—and thank God for it, I say. At least it'll get us all out of Crestview. The kids will love it and Robin will have her own room just for music. You could have a proper study. You yourself said it was good value for the money. So what's stopping us?"

Quite without meaning to, she had pushed him into a moral corner. "Well," he conceded, "I suppose technically you're right. We could just about swing it, if we're careful. And I can see it means a lot to you. But of course"—he searched until he found the face-saving device—"of course I would have to examine the contracts very very carefully before we commit ourselves. Real estate isn't exactly your line of country."

"You're the expert"—she nearly wept with relief—"and I know you'll make the right decision, although I'm afraid it'll have to be settled this week. Ellie says she can't keep it off the market much longer."

"I'll think about it and let you know by Friday. Will that be all right?" But his look let her know already the battle was over. She leaned across the table with a radiant smile. "Is it all right to kiss your husband in public or is that considered bad form?"

"The beige? What do you think, Dasha? The beige with that little fleur-de-lys scarf, or do you think that's too dressy? Maybe I should just wear a skirt and blouse."

"The beige is lovely, Charlie, very becoming. There's nothing to be nervous about."

Her mother-in-law had spent half the morning scrutinizing her wardrobe in an agony of indecision.

"But there's nothing to worry about," Dasha said for the tenth time. "All I'm asking is that you meet Ben McCabe. Just meet him, that's all, and if you don't like each other no harm done."

"That's all well and good for you to say, dear, but let me tell you it's very strange being 'fixed up' by my daughter-in-law."

"Now, now," Dasha soothed. "It's just a Sunday dinner. That's all. And if you don't care for Ben, so it's a couple of hours out of your life, that's all. How long can it take to get through a meal?"

It could take forever, Dasha discovered, in psychological if not absolute time. She and Jordan introduced one topic after another as conversational bait, but no topic lasted more than three rounds.

"I understand you're an opera nut, Ben. So's Charlotte—especially when it comes to Italian opera."

"Oh really, Mrs. Croy?" Ben picked up the gauntlet. "Have you seen the new *Bohème* at the Met?"

"Yes."

"Did you see it with Pavarotti singing?"

"No."

"With Domingo?"

"No."

"Charlotte saw it with Carreras," Jordan volunteered.

"Oh, did you like him?"

"No." And that was that.

The poor woman was utterly tongue-tied. Even crime-in-the-streets, that conversational standby of all New York dinner parties, failed to get a rise out of her. The evening inched along in a slow-motion agony.

As for Ben, a sweet and gentle man, he had the good grace not to consult his watch more than half a dozen times, and even then always furtively. Dasha could scarcely wait to get the dessert served and the dinner over. She handed round the coconut cake.

"My wife's specialty," Jordan said. "She makes it with freshly ground coconut. Have some, Ben. It's delicious."

Ben duly smiled, swallowed a mouthful politely, then choked.

"My God!" Dasha sprang to her feet. "There must have been a piece of shell in there. Quick, Jordan, get some water. A bit of bread, anything! My God . . . the man's turning blue!"

Suddenly, there was Charlotte, streaking across the room like a bolt of lightning. In one furious motion, she hurled herself against the back of his chair, grabbed Ben around the ribcage with both arms, and jerked him upward with such force that the two of them toppled to the floor amid a landslide of silver and coconut cake.

"Are you all right?" she was shouting. "Mr. McCabe, are you all right!"

He lay there white and motionless, gasping for breath.

"Please . . . " Charlotte straddled him and began beating his chest with her fists. "Please say something."

Ben McCabe took a deep deep breath, looked up at the dark-eyed woman lying astride him, her face filled with anguish, her body pressed against his in a conjunction as intimate as the act of love.

"We can't go on meeting like this," he said.

And Charlotte Croy burst into a whoop of hysterical laughter.

"Listen to 'em," Dasha whispered to Jordan later. "They're cackling like teenagers. I must say, though, that's one hell of a way to break the ice. Where did your mother learn that trick, do you know?"

"She said she saw a first-aid poster up in a restaurant. I guess she reads that kind of stuff."

"Well, thank God she did." Sasha sighed. "I thought we were going to have a corpse on our hands."

When Ben finally left at one o'clock, Charlotte was all over her for details.

"He's very nice, really very cultivated, but a little on the shy side, I thought. What did you say he did for a living?"

"I believe he owns a photography shop."

"Oh." Charlotte's face fell. "I thought perhaps he had something to do with the arts."

"Charlie"—Dasha could read her mind—"not everybody can be a Martin Croy. If you don't like Ben, that's one thing. But if you do, why start raising barriers? He's a nice man, a *gentle* man. And he earns his living in an honest, reputable manner. You can't tell me you didn't enjoy his company once you got warmed up."

"Well, yes I did," the older woman conceded. "Still, when one is used to the company of intellectuals . . . "

Nonetheless, when Ben asked her to the theater the following week she went cheerfully enough. By the time autumn rolled around they were a regular Saturday night couple. Would they ever get married?

Dasha thought about it intermittently, but she had many other things on her mind. The office, naturally. The kids' progress. The move to Park Avenue. And out of a clear blue sky, the question of David.

Alex called one October evening in a state of near panic. Had Dasha heard from her nephew?

"Just a postcard saying he arrived in L.A. Why?"

"He's disappeared." Alex's voice was thick with anxiety. "He registered for school a couple of weeks ago and nobody's seen him since. I thought he might have called you."

"No." Her stomach turned queasy. "Just that postcard, that's all. You think something's happened to him?"

"I don't know. California's such a freaky place. Everybody out there is into drugs, crazy politics, kinky sex. Lord knows what trouble a boy can get into. God help me, Dasha, but I keep remembering Charles Manson and now there are those horrible Hillside murders."

"Oh, Alex!" she groaned. "Don't even think of such a thing."

"It's impossible not to. I put a notice in all the L.A. papers—the underground ones, too. But nothing! I'll give it another twenty-four hours, then I'll call in the FBI."

Weeks passed. There was no further word and Alex stepped up the search, adding a team of private investigators to the government effort. Dasha grieved for him.

Then, on Christmas Eve, David telephoned person to person.

"Where are you?" Dasha cried. She could hear coins being dropped into the phone box. "Where are you calling from?"

"It doesn't matter." The voice was cool and emotionless, yet unmistakably it was her nephew's.

"What do you mean, it doesn't matter? Your father is climbing the walls."

"Then tell him to stop, Auntie. Tell him to call off the cops. You can assure him that I am alive and well and happier than I've ever been before . . . "

"But where?" Dasha pleaded.

"And you can tell him one more thing. I've found a *real* father at last."

With that he hung up. The call had lasted less than a minute, but at least she could assure Alex that his boy was alive. As for the utter cruelty of David's final remark, she could spare her brother that. The poor man had suffered enough these past ten weeks.

For months after, she left a phone number behind wherever she went in hopes that David would contact her again. But he never did.

CHAPTER TWELVE

☐ Frank.

What was there to say about Frank Hunicutt except that for about a year now she had been half in love with him? Well, maybe half was an exaggeration, and maybe "love" was the wrong choice of word. "I admire him tremendously," she told Jordan. "He has such energy, such enthusiasm. I've never known anyone who enjoys life more."

There was nothing between them, of course. They were both respectably married people who also happened to be friends and colleagues. Inter-office dalliance was frowned upon at Slater Blaney. And though the dining room buzzed continually with gossip and backbiting, it was of a professional rather than sexual nature.

"When you put in an eighty-hour week," one associate griped, "who has the time to screw around?"

"Time!" Dasha laughed. "Who has the energy?"

Yet though she could certainly vouch for her own marital fidelity, she couldn't do as much for Frank's. He, of all people, *would* have the energy. Indeed, it seemed unlikely that a man with such an exuberant appetite for life could ever be thoroughly domesticated.

In fact, she had spotted him one afternoon in a Hamburger Heaven —the last place in the world for a senior partner to be lunching— snuggled in a back booth with a very young, very pretty airline stewardess. The buttons on the girl's blouse were half undone, her hair was rumpled, and Dasha's unmistakable impression was of a lunchtime "quickie." Rather than embarrass him, Dasha decided to sneak out unobserved. At that exact moment, he looked up. Their eyes locked for perhaps two seconds. Then he smiled, nodded briskly, and went back to his conversation without the faintest show of discomfort. Dasha left without a word and neither of them ever mentioned the incident.

His love life was his business, she felt. Not hers. What *did* concern her was the possibility that their own relationship might serve as fodder for the office rumor machine. The thought wouldn't have occurred to her had it not been for a casual chat with Miranda Richmond, whose office was across the hall.

They were having coffee one morning when Miranda asked her bluntly, "Are you having a thing with Frank Hunicutt? I'm not being judgmental, just curious."

"My God!" Dasha nearly spilled her coffee. "What a thing to say, even in a joke. Where did you get such a notion?"

"Okay, okay," Miranda pleaded ignorance. "Sorry I even mentioned it. It's just that I know how close you two are and I thought . . . "

"Thought what?"

"Well." Miranda shrugged. "I have it on very good authority that Hunicutt is one of New York's greatest swordsmen. 'Love 'em, lay 'em and leave 'em,' as the saying goes, and I was just curious if he'd ever made a pass at you."

"I can assure you he hasn't. Nothing of the kind. Why? Has he ever made a pass at you?"

"No such luck! Although I wouldn't mind waking up with *his* head on my pillow some morning. That is one very sexy guy."

"Well, sorry I can't satisfy your curiosity," Dasha answered stiffly, "but there's absolutely nothing between us."

Which was only partially true, for in another sense there was everything between them—everything but physical love. With the sweep of a master magician, he opened invisible doors and drew her up into his world, a world of challenge and infinite range. "You and I can move mountains," he seemed to say, "for together, everything in life becomes possible."

He filled her with a sense of wonder, the result being—often as not —that she surpassed her own expectations.

That was his charm, his genius. It was also, she recognized, the chief reason why—in a business crowded with men of wit and tact and ability —Frank had risen so high and so swiftly.

He was a superb executive, a master craftsman of the negotiated deal. Yet behind the bonhomie, there was a subtle and observant mind. More than a lawyer, he was a politician. A psychologist with sure instinct for other people's strengths and weaknesses. "You must always remember," he told her, "that you're not dealing with textbooks or principles of jurisprudence. You're dealing with people—brave, frightened, greedy, rash, stupid, clever, unpredictable people. The trick is in knowing which ones to trust, which ones to tackle, and which ones are out for your blood."

"Should I trust you, Frank?"

"With your life."

She did, and he was an extraordinary guide through the minefields and booby traps of the corporate jungle. He was a font of practical advice, sharp insights. "Discount everything Grayson has to say by half," or, "Never confide anything, not even what you had for breakfast, to Ginny Walsh. She's married to an examiner from the SEC." Or—upon going to meet a new client—"Sit down as soon as you walk into his office. He's intimidated by tall women."

More than once when she had chosen a highly arguable course of action, he had gone to the wall for her. "Of course Dasha's right," he had thundered at a nervous client. "How could you possibly question the quality of her advice!" Privately, he told her later, she had probably cost the poor bastard a hundred thousand dollars. "However"—he shrugged —"it's not a mistake you're likely to make again."

And through it all ran the constant thread: *You are going to be a magnificent lawyer. One day. One day soon.*

She adored him. And while logic told her that Frank's special magic was not reserved for her alone, within the firm there was no question that she uniquely had been singled out, the one associate among a hundred to be chosen as his protégée and confidante.

They communicated.

"I can talk to you, Dasha," he would say now and again. "We're on the same frequencies." And she could talk to him as well, lobbing out ideas and tacks that a less imaginative man would have balked at. She had a healthy respect for his intellect. They fell into an easy verbal shorthand, conscious of stumbling on the same ideas, arriving at the same conclusions, laughing at the same jokes.

"Christ," Frank would say sometimes, "it's such a relief not having to spell everything out. *You* do it, Dasha"—he would delegate authority to her. "You know what I want."

Often at the end of a particularly hectic day, he'd invite her to his office, pour her a drink, put his feet up on the desk in total disregard of the rules of caring for antique furniture, and the two of them would spend a pleasant half-hour simply unwinding.

He rarely drank, Dasha noticed, although his bar was always lavishly stocked. Sometimes he would pour himself a finger of scotch, then leave it virtually untouched; more usually his tipple was coffee or iced tea. She wondered if he had had problems with alcohol. But perhaps he simply preferred to remain sober. To let others make fools of themselves. *"Après ski,"* Frank called their get-together. They'd talk about work, politics, their children, themselves, each other, but mostly about who was doing what to whom, both in the office and out.

Almost the only people about whom he never gossiped were the two who aroused her curiosity most: Amory First and Clarisse Hunicutt. To her dismay, she had never met either. Perhaps Frank felt she wouldn't fit in their social milieu.

Perhaps she wouldn't. She had no way of telling. She tended to accept F. Scott Fitzgerald's submission that the rich *were* different; and while Dasha didn't think she would be so gross as to drink out of fingerbowls—recalling Andy McCabe's image—neither could she be certain that she would feel at home in that kind of environment.

Amory First particularly had a reputation as a snob and social climber: on the board of half a dozen museums and universities and hospitals, a man determined to buy his way into the most secluded level of the American establishment. He bred racehorses, Dasha had heard, and collected Fabergé, which certainly limited the areas of small talk. Nonetheless, she was curious, especially as the man appeared to be such a contradiction in terms. The King of Crap was, by reputation, a considerable aesthete.

So it was exciting and faintly intimidating to be invited, one day in late June, to a house party at the Hunicutts' in Southampton.

"It's time you met Amory," Frank said, "since you're going to be dealing with him directly one of these days. We're having a party at our summer place on Sunday and he'll be there. But if you and your husband are free, why not come out Saturday and stay for the weekend? We'd love to have you and Clarry's invited some interesting people, so it should be fun all around. Medium formal. Bring a swim suit and if you like to ride, we keep horses."

"Jordan'll like that. And is there anything I should bear in mind when dealing with Mr. First?"

Frank shook his head. "Just be yourself, Dasha, and try to take him as he is."

Before packing for the trip, she checked with Frank's secretary as to what constituted a "medium formal" weekend at the Hunicutts', then went out and bought a pile of Perry Ellis sport clothes and a de la Renta chiffon dress.

"Some layout!" Jordan said as he pulled into the drive. "Well, I guess we're finally going to see how the other half lives."

"The other half of one percent you mean. My God, Jordan, if this is their summer place . . . " Her voice trailed off in wonder.

It was enormous—a rambling clapboard mansion, set amid flowerbeds and acres of emerald lawn, vaguely Georgian in design, and as white and fresh as though it had been painted yesterday, with generous porches running the length of the house. Everything sparkled in the sun, clean and unstrenuous. Gatsby might have lived here, Dasha thought, and thrown those legendary parties on this lawn overlooking the sea.

At the end of the driveway a woman in tennis whites was grooming a Labrador. Jordan stopped the car, and Clarisse Hunicutt came over and introduced herself. She was very tanned, very pretty, with fine straight blond hair and the slim easy elegance of an Estée Lauder model. Only the laugh lines around her eyes gave the faintest hint of middle age.

"Dasha!" she greeted her like an old friend. "How good of you to come. I've heard so much about you. And Mr. Croy, may I call you Jordan? We don't stand on ceremony around here, you'll find." Before Jordan had a chance to protest, she grabbed one of their suitcases and led them through the house and upstairs to a spacious bedroom.

"Now do get out of your city clothes and make yourselves at home. Frank's down at the pool with the other guests and we can join them whenever you're ready. But perhaps you'd like me to show you around the house first?"

"I'd like that very much," said Dasha.

And Clarisse shot her a grateful smile. She is very pleased, Dasha thought, very pleased indeed to be doing the honors of the establishment.

For all its size, or perhaps despite it, the house was wonderfully comfortable, surprisingly intimate. There was no hint of the professional decorator; rather, a sense of private people indulging private tastes with the simplicity that only great wealth can buy.

Wicker and wool and cotton and wood and leather—everything was warm and weathered to the touch. White gauze curtains billowed in the ocean breeze and each room seemed to offer a different invitation to pause and enjoy an hour of lazy self-indulgence. Sit down on this window seat, stretch your legs out on that chaise, linger here over a long cool gin and tonic, relax there with a brandy by the fireplace. The house abounded with quiet biographical touches: needlepoint cushions, family pictures, photos of ancient pets and young children. Dasha paused before a wedding photograph of quite the handsomest young couple she had ever seen. The bride was wearing yards of pearls and acres of lace. The groom looked intensely proud and happy. Dasha caught Clarisse's eye and smiled. "Lovely."

And for one aching moment she envied her. To live like this, to be really rich, truly beautiful, to have a husband as dashing and vibrant as Frank—who says you can't have it all?

At poolside, a lunch of lobster salad and Vouvray was waiting. As she and Jordan walked down the flagstone steps to join the rest of the party, Dasha felt a tweak of self-consciousness about being seen wearing only a bikini. It was a profoundly unlawyerly garment and Frank was, after all, a senior partner. Yet informality seemed to be the order of the day. Frank himself was wearing black swim trunks that seemed little more than a jock strap. French, she imagined. The kind of thing they wore on the Riviera. Jordan would die before he'd appear in public like that.

But of course this wasn't public; it was the Hunicutts' own turf, and Dasha had to admit the man looked magnificent. He had the physique of a football pro, broad in the shoulders, narrow in the hips. Miranda's words came back to her. One very sexy guy indeed.

He pushed back his sunglasses, gave her a welcoming smile and a look of unmitigated approval. "Why, Miss Jones! You're beautiful without your pinstripes."

Dasha thought it a funny remark. She was half tempted to answer "You too," when she became conscious of Jordan, standing beside her, frozen with anger. She didn't need to look. She could feel his resentment. It was tangible, sharp and cold as the north wind. *He's furious,* she realized. *Jordan is absolutely furious.*

Clarisse, too, must have sensed his rage, for she broke in quickly with a pleasant giggle. "Oh now you mustn't mind Frank," her voice rich with conjugal affection. "He says that to everyone in the firm from Blagden Geere on, and you should see *Blagden* in a swim suit. Now I'd like to introduce you to our other guests." And she finished with a swirl of names and chatter.

The awkward moment passed, to be followed by an easy afternoon. They swam, snoozed, played tennis, lounged on the terrace, small-talked the hours away until dinner. The two Hunicutt boys were home from Yale, healthy and handsome as their father, popping in every now and then with a crowd of college friends. "Aren't my boys gorgeous?" Frank said, rumpling his older son's hair playfully while Chad gave an unembarrassed laugh.

"Dad has no shame," he said to Dasha.

"None at all," Frank returned happily.

Dasha was struck with how close the family was. They had a limitless supply of nicknames for each other, some foolish, all affectionate. It amounted to a secret language. By afternoon's end, Dasha decided she had fallen in love with the entire family.

At six, the Croys went upstairs to dress for dinner.

"Well, what do you think?" Dasha could hardly wait for the privacy of their bedroom.

"*She's* charming," Jordan emphasized.

"They all are." Dasha was conscious of the omission but glossed over it. "I've never seen so many good-looking people all in one place. And that lobster salad—mmmm, gorgeous."

But Jordan, still in his swim trunks, was taking stock of himself in the mirror. "Do you know, we were the only pale people there? That was one of the world's greatest collections of expensive tans. Made me feel like a pauper."

"That's silly."

"Very well then, I'm silly. Dressing for dinner!" He looked in the closet where his clothes were hanging out. "Of all the high-falutin' nonsense."

"Now don't be a spoilsport," she teased him. "Besides, you'll look terrific in a dinner jacket. Let's get dressed and go downstairs."

Like a fish in water.

That was how she felt from the moment she sat down to dinner.

They were sixteen in all, seated at a single long table that dazzled with china and crystal and the gleam of white Belgian linen.

Clarisse had placed Dasha between the French cultural attaché and the author of the year's hottest novel. Simply two of the most delightful men she'd ever met. Dasha couldn't remember when she'd enjoyed herself so much. Jean-Pierre was fascinating—a mountain climber, an amateur pianist, and also, to be sure, an outrageous flirt. But that was half the fun, and anyhow one shouldn't go through life without ever having exchanged *doubles entendres* with an attractive Frenchman. Moreover, everybody was flirting with everybody.

Except Jordan. Never Jordan, who was sandwiched between the attaché's wife and a very pretty redhead, and talking to neither. He looked dour and faintly intimidated. He wasn't used to sitting so far away from his wife at dinner parties.

Several times early in the evening, Dasha tried to catch his eye, just to wink and say a mental *Hey there, relax! These are charming people.* But Jordan's eye refused to be caught, wavering neither to left nor right. His attention seemed to focus solely on the soup. And very good soup it was, a crayfish bisque made with sherry.

Oh well, Dasha gave up. If it made Jordan happy to be miserable, then let him be miserable. She refused to let his mood spoil her own evening. It was a marvelous party. She had never felt so elegant, so attractive, so downright sexy. Maybe it was the dress. Oh, the power of a wisp of chiffon!

And maybe, too, that was where the evening had started souring for Jordan. With the dress.

"You're not going to wear that thing without a bra, I hope?" he'd said when she slipped it on. "Your nipples show through."

"It's not the kind of dress you can wear with a bra," she explained. "Funny. I could swear I showed it to you when I bought it."

"You held it up, but you didn't show me what it looked like on. Really, Dasha, I find that a bit much. After all, we hardly know these people . . . "

"Oh, for heaven's sakes, Jordan. You're beginning to sound like my father. It's a dinner party, not a PTA meeting."

In fact it was a great dinner party. Dasha looked to the far end of the table to reward her hostess with a smile, as the butler filled a fresh wineglass with a ruby-red Bordeaux.

Across the expanse of spotless linen, Clarisse smiled back, spilled her wine, then rolled her eyes with a mock "Oh my!" Dasha raised her own glass in a playful toast, and after that the decibels got louder.

By evening's end she had got an offer to spend a week cruising the Greek Islands, heard the plot twists of next year's best seller, been invited to three dinner parties, and received a terrific stock market tip. She floated upstairs in a happy buzz.

"What a sensational party," she said, putting away the offending chiffon. "It really was."

"If you say so," Jordan muttered.

"You can't blame me if you didn't have a good time, Jordan. They were nice people, interesting people. You would have had fun too, if you'd unwound a bit and joined in the conversation. That was a very pretty woman sitting next to you, by the way, the little redhead. Who did she belong to, anyhow?"

"About everyone, as far as I could figure out. She's been married four times, can you imagine? I think she was measuring me for number five. Where do we summer, she wanted to know, and do we like hang-gliding?" Jordan did an imitation of the accent known as Long Island Lockjaw. "I told her there wasn't a helluva lot of hang-gliding going on at Jones Beach. That shut her up fast." He shook his head solemnly. "I know I'm being a lousy sport, but I don't like these people, Dasha. I don't feel at ease with them. They stink of money. If I had my druthers, we'd be heading for New York this very minute. And as for class, I notice even our beautiful hostess spills her wine."

Dasha sighed and sat down on the counterpane. "Clarisse did that deliberately, you know."

"Don't be silly. No one ruins an expensive tablecloth on purpose."

"I watched her, honey. She spilled the wine deliberately. I presume she thought sooner or later somebody else would ruin the tablecloth so she did it first to spare their feelings. And that, my dear Jordan, is what I call class."

"That's what I call stupid."

"Well, there's no point in arguing about it. Anyhow, I'm afraid you'll have to stick it out another day. I'm supposed to meet First tomorrow. Big lawn party. I saw them setting out the tents this evening. I had rather hoped you'd enjoy it. And you would if you'd just relax."

She kissed him and switched off the light. The room was fragrant with flowers and the smell of the sea. She walked to the window for a last look at the ocean.

Down below her on the headland she could make out a figure in the moonlight, a man in an evening shirt holding a tennis racket. There was something surrealistic in the combination. Then she recognized the figure as Frank Hunicutt. He was standing at the edge of the dune, a massive silhouette against the horizon, smashing tennis balls down into the ocean with the force of a pro. One after another after another. In the moonlight the white of his shirt was luminous.

Such energy! Dasha smiled and climbed into bed.

In the distance a band was playing a medley from *Annie* while an army of waiters handed round champagne in tulip glasses. Like everything else in the world, nature had bent over backwards to oblige the Hunicutts by providing them with the perfect day for a party.

The guest list ran to well over a hundred, half the summer population of the Hamptons, Dasha ventured. And, as Alex would have said, the half that counts. There were tennis stars and diplomats and corporate chiefs; writers, actors, a sprinkling of journalists, a dash of academics; the conductor of the Philharmonic, the newest sensation of the Alvin Ailey Ballet. And, as was to be expected, a heavy helping of lawyers and judges. Amory First must be somewhere in the crush and Frank would introduce her during the course of the afternoon. It was a prospect she approached with mixed feelings.

A few days earlier she had tried to pump a couple of her contacts over at FBC as to what she might expect. Frank had been so uncharacteristically cryptic on the matter. "Do you think First will like me?" she asked one of the network executives.

"Who can tell?" He shrugged. "Reading Amory First is like trying to decipher black ink on black paper at night when the lights are out." Another FBCer described him as "a man who drinks Château Lafite and pisses ice water." And yet another refused to discuss Amory First at all. "For all I know, this place may be bugged," he mouthed.

She would meet him soon enough. In the meanwhile, the day was young, the canapés delicious, and there were plenty of other friends to say hello to. Executives from the network, fellow lawyers from the firm. She'd always wanted Jordan to know more about the people she spent the largest part of her day with and this seemed the ideal opportunity.

"Come on, darling." She snatched his arm and steered him over to a boisterous gathering at the edge of the pool. "I'd like you to meet . . . " The names tripped off her tongue. "Bill Baxter. Samantha Devlin . . . and this is Carter Brice you've heard me talk so much about." She handed Jordan a glass of champagne, then stepped away for a minute to talk to someone else.

"Sorry." Carter Brice cupped a hand about his ear to shut out the din. "I didn't catch your name."

"Croy. Jordan Croy."

"What? Ah, then you're Dasha's husband. We think your wife is someone very special, you know. One of the sharpest lawyers with the firm. She has all the making of a first-class corporate litigator."

Jordan nodded, sighed, permitted the waiter to give him a fresh glass of champagne. "I happen to be an attorney too," he remarked.

"Oh?" Carter's expression perked up. "I had no idea that Dasha was married to a lawyer. Which firm are you with?"

"I'm not with any firm. I have a small independent practice uptown." He swallowed off his champagne. "No corporate clients, no bankers beating down our doors. Just something we locals call storefront law. Perhaps you've heard of it?"

"Ah, yes." The older man's interest deflated as quickly as a pricked balloon. "I'm sure that's a very rewarding specialty."

Unaccountably, his remark struck Jordan as hilarious.

"Rewarding! Why, sir, you have stumbled upon it. *Le mot juste*, as they say in Spanish Harlem. The very term I myself would choose to define my practice. I'll have you know, sir, that I endow whole universities with the proceeds, and with what's left over I stamp out starvation in Biafra."

And then it was Carter's turn to laugh.

"Very funny. But you better watch that champagne, pal. It can be very sneaky."

Jordan ambled back to where Dasha stood chatting with friends.

"Grand party," he murmured with a feel-no-pain smile. "Super party." Then he moved off in the general direction of the buffet. Dasha watched his progress from under half-closed lids. He seemed pleasantly animated today. Gregarious. He'd apparently had a nice chat with Carter Brice and now he was talking with his red-headed dinner companion from the previous evening. With a sigh of relief she presumed that Jordan had finally taken her advice and was unwinding. Now they could both enjoy themselves. It *was* a super party and getting better all the time.

"Ah there you are!"

Frank Hunicutt came and drew her off and began steering her across the lawn. "You ready for your big moment? Amory First is over there on the verandah. Come on, I'll introduce you." Instinctively, Dasha smoothed down her dress. She was looking well today, elegant yet businesslike, no nipples showing. Quite within the bounds of decency. She grinned up at Frank. "Ready when you are."

He was sitting in a wicker chair on the porch, a man in a soft linen suit sipping a glass of milk. A cordless phone lay at his elbow. White on white on white. He made no motion to rise.

Translucent. That was the word that came to mind. Translucent as antique porcelain. Dasha had the eerie sense that if Amory First were to stand before a strong and merciless light, she would be able to see through him. He looked his age, which she knew to be close to eighty, yet in an eerie way almost untouched by time. The skin was smooth, milky pale and luminous, the hair a quiet polished silver. And the eyes . . . ah, the eyes.

It was not enough to say they were gray as steel and cold as death. They were not really eyes at all, but a high-tech precision instrument. A calculator, fast and efficient, that looked you over, totted you up, sized up your strengths, subtracted your weaknesses, finally arriving at some secret bottom line you could only guess at.

Is this person important? She tried to read his gaze. *Is this person useful to me? Exploitable? Someone worthy of my time and attention? Is there something to be gained from this particular specimen?*

There was nothing remotely sexual in his appraisal, indeed nothing personal at all. It was similar, she imagined, to being examined by a CAT scanner in a hospital, a procedure that was probingly intimate and utterly impersonal all at once.

"Croy," he murmured in a voice that was nearly inaudible. "Croy. That's a familiar name."

"Dasha is the one who conceived the Pendleton merger," Frank offered. "And one of our most gifted younger attorneys. We expect to get her more and more involved with FBC."

"Of course." First gave a thin cold smile, and the calculator eyes clicked *Worth my time.* They shook hands. Hers was moist, his parchment dry. "Won't you sit down? I find it instructive," he said to no one in particular, "that in a firm that employs two hundred attorneys it took a young associate to solve a simple technical problem." Dasha was uncertain whether this was meant to be a dig at Frank or a compliment to herself. She said nothing and First continued. "However, I suppose an old man should be grateful to get competent legal advice no matter what its source. Perhaps I shouldn't be keeping you from your guests any longer" —he dismissed Frank with a flourish of the fingers—"and now, young lady, now that that execrable band has stopped its caterwauling, we might enjoy a little quiet conversation. I'd be interested in hearing your views about the new FCC ruling on piggybacks and what you think of our chances should we choose to appeal."

You don't horse around, Amory baby, do you? she thought. Was this Frank's idea of a "social" meeting? Was this the old tycoon's notion of small talk? Dasha knew where her duty lay.

"The problem as I see it . . . " she began. He heard her out with an air of intense concentration. Painfully aware that she was under inspection, she picked her way through the legal underbrush with consummate care. *You're doing good, kid,* an inner voice assured her, and she could see the response in First's rhythmic nod.

"Yes," he said when she finished her piece. "You may be right. However . . . "

He had a low voice, hardly more than a whisper, and she leaned forward, straining to catch his words.

Thrmmmmm . . . an electronic howl surged through the amplification system and rolled across the lawn in a cosmic burp. Then, over the microphone, magnified tenfold, came the *whumpp* of a guitar and a familiar voice sang out:

> *"If we can put a man on the moon,*
> *Why can't we cure the common cold?*

C'mon, everybody, let's all join in . . . "

Amory First's eyes narrowed into slits. "What in God's name is that?"

What in God's name indeed! What in God's name had got into Jordan to jump up on the bandstand and make such a damn fool of himself? Or *her?*

Booze, of course. Booze and jitters had got into him. Or did he really believe that was still a funny routine? Christ almighty, where was his judgment? That may have been a hot number fifteen years ago on campus but dear God, not here! Not now!

An embarrassed titter ran through the crowd.

She wanted to die. She wanted the floorboards of the porch to open and swallow her up forever. In that instant she never wanted to see Amory First again. Never wanted to see any of these people again. She forced herself to look up on the bandstand where Jordan was clutching the mike in a floundering effort to steady himself. For one heart-stopping moment, he teetered and threatened to fall face forward into the crowd. Then, mercifully, Frank Hunicutt materialized beside him, switched off the mike with an imperturbable smile and, placing a strong arm around Jordan, led him off into the house.

"Who *was* that joker?" First asked, when the din died down.

Dasha hesitated. She would have given anything to be able to lie, pretend ignorance, but that was a coward's way out. Never apologize. Never explain.

"That's my husband."

First looked at her and for an instant she fancied she saw a glint of amusement in his eyes. "Then Croy is your married name," he mused. "It still rings a bell."

Dasha made the connection. "Perhaps you were thinking of Martin

Croy, the television scriptwriter? I believe he was quite well known in the early fifties."

"Ah yes." The calculator eyes had turned inward in search of some bit of data long since filed away. "The Martin Croy affair. Yes, now I remember. Was he some relation?"

"My husband's father."

"Indeed!"

Dasha was intrigued by his use of the word "affair." It struck her as an odd term to describe what had been a personal tragedy, but this was not the time or place to ask. Now having retrieved the information he had sought, First looked at Dasha with an enigmatic smile. He murmured "Like father like son" in such an ambiguous tone that she couldn't tell whether it was said as a question or a judgment. Then the eyes snapped shut, the file was closed, and the old man resumed his denunciation of the FCC.

She left the party as soon as was decently possible.

Dasha drove home in a black rage, hardly trusting herself to speak, while Jordan huddled in the back seat, drunk and dead to the world.

Forgive, all the wisdom of their years together urged her. *Forgive and forget.* It was not as though Jordan were a confirmed alcoholic who made a habit of disgracing his wife in public. It was a one-time-only lapse.

But what a time to pick! And what a place! It took all Dasha's willpower to keep her from pulling over to the side of the road and giving full vent to her tears, her frustration. She wanted to beat her hands on his chest, to shake him into consciousness. How *could* you? *How could you do this to me!*

But instead she followed the advice she gave her more volatile clients. She would cool it. Sleep on it. Not even mention it for the rest of the day. And maybe it wouldn't look quite so grim in the morning.

At home, the children watched mystified as she and Charlotte dragged Jordan's passive hulk into the bedroom.

"What's the matter with Daddy?" Geoff wanted to know.

Dasha pursed her lips. "Daddy came down with a touch of the flu. Now get your coats on and we'll drive Grandma home."

He woke up in the middle of the night, sober but miserable.

"Are you awake?" he whispered to Dasha.

"I'm awake." She sighed. "How are you feeling?"

"I'll live," he murmured. "Unless you have other plans for me. Dasha . . . ? Dasha?" And when there was no reply, "You want to talk?"

"Go to sleep, Jordan. It can wait until tomorrow."

"I'm sorry," he said softly. "I'm awfully sorry."

That was it! The words were a match to kindling, all it needed for her to forgo her good intentions of cool and calm.

"*Sorry!* Well that's just great! You disgrace me in public, you humiliate me before my most important client . . . and you're *sorry!* Well, I'm a helluva lot sorrier." She burst into tears. "I wanted to crawl into a hole in the ground and disappear."

"To be fair, Dasha, you did keep nagging me to socialize. Unwind —that was your word, as I recall. So I unwound. Okay, maybe a bit too much."

"So now it's my fault?" Her voice rose an octave. "You make a spectacle of yourself and now it's my fault! I don't know how I'll show my face in the office tomorrow."

"Honestly, Dasha." He switched on the light. "You make it sound like it was the end of the world. Perspective, perspective! So I had too much to drink and made an ass of myself. It's a misdemeanor, not a crime, for God's sakes. There were plenty of guests in a lot worse shape than I was. Jesus! I saw a federal judge throwing up in the swimming pool."

"You are not a federal judge," she reminded him.

"Goddam right I'm not!" he exploded. "I'm not much of anything, am I? I'm nobody in the world except the guy who has the privilege of being married to Superwoman Dasha Croy. Well, I don't need you to tell me that I'm strictly minor league. I've had a whole goddam weekend of it. I got the feeling I was there under false pretenses, a gate-crasher riding on your coattails. 'Which firm are you with?' that Brice guy asked me. It was like some dumbo kid's game . . . *my firm's bigger than your firm.* And when I told him what I actually did for a living, he looked at me like I was an ambulance chaser. Real contempt. I read it in his eyes, Dasha. And sometimes I read it in yours."

"Oh Jordan!" His words had hit below the belt. "Now *you're* the one who's taking the whole business too seriously. This contempt you say you feel, it's all in your mind."

"Is it? Well, could be. And could be Brice was right—that's all I am, a two-bit ambulance chaser in a polyester suit who somehow slipped past the doorman. And my bet is Hunicutt sees me pretty much the same way. What am I . . . five, six years younger than he? And there he is pulling down a million bucks a year and here I am, still sweating it out on Columbus Avenue."

"You're talking nonsense, Jordan. You can't compare yourself to him. He's a man who was born with every conceivable advantage . . . "

"But *you* compare me to him. I saw the way you looked at him when we went down to the pool. Yes, I agree, he's the man who's got the world by the nuts. Money . . . power . . . the whole shebang. And that's what you think I should be, too. But I won't. I can't be. And I'll tell you something else—I'd never want to be. I hated it, Dasha." His voice was cold sober now, and she could detect a note of desperation. "I hated every minute of that fucking weekend. I'm not like you. I don't have that same ability to kid around and compare notes on how I spent my summer . . . not when I'm sitting next to a Vanderbilt heiress or the head of some Fortune 500 corporation. They're not my kind of folks, Dasha, and they never will be. What's more, I don't really believe they're yours. I watch you with them and you're perfect, you truly are. You wear the clothes, you talk the jargon. You've got all that hotshot executive stuff down pat and you sure pull it off. I look at that person and she's a stranger. But that's not you, Dasha. You can't make me believe that's really you."

"Then what's me?" she cried out, anguished. "Is it the real me in the kitchen making meatloaf . . . the real me ironing children's overalls? Why is one less real than the other? If what you're saying is that I'm not the same person I was ten years ago, fifteen years ago, all I can answer is . . . of course not! How can you expect me to be? Of course I've changed."

"I haven't," Jordan said. It was not a guilty plea or an alibi, merely a statement of fact.

It was true. He hadn't changed. She looked at him in the muted light of the bedside lamp, and he could have been the same Jordan of their wedding day. A little thinner on top, a little thicker around the middle, perhaps. But in all other particulars he was the same man she had married.

Why don't they write songs the way they used to? he had said that very afternoon when the band was playing a current hit from *Saturday Night Fever*.

It was a chronic complaint of his.

Life was speeding by too fast, altering too rapidly, substituting the worse for the better. His tastes had crystallized in the early days of their marriage and now he looked back upon that time as an almost idyllic era when the songs had been more melodic, the tomatoes tastier, the movies funnier. When even the Yankees had played a better brand of baseball.

"You're too young to be nostalgic," Dasha had said to him on occasion. He in turn charged her with loving change for change's sake. "Newer doesn't mean better," was his response. No, Jordan hadn't changed.

"I haven't changed." He cupped her face in his hands and looked at her with a longing that made her heart ache. "In all these years I haven't changed. For better or worse, I'm just as crazy in love with you as ever."

"Oh Jordan!" It was the last thing she had expected him to say. She had been geared for accusations, recriminations, anything but a simple confession of love. A wave of guilt overwhelmed her. Guilt and a swift lash of panic. They had never before come so close to the edge.

What kind of madness had possessed her to make such an issue of a single lapse in all the years of their marriage? Only ten minutes earlier she had been almost ready to leave him for what had been a minor social embarrassment. Even more incredible that she should think of herself, for even one minute, as someone separate from him.

This was Jordan, for God's sakes, the one person who mattered most in the world. No, he hadn't changed, thank God. He was the same Jordan she had fallen in love with on a crisp autumn night in Northampton. The Jordan who had been her first love, her last love, her only love. The man she had turned to and trusted at every crisis in her life. The Jordan who had fathered her children, shared her joys, dried her tears, who had seen her through law school, placed her happiness first, supported her every step of the way.

And this was his reward. To be screamed at and abused simply because he had one drink too many at a party.

Suddenly she was in his arms, smitten with remorse. "I'm sorry," she said. "I've behaved unforgivably . . . the things I said. The way I talked to you. I don't know"—she began sobbing—"I don't know what's me and what isn't any more. I'm so confused. All I know is that nothing, *nothing* can ever be more important than you, us. I must have been a little bit crazy."

She lay in his arms for a long time weeping uncontrollably and he comforted her, loving and unjudging, as he had done so many times before. When the tears subsided, she kissed him and whispered in his ear. "What is it you want, darling? Do you want me to quit the firm? Stay home the way I used to? If you do . . . if it means that much, then tell me honestly."

He drew her from him to look at her more closely in the lamplight, her hair a dark tangle, her face stained with tears. "Do you really want to leave Slater Blaney? Be frank with me, Dasha."

She shook her head. "I don't, but I'm willing to, Jordan, if that's what it takes to get us back on the track. All you have to do is ask and I'll give up the job tomorrow. And I would hope to do it graciously." She drew a pained breath and fought back another round of tears. "But I want to know now, tonight, Jordan, before I get any more involved. I need a firm answer, yes or no. Because"—a swift pang of regret flooded through her; already she missed that damn place, missed it as one might miss a stillborn child—"because I can't promise you that I will ever make this offer again. That I'll be able to. That place, as you know, casts a spell. So tell me now, this night, and I'll do it. But dear God, don't ever ask me again."

"You really would? You would do that for me?" His voice shook with emotion. "My darling Dasha, what can I say? I couldn't accept such a sacrifice, I couldn't possibly. Sure, I have occasional fantasies about how nice it would be to come home from the office and find you there waiting for me with a smile and dinner on the table and did I have a hard day at the office. Just like old times. It's probably what most men want at heart; but I don't kid myself. You'd go bananas in a situation like that, now that you've had a taste of the world. Probably wind up putting arsenic in my morning coffee. And no jury"—he laughed limply at his joke—"would find you guilty. I'm not such a hopeless troglodyte as all that, Dasha. I want to be fair. Stay with the firm. I'd only ask one thing of you."

"Anything, my darling." She could barely mask her relief. It was a last-minute reprieve from the firing squad. "Anything within reason— or without."

"All I ask is that you don't push so hard at the office, slow down a little, try to make more time for the rest of us. So what if you don't make partner? It wouldn't be the end of the world. You know, Dasha, we haven't had even a decent weekend together this last year, let alone a real vacation."

"I know, I've been . . . "

"Busy," he broke in. "That's all I ask, that you be a little less busy from now on. You know what I'd like?" He gave his old crooked grin. "I'd like us to have a second honeymoon. A first one, actually. We never did have a proper going away. Tell you what, when school starts in the fall, let's leave the kids with my mother for a couple of weeks and go away somewhere, just you and me. Someplace lush and romantic and we won't have anything to do but eat and drink and make love. What do you say, Dasha?"

"My own dear sweet Jordan." She placed his hands on her breasts. "Let's begin that honeymoon right now."

They made love, strong and fierce and bittersweet till daybreak crept through the curtains, then lay back replete and happy in each other's arms. This is how it should be, Dasha thought as her eyes grew heavy with sleep. This is how it's always going to be.

In the afterglow of love, she made a silent pledge to do as he wished. Slow down, ease off, apply the brakes on her ambition. It was an utterly reasonable request. She would have a good career, if not a great one, and she would also have Jordan's love into the bargain.

CHAPTER THIRTEEN

☐ It was the quiet season—the last sleepy week before Labor Day, and for once the Slater Blaney pressure cooker was running at half steam. Summer had slowed the courtwork down to a trickle, vacations had taken their toll of both partners and clients. Frank had gone with his sons on a golfing tour of Scotland, and Dasha had profited in his absence by catching up on her own family life. And by her own admission there'd been a lot of catching up to do.

For the first time since joining the firm, she enjoyed the amenities of quiet evenings at home and long lazy weekends with the kids. Even the occasional afternoon.

In fact—she checked her watch—maybe she'd cut out early today and take the children to see that new *Star Wars* movie, what was it called? Oh yes, *The Empire Strikes Back.* They'd probably love it. Unless, of course, they'd seen it already, which was always a possibility. Not that she remembered either of them mentioning it, but that didn't prove anything. The lines of communication had grown a little frayed in the last year or so.

In which case, today was as good as any to start getting back in touch.

"All quiet out there?" she buzzed her secretary.

"You could shoot moose in the hallway."

"Then I think I'll quit early today."

"Have a good one."

"You too."

188

She was halfway out the lobby when her beeper went crazy, and next thing she heard was Fran's excited voice on the phone.

"Amory First just called. *Himself,*" Fran emphasized. "He wanted Mr. Hunicutt to go over there right away."

"Frank's in Scotland . . . "

"I know. I told him. Then he said, in that case he wants *you* to get over there on the double and watch some kind of television show."

"Did he say what it was about?"

"Nope, just that you should preview this program in their screening room and see him as soon as you're done."

The request puzzled Dasha. As the outside counsel for FBC, Slater Blaney concerned itself with matters of corporate policy, but almost never with program content. That was the job of the network's in-house counsel.

First Broadcasting had always maintained a sizable staff of attorneys on its payroll for the purpose of handling its day-in day-out affairs. Not a day passed but that someone somewhere tried to haul FBC into court to make a quick buck before a jury. FBC's house counsel usually made short work of them, but even when the cases went full term, Slater Blaney was never involved. Which made Dasha wonder, as she settled into the gold plush chairs of the FBC screening room, what today's command performance was all about.

"Hi." A short heavy man with a stubbly beard came over and shook her hand vigorously. "You the lady from the law firm? I'm Ken Lafferty."

She recognized the name as that of one of America's most controversial filmmakers. She admired his work, particularly the documentary on the Ethiopian famine victims that had won him an Emmy a year earlier.

Definitely a crusader. Definitely an artist. Just as definitely, not the type one would expect to find hanging out at Schlock Rock. "What's a class act like you doing in a place like this?" she wanted to ask him. But instead she said, "Can you tell me something about what I'm going to see?"

"First I'd like to clarify. Technically this film isn't a documentary. It's what we call in the trade a docudrama. Which means we've used actual footage wherever possible, and where it's not, we use actors to portray the actual people. But always in their own words, you understand. There's nothing new about docudramas, though, as a rule, they usually deal with characters out of the history books. Guys who are dead and buried. *Capisce*?"

Dasha nodded. "Except this one isn't about somebody who's dead and buried. Right?"

"Right. Now the show you're going to see is the pilot in a series called "First Insights." The idea is that each program will report on . . . it could be a political scandal or a movement or a personality, but the important thing is, it'll be a topic that has never been exposed to the public scrutiny before, the reason largely being that the people involved refuse to cooperate with the press."

"I see. And the target for tonight is?"

"The Reverend Elijah Kim, and I use the term 'Reverend' advisedly since our good friend appears to have earned his degree in theology through one of those five-dollar mail-order houses. He's a former junkie, an ex-con, although that's not normally the kind of thing I'd hold against a man. At any rate, Kim claims to have kicked the habit through divine intervention while sitting all alone in a cell in Los Angeles County Jail. There he was praying for a fix when, literally, God came to him and tapped him on the shoulder. Who says the Age of Miracles is over? So now his mission in life is to go forth and save American youth from the perils of heroin."

"That's sounds commendable enough."

"Oh, it is commendable. So very commendable that Kim has managed to drum up fortunes in donations. He's boondoggled some top corporations into coughing up sizable sums, but what happens to the money is less clear. One thing is certain, about two million of it has gone into building a huge mansion near San Francisco. All for the good of the kiddies, of course. You won't believe the figures although they're all in the program. Verified, too. In fact, everything you're going to see has been verified by me personally. If it were only another fund-raising scam, it wouldn't matter so much. The thing is that over the last few years, our Mr. Kim has developed quite a following. Teenagers, mostly, a bunch of mixed-up weirdos, dropouts, plus a lot of middle-class sons and daughters too. All told, they number maybe fifty thousand. The Kimfolk, they call themselves. Maybe you've caught their act?"

"You mean those kids who hang out at the airports, the ones with the straw hats and blazers? They look harmless enough to me."

"They're not harmless once Kim gets his mitts on them. Believe me, Dasha"—Ken gripped her hand with fervor—"this guy has 'em hypnotized. They're zombies, walking talking zombies, clean-cut on the outside, burnt-out on the inside. I know. I've tried to interview them and it's like drowning in a sea of cotton candy. There's nothing to get hold of, they have no will of their own. All I could think of was that madman Jim Jones and his Kool-Aid cocktail party down in Guyana. How many died?"

"Good Lord, Ken!" Dasha could see a multi-million-dollar libel suit staring her in the face. "Your program doesn't imply that this is going to be another Jonestown!"

"Nope. I've been a good boy. In fact, I've bent over backwards to show both sides of the controversy. It's for the viewer to draw a conclusion. And everything you're going to see and hear on this film has been vouched for. I've got releases, sworn statements, all the paperwork anyone would need to back it up. But how about letting the film speak for itself?"

Which it did. Admirably. Powerfully.

Ken Lafferty had contrived an extraordinary mixture of live footage and convincing dramatic reenactment. Dasha could hardly tell which was which. The kids at the airport were real. The Reverend Kim was a tall egg-bald actor. The great rambling estate in California was real. The phalanx of armed youth training on its lawns like a commando squad . . .

"Is that scene real or staged?" she asked.

"Real."

Deep within her a hard ball of anger began forming.

The camera cut to a crew of newsmen battering at the massive iron gates that barred the Kim estate from the public. Behind the wrought iron, teenagers jeered and screamed abuse. They were like madmen. One of them, a tall skinny boy with hollow eyes, brandished a menacing fist at a reporter. And that was real.

Too real.

"Stop the film." Dasha clutched the armrests for support.

"Pretty powerful stuff, huh?"

"Yes." She gasped for breath, found it. "Could you . . . could you please rerun the last couple of minutes in slow motion?"

And there he was. Pale, thinner than when she saw him last, remote and other-worldly with his haunted eyes and shaven head. David Oborin.

191

There could be no mistake. Dasha clapped a fist to her mouth to stifle a cry of rage. Of anguish. Then struggled to regain her composure.

"Okay?" Lafferty asked. "You want to see the rest of it now?"

She was too shocked to do anything more than nod, while the film unrolled in horrifying detail.

David, sweet troubled David in the hands of this monster! David brainwashed, for there was no question of the techniques involved. And not only David but how many thousands of other boys like him—lost, lonely, unhappy at home, in search of false fathers, pat answers. Today it was her nephew. Tomorrow—who knows?—it could be her own vulnerable son!

When the lights went up, she was still trembling.

"Dynamite, huh, Dasha?" Abe Riskin, the network's chief of programming, had joined them in the screening room. "You look as if you've seen a ghost."

She made a huge effort to pull herself together.

"I think," she said, "I've seen a lot of them." Ken Lafferty's reference to Jonestown no longer seemed so impossible. "I have absolutely no doubt that the show should be broadcast. It deserves the widest audience possible. I for one am glad I've seen it. Clearly the man must be stopped. But surely, Abe, your staff lawyers have already gone over the content with a fine-tooth comb? They're much better equipped than I to say whether it's libelous."

"They don't believe it is."

"Then what *is* the problem?"

"The problem"—Abe looked anxious and unhappy—"is Kim himself. Frankly, he's got everyone scared shitless. He's a litigious bastard, you know, which is why there's been so little coverage about him in the press. They say he netted millions in an out-of-court settlement with *Sunset* magazine. And believe me, their story wasn't half as gutsy as ours."

"Then why the hell did they settle?" Dasha was outraged.

"Rumor has it there was strong-arm stuff involved."

"Such as . . . "

"Such as witnesses disappearing or retracting statements under oath. A reporter's watchdog got poisoned. An editor found a rattlesnake in his coat closet. Of course nobody could prove intimidation."

"I see," Dasha said thoughtfully. "And I can understand everyone's caution. I'm curious about one thing, though. In the past, FBC hasn't exactly demonstrated leadership, let alone courage, in the crusading-reporter department. I've always associated you with quiz shows and soaps. So this is quite a radical departure."

"It sure is," Abe agreed. "It's one hell of a pioneering show and I wish I could say it was my brainstorm. But it isn't. It was Amory First's idea."

"Really! All I can say is I'm pleasantly surprised. I've always felt it was shocking, the way the network has dragged its feet on public affairs coverage. Matters of conscience, so to speak. I'm glad Mr. First has had a change of heart."

Her remark made Abe laugh. "Listen"—he lowered his voice to a whisper, and she remembered that at FBC the walls were rumored to have eyes and ears—"it's got nothing to do with public interest. First couldn't care less. What it's all about, frankly, is that the old man wants to be invited to dinner at the White House."

"I beg your pardon?"

"You didn't hear it from me, but the President is setting up a National Commission for the Advancement of the Arts. The chancellor of Columbia is on it, Pope-Hennessy from the Met, David Rockefeller, even a Rothschild or two, and First would give his soul to be one of their number. Well, I don't need to tell you where he stands in the cultural establishment."

"The King of Crap," Dasha murmured. "Only he doesn't want the title any more. Is that it?"

"That's it indeed. The idea is that this series will blow the stink away, and he'll emerge as one of our most reputable, most public-minded broadcasters. Integrity is his new middle name. You should see the programs we've got lined up—on the asbestos scandal, the treatment of mental patients. Really top-drawer quality stuff."

"I understand," Dasha said. "But what's the rush? I'm still uncertain why I'm here today."

"The rush is"—Abe shook his head in wonder—"that First is attending a dinner party tonight and some friends of the President are going to be there. He wants to wow the dinner guests with this incredible announcement. Amory First, Public Servant. He figures the show will win him an invitation to dinner on Pennsylvania Avenue, plus, of course, a seat on the Presidential Commission."

"Well." Dasha straightened her jacket. "A lot of good works have been done for lousy reasons. I've got to go now. I have a meeting with Mr. First in five minutes."

"You don't have a meeting with Amory First." Abe laughed. "You have an audience."

Black, white, silver, crystal. It was more like a photograph of a room than any actual room she had ever seen. White rug, onyx tables, silver fireplace, ebony chairs, Dürer etchings, Brancusi marbles: the effect was dazzling. Frigid. There was no hint of color anywhere except for the four television screens built into the long wall which silently showed the offerings of each major channel.

She crossed to where First sat on a black leather divan click-clicking beads on a polished abacus. Her footsteps were soundless and when she spoke, her voice was drained of overtones. The walls were lead-lined, Frank Hunicutt had told her, the windows made of one-way glass. The old man had a terror of being spied upon.

"Should I sit down, sir?"

"Please, Mrs. Croy." He indicated an armchair opposite.

"Let's discuss Kim," he said abruptly. "You saw the program. I'm not interested in what you thought of it on aesthetic grounds. I merely seek your advice as to whether it can be shown with impunity. My lawyers here seem to think not. I wanted an outside opinion."

"I'm not an expert in libel law," she began.

"Frank Hunicutt said you had"—he interrupted—"guts, I believe his word was. It's why I asked for you in his absence. I've already had a heavy dose of mealy-mouthing from my counsel here. What I want is a hard-and-fast answer. Should I broadcast the program—yes or no?"

Dasha took a deep breath. She knew it was FBC policy to avoid litigation wherever possible, but First wanted a response. He wanted it now. She could feel him champing at the bit like a racehorse and all she could go with was her instinct. That monster had to be stopped. Exposed to public scrutiny. There was a moral imperative here. She would never forgive herself if she backed off now. Never be able to erase the image of David. Perhaps she wasn't acting like the cold-blooded lawyer this very minute. But there were more important things in life.

"Show it," she said passionately. "By all means show it. You have a vital film here, one that deserves to be seen. I think, too, that Kim will probably sue on one pretext or another. You should be advised of that. However, if you believe in it and are willing to back it in court if necessary, then it's not so much a legal decision as a moral one. And with all due respect, sir, the moral decision must be—Show it."

"Are you speaking for yourself or for the firm?"

"For both." The words rang out sharp and clear.

"Bravo!" First had heard what he wanted. "Frank was right. You do have guts. And I agree, the film deserves to be broadcast. Well, let Kim sue, if he thinks it'll do him any good. I'm not the man to lie down and play possum for some two-bit preacher."

"Win or lose, it's my duty to point out you're bound to incur substantial legal costs if it comes to trial."

"Kim be damned and the expense be damned," First replied. "Although naturally I expect to win. That's one of the reasons I retain Slater Blaney."

They spent the next half hour exploring options, with Dasha, now that she had his confidence, expressing her views with less and less hesitation. He may be the world's biggest son of a bitch, she decided, but he was a *smart* son of a bitch. She could talk to him.

As the interview drew to its close, she gathered her courage and asked for a few extra minutes of his time.

He looked at his watch. "Ten minutes, Mrs. Croy. I have a dinner engagement this evening."

"I'll be brief, Mr. First. I would like you to satisfy my curiosity. When we met at the Hunicutts' earlier this summer, you mentioned something about my husband's father, Martin Croy. What really happened? All I know is that he died in a car crash."

"Ancient history." The old man shrugged. "Ancient history and best forgotten. Besides, there are certain confidences involved."

"I'm a lawyer," Dasha assured him. "And you're my client. I know how to keep secrets."

He hesitated for an instant, then reached for a switch under the table, clicking off the four television sets. As if, she thought, he didn't even want the screen to overhear.

"Very well," he said. "I'll tell you what you want to know."

She left FBC that evening with a great deal on her mind. First, David. She'd have to notify Alex, of course, then see to it that he didn't appear in the film's final cutting.

Then there was the business about Martin Croy. What she had heard was deeply disturbing, but the old man was right. It *was* ancient history and there could be no point in unearthing it ever again.

Finally, she wondered if she had been correct in advising First to run the Kim show. The prudent course would have been to dissuade him. Better safe than sorry—that was a basic tenet of the downtown bar. Or as Andy used to put it, "When in doubt, weasel out." And she had plunged into the decision head first. Heart first, too, quite honestly. Out of anger. Out of righteous indignation.

If only Frank had been there, he would have known what to do. She had never missed his guidance so acutely.

The next two days were spent tracing him down. She phoned several Scottish golf courses before she finally located him at the clubhouse of St. Andrews.

"I hate to interrupt your vacation," she apologized, then gave him a precis of what had happened. "What do you think? Did I do the right thing?"

"Absolutely." He sounded blithely confident.

"And if Kim sues . . . ?"

"If he sues, we make a million bucks in fees. Don't worry about it."

"The thing is, Frank"—she had to confide in him—"I'm afraid I urged First into that decision for some very unprofessional reasons"—and she poured out the story of her shock at seeing David on film, her decision that something had to be done. Her anger at Elijah Kim.

Frank heard her out without saying a word.

"Am I fired?" she asked softly.

"You still did the right thing," came the answer. "And when we go to court, I want you to keep some of that holy rage on tap. It's good stuff to have in a crunch."

"Thanks." She felt the weight slip from her shoulders. "And while I have you on the phone, can I ask one more question? Did you really tell Amory First I had guts?"

"Nope," Frank said. "I'm afraid I've been misquoted."

"Oh!" She was mildly disappointed.

"What I really said," Frank continued, "is that you have balls."

CHAPTER FOURTEEN

☐ The Rio Verde Ranch was, in both style and substance, as far as it was possible to get from mid-Manhattan without leaving the continental USA.

"Come out on the terrace," Jordan said exultantly, their first night in Arizona. "Now look up. You know what those funny things are up there in the sky? No, they're not spotlights or police helicopters or reflected neon from Joe's Bar and Grill. They are—my dear lamb chop —what are known as stars. You may have read about them in college textbooks. Christ, when was the last time we looked up and actually saw a sky full of stars, will you tell me? Not in Manhattan, that's for sure. And God!"—he breathed in a full measure of the crisp desert air—"just fill your lungs, will you? It's glorious here . . . really glorious!"

"For three hundred bucks a day," she laughed, "it *should* be."

He put his arm around her to ward off the desert chill. "Makes you wonder why anyone puts up with New York—the filth, the rotten air. You could get drunk just inhaling out here. This, my love"—he pulled her closer—"is going to be the best vacation two people ever had. And you can't say we haven't earned it."

They certainly had.

With the recent explosion in co-op housing, Jordan's practice had picked up briskly, and after much consideration, he decided to hire a paralegal to help him handle the paperwork. His new assistant was a petite and conscientious Japanese girl with sloe eyes and glossy black hair that ran halfway down her back.

"Should I be jealous?" Dasha teased. "She's awfully sweet, all ninety

197

pounds of her." And Jordan answered earnestly, "Michika's very good when it comes to writing up mortgages," until Dasha felt impelled to explain she was only kidding.

For her, too, New York had been increasingly hectic—long hours largely spent in ensuring that the Kim broadcast be airtight and impervious to arbitrary lawsuits. Every word, every frame of the film had been gone over with Ken Lafferty at least a hundred times. "There's a difference between being fearless and being foolhardy," she kept reminding him. "So let's stick strictly to hard facts."

However, self-styled reverends and sloe-eyed paralegals were out of sight now, replaced by a sweeping landscape of limitless desert and velvet sky, a sense of infinite freedom and infinite time. Two whole weeks, in any event. They began the evening with peach margaritas and barbecued steaks, then topped it off with double brandies in the fieldstone lounge.

"Do you know"—Jordan swirled the cognac in his snifter—"that this is the first truly carefree vacation you and I have ever had together? Without worries, without work . . . "

"Without kids," Dasha completed his thought. "It's a weird feeling, isn't it? Almost as if we were playing hooky."

"Or enjoying an illicit assignation," he replied.

The notion made her smile. She looked around the lounge. It was crowded with well-fed, well-dressed people, for the most part middle-aged. And then she looked at Jordan over the rim of her glass. In the intimate light of the hurricane lamps, he looked wonderfully handsome —youthful, romantic as the night they had met. Decidedly he was the most attractive man in the room.

"Let's pretend we're not married," she said. "Or at least not to each other. Two lovers who are doing their damnedest not to be caught." The brandy had given her a heady buzz. Her body felt warm, glowing.

"Why?" He looked at her puzzled. "Was sex better for you before we were married?"

"Not better necessarily"—her eyes grew bright—"but fresher, perhaps. And it did have that added excitement."

"Forbidden fruit." He laughed.

"Yes, forbidden fruit." She leaned toward him, then slipped her hand beneath the table, touching his knee, climbing his thigh. She spread her fingers to cover his penis, suddenly hard beneath the Western jeans.

"Jesus, what are you doing?"

"Ssshh! My husband may be watching, so I must go now." She whispered urgently, "You should know that he's wildly, insanely jealous. If he finds us together, he will kill you. You mustn't look in my direction. Just pretend we're strangers and finish your drink. But if you come to my room at the stroke of midnight, I will be waiting." She withdrew her hand with a long slow stroke.

"Can you tell me your name?" He had fallen in with her fantasy. No, she shook her head.

"My name doesn't matter, nor does yours. The only thing that matters is that I want you to take me to bed."

"How long will we have together?" He reached for her hand.

"How long can you make love to me?"

"I can make love to you all night."

She picked up her bag, got up, and walked past him, brushing her breast against his shoulder.

"Room 605 . . . midnight. Tell no one."

By the time she reached her room she was in an extraordinary state of arousal, and when Jordan arrived a few minutes later, he found her naked, her nipples and thighs scented with the heady smell of Opium. She had drawn the curtains wide to let the moonlight flood into the room.

"Here!" She took his hand and placed it between her legs with a delicious shiver. "Feel how much I want you. Now don't say a word, just let me undress you at my pleasure."

She drew his clothes off slowly, with soft stroking fingers until his flesh gleamed cool and white in the darkened room. He knelt before her. She couldn't see his face, only feel his lips against her belly, sucking on her breasts. In the eerie light he might, indeed, be anyone. A demon lover never to be met again.

"Lovely." He suddenly lifted her up with brute arms and carried her off to bed. "What a lovely loose woman you are . . . whoever you are. Do you know what happens to loose abandoned women?"

"No," she said breathlessly. "What happens to them?"

"I'll have to show you."

He thrust her hard against the pillow, then covered her face with butterfly kisses. Then he was on his knees straddling her with all his force, grooving his rock-hard penis down the length of her body, kneading her buttocks with authoritative hands. She lay hot and blissfully helpless beneath his grip.

He thrust himself hard and deep inside of her, plowing into her with a relentless rhythm, filling her with wave after wave of consuming fire.

They made love with all the ardor of youth, all the freshness of strangers, sharing fantasies until the break of dawn.

"My demon lover." She kissed the curly hairs of his belly moist and sweaty in the morning sunshine. "My dear demon lover. What a splendid idea that was."

Jordan fondled her hair and laughed. "I think I'm going to be muscle-bound for days. Was that really me playing Dracula? Good God. But you're right, darling. It was something else!"

Neither of them ever referred to that night again. In retrospect it was faintly embarrassing. Yet it set the tone for a renewal of old intimacies and easy affection.

The other guests must have presumed them to be lovers or newly-weds, and for the first few days left them spectacularly alone. The Croys swam, hiked, spent long leisurely hours exploring the countryside on horseback. But before the week was out, their natural sociability began to surface.

Among their new acquaintances was a short, chunky property developer from Tucson. Bernie Gross was, in fact, a transplanted Brooklynite, but he viewed the Sun Belt with the proprietary fervor of a convert. He and Jordan hit it off immediately, two men with a talent for instant friendship.

"You gotta do it, Jordan." Bernie clapped an arm around him. "You gotta shuck that city dust off you and move out to where the earth people are. This is where it's happening—the land of opportunity. Some of the fastest-rising property values in the country. A regular building bonanza. You know, a good real-estate lawyer could make a bundle. How about it?"

"You'd have to talk to the boss." Jordan laughed, but he was flattered.

"Well, boss?" Bernie turned to Dasha.

"I'm afraid I'm a city girl." She smiled.

"That's what my wife said," Bernie countered. "And now I couldn't drag her back."

Of course it was a pipe dream, but it was one that Jordan responded to, especially at the end of a particularly blissful day.

"Wouldn't it be great," he fantasized as they stood on the terrace watching the red sun tumble down behind the horizon, "to move out here with the kids? Real air, real country, real people."

For a moment she fell in with his dream. But only for a moment. It was too distant from any world she understood. "Real mosquitoes, too," she said. "Let's go in, sweetheart, before I get eaten alive. You know me and mosquitoes. Besides which," she recalled, "tonight is when the Kim program is being broadcast. I imagine you'd want to see it after all this talk."

"Yeah . . . sure." He turned away from the sunset reluctantly. "That's why we came out to Arizona, to watch a television show."

They sat up in bed eating tacos and drinking margaritas while the show unrolled on the screen. There were no surprises. Except, Dasha discovered, the surprise that it was still as powerful and moving as when she had seen it the first time.

"What do you think, darling?" she asked Jordan, when it was over.

"Very disturbing stuff." He shook his head. "Poor David!"

"I did the right thing, then?"

"What do you mean?" Her question puzzled him.

"I mean, in recommending that First go ahead and broadcast it."

"Why, Dasha, you're making it sound as if it were *your* decision. Like you personally are responsible."

"Well, in a way that's true, you know. If I had argued forcefully against it, that program would never have seen the light of day. But I urged First to go ahead."

"Okay, if you say so." But Jordan was patently unconvinced. She shook off a quick flash of annoyance, sensing that Jordan begrudged her any claim to power. But it wasn't worth arguing about—not on this second honeymoon, with another full week of pleasure yet to come.

"I'm glad you enjoyed it." She nestled into his arms. "What do you want to do tomorrow, darling? You want to take that trail that goes down to the Indian reservation?"

They spent the rest of the evening making plans.

They were breakfasting on the sun deck—western omelette, home fries, fresh watermelon juice—when the waitress came over trailing a phone.

"A long-distance call for you, Mrs. Croy. Shall I plug it in here?" And the next thing she knew, Frank's voice was bridging the two thousand miles.

"Pick a number, Dasha, any number."

She clapped a hand over the phone and mouthed to Jordan, "Kim's suing."

"I can't begin to guess, Frank. You tell me."

"How does one billion dollars hit you?"

For a moment she thought she'd misheard. Or maybe Frank had a head cold. "Is that with a 'b' as in bilious or with an 'm' as in mother?"

Frank laughed appreciatively. "That's right. The mother's suing for a billion. And you'll never guess on what grounds."

"Libel? Slander? Invasion of privacy?"

"Guess again."

"Double parking? Practicing ukulele without a license? Come on, Frank, give. I'm running out of complaints."

"Right, Dasha. Here goes. The nature of the charge is 'false light.' "

The words meant nothing to her. "False light," she repeated. "Is that something new in legal parlance or did I sleep through the pertinent class back in law school?"

"False light," Frank explained, "is nothing to do with either slander or libel. It consists in putting one man's words or thoughts or ideas into somebody else's mouth—in this case, an actor's—thereby placing that person in a false light. Kim's contention is, you see, that his life is his exclusive property . . . his most precious commodity. He owns it, therefore no one else has the right to portray him, let alone exploit him for commercial gain. The fact that the show was entitled 'The Elijah Kim Story' merely proves his point, he contends. We've robbed him of himself. Ergo, he'd like your basic quarter billion dollars for placing him in a false light, plus triple that in punitive damages."

"Very cute," Dasha said, "but I can't think it will stand up. Why, if you carry that thesis to the logical extreme, you couldn't do a Bette Davis imitation at a block party. And yet"—she began to envision pitfalls, play devil's advocate—"and yet, in a sense, the program did preempt his own story. Say Kim was planning to write his autobiography or produce his own movie, in that case he could have a legitimate grievance. Am I crazy, Frank, or is there really a case to answer to?"

"Could be. This false light idea has been kicking around quite a bit lately, although it's yet to be fully tested in court. And if you're crazy, so is Roger Hazzard. Kim's retained him, and you know what that means."

Indeed she did. Roger "The Bomber" Hazzard was probably the toughest, meanest, *winningest* attorney in the country—F. Lee Bailey and "Racehorse" Haines notwithstanding. Juries adored him, judges respected him, opposition lawyers treated him with fear and loathing. He was, by all accounts, a master of invective, a superb tactician, a man capable of inflicting sudden death in the courtroom. Hence the nickname.

She felt a frisson of excitement. To engage in hand-to-hand combat with the Bomber was an opportunity not to be missed.

First Amendment. Her mind was already engaged in scanning the possibilities. It would have to be a First Amendment defense. Definitely. Cut through the "false light" verbiage, and those were the issues at stake: freedom of the press, fair comment pitted against a man's right to control how the world perceived him. *Whose life is it anyway?* That's what Kim was saying, in effect. It was a fascinating challenge and she could hardly wait to plow into trial preparations with both hands. Already her pulse was racing in anticipation, the blood rushing to her brain.

"Let's see . . . There was *Sullivan versus The New York Times, Miami Herald versus Tornillo.*" The cases, the precedents began unfolding even as Frank was talking on the phone.

"So," he concluded, "while I hate to spoil your fun"—*Spoil her fun! This was the fun*—"I'm afraid we need you back at the office right away. How soon can you get here?"

She began calculating: a half-hour to pack, two-hour drive to Phoenix, check the desk and see about afternoon flights . . . She turned to Jordan.

Beneath his tan, he was pale with rage, his hand gripping the coffee mug so hard the knuckles showed white. Dasha made a massive effort to control her emotions, to disguise the longing she felt to be back in the office.

"I'm sorry, Frank, today's out of the question." Each word cost her. "My husband and I have plans for the day. I'll try to get out tomorrow."

"Don't sit on it."

"I'll see you tomorrow, Frank."

She hung up the phone. "I'm sorry about that, darling . . . " But Jordan interrupted her, tight-lipped: "Let's go riding."

They saddled up, with Dasha as usual picking the gentlest, sturdiest horse she could find. Within the hour they had started down the unfamiliar trail that led to an ancient Hopi burying ground. The path was winding and strewn with rubble and sharp rocks. This once, Jordan showed no interest in reining in and making allowances for Dasha's lack of expertise. For a city boy, he was a surprisingly good horseman. He had a natural feeling for the pace and temperament of his mounts and they responded in kind. To Dasha, they remained alien creatures.

Now on this bleak and lonely trail, he broke into a gallop, widening the gap between them. "Hey, Jordan," she tried calling to him. "Hold your horses. What is this, some kind of game?" But he rode on without looking back. And as he vanished momentarily behind an outcropping of cactus, all the carefully nurtured warmth, all the rekindled intimacy of their second honeymoon vanished with him.

He was trying to wear her out, she decided angrily. Show her up. Well, she was damned if she was going to break a leg in this godforsaken terrain trying to out-macho him on horseback. She continued on the path at a measured pace, not catching up with him till well past noon. He had found a patch of shade beneath a clump of piñon trees and had spread out their lunch on a picnic cloth.

Dasha dismounted and tied up her horse.

"Would you like a barbecued chicken leg?" he asked. "They're delicious."

"I'd like an explanation"—she sat down on the ground beside him —"as to why you rode off and left me behind."

He munched on the chicken leg, then gave her a cryptic smile. "Come on, Dasha, you're a big girl now. You don't need me to look after you." Then he went back to his lunch in silence. She watched him finish the chicken, lick his fingers with a show of gusto, then go to work on the potato salad.

"I had hoped," she said finally "that our last twenty-four hours here could have been as pleasant as the rest of the vacation."

Jordan opened a beer with exasperating deliberation.

"It may be *your* last twenty-four hours here, but my vacation doesn't end until Sunday. How about a beer while it's still cold?"

"If you want to stay"—she tried to keep an even tone—"by all means do. There's no reason your vacation should be ruined."

"None at all."

"In which case, perhaps I'd best be getting back to the hotel. Maybe I can still get a plane out tonight."

She rose with a heavy heart and had begun to untie the horse when he sprang up and caught her by the arm.

"Don't go!" He had dropped the sarcasm, the aloof pretense. "Please, Dasha, don't go! Call the office and . . . and opt out."

She looked at him in astonishment. "Are you serious?"

"Dasha, there are fifty lawyers up there who could handle it just as well as you. Experienced trial lawyers. I beg you, don't get any more involved."

"But I have to, Jordie! Don't you see? I've been handed a one-in-a-million chance to be part of a case that might make legal history. What's the matter?" Jordan's anguish was contagious. "Do you think we're going to lose?"

"Winning, losing . . . " He shook his head in despair. "Is that what everything comes down to? I wasn't thinking about the case, Dasha. And I don't care who wins or loses. I was thinking about us, our marriage. My God, cases like this eat lawyers alive. It's going to be as hard on me as it will be on you. And what about the kids? They see little enough of you as it is. How about giving them some thought?"

"Believe me, Jordan," Dasha broke in, "they're on my mind constantly in *and* out of the office. Not a day goes by, not a meeting runs overtime but that I don't question my choices, worry if I'm short-changing them. Should I be here, should I be there? Am I missing out on whole chunks of their lives? Am I spreading myself too thin? I wish I had easy answers, but I don't. Maybe if it were some other case, different issues involved, but *this* . . . Jordan"—she gripped his hand fervidly—"this case means so much to me personally. I didn't go looking for it, but now that it's here, I'd never forgive myself if I copped out. I realize it's going to be a sacrifice all around, cut into our private lives. But don't you see . . . don't you see what's at stake?"

"*I* see." He put his arms around her and scoured her face with a disturbing intensity. *"I* see. I only hope *you* do. Now come sit down and have a bit of lunch and we'll both go back to New York tomorrow."

She managed to swallow a few mouthfuls of chicken, and they spent the rest of the afternoon poking through the remains of ancient pueblos as if Slater Blaney and the Reverend Elijah Kim didn't exist.

"Time to go," Jordan said as the sun began lowering. "Saddle up, and I'll race you back to the hotel."

No sooner had she mounted her horse than Jordan was off in an explosion of dust, a clatter of flying rocks. A half-hour later, he was waiting for her at the stables when she arrived covered with dust and sweat.

"Well." He handed her down from the saddle. "It's nice to know there's still something I can beat my wife at."

CHAPTER FIFTEEN

☐ There are certain cases that spark public interest less for the issues than the personalities involved. Patty Hearst was surely more than just another bank robber, another kidnap victim. She was a millionaire's daughter. And the image of Jean Harris standing over the body of the Scarsdale Diet doctor was not to be confused with your routine Saturday night shoot-out, but was perceived as a monumental saga of sex and snobbery.

So, too, the confrontation between the Reverend Kim and FBC instantly triggered an outpouring from the media. *The Billion-Dollar Battle,* the press dubbed the affair. As for the public, Dasha quickly realized they couldn't care less about the fine distinction between the libel laws and the doctrine of "false light." What delighted and provoked was the prospect of two flamboyant figures going at each other's jugulars.

When questioned by a reporter on the matter, Amory First had made a single statement ("I stand by my employees") and refused to be drawn further into the dispute. Privately, however, he had fallen into a low angry simmer. The billion-dollar lawsuit hardly ruffled his feathers; he expected it to be thrown out of court. But the fact that the broadcast had not fulfilled his social ambitions was a source of constant irritation. For all his efforts, he had neither been invited to dine at the White House nor asked to serve on the Presidential Commission. "So much for public service broadcasting," he sneered. "From now on I'll give the peasants what they want." The "First Insights" series was dropped in favor of a sit-com about unmarried mothers.

Elijah Kim, however, showed no such reticence. One could hardly turn on the evening news without seeing "Bomber" Hazzard making some statement on his client's behalf. The day after filing charges at Federal Court in San Francisco, Hazzard called a press conference and announced to the assembled reporters: "When we collect our billion dollars, we plan to spend every penny of it on good works."

The Reverend Kim, he explained, had no interest in amassing worldly goods. He was a simple man who had chosen a simple life. Having God by his side, he asked nothing more for himself. The man's only concern was the health and welfare of American youth, his sole ambition to combat the curse of narcotics that was destroying so many innocent lives. To this end he dreamed of establishing a chain of refuges —"Havens of Help," Hazzard termed them—in the midst of urban ghettos for the cure and rehabilitation of addicts.

"That was some grandstand play," Dasha said to Frank the morning after Hazzard's news conference. "Already the man's managed to bribe just about every prospective juror in the country. Who'd deny those poor ghetto kids a Haven of Help—even if it does come out of our hides? I hope this case isn't going before a jury."

"Tom Hatt thinks it should."

"Yes, I know."

That was a sore spot with Dasha.

As the most experienced of Slater Blaney's trial lawyers, Thomas Hatt automatically took charge of the FBC defense team. "Litigation is war" was his motto. He was a man of monstrous ego who lived for the joy of combat, never happier than when marshaling his troops with the vigor and venom of a Marine Corps general, and you could pay him no higher compliment than to call him a hard-nosed, single-minded bastard.

A long, juicy trial was his definition of fun, and no amount of reasoning—least of all Dasha's—was going to rob him of the thrill of playing to a jury.

Jordan, certainly, found nothing at all thrilling in the Kim case, or its effect on their lives. He thought the notoriety unwarranted, and the fact that his wife played a leading role in the proceedings merely added to his sense of umbrage. His fellow lawyers quizzed him about it constantly. How was Dasha doing? What was the thrust of Slater Blaney strategy? Was it true that FBC was planning to lodge a countersuit?

"I don't know," Jordan would answer frostily. When Robin came home from school one day remarking that her English teacher—of all people—had pumped her for behind-the-scene insights, he was furious. "I will not have this ridiculous case become the sole source of conversation in this household." He forbade any discussion of it at mealtimes.

Yet like Canute unable to turn back the tide, the more he protested, the deeper the waters of controversy swirled about him. He retaliated with a subtle campaign of indirection. The forthcoming trial itself was never mentioned, nor was there any criticism of the hellishly long hours that Dasha was putting in. Instead, Jordan would seize upon some minor household matter, some petty detail gone awry, and build a little prickly edifice about it.

"You wouldn't happen to know where I might find such a thing as a safety pin around this establishment, would you? Not that it's a matter of overweening urgency but Geoff went to school this morning with the top button missing from his jacket and I thought, this cold weather, if perhaps you might tell me where I could locate a safety pin—I might patch it up for tomorrow morning."

"For God's sakes, Jordan." Dasha slammed her papers back into their file and went to fetch her sewing box. "You could sew a button on too, you know."

"Well, of course, Dasha, if you'd just show me how. I don't see what you're all upset about. How could you know Geoff had a button missing? You haven't seen the boy since yesterday evening."

Then there was the business of the sauerbraten.

"Remember that terrific pot roast you used to make?" he asked her one evening when she was reading through a deposition. "Oh, sorry, Dasha, I didn't mean to interrupt."

She looked up briefly. "You have my undivided attention, Jordan. What kind of pot roast?"

"The one made with the vinegar. You used to serve it with red cabbage. What was it called?"

"Sauerbraten."

"Sauerbraten," Jordan sighed. "Delicious. We haven't had that in ages."

"It takes three days to marinate, Jordan, and about six hours to cook. I don't have the time to make sauerbraten."

"Oh, I know!" His apology was fulsome. "I wouldn't dream of

asking you. I just was wondering . . . perhaps if you gave my mother the recipe?"

"It's in *The New York Times Cook Book.*" Dasha returned to her work. "All you have to do is look it up."

"Oh fine. My mother will be delighted."

Two nights later he brought up the sauerbraten again. "I looked in the cookbook and actually there were two recipes. One called for parsnips, the other didn't. Do you remember which one you used to make?"

"No I don't, Jordan."

"Sorry for the interruption. Parsnips . . . parsnips . . . " he murmured. "Are they something like turnips? I wouldn't know what to look for in the supermarket."

"Oh for Chrissakes!" she exploded. "You want the goddam sauerbraten, I'll get you sauerbraten."

"Dasha, I don't want you to fuss."

She didn't answer. Instead, she went to the telephone and called the Heidelberg Rathskeller.

"Do you people deliver?" she asked. "You don't. Oh Lordy me, I'm simply devastated. Do you think you might make an exception just this once? It's terribly important. Please let me explain. You see . . . my husband and I had our wedding dinner at the Rathskeller twenty years ago tonight. We had—I can still remember it—your wonderful, wonderful sauerbraten. And every year on our anniversary we've gone back to your restaurant. And we hoped to this year again. But last month . . . well, you see my husband had a stroke. He's . . . he's partially paralyzed and we don't know if he'll ever walk again. I shouldn't be asking you, but it would mean so much to both of us. You will? Oh you lovely, lovely man! Yes, two orders of sauerbraten, some of your nice red cabbage, and apple strudel. If you just put it in a taxi as soon as possible. . . ." She gave him the address, thanked him effusively, and hung up. "Well, Jordan, it'll be here in twenty minutes."

"That was the most appallingly vulgar display I've ever seen."

"You wanted sauerbraten, you got sauerbraten. So what's the problem? *Now* can I work in peace?"

They had entered a state of undeclared war.

Increasingly, Jordan resented the social demands he felt were made upon him on his wife's behalf. Invitations from Dasha's friends were accepted only under duress and once on the spot, Jordan usually clammed up to the point of being surly. "I have nothing to say to these people." As far as he was concerned, social life began and ended in Crestview. Like old songs, old friends were the best. With people from Dasha's world he was withdrawn, sullen. Life became a progression of awkward evenings.

When the Hunicutts invited them to be their guests at the April in Paris Ball, Jordan flatly refused.

"Joe Sincere" was his term for Frank Hunicutt, uttered in a mix of envy and mockery. From the moment Frank had led him, drunk and dazed, off the bandstand at Southampton, Jordan had harbored a profound dislike for the man. It was bad enough that his wife's boss had the world by the tail. That he was rich, successful, charismatic. Jordan might have forgiven him that much. What was unforgivable was that Jordan had lost face in front of him. That day in Southampton marked the nadir of his self-esteem.

"I am not about to get dressed up in a monkey suit," he now told Dasha, "for the privilege of being patronized by Joe Sincere."

"Well, I can't very well go alone."

"Then find another escort."

"Maybe I will."

Dasha didn't know what to do. She couldn't imagine going to a charity ball alone. That was humiliating. Yet in this instance, she felt relieved that he had opted out.

God only knew what he would do. On unfamiliar turf he was like a time bomb, ticking and dangerous, capable of exploding at any moment. And when she turned down the Hunicutts' invitation claiming pressure of business as an excuse, she realized with a shock that she felt as much relief as regret.

I am ashamed of him. Heaven help me. I'm ashamed of my own husband.

By spring, however, balls and dinner parties were the furthest thing from Dasha's mind, pushed aside by the demands of pre-trial discovery.

"I don't want any surprises at the trial," Tom Hatt reiterated. Every document, every deposition by a witness would have to be obtained, scrutinized, poked for holes well in advance of the court date. To Dasha fell the task of examining and cross-examining dozens upon dozens of witnesses, their every word recorded and transcribed in what amounted to a trial in miniature.

With one or two exceptions they were a rag-tag lot, people who bordered on the bizarre. There were former junkies, psychological orphans with dirty fingernails and earnest eyes. Worse yet, they nearly all lived in the San Francisco area. For months she commuted with such regularity that she came to know all the flight schedules, all the airline menus, even most of the stewardesses by heart. She'd usually fly out on a Wednesday, work through late Friday evening, then catch the red-eye special back, arriving in New York with the dawn.

She kept a permanent room at the Drake with a closet full of suits to spare herself the hours spent packing and unpacking. During those months San Francisco became a second home. Which is to say she saw as little of it as she saw of New York or her family these days.

Life had taken on a hectic, dreamlike quality. Time, space, the world beyond had no importance. The baseball season started. School ended. Roses were coming into bloom. None of it was real. Nothing existed but the case. Nothing mattered but winning it.

Weekends were spent in conference with whatever members of the team were in town. It was a time for planning strategy, synchronizing data, getting the last details into place.

Tom Hatt was in charge of these marathon meetings, with Dasha second in command. Frank Hunicutt rarely attended. He was not a trial lawyer, he insisted. Litigation was Tom Hatt's department. Frank's job was keeping Amory First from blowing up.

"Are we going to win, Tom?" Frank asked when he showed up one Saturday afternoon. "My old man over at Schlock Rock is getting jumpy. He wants an interim report."

Tom answered with a thumbs-up sign, cocky as ever, and Dasha wished she shared his firm optimism. The documentation that Ken Lafferty had given her at the time of the broadcast, his signed releases, the sworn statements that had seemed so solid—all looked less substantial given the character of the people who had made them. Now she was openly apprehensive.

She wanted desperately to share her anxieties with someone she trusted. With Frank. He must have read her mind, for when the meeting broke up, she found him waiting for her by the elevator.

"Are you dashing off somewhere or do you have time for a drink?" he asked.

Saturday night. Robin was away at music camp. Geoff would already be in bed. As for Jordan, he had invited some of his old Crestview friends over for an evening of nickel-dime poker. And when his guests left, he and Dasha would begin another round of war games. That was one virtue of those long hours she put in at the office: They spared her from Jordan's air of wounded sensibility.

"I'd love a drink, Frank. Maybe even two or three or four."

"Right." He shepherded her into the elevator. "Do you think you could manage a bite of dinner? You look thin. I worry about you. Let's pig out at Windows on the World."

Ten minutes later they were ensconced in creamy beige banquettes, nibbling canapés and looking down upon the Jersey coast from a glittering aerie a hundred and four stories high.

"You can practically touch the sky here," Frank remarked. "Even after all these years I'm a sucker for views. I guess that comes of being a small-town boy."

"Funny. I always assumed you were from New York."

"Gloversville, New York," he said. "Population twenty-five thousand. We moved there when I was a kid. My mother thought it would be a good place for me to grow up, its principal virtue being the distance it put between me and my father."

He ordered them both double scotches.

"I thought you didn't drink," she said.

"I never drink on the job. You know, like a trapeze artist or an airline pilot."

She laughed. "But you don't drink at dinner parties either, I notice."

"Dinner parties, my dear Dasha, are also part of the job, as you'll realize when you make partner. However, I'll be delighted to drink with you."

He swallowed his scotch and called for another round. *Whoa there,* she cautioned herself, *you're getting a wee bit high. And so is he. Watch it.*

Nonetheless, it felt achingly good to be here with Frank, relaxed. Basking in his glow. She'd never seen him so unguarded before.

"Confusion to our enemies." He gave the classic pre-trial toast. They clinked glasses and chatted casually for a while. Then he leaned over and, taking her chin in his hand, swiveled her face toward him. His fingers were warm and smooth against her skin.

"What's troubling you, Dasha? And don't tell me 'nothing.' I know you better than that."

My husband, she wanted to say. *My marriage. The fact that I don't even want to go home tonight.* But she didn't say it. She wasn't *that* high, thank God.

"The Kim case, Frank. What else? Honestly, you should see some of these creeps I've been deposing out in California. The thought of putting them on the witness stand gives me the willies. These flakes can't even remember what they had for breakfast, let alone what happened two years ago. Tom Hatt keeps saying not to worry, that they'll be fine, but . . . " She sighed. "I don't know. I haven't got a notion what makes a good witness."

Frank sipped scotch number three and smiled.

"Clarry," he said.

"I'm sorry?" Had he forgotten that it was Dasha by his side?

"My wife. Clarisse. She'd make a good witness, a great witness. I sometimes think she missed her calling. She's a remarkable woman, Clarry is. Everything you'd want going for you on the witness stand. Did you know she has total recall?"

"No I didn't." Dasha giggled.

"It's true. Clarisse can go to a dinner party and tell you ten weeks later exactly what every woman in the room was wearing, the color of her nail polish, the name of her decorator and whether the service was Royal Worcester or Minton. My wife"—he shook his head in admiration—"can tell the difference between sterling and silver plate at a hundred paces. In her next incarnation, she's going to come back as a buyer for Bloomingdale's. No detail of hemline would ever go unremarked. Yes indeed, Clarry would make an excellent witness, except of course she'd never show up in court. You see, everything that has to do with law and lawyers bores her silly." He smiled at Dasha. "Including me."

"Oh come on, Frank." Dasha was astonished at this turn of conversation. "You couldn't possibly bore anyone."

He laughed. "That's sweet of you to say, Dasha, but I have an immense capacity for driving poor Clarisse to distraction. All I have to do is mention the office and she falls into instant coma. 'Oh Frank, that's so dull'—her favorite phrase for the merest mention of business, be it a takeover battle or a lawsuit that's got you with your heart in your mouth. 'Oh Frank, that's so dull.' Yes, I'm afraid I bore my wife to tears . . . "

And she bores me.

Frank didn't have to finish the sentence. Dasha read it in his eyes. Perceived the emptiness that lay behind the facade of that Southampton domesticity. So many years of marriage, so many children. Was that what it always came down to. Boredom? Fatigue? A polite charade one performed out of habit? She wanted to reach out, take his hand, add her own confession to his. But Frank suddenly averted his eyes.

"I bore my wife and now I'm afraid I'm boring you." He waved for the waiter, who came bearing French bread in a silver bowl. "Now, let's order everything good on the menu. After all, I can't send you home to your husband on an empty stomach." He called for pâté, oysters, salmon mousse, roast squab, wild duckling, all to be washed down with a superb Montrachet.

"I have gargantuan appetites." He surveyed the riches of the table. "I hope you realize that."

"For food?"

"For everything." He laughed, and placed a succulent piece of duckling on her plate.

Unbeckoned, the image of Clarisse Hunicutt—spotless, delicate, aloof—flashed through Dasha's mind. Another image, too, of Frank smashing tennis balls into the nocturnal sea. At the time she had seen his gesture as one of exuberance. Now she recognized it as a venting of frustration.

For all that Dasha cared for Frank, for all that she admired and respected him, there had been until tonight a measure of awe in her emotions. His life was too grand, too distanced from her. Only tonight did she glimpse him as vulnerable. The evidence lay before her on the table, in the very lavishness of the dishes arrayed.

What pleasure he had taken in ordering the richest, most expensive items on the menu. In ordering far more than they could possibly eat. It was the pleasure, she realized, of someone for whom enough would never be as good as a feast. The pleasure of a poor boy grown rich.

Her heart went out to him. Now that Frank had breached the wall between them, she felt she could speak openly. "You're endlessly surprising. You know, I never would have figured you as a kid from Gloversville."

"What would you have figured me for?"

"A Social Register type. A rich man's son."

"My father was a rich man's son," he replied. "Not me. He was the perfect model of an Old New York blueblood. He never worked a day in his life. By the time I was born, he'd pissed away a million dollars, and a few years later, he forfeited whatever was left for love."

"That sounds romantic." Dasha was intrigued.

"No, only foolish."

At the threshold of middle age, Frank Hunicutt Senior had fallen in love with a married woman. "Now Sara wasn't some little bit of nooky, mind you, hardly your proverbial chorus girl. She could have been a clone of my mother. Same background, same age. They even sounded alike, with their Chapin School accents. I can't believe he could have told them apart in the dark."

The two besieged lovers ran off to the South of France, then returned to New York, where they married. For as long as she lived, Frank's mother never got over her husband's desertion. "Her whole life, her whole excuse for existence was focused on this sense of injustice. Her greatest hope in life was that my father would live to rue the day. She made a career out of bitterness. Bitterness and booze. As for him, he seemed neither more nor less happy than he had been when he was married to her."

Love, Frank seemed to be saying, *romantic love is the sorriest of all delusions.*

Frank had gone to Groton on scholarship, worked his way through Harvard, and when he came to New York—an ambitious young lawyer —joined Slater Blaney as an associate. "I wanted to be the best in my field, make waves, have lots of influence. It was that simple."

Dasha felt a chill pass over her. The sentiments were familiar. Jordan had voiced them himself years ago.

"It was not my plan to marry the boss's daughter, odd as that may sound," Frank continued. "I didn't plan to marry at all, given the example of my parents' domestic life. But she was enchanting. You can't imagine how lovely Clarry was at twenty. And timid, like a fawn. What they used to call 'a nice girl.' I don't know if they have them any more. And I thought I'd go crazy if I didn't go to bed with her. Only I didn't put it so crassly then . . . not even to myself."

To a young man in love, her every shy silence appeared to be a well of profundity, her every little mannerism the epitome of charm. And she *was* charming. Charming then, charming still. She was the girl he had married years ago—pretty, sweet, kind to the dogs and servants.

Frank stopped abruptly.

"If you'll excuse me, Dasha, I see an old client of mine waving to me over there. Someone I've been trying to lure back into the firm. Can you spare me for five minutes while I pop over and say hello?"

She watched him walk across the room, then seat himself beside a heavyset man in banker's pinstripes. A moment later the two of them were deep in conversation. That was the Frank she knew, the office persona, making rain whenever the occasion presented.

She thought of the private Frank. What he'd said—and what he'd left unsaid. Clarisse and Frank. She and Jordan. That crazy intoxication of young love. That passionate belief that what you wanted at twenty you would want forever.

But life wasn't like that. People changed. They grew. And sometimes they outgrew each other. For all the sterling intentions of your wedding day, you couldn't sustain that state of emotional heat, couldn't preserve it like an insect in amber.

Yet what did you do with all those years of marriage, all that equity tied up in children and habit and memories?

How did you fill the emptiness?

For Frank, the answer was pretty stewardesses with rumpled hair. For Dasha, the Kim case. There had to be something more.

She wanted—oh God! not longer and longer hours in the office, but that indefinable "something more." No. Not something more. *Someone* more. Someone to whom she could entrust every thought, confide every anxiety. A partner. A true life partner with whom she could share her work, her deepest aspirations. Strong, unjudgmental, loving. Yes, loving. Ardent. Someone who would bury her with the act of physical love. Possess her totally in mind and body.

Across the room Frank caught her eye and smiled. In his smile she read a warmth, a yearning. He was trying to break out of the conversation, but the elder man had him pinioned.

Dasha drained her glass of the last golden bead of Montrachet.

Frank. Dasha and Frank.

How blind she had been not to recognize the absolute inevitability of Dasha and Frank. Every minute, every day of the last two years had been leading to this. Jordan had recognized it that day at the pool. Miranda had sensed it in the office. Only Dasha had not perceived it until now. They would be lovers. They would be lovers before this night was done.

The waiter came, refilled her glass. In a fevered flush, she looked over again to the banker's table. *Come. Come to me now.*

As if psychic, Frank rose to take his leave. A recessed spotlight caught the burnished glow of his hair, outlined the massive shoulders, carved his profile in strong sensuous strokes. She felt her heart turn over, her nipples tauten.

Come to me.

He came to her. Sat down by her side.

"Frank." Her voice sounded distant, disembodied; in that moment their eyes met. Her mouth was too dry to say anything else. Instead, she placed her hand on his lips.

I can read your mind, Frank. Can you read mine?

He sat perfectly still, eyes fixed on hers. Then he kissed her fingers. And then, very very slowly, Frank shook his head.

No.

Nothing had been said. Nothing had happened. Except in Dasha's heart.

"I'm sorry." He turned his head and signaled the waiter for the bill. "I'm afraid I've had rather too much to drink tonight, Dasha. And perhaps you have, too. If I've said too much, perhaps you'll forget it. What time is it, ten-thirty? I have a car coming around at eleven to drive me to the Hamptons. May I drop you off at home?"

"No, Frank." She swallowed down the pain in her throat. "I'll be fine in a cab. I really . . . I really have to get going. Thanks for dinner."

"Perhaps some other time."

"Perhaps."

Why, she pondered in the cab ride home, why had he backed off from such a clear invitation? Was she less attractive, less interesting than an airline stewardess?

But of course Dasha knew the answer. It was precisely that she was not a stewardess. She was Dasha Croy, his indispensable right hand, his heir apparent. Nothing between them could ever be casual. Nothing could ever be so simple as a drunken roll in the hay.

Because *that,* she realized, was what tonight would have been. And he was right in turning her down. "Perhaps some other time," he had said. Perhaps never.

Dammit.

She rolled down the window and let the night air cool her face. Sober her up. She was still tipsy. Tipsy, lonely, aching with disappointment. She couldn't believe she could desire a man so much.

"Driver, will you take me twice around the park before letting me off?"

By the time she got home, the ache had quietened to a dull throb.

The poker game was just breaking up as she walked in the door. Jordan was busy emptying ashtrays and putting away the chips. In the hall she bumped into one of their old cronies from Crestview.

"Hi, Randy. How's Lorna, the kids?"

"Fine. You?"

"Not too bad." She helped him on with his coat.

"I hear you're working on that big legal case. What's he like, by the way?"

"Who?"

"The nutso preacher. Is it true that he gets to sleep with all the girls?"

"I wouldn't know, Randy. Never met the man." She was conscious of Jordan standing in the doorway. "I'm afraid I'm just a laborer in the vineyards. Goodnight."

She opened a window. The air was thick with tobacco smoke.

"How was the game, Jordan? How'd you do?"

"Pretty good. Won twenty bucks, give or take. If you're hungry, Dasha, there are some salami sandwiches in the refrigerator. Or have you eaten already?"

"Yes, I've eaten. I had dinner with . . . "

With Joe Sincere. Christ, that was all he'd need to hear.

"We had dinner sent into the conference room," she muttered.

"Booze, too, by the smell of it. You reek like a tavern."

"Yeah, well . . . All work and no play. Isn't that what they say?"

She looked at him and thought of Frank.

Two poor boys who had become lawyers. Two self-made men. The difference was in what they had made of themselves.

"If you don't mind, Jordan, I'll turn in now. I'm pretty tired."

"You go ahead. I'll clean up in here."

Through a leaden sleep the phone jangled in her eardrums.

"Goddam." Jordan stirred beside her. "Who calls at six on a Sunday morning? Gotta be your office. No one else would have the nerve."

She picked up the phone. A woman's voice. Someone crying, pleading in a Spanish-accented English.

"It's for you, Jordan." She handed him the phone.

"Yes," he was saying. "It's Sunday . . . I see, I see." He gave a heartfelt sigh. "I'll be there within the hour."

"What's up, Jordan?"

"Client." He got out of bed and began pulling on his shorts.

"At six A.M. Sunday? Must be a pretty important client."

"Woman I negotiated a lease for a couple of years back. Nice lady, a Cuban refugee. She runs a coffee shop over on Amsterdam."

"What's the emergency? Her lease just expire?"

"Don't be a smartass. As it happens, her son was arrested for rape a few minutes ago. I told her I'd be down there right away. Could you fix me a cup of coffee before I leave?"

"How come she called you?" Dasha frowned.

"Because I'm her lawyer, that's how come."

"But, Jordan . . . " she protested.

"Will you make me a lousy coffee or do I have to do it myself?" She went into the kitchen and turned on the coffeemaker while he ran an electric razor over last night's beard.

"I hope," she said when he sat down at the table, "that you're not going to get personally involved in it. Rape." She shuddered. "It sounds so ugly. Why don't you call up Bob Rubinoff right now and let him handle it? He does all your criminal stuff, doesn't he?"

"What's the matter, Dasha. Do you feel I'm not competent?" Jordan's voice took on a dark edge. "I passed the same courses at law school as everyone else. I qualified in the same bar exam."

"It's not a question of competence," she ventured. "Just practical experience, background. I mean, you've really never done any criminal law, just like I've never done any real estate. We all have our specialties. Honestly, Jordan, don't you think it would be better all around if . . ."

"That does it!" Jordan slammed his mug down on the counter. Hot coffee splattered all over the tiles. "For years, for *years* you've done nothing but bitch about how I let my career languish in the backwater. Step up. Be bold. Go for it! That's all I ever heard from you, and now when I do move out beyond the beaten path, you have the incredible gall to stand back and belittle me! Why? You think I'm such a slob because I don't have million-dollar clients? Well, this poor Romero kid is just as much a human being as Amory First, and just as entitled to a defense. More so, I venture. Jesus, Amory First has raped the whole American public!"

"This is a ridiculous conversation!" She was trembling with rage. "And you're talking like a fool."

"Like a fool, huh?" Jordan began to shout. "Well, let me tell you, I'm sick and tired of sucking hind tit around here. Hearing about *your* cases, *your* precious clients. You think you're the only one who knows anything about the law and I should be grateful for the privilege of having married you. I'm every bit the lawyer you are, Dasha. A damn sight better, in fact. When we were in law school, I mopped the floor with you as I recall. My God, you couldn't even string two words together in a moot-court proceeding. You were pathetic! So much for Dasha Croy, the lady hotshot."

"I *let* you win." The words spewed out in an angry hiss, said and gone forever before she could call them back. But Jordan, white with anger, hadn't heard—thank God! Or if he had, then he didn't acknowledge.

"You conduct your career and I'll conduct mine!" He snatched a jacket and headed for the door. "Today I'm the one who works all day Sunday and you can damn well baby-sit for a change!"

He slammed the front door with such violence, the coffeepot slid off the counter and hit the floor with the impact of a bomb.

"Oh God!" Dasha stood, her fists bunched with fury, surveying the wreckage around her. "You stupid son of a bitch!"

Pulling herself together with a massive effort, she went to fetch a dustpan from the hallway broom closet. Then she saw him.

Geoff.

He was standing at the pantry door in his pajamas. Silent. Stricken. How much had he heard?

"Geoff!" she cried and ran to throw her arms around him, but he fled her embrace like a streak of quicksilver and darted down the hall.

"Geoff . . . you don't understand. It wasn't really what it seemed."

He froze for a second before the door of his room. His eyes were black, blazing.

"I hate you," he whispered. "I *hate* you!" Then he ran inside the room and shut the door in her face.

"Please." Dasha pounded at the door. "Please, let me in, Geoff. I beg of you . . . let me explain."

The key turned in the lock.

She pounded for what seemed an eternity. Pleaded. Promised. Threatened. Cajoled. Then dragged herself back to the kitchen. Broken glass lay everywhere. The coffeepot had fragmented into a thousand pieces. Shattered. Destroyed. Like family happiness.

She folded her arms on the wooden tabletop and wept.

CHAPTER SIXTEEN

☐ Two weeks before the Kim trial was scheduled to open in San Francisco, Blagden Geere called Dasha into his office and, over a cup of Earl Grey tea, blandly announced that he had decided to take over the case himself.

His decision left her speechless. The assignment was one that would drain the life's blood out of a man half his age and Blagden Geere was eighty, born with the century, as he occasionally remarked. The march of years had dulled the edge of his brilliance, played hide-and-seek with his memory. He sometimes nodded off in mid-sentence. For all his ancient victories, the old gentleman was no more capable of mounting the FBC defense than he was of running the marathon.

Yet to Dasha's chagrin, his mind was made up, the rheumy old eyes bright with anticipation. "It will be," he told her, "my last case. I will end my career in a blaze of glory."

Dasha made her escape and minutes later burst in unannounced on the Monday meeting of the senior partners. Frank, Tom, Porter, J.J.—they were almost all present, thank heavens.

"Gentlemen," she said breathlessly, "I know you'll forgive the intrusion but—" She was halfway through her piece when Tom Hatt broke in with "Disaster. He'll be a laughingstock . . . "

"And so will Slater Blaney." Porter Collins stepped in. "He's got to be stopped before this goes further."

But deflecting a senior partner was more easily said than done.

Especially when that partner owned the biggest single chunk of the action. There were rules, rights. No senior could be retired against his will, be he blind, deaf, dumb, or senile. "The firm looks after its own" was one of Slater Blaney's proudest boasts, though now it seemed more a matter of the firm looking after the infirm.

"But surely," Porter said, "the old boy will listen to reason."

"With all due respect," Dasha offered, "I don't think reason is going to obtain. His heart is set on it."

A ripple of alarm ran through the room. "Jesus," Tom Hatt groaned. "How do we break the news to Amory Fist that we've just entrusted his billion-dollar defense to Rip Van Winkle?"

"Now, now," Frank soothed. "I'm sure Blagden can be talked round."

"Dasha says the man won't be reasoned with."

"Who said anything about reason! Is he in his office now?" Frank turned to Dasha. "Fine! Then come along with me and don't say anything. Just follow my lead and we'll play it by ear."

Five minutes later they were at his door.

"Franklin." The old man held out his hand. "What a pleasure to see you."

"And what a pleasure to see you, Blagden." Frank pumped his hand with genuine warmth. "Dasha just told me the splendid news about your taking over the defense of the Kim case. We're all just delighted."

She watched in astonishment as Frank continued buttering the old man up. Lord only knew what he had in mind. Now Frank was asking him if he planned to use some of the techniques he had employed in his historic cases: in the the old South, in Washington, in Nuremberg . . .

As if on cue, Blagden took off on a nonstop voyage into the past. Names, dates, ancient memories ran together until despite herself Dasha's eyes glazed over. As for Frank, he was listening with every show of respect. "Yes." "Oh really?" "You were absolutely right, Blagden."

When Geere finally ran out of steam, Frank was looking at him with an expression of pure rapture.

"Listening to you, Blagden"—he shook his head in wonder—"is like listening to history come alive. The history of this country. The history of Slater Blaney, too, and you could say in many ways they're one and the same. It's a shame really that no one has ever written an official history of the firm. It would be such an inspiration for young lawyers like Dasha here to understand the Slater Blaney heritage. General readers, too, I would think. I was having dinner the other night with Alfred Knopf—you know, the publisher?—and he was remarking the same thing. In fact, I planned to bring the matter up at the next committee meeting."

"What a good idea!" Geere had popped to attention.

"I'm so glad you think so, Blagden. What I was planning was, we'd hire a ghost writer, some clever lad who's good with words . . . In fact, maybe when the Kim case is over, you could spare him a few hours of your time . . ."

But Blagden Geere had stopped listening halfway through Frank's speech.

"A *ghost* writer!" He was incredulous. "You would turn this firm's history over to a paid ghost writer? A commercial hack? What absolute rubbish. No outsider could ever write the Slater Blaney story. And damn few insiders, for that matter. Nobody knows the firm the way I do. Fifty years at the heart of it, Frank. Fifty years of Slater Blaney. That's a pretty good title, don't you think? *Fifty Years of Slater Blaney.* Or maybe *Slater Blaney: The First Half Century.*"

"I prefer the second," Frank said. "I think it shows the story isn't over. That the past is prologue."

"Yes." Geere nodded. "You may be right. You know, Frank"—his voice grew confidential—"nobody can write that book but me."

"I know, Blagden, but"—Frank shrugged—"you're needed too much on the Kim case. And for all we know that might take another year. No, no, we'll just find ourselves a competent ghost writer . . ."

"You'll do no such thing!" Geere protested and spent the next ten minutes arguing Frank down. "Why this book, this history would be the capstone of my career." Before her eyes, Dasha could see Geere expanding with pride and purpose. He glowed with happiness. "The very capstone! Franklin, my boy, I hate to overrule you but seniority has its perks. As for you, my dear"—he turned to her with a glorious smile—"I'm afraid you'll have to soldier along without me on the Kim case. Now, now," he cautioned. "Don't cry."

But the tears in her eyes were genuine. Frank had done it. He had saved the day. He had saved the case. Above all, with his exquisite tact, his sensibility, he had saved the pride of a grand old man.

"You were wonderful," she said the moment they were out in the corridor. "You were simply wonderful."

What she really meant was *I love you, Frank.*

"I love you, Dasha," Jordan said. "In spite of that godawful scene last month, in spite of all the ghastly things we've said to each other, I still love you, Dasha. And I can't have you going away tomorrow with everything hanging between us this way. I want to know: Are we going to stay married or aren't we?"

"This isn't the time." She paused in her packing. "I don't think I can handle it right now. Not with what looks like a two-month stint in San Francisco staring me in the face. You know, Jordan, maybe we should think of my going away as a trial separation. Use the time to see how it works, whether we can manage without each other."

"And the children? Will it be a trial separation for them, too?"

"Oh Jordan!" She was sick at heart. "I'll call home every day. Come to New York whenever I can. I told you that."

"Did Geoff say anything to you about wanting to go to boarding school?"

"No!" Dasha sat down on the bed in astonishment. "Although he hardly ever says anything to me, period. But this is the first I've heard about his wanting to go away. What reason did he give?"

"Oh, the usual. He'd like to live in the country, maybe even keep a pony. He keeps saying it would be fun to sleep in the dorms. Make lots of new friends."

"Plus which, he'd have gotten away from me," she cried out. "That's it, isn't it?"

"No, Dasha. Geoff never said any such thing."

He didn't have to, she thought. His resentment was tangible, as stinging as a door slammed in the face. Or a blow aimed directly at the heart.

From the moment he had witnessed that ghastly Sunday morning scene, he had done his best to avoid her.

A week passed before he even spoke to her, a week during which he looked only to Jordan and his sister for his needs. And when Dasha did, finally, reestablish conversation, he managed to confine it to the most neutral topics. His guard was always up, and she found it virtually impossible to make eye contact with him.

She took him to see a highly recommended psychotherapist, a warm and grandmotherly woman whom she thought he would adore, but after three visits he refused to go back.

"There's really no point," Dr. Hirsch said, "in trying to force him to come here against his will. I'm afraid that would be counterproductive."

"But what can I do?" Dasha wept. "There must be something. We were so close when he was a baby, I could practically read his mind. But now he shuts me out. You know what he does when I try to get close to him? He puts on his Sony Walkman, rock music I suppose, and then he pretends he can't hear me talking . . . He loves horses"—Dasha honked into a tissue—"did he tell you that? He's just crazy about animals, so a couple of weeks ago I took him out to Belmont—just the two of us—so he could see some really beautiful horses. I thought it would be a marvelous treat. We went to the clubhouse, had a lovely lunch, and then I told him that if he liked, I'd bet on a horse for him. Any one he wanted. He picked a name, a real long shot. Well, anyhow, I placed a two-dollar bet and damned if the horse didn't come in. So there is Geoff . . . first time in his life at the racetrack and he's just won himself nearly fifty dollars. Terrific, huh? So I say to him, 'Let's go collect your winnings,' and he looks absolutely crestfallen. In fact, he's crying. 'What's the matter?' I ask him. 'What's wrong?' And you know what he said? He said he didn't want the money. He didn't want it because it meant that for his horse to win, all the other horses had to lose. Well, they had feelings, too, didn't they? I tried to explain to him that that's the nature of horse racing. There's only one horse that can come in first. Otherwise there's no sport. And that the horses understand that, too. He got so upset we wound up leaving the track. He's so vulnerable. So terribly vulnerable. And the irony of it is—that was the first substantive conversation we'd had in a month. I don't know"—she started crying again—"I don't know how I can keep from hurting him. What is it, Dr. Hirsch, what is it that he wants of me?"

"I think"—the elder woman looked at her with wise brown eyes —"he wants you to be—ordinary."

Now as she finished packing her bag for the trip, she said to Jordan, "Perhaps Geoff is right. Perhaps boarding school wouldn't be such a bad idea. But one where there's not too much pressure. As soon as I get back from the coast I'll start looking into it."

Everything would have to wait until she came back from the coast. Even life itself.

On the plane to San Francisco, Dasha chose to sit alone. She needed these last few free hours for emotional housekeeping.

Jordan had driven her to the airport and the children had come along for the ride. Even Geoff, now that she was leaving, seemed to draw slightly closer. They had all kissed one another goodbye in the departure lounge with every show of affection and care. They had, in fact, for the first time in months, appeared in public as a loving and united family.

There were nearly a dozen other Slater Blaney people making the trip, but hers was the only family that had come out to the airport, had squeezed out the last moment right up until the time the plane boarded. Once again, Dasha was struck by the very special quality her marriage had always had. The Croys were, first and foremost, a family.

Yet here she was seriously considering whether all those years were about to end.

Life without Jordan? It boggled the imagination.

The sun rises in the East. Paris is the capital of France. Dasha is married to Jordan Croy. For all her adult life those had been equally immutable propositions.

Her upbringing, her values had been shaped around the solidity, the permanance of marriage. Family.

Suppose she decided to leave him. What reason could she give? While divorce courts no longer demanded a string of justifications, Dasha herself did. Not legally. Morally. You didn't destroy a thirteen-year-old marriage on a whim. Not with children involved. Not without some real and unbearable grievance.

And what was her grievance against Jordan? The fact of her success? No. That was *his* grievance against her; that she wanted the chance to be—not a small fish in a big pool, as Jordan had once charged, but a big fish in a big pool. In an ocean.

228

Jordan was right that she worked only for the benefit of the rich and privileged, and that great law was something more than pandering to the wealthy and powerful.

In the past, great law had been the hallmark of Slater Blaney. It was Ralph Slater confronting a Southern lynch mob. It was Bill Blaney framing legislation for Roosevelt. It was Blagden Geere at Nuremberg. Not in recent years, though.

Yet it could be so again. Vital issues were at stake in the Kim case. The freedom of the press. The guarantees of the First Amendment. It would be a privilege, an honor to be part of the winning team that wrote legal history.

But of course Jordan understood that. In fact she suspected it was at the root of his jealousy—the jealousy that was making their life together such a nightmare.

No, she couldn't go on with him. Not the way they'd been living —more like adversaries than like married people. Yet neither could she imagine a life without him.

On her own. The idea was frightening. She had never lived alone. Never been without the love, the structure of a man in her life, be it father or husband. Perhaps if Frank Hunicutt were waiting in the wings . . .

No, she mustn't even permit herself such thoughts. Frank was a married man and she, despite the intensity of her feeling for him, was not a homewrecker. It was just as well he wouldn't be coming out to the trial. Probably as well if she never saw him again. No. That too would be unbearable. As unbearable as her situation with Jordan.

She arrived at San Francisco no closer to a solution than she had been five hours earlier. At the airport a fleet of black Cadillacs was waiting to take them to their hotel.

Tom Hatt indicated that Dasha should join him in his limousine.

"Did you have a pleasant flight, sitting there all by yourself?"

She gave a noncommittal answer about catching up on her sleep.

"Good," he said. "Because from now on only one thing is going to matter to you, be it morning, noon, or night." He drew his body taut like a fighter prepping for the main event. "Winning," he whispered. "Clear your mind of everything else except *winning!*"

IT IS BETTER TO ENTER A TIGER'S MOUTH THAN TO ENTER A COURT OF
LAW. OLD CHINESE PLOVERB. LOVE. GOOD LUCK. FRANK

She walked into the federal courtroom, keyed and buoyant, with Frank's
telegram tucked away in her handbag like a rabbit's foot.

The day before the trial began, Judge Armand Loewenthal had asked
all the participating lawyers to see him in chambers, providing Dasha
with her first good look at Bomber Hazzard.

He was in his fifties but appeared younger from a distance, the skin
taut and smooth as a baby's. Close up, however, she could make out two
curious hairsbreadth scars at the base of his ear. Combat wounds?
Vampire bites? Then it struck her—he'd had his face lifted. Twice.
Son of a bitch! She smothered a smile. And they talked about women's
vanity!

The judge counted heads, then asked: "Have both sides considered
the possibilities of an out-of-court settlement?"

Hatt and Hazzard exchanged glances—two trial lawyers who could
barely wait to get at each other's throats. "It's non-negotiable," one
breathed and the other nodded. The judge looked at them and sighed.

"In which case my next question is, Is there any chance we'll be
finished by Christmas?"

Hazzard adjusted his bow tie. "By Christmas, your honor, do you
mean Christmas 1981 or Christmas 1982?"

Loewenthal made a face. "I'll see you all at ten o'clock tomorrow
morning."

Everything that could be researched in advance already had been, beginning with the judge himself. Firm but fair had been the verdict. Next,
Slater Blaney had hired a team of consultants to work up a computerized
profile of their ideal juror, the kind of person with a built-in anti-Kim
bias. White married female non-professional, came the answer. Between
thirty-five and fifty, middle class, teetotal, preferably with teen-aged
children. "Gee," Dasha said to Tom Hatt when they read the report, "I
could have told you that. The problem is, go find them. According to
the report, your basic all-American apple-pie mom is going the way of
the dinosaur. Frankly, Tom," she reiterated, "I think we should go for
a bench trial, argue the case on its merits, not its emotions. And if you're

dead set on jury trial, at least insist on a change of venue. San Francisco isn't exactly Middle America."

"Rubbish!" Hatt was determined that nothing would rob him of a public forum. He loved the fanfare, the chance to play to the crowds. "People are the same everywhere. Believe me, Dasha, I'll have those jurors weeping into their Kleenexes. It's going to be bleeding hearts all the way."

In fact, it took three full weeks to form a jury, and a very mixed bag it was—youthful and largely blue-jeaned, with not an apple-pie mom among them. Still the research had prepared her for that. What it hadn't prepared her for, what had always been the great imponderable, was the character of Elijah Kim himself.

The first time he appeared in court, she felt herself in the presence of a master. He resembled the actor who had portrayed him on TV insofar as he was tall, bald, and bearded, but in person he exuded a warm, almost folksy quality that had been absent in the broadcast. Kim was fatherly. Neighborly. He greeted each member of the jury with a smile.

For the trial, Kim had abandoned his flowing white robes, turning up each day at the plaintiff's table in soft shirts and the same rumpled tweed suit. His shoes, she noted, needed polishing. It was a nice, albeit calculated, touch. By comparison, the Slater Blaney lawyers looked cold and snobbish in their impeccable East Coast tailoring.

Even Tom Hatt was taken aback. Already, the popularity contest he'd envisioned was threatening to boomerang. Tom had counted on screaming mobs of Kimfolk, courtroom disruptions. But the hysteria never materialized, undoubtedly on Kim's instructions, and the howling crowds that jammed the courthouse steps weren't groupies at all, but newsmen and TV crews, all hungry for the latest tidbit.

"You talk to 'em, Dasha"—Tom Hatt paled the first time he encountered the horde. "You're prettier than I am." Next thing she knew, a microphone was thrust in her face, and she found herself the unofficial spokesperson for their team.

Her misgivings deepened when Kim took the stand.

"I am a simple man," he announced in a rich, earthy baritone. Dasha felt a quiver of apprehension. "A private man. The only thing I have in life that is of value is my story."

And what a story it was, as it unrolled. Emotional dynamite, packed with the drama of crime and punishment, of addiction and triumph, of redemption and rebirth.

Since his conversion, Kim claimed, he had dedicated his life to saving America's troubled youth. To this end he had crisscrossed the country, begging bowl in hand, seeking funds on their behalf. He had even, much as it hurt, encouraged the kids themselves, poor things, to pitch in by selling carnations at airports.

"Kids." Dasha balked at the word. Suddenly, they weren't Kimfolk in his terminology, but helpless kids, soft and vulnerable as her own two children. Instinctively, her mind streaked across three thousand miles.

It was late afternoon in New York. Robin and Geoff should be home from school right now—practicing, doing homework, downing milk and cookies. What if they weren't? What if they were "hanging out" in some unknown place, unsupervised, headed for trouble? Ridiculous, she assuaged her own doubts. They were good, decent children.

So had her nephew David been—good and decent. She repressed a nervous tremor and forced her attention back to the courtroom.

Ever since the broadcast, Kim was testifying, he had been treated like a pariah. Donations had dried up. Corporate grant-givers didn't want to know him. His followers were subjected to abuse. "All because"—his voice trembled with righteous indignation—"FBC implied I am some sort of lunatic, a menace. All because FBC has shown me in a false light."

At last the magic words, powerfully placed. God, the man was a consummate actor, far better than the counterpart who had played him on TV. She had to keep reminding herself Kim was a fraud, a schemer, a multi-millionaire.

"And all I am is a simple man."

In the jury box, a moist-eyed college student blew her nose into a tissue.

The moment court broke, Dasha called home.

"Hi, Mom," Robin answered. "What's up?"

"Just called to say hello." Dasha felt instant relief. "I was thinking about you guys in court today. Everything okay?"

Fine, her daughter assured her. In fact better than fine. Geoff was playing Monopoly, Robin was practicing. Her piano teacher was organizing a little recital on Sunday and Robin was going to play a Mozart sonata. "My first time with a real audience. Of course it's only other kids' parents . . ."

"What time Sunday?" Dasha began a rapid calculation: Take the red-eye special Saturday night, sleep on the plane, arrive in New York in time for breakfast, go to the recital, catch the last flight back on Sunday. With luck it could be done.

"And what do you mean it's only other kids' parents," she now told Robin. "I'm gonna be there too!"

The trip was hectic and totally exhausting, not an awful lot more than "touching base." Nonetheless, it was worth it, even though Tom Hatt had been furious when she turned up bleary-eyed on Monday morning.

"We have all-day meetings here on Sunday, remember? Don't ever go shooting off like that again!"

In fact, the opportunity never arose, for as the trial hit its stride, the pace became relentless. For two solid months her only contact with her family was rushed and fervent phone calls jammed in between the hectic work schedule and the four hours' sleep she permitted herself each night.

Every waking moment that wasn't spent in court was spent in conference—sifting through transcripts, planning tactics, preparing for the next day's onslaught, grappling with the mountain of words. As the parade of witnesses marched up to the stand, Dasha's worst fears were being confirmed.

They were scared, she realized; scared or suborned or simply lame-brained. In any event, they preferred to face the judge's wrath and the threat of perjury charges to whatever vengeance the Reverend Kim might wreak.

One of Dasha's key witnesses, a middle-aged accountant who once had handled Kim's books, disappeared two days before he was due to testify. Hatt engaged a private detective to track him down.

"It looks like your Ira Leitner flew the coop," Tom Hatt broke the news to Dasha.

"He wouldn't do a thing like that," Dasha insisted. "Ira's not a Kimfolk. In fact, he's straight as they come. Something's happened to him. I'd stake my soul on it."

"Yeah . . . well, what happened was an all-expenses paid trip to South America on Wednesday, according to Pan Am. So much for your knowledge of human nature."

Dasha let the slight pass, but inside she was simmering.

Tom Hatt was looking for a scapegoat. He had misjudged the case from the outset, misunderstood the temper of the times, and now was in the market for a fall guy. And who better than Dasha, who had called the shots, right? On the day of Ira Leitner's no-show, it was left to Dasha to face the press.

"What happened to your star witness?" one reporter teased.

"No comment!" Dasha tried to edge her way past.

"Can you amplify that?" It was Katie Evans of the *Chronicle*. She had always been very nice to Dasha.

Dasha forced a smile.

"Absolutely no comment," she amplified.

Jordan called her later that night. "Guess what? I saw you on the Eleven O'Clock News."

"Really?" She was still shaken by the events of the last few days. "How did I look?"

"Poor baby," he commiserated. "You looked absolutely wiped out."

The words were unexceptionable, even sympathetic, but she heard —or imagined—something in his voice. A soft, almost inaudible note of self-satisfaction. *I told you so.*

After the Leitner fiasco, it was all downhill. There were dozens more witnesses, some good, some pathetic, but the tide had turned.

The jury was drowning in a sea of testimony. The sophistication of the issues had long been submerged, and as the trial moved into its final stages, night and day running together without a break, Dasha teetered at the edge of collapse. In the midst of a crowd, she felt isolated. Utterly alone.

Hatt was now openly hostile. Judge Loewenthal coolly contemptuous. Bomber Hazzard took particular pleasure in baiting her. "Girlie," he called her, and when no one was watching, amused himself by winking at her—a broad vulgar wink that might have come from a comic strip.

As for Jordan, three thousand miles distant, he seemed to be taking a subtle pleasure in forecasting disaster.

"You win some, you lose some," he said on the phone. She hung up without replying.

Now, sitting alone in her hotel room, she was more depressed than she had been in years. The recent months had taken a dreadful toll. There had been no break, no laughs, no let-up of pressure. Tomorrow both sides would present their final arguments. The judge would charge the jury. The jurors would withdraw to deliberate. After that, there was nothing more she could do. Except wait. Wait for the worst.

If only there were someone to share the agonies of that long vigil with her. Someone to give her comfort, encouragement. She yearned for respite. For warmth and approval and loving arms around her. She yearned for . . .

"Frank?" It wasn't a greeting. It was a cry for help.

"Is that you, Dasha?" There was crackling on the line. "You're psychic. I was just sitting here in my office thinking of you. How are you?"

"Fine," she answered. God it was wonderful to hear his voice, even with this lousy connection. "Fine," she repeated, then suddenly the months of pent-up emotions overflowed in a cataract of tears. "No, I'm not fine . . . I'm awful. Everything's awful. It's all falling apart before my eyes. Oh, Frank, Frank, it's as if the whole world is out of tune."

There was a brief silence at the other end.

"Hang in there, Dasha," he said softly. "Everything's going to be all right. I'll take the first plane out in the morning."

CHAPTER SEVENTEEN

☐ "North, south, east, west? Where would you like to go?" He folded his arms over the steering wheel of a rented Mercedes, leaned his head forward, and swallowed her whole with his eyes. "Marvelous!" he murmured. "Fantastic bloody marvelous that you and I are finally going to be lovers! My clever beautiful Dasha. Do you know how long I've ached for you?"

They were parked in a narrow side street a few blocks from the courthouse and Dasha could scarcely believe he had come. That he was taking her away. It was all so dreamlike.

Barely an hour earlier he had slipped unnoticed into the rear of the courtroom, miraculously caught her eye as Loewenthal was addressing the jury. Caught *her* eye—no one else's.

"Soon," he formed the word silently. Or perhaps it was "You." What difference did it make? They both meant the same. *Soon you* will be in my arms. Then he raised his forefinger to his lips and left.

She sat quietly until the jury filed out and the courtroom had emptied, the crowds had gone home. There was a great putting away of papers, snapping shut of briefcases. "You want to join us for lunch?" Tom Hatt asked, but she shook her head no. "I'd just like to sit here for a few minutes."

In the empty courtroom he had come to her, folded her into himself with a single sweep of his powerful arms, buried his lips in her hair.

"Poor lamb! It's time you got out of here. I've got a car downstairs. Let's try and avoid the front exit. There are a hundred reporters out there

236

just lying in wait for you. Unless you were planning a press conference?"

"No, no! Is there a back way?"

"There's always a back way." He laughed, and smuggled her through a warren of unfamiliar corridors out into the street. She held her breath until she'd achieved the safety of a car, then let out an enormous sigh, flung her arms around Frank, and kissed him.

"I'm drunk," she said. "Eleven o'clock on a Friday morning and I am drunk with freedom. I feel like a kid out of school . . . "

"The jury won't be back till Monday at the earliest. Even later if we're lucky. Where would you like to go, my darling? Shall I charter a plane and take you to someplace outlandish?"

But she was too excited to think. "Just drive," she said. "Drive. Anywhere. You decide."

They were a half-hour down the coast road before it struck her.

"This is crazy," she said. "I should have gone back to the hotel and packed a bag. I don't have any makeup, any clothes. I can't spend a weekend in a black gabardine suit."

"You won't need any clothes, Dasha."

"Seriously, Frank . . . "

"Okay, we'll stop and get a pair of jeans."

"And some tops."

"Perhaps"—he considered—"perhaps a T-shirt or two."

"And I'll need some underwear."

"No underwear," he laughed softly. "I absolutely draw the line at underwear." He took a hand from the wheel and placed it on her stockinged thigh. "No, darling. I want you naked underneath at all times."

His words, his touch, even the rolling motion of the car—it was all too devastating, too lubricious. She wanted to slide his hand up her thigh. Except he would discover how hungry she was for him. It was indecent. She made an effort to mask her arousal with small talk.

"Where are we going, or is it a secret?"

"No secret." He put his hand back on the wheel. "We're going to the Monterey Peninsula . . . the Big Sur country. Have you ever been there?"

She shook her head, and he laughed again. "What a deprived existence you lead. Here you've just spent three months in California within driving distance of paradise, and all you know is the courthouse and the Drake Hotel."

"What's it like in Monterey?" she asked. "What are the main attractions?"

Already the scenery was changing. Every turn of the road brought a new vista: great groves of redwood, pristine beaches lying empty and seductive in the noonday sun. Had it been summertime and not November, they might have stopped here, walked hand in hand along the ocean, kissed in the surf, made love on the fine white sands. She would have liked that. She had never made love on the beach.

She looked at Frank. His eye was on the road, his lips curled in a half-smile of anticipation. "And what will we do when we get there?" she whispered, certain what his reply would be.

He glanced over to her and grinned.

"In answer to your first question, it's magnificent country, unlike anything back east. The local attractions include a rich and varied bird life, an island where sea lions breed, and an excellent variety of red snapper. That's in answer to your second question. As for your third question: When we get to Monterey, we will find ourselves a very pretty hotel, white clapboard preferably, high on the cliffs overlooking the sea. And then . . . "

"Yes?"

"And then, my darling Dasha, we will make love to each other to the point of utter exhaustion." He pulled off the road for a minute and kissed her throat, the nape of her neck. A dozen small tender kisses.

I want you now, Frank. Here by the side of the road in broad daylight with a thousand cars whizzing by each hour. I want you to make love to me now.

"Let's go." He turned the key in the ignition. "We've got to get you some jeans."

Twenty minutes later they were wandering through a vast roadside shopping center. Huge, unadorned, mercilessly lit with bluish overhead fluorescents. "Wonder-Mart Discount," Frank laughed. "I love the name. They seem to have everything here from kerosene lamps to—ah, there we are. Women's clothes."

He ferried her swiftly across acres of linoleum, weaving in and out among the other shoppers, pausing every now and then to snatch an item from a counter. A tattersall blouse, denim shirts, some sweaters. He held up a skimpy top that read: MY PARENTS WENT TO PEBBLE BEACH AND ALL I GOT WAS THIS LOUSY T-SHIRT. "Love it!" He added it to the heap. "Jeans, jeans— Ah, there they are!" He seized upon a counter stacked high with Levi's and began tearing through the pile.

"Frank," she was laughing. "Let me catch my breath."

"What size are you, ten, twelve?"

"Twelve usually, sometimes fourteen."

"Really?" He gave her rump an affectionate pat. "I would have thought less. Right, then!" He extracted several pairs from the stack. "Here you go!"

He began pulling her in the direction of the fitting rooms. "You better try 'em on, don't you think?"

"Okay, I won't be a minute." She reached to take the clothing, but instead, he had followed her into the tiny dressing room, slipping unnoticed past the guard. Once inside, he closed the door swiftly.

"Fantastic!"

The garments slithered to the floor, and he was standing tall behind her, smiling at their reflection in the three-sided glass, cupping her breasts in his hand. She felt the urgent pressure of his penis against her spine.

"Frank! This is insane."

"Insane? It's marvelous!"

"Well, my God! There may be closed-circuit television in here for all we know . . . "

"In which case," he said, "the store detective is about to witness some truly superior lovemaking. And we will try to be very very quiet."

Given the size of the room, hardly three feet wide, simply undressing was an act of consummate skill. It could only be done one person at a time, one item at a time. Far easier to undress each other in slow, loving stages. At last she stood before him, naked, trembling, under the shadowless fluorescent light while in the distance the Muzak scratched out a string of tunes from *My Fair Lady*. Then she looked into his eyes and saw that she was beautiful.

"Beautiful," he whispered. "But what's this?" He ran a finger down an ancient scar line.

"I had an appendectomy when I was eight."

He was on his knees before her, his hands caressing her breasts, his lips on her flesh. "Sweet scar," he traced its outline in kisses. "Sweet lovely belly." He rubbed his cheek back and forth against the curl of her pubic hair and breathed in her scent. He opened her labia gently with the tip of his tongue, then sliding his hands down her buttocks, pulled her close.

"I think I shall eat you alive. For a start. Beginning right here."

He had names—intimate, erotic, often obscene, always tender—for every part of the body, every act of the flesh. It was almost like making love for the first time, with every caress, every word a discovery. The scent of his skin was different, the taste of his semen. He had a tuft of wiry hair at the base of his spine which surprised her, delighted her. It was so totally unexpected.

And while the Muzak played Strauss and Gershwin and Porter and Kern *ad infinitum,* they explored each other's bodies in the litany of love. Until at last—bathed in sweat, drenched with pleasure, exhausted by the efforts it had taken not to cry out again and again for sheer joy—Dasha felt her legs about to give way.

"I'm going to fall."

"Poor darling." He kissed her hair, then gathered up the clothes. "Yes, I think we've exhausted the possibilities of the Hotel Wonder-Mart."

Despite herself, she giggled. "And they didn't give us enough towels."

They made their way out past an astonished security guard.

"Hey, what are you doing with those clothes, buddy?"

"We'll take them all," Frank replied. "Tell me, do you people accept the American Express Gold Card?"

"Are you all right, darling?" He opened the car door for her. "You look a bit pale."

"I'm fine, Frank. Filthy, sweaty, sticky, but fine." She leaned over and put her lips to his ear. "But you know what I would like?"

"A hot bath?"

"What I would really like," she murmured, "is to find a pretty hotel overlooking the sea at Monterey . . . "

It was Sunday afternoon before they emerged from the hotel room, and by then her life had been changed beyond recognition. She had always thought herself a sensual woman—amorous, uninhibited—but only now did she discover the full measure of her sensuality.

Frank was, she realized, a man of enormous sexual experience, an enthusiastic lover absorbed in all aspects of physical pleasure.

"I always wondered what your nipples would be like," he said. "I had envisioned them a bit darker."

"And when did you envision them?"

"The first day I ever saw you."

"Oh really, Frank." She turned scarlet.

"Yes, really. And do you know that when you're aroused, your left nipple gets slightly firmer than your right one? Don't laugh. It's true." He rubbed his cheek gently across her breasts. Then, as soon as she responded, he pressed her own hands gently against her nipples. "Feel yourself. Can you feel the difference?"

Nothing shocked him, nothing shamed him.

"Nor should it you, darling. Every part of you, inside and out, is full of all kinds of erotic capabilities."

She laughed. "Maybe to you, not to me. Feet, for instance. Why, if anyone even touches the soles of my feet, I jump a mile. They're not erotic. They're just plain ticklish. And as for toes!"

"Why, Dasha," he said. "Feet are incredibly sexy things. They drive me up the wall. Let me show you."

They were lying naked in bed at the time—when were they not? —she was half-upright against the pillow as he spread her legs gently. He put his lips to her, then kissed a liquid path down the inside of her thighs, nuzzling in back of her knees, tasting the hollows of her ankles.

Then, crouching lightly atop her, head to heel, he inserted his tongue between her toes. It was an extraordinary moment—a sexual entry, almost a form of penetration, as he slid his mouth from one to another, devouring them, sucking each one in turn, exploring every minuscule crevice. With the same relentless rhythm his thumb was massaging her clitoris. And with the same rhythm, his testicles lapped against her breast.

Every part of her body responded. Beneath his caresses, toes were no longer toes. They were pleasure points, hardly distinguishable in this sensual miasma from any other part of her body.

After a long sated while, he pulled off her. "Did you like that, darling?"

Her only answer was the softest moan.

"Yes, toes are delicious things." He smiled and laid his head across her belly. "I think next, we'll have to work on your soles."

Then suddenly it was evening, and the light was fading fast.

"Time out." Frank tossed a pair of jeans and a sweater over to where she lay on the bed, languid and satiated. "Let's get some fresh air. A nice brisk walk."

"You're fantastic." She looked at him in adoration. "Where do you get the energy?"

"Same place I get the energy for everything else. Come along, love. Put on those Wonder-Mart duds of yours and we'll go for a stroll along the beach."

She slipped into jeans and the Day-Glo T-shirt, topping it off with a bulky orlon sweater.

"How do I look?"

"Deeply awful," he laughed. "And incredibly sexy. Let's get out of here before I throw you back into bed yet again."

They walked along the beach with only gulls and a passing sandpiper for company. Then when night drew in, they gathered driftwood and lit a fire in a sheltered cove.

"We should have brought hot dogs," Frank said.

"Then we could sit around the fire and tell ghost stories," she answered. "Just like camp. You know, I still can't believe it."

"Can't believe what?"

"I can't believe we're here. I can't believe the things we've done together these past few days. I can't believe how crazy mad I am about you. I have a confession to make, Frank. I've never had a love affair before, and it's very hard for me to be casual about it. I'm not like you that way. You've had a lot of women, haven't you?"

"Do you want me to lie to you? I wouldn't, even if I could. Although I must say Hamburger Heaven was the last place I ever expected to run into a colleague from Slater Blaney. Yes, Dasha, I've known other women. I love women. I love the way they smell and taste, I love the feel of their bodies, the sound of their voices, the texture of their hair. Sometimes, but not too often, I love their minds. Yes, Dasha, I've had affairs and I suppose, by your lights, a lot of them. Yet I can truly say I've never had an affair with anyone like you. Anything like this. I've wanted you from that first day you walked into my office. I remember it vividly. It was a miserable day, gray and rainy, and you were wearing the most boring somber black twill suit, just like an undertaker. And all I could think was: *'The sun just walked in.'* You were so alive, so vital. The moment I saw you, I knew that one day we'd be lovers. We're suited, you and I—you know that, don't you?" He leaned forward and took her face in his hands. "In bed, out of bed, every which way."

"What happens when we get back to New York?" she asked.

"We'll see each other. My God, you don't think this is the end of it? It's just the beginning!"

"And what about . . . " she started to say "Clarisse," but found it hard to articulate the name. She liked Mrs. Hunicutt, liked her tremendously. Suddenly she was acutely conscious of having betrayed her. "And what about your wife? Does she . . . does she have affairs too?" She desperately wanted Frank to say that theirs was an open marriage. Contemporary, uncommitted. That Clarisse had an army of lovers. It would have eased some of the guilt.

"Clarry?" Frank shrugged. "I don't know. It's hardly the kind of question one asks one's wife."

And by his tone, Dasha was certain she did not. But he wouldn't let it go at that.

"This is between us, darling. Clarisse doesn't enter into it. Nobody enters into it except you and me." *After all*—he didn't say it, but the words hung in the air—*you're married, too.*

He changed the subject. "I'm afraid we're going to have to go back to San Francisco in the morning. I spoke to Tom Hatt while you were in the shower. He thinks the jury will be returning quite soon."

"We're going to lose, Frank. I can feel it in my bones. And I feel in large part responsible. Tell me, was I wrong in helping to get that show on the air?"

"No, you were right—both you and First—although you were right for all the wrong reasons."

"What do you mean?"

"You wanted the program shown for moral reasons. First wanted it for personal reasons. But there was only one good reason for that program to have gone on"—he paused to consider his words—"because it made excellent business sense. Amory made a serious mistake in cancel-ing the series. It could have pointed FBC into a whole new direction. Times are changing. People's expectations are more sophisticated than they were when he started in the business. But old Amory, he doesn't change. As a result, he's running the network into the ground. Their stock is falling, their shows are degenerating. And this mania for acquisition is suicidal . . . indiscriminate. . . ."

"In other words, you think First should retire. Most likely he should, but he'll never do it, you know. Not as long as there's breath in his body. Besides, who could ever take his place?"

"*I* could," Frank said softly. "And some day I will . . . some day soon."

She was surprised. "I thought you were so happy at Slater Blaney."

"Happy—but not content."

There was the challenge of FBC, he said. The challenge of taking one of the hundred biggest corporations in America and making it into one of the fifty biggest. He had already determined which divisions were to be sold off, which expanded, mapped out executive shuffles, overseas opportunities.

For a man like him, that challenge was irresistible.

"And you, Dasha." He turned to her in the firelight. "What is it you want? Your secret ambition? I asked you once before and got the usual answer."

She had trouble forcing her mind to the question posed, for at this moment in her life she had no ambition other than being with him, sharing his dreams, basking in his warmth. She would rather have talked love than talked shop. But he was looking at her with an air of expect-ancy, and she fumbled for an appropriate answer.

"It's still the same one, Frank. I'd like to make partner some day."

"Why?"

"*Why?* What an extraordinary question! Well, of course the money would be marvelous. And then . . . " She was temporarily at a loss for words. The office was three thousand miles away. Another planet. "I guess it's that I want to practice law at the top level, I want to serve my clients well, be the best, most skilled advocate I possibly can. I'd like some day to see the firm do more *pro bono* work, get involved in important issues . . . " But even as she spoke, he was shaking his head no.

"Those are rationales, Dasha, not reasons. I'm not impugning your idealism, but there's one word that's been curiously and consistently absent from all your talk of aspirations. Going way back. And that word is 'power.' Never once have I heard you say you want power. I suspect it's a dirty word in your lexicon. Like 'cock'—to use another word that upsets you. At least it did until a couple of days ago. I get the idea you think that they're both of them exclusive male prerogatives."

"Don't try to shock me, Frank." She pulled away from him. "And please don't make fun of me."

"Goddammit!" he roared. "I am not making fun of you. I'm trying to tell you something about yourself. You seem to think there's something shameful about wanting power. Always thrusting that concept away from you. There's something in you, Dasha—what is it, the residue of all those years of housewifery?—that is profoundly ambivalent. I watch you at work and you can act so marvelously self-assured. Yet at other times you have this expression as though you stumbled into the wrong world by mistake. And God forbid you should show naked ambition. Well, let me tell you, darling, there's nothing inherently wrong about being ambitious, wanting to run things, take control. Power isn't male or female, good or evil. It's neutral merchandise. What really matters is how you handle it. And you, I think, would handle power both well and wisely."

"I don't think I am that ambitious, Frank."

"You didn't think you were that sensual, either, until these past few days. I suspect I know you better than you know yourself, so I won't let you off the hook, Dasha. I want you to be all that you can. I always have done. And at the least, I want you to try for it. Try stretching your dreams a mile further, beyond the mere fact of making partner. Try envisioning the next level up. Maybe you'll take over the firm one day. Slater Blaney and Croy. You smile, but some day—why not? And now think a step beyond that . . . "

"To what, Frank?" She stared at him incredulous. "To the president of the Bar Association? To the cabinet? To the Supreme Court?

"Why not?"

"Oh Frank, darling, talk sense!"

"I am talking sense"—he lowered his voice—"but you're not yet ready to listen. You cling to this myth that you're just a garden-variety wife and mother who happens to be gainfully employed. Because to take it that one step beyond, to really face up to your ambitions, that would be . . . what? Unladylike? Unfeminine? A kind of indecent exposure? I'll leave the choice of terms to you. But what it comes down to in your heart of hearts is that you feel women shouldn't want that kind of thing. Like admitting to a sexual perversion. Because you still are sexist, Dasha Croy. But if you can't see where you're heading, I can. Think about it when we're back in New York."

With that he began throwing sand on the embers until the fire was extinguished.

"And when I'm the chairman of the board of FBC," he said in the darkness, "and you're in command at Slater Blaney, I'd like you to be my attorney. It'll be your responsibility, Dasha, to see that I stick to the straight and narrow—to be my upright New England conscience. Just think how much power you'll have over me."

She couldn't tell if he was joking or not.

"In the meanwhile," he concluded, "I'll settle for going back to the room and having lots of wonderful sex."

And he certainly wasn't joking about that.

Late Monday afternoon, a bleary-eyed jury announced that the Reverend Elijah Kim had indeed been portrayed in a false light. They assessed the injury endured as being worth $130 million.

On the courthouse steps, Dasha faced the reporters for what she sincerely hoped was the last time. "We plan to appeal," she said tersely, then escaped to rendezvous with Frank.

The drive back from Monterey earlier that day had been made in cold, gray drizzle.

"Back to reality," Frank said, as they pulled into San Francisco.

"I thought reality was what we had in Monterey," she replied. "Or was that fantasy? I don't think I can tell them apart any more. Does anyone else know you're here, darling?"

"Only Tom Hatt and Amory. I told them I wanted to be here for the grand finale. I think, love"—he drew up in front of her hotel—"it would be prudent if I dropped you off first."

"And when will I see you?" She had the panicky notion that Frank might suddenly vanish in the San Francisco fog as noiselessly as he had arrived.

"Come dine with me tonight. I'm staying at the Fairmont."

Inside at the desk, there was sheaf of messages waiting. *Jordan called. Mr. Croy called. Your husband called. Call home.* There must have been twenty in all.

She flew to her room like one possessed. Incredible. Unforgivable that in three whole days she had given hardly a thought to her husband. Hadn't talked to him . . . talked to the children! God only knew if they were all okay.

She reached him at the office immediately.

"Dasha! Where the hell have you been? I've been phoning you every hour on the hour since Friday afternoon."

"Is everything all right there?" Her voice broke with anxiety.

"Everything's fine, except I've been worried sick about you!"

"I . . . I don't know what to say, Jordan. It was all so tense, so nerve-racking this last week, that when the jury went out, I . . ."

"You what?"

"I just rented a car and drove." The lie stuck in her throat the first time, but with repetition it grew a little easier. "I had to be by myself, don't you understand that? I spent the weekend walking on the beach. I never dreamed you'd be so worried."

"Jesus!" He heaved a sigh of relief. "I damn near called out the cops. How *could* you be so inconsiderate!"

He finally hung up, but not before exacting a promise that she would come home the following morning. "What is there to keep you, now that the trial's over?"

The conversation weighed on her throughout the day, mitigating even the monstrousness of the jury's findings.

She had expected to lose in court, had been geared for it. What she hadn't been prepared for was this burden of guilt. Now, on her way to meet Frank at the Fairmont, she was fighting a losing war with herself.

The honest thing would be to face up to Jordan as soon as she got home. *I've fallen in love. I'm sorry. It's over.* But she couldn't even play the picture in her mind's eye. It was too cruel, too frightening. First, she'd have to discuss it with Frank.

He was entertaining half a dozen guests when she got there, West Coast executives from FBC. "This is my associate, Dasha Croy," he introduced her formally, while the network people clucked about the Kim case, about ratings, about business, about this and interminable that.

"Ah." He rolled his eyes when they finally left. "I thought they'd never go."

"Couldn't you get rid of them?" She was vexed at having their last night together spoiled by a round of political finagling.

"I just did. Now, now, Dasha, don't be cross just because you haven't been fed. I'll order dinner in, if that's all right? By the way, I bought you something this afternoon. Something quite pretty. I hope you like it."

He went into the bedroom and came back bearing an oblong package from Gumps.

She opened it. Inside was a slim black leather case.

"It's very nice," she said. "Is it for makeup or for carrying documents?"

He looked at her, puzzled. "The case isn't the present, darling. The contents are."

Jade. The greenest jade imaginable. A long link-chain necklace, perfectly formed, ending in an oval pendant on which a carved dragon held sway. The dragon had emerald eyes. The workmanship was exquisite.

She stared at it speechless, hardly daring to take it from the case.

"The dragon's eyes are the color of your eyes, Dasha. The interesting thing"—he plucked it lovingly from the box and held it against the light—"is that the entire necklace is carved from a single piece of jade. Jadeite, actually, from Yunnan. The Chinese, you know, considered this particular type of jade the most precious gem. It's supposed to embody the five cardinal virtues—charity, modesty, courage, justice, and wisdom."

"Not fidelity?"

"I don't think that sexual fidelity, assuming that's what you had in mind, ranked very high with the Chinese mandarins. Here, let me put it on you."

The jade felt cool at her throat. His hands felt warm. The dragon nestled in the hollow between her breasts.

"I couldn't accept such a gift, Frank," she said with reluctance. "I would feel like a concubine."

"I'm not trying to *buy* you, darling," he murmured. "I'm trying to please you. Take it. You must. I spent the whole afternoon at Gumps picking it out."

"But where would I wear it? How could I possibly explain it to Jordan?"

She ached to have Frank say, "Tell your husband the truth. Tell him we love each other. Tell him, and I will tell Clarisse." All it would need was that one sign from him, that word of command.

But he let the moment pass. Instead, he traced the path of the jade links and rested his hand on her breast. "Then wear it for me, darling. Wear it only for me."

"And if I don't take it?" Her voice began to tremble. Just as intuitively, her body began to respond. "What then? Will you give it to your wife?"

"If you don't take it," he said, "I'll leave it on the dresser as a tip for the chambermaid. And she'll be the richest chambermaid in California. Now stop all this nonsense, darling, and get into bed. I'll have some dinner sent up to the room."

When the waiter knocked a short while later, Frank went to answer the door, completely naked. He had done that before, in Monterey, and it never ceased to embarrass Dasha.

"Have you no shame, Frank?" she said when he returned.

"Nope."

"No modesty?

"I certainly hope not."

"You know, sometimes I think you're a thoroughly amoral person."

He laughed. "Is that meant as a compliment?"

The following morning she flew back to New York.

"Back," as Jordan put it, "into the bosom of your family."

CHAPTER EIGHTEEN

☐ "You like to take risks."

Those were among the first words Frank had ever spoken to her, and they were proving prophetic.

Once back in New York, the affair rocketed out of control, and Dasha, lost to all discretion, could scarcely believe her own recklessness. It was a shared madness: the element of danger, the constant risk of exposure merely heightening the acuteness of each sensation.

A meeting over at FBC.

There had been twenty people present—lawyers, executives, financial analysts. Across the distance of the conference table, while First himself was speaking, Frank had mouthed, *"I want you. I want you now."* Ten minutes later they were coupling like animals in heat in the control room of a darkened studio.

A bitter night in February.

She had been working late in her study while outside, snow blanketed the city. One room away, Jordan lay sleeping. Then the phone rang.

"What are you doing? What are you wearing?"

"Old bathrobe and slippers. Why? Where are you calling from?"

"My car. Throw a coat on over and come down to me. I'm parked right in front of your building . . . "

And they had made love in the back seat of a Rolls Corniche, screened from the rest of the world by nothing more substantial than a snow flurry. A few feet away, Dasha's doorman peered out onto the frozen street, oblivious.

At the firm.

He had private wires installed in both their offices so they could reach each other at any time without going through the switchboard. No one else had the number. No one else even knew of its existence.

When the phone rang, it could only be Frank. Frank wanting her, arranging their next assignation. Frank pushing every thought out of her mind but the pleasures they would be sharing. She would respond to its ring reflexively, like Pavlov's dogs—only the reward that spurred her was sex, not food.

That winter, Frank sublet a loft from an artist in SoHo. It was a peculiar area, not far from the office, yet in every other way remote and exotic. An area populated with small galleries, trimmings shops, wholesale fabric merchants.

The loft itself was a single vast stark room furnished by its absentee owner with little more than abstract canvases, a few uncomfortable chairs, and a king-sized mattress on a bare floor.

They met there lunch hours, early evenings, sometimes first thing in the morning before the work day began. She explained her early departures from home by informing Jordan she had taken up jogging.

For eight months she met Frank there almost daily. In winter the place was an icebox, in summer an inferno. But what did it matter? She need merely open the door and nothing existed but the prospect of lovemaking.

How could Jordan not know! How could he be unaware that she was living her life in a constant state of arousal? How could he not smell another man's scent on her skin? How could he be blind to the hundred signs of total sex? She hardly dared ask herself.

She had come home from California with a sense of trepidation, certain that the moment she stepped off the plane, Jordan would realize what had been going on. You didn't spend half your lives together without developing some kind of sixth sense.

He was waiting for her at the airport, looking unfamiliar in a half-grown goatee, clutching a bunch of roses.

"The flowers are in case you didn't recognize me after all this time, what with the whiskers. Three weeks since I saw you last. I was afraid you wouldn't get here in time . . . "

"In time for what?"

"Why, Christmas, of course. I held off sending out the cards till you got back."

He appeared genuinely happy to have her back, affectionate and unsuspecting, and if Dasha had any lingering thoughts about coming clean with Jordan, they were immediately smothered in the warmth of his welcome. She simply didn't have the heart.

Once home, she threw herself into a frenzy of holiday preparations. "We'll have a real old-fashioned Christmas," she promised. "I'll make roast goose with the apple stuffing that you liked so much, a nice home-cooked plum pudding. We'll invite my father, your mother. . . ." In the back of her mind was the lingering notion that adultery might be paid for, neutralized by showering her family with a cornucopia of food. She cooked. She sent out cards. Did her best to present a good front. Yet every time she looked at Jordan, the words kept running through her mind: *I'm sorry.*

"I thought Ben was coming," she said to her mother-in-law as the family sat down to Christmas dinner. A place was set for him as a matter of course, but at the mention of his name, Charlotte grew agitated, and remained subdued throughout the meal.

Notwithstanding, the afternoon went well. The goose was superb, the plum pudding indecently fattening. After dinner, Robin played Mozart sonatas with her grandfather. The two had a real rapport, musical and personal.

"Have you considered sending her to the Curtis Institute in Philadelphia?" Max asked that evening. "Presuming that Curtis will accept her. It's an all-scholarship school, you know. However, I'm convinced she has the stuff, and she ought to be living in a total musical environment."

"I sing in the shower," Jordan volunteered.

"You will have your jokes," Max went on unperturbed. "However, Robin's thirteen now, a crucial time in a musician's development. And she herself is anxious to go."

"You've already discussed it with her!" Dasha was horrified.

"Actually," Max said, "she asked me to bring the matter up with you. She was afraid you'd say no."

"Damn right!" Jordan exclaimed. "I want her home. As it is, we'll be losing Geoff to boarding school next year. I don't want to be without *both* my chicks."

But later, getting into bed, the topic surfaced again. "You know, I couldn't help thinking when I wanted go to law school, how afraid I was to approach my parents," Dasha said.

"But Robin's so young," Jordan protested.

"Young, but very mature in a lot of ways. Well, first of all we'd have to see if she can pass the audition. Meanwhile, I'm turning in." She gave Jordan a casual peck on the lips. "Goodnight, Jordan. Merry Christmas."

"Goodnight? Just like that?" He placed a tentative hand on her breast, and began rotating it gently, his usual prelude to the act of love.

Instinctively, she recoiled.

"Please, Jordan, not tonight. I'm just bushed from all that cooking."

"You're always bushed these days, Dasha. It's too hot, it's too cold. You're too tired. Ever since you came back from California. Of course! It's my beard. That's it, isn't it? My beard turns you off."

Without further ado, he scooted into the bathroom, returning fifteen minutes later clean-shaven.

He climbed back into bed, smelling of witch hazel. "There now, that's better, isn't it?"

Dasha shut her eyes. *He will put his right hand on my nipple. His left hand on my crotch. We will French kiss for two minutes. Then he'll climb on top of me and murmur Darling . . .*

"Darling . . ."

She tried, first, not to think of Frank. That was merely compounding adultery. Then she tried thinking of him, pretending those were his arms around her, not Jordan's, trying desperately to respond. Then she tried to hold back the tears while Jordan pumped and heaved in an act that afforded neither of them satisfaction. After what seemed like an eternity, he gave a groan of dismay and rolled off her.

"I'm sorry, Dasha. I guess I'm not up to my usual standards tonight."

"That's all right." She was relieved. "We're both pretty tired."

He sat up in bed, thinking things through in the darkness, while Dasha pursued sleep without success.

"I have a confession to make," he said finally. His voice was grim.

"A confession?" She was instantly awake.

He must have had an affair when she was on the coast. Perhaps even a serious one. He had—my God!—he had got her off the hook. If so, it was an invitation for her to be honest with him, to clear the air once and for all. She held her breath and waited.

"It's been bothering me the entire last month, and . . . I've never kept any secrets from you, Dasha."

He had gone up to Buffalo to work out a custody settlement and Michika had come along to assist. The negotiations had taken longer than expected so they decided to spend the night up there. They had checked into the Sheraton, gone out to dinner. "Maybe I had a little bit too much to drink, maybe she did as well. Maybe it was just because we were a long way from home. In any event . . . "

They had wound up in Michika's room for a nightcap, turned on the radio, found some music. She asked him to dance. It was very romantic, very sexy. "And the next thing I knew we were peeling our clothes off and climbing into bed."

"I see," Dasha said. Yet she didn't. Instead, she began to tremble. She had trouble visualizing Jordan making love to someone else.

"And there we were, lying in bed, all over each other . . . "

"I don't need this, Jordan," she interrupted.

"And all I could think of"—his voice was anguished, almost angry —"was *I don't want to be here. I don't want to be with anyone but my wife!* There I am with a mile-high erection, in bed with a lovely girl. I mean she was so sweet, so willing—I guess she has a bit of a crush on me. And all I could think of was you."

"But what happened?" Dasha cried.

"What happened is that I grabbed my clothes, got into the car, and drove five solid hours back to New York. Straight through the night, because I had this crazy notion that you'd be there waiting for me. Sure I knew you were in San Francisco. In my head I knew that. But in my heart, I somehow believed you'd be home. That you'd sense how much I needed you. Because I really did. And when I got home, of course, you weren't there."

"And with Michika . . . then you never did . . . ?"

"No. Almost, but—no."

His confession was a confession of fidelity.

"I don't see what you're punishing yourself about, Jordan."

"I feel guilty because I *might* have. I came so close. I feel guilty because I had to let Michika go."

"You *fired* her?"

"We couldn't go on working together as though nothing had happened. You can see that, surely?" He hugged Dasha close, and there was a desperation in his embrace. "Don't ever again go away for so long, darling. Don't put me in the path of temptation like that."

Her only answer was to burst into tears.

"It's tearing me in half." She told Frank the story as they were lying in bed in the SoHo studio. "Here we are. We've just made sensational love and what am I talking about? Jordan. Crazy! Because when I'm with him, all I can think of is you. Oh God, darling! I feel like such a cheat. Such a goddam hypocrite."

"Then leave him, Dasha. Leave him and be done with it. I know you feel indebted to the man, darling, and I respect you for your loyalty. But you can't spend the rest of your life chained to the stake simply because you fell in love when you were an eighteen-year-old kid."

"And I should leave him simply because I fell in love again at thirty-six? When he's been so faithful? Is that his reward?"

"There's more to it than that, Dasha. I've *seen* you two together. You don't fit any more. The point is, he's still a college sophomore and you're not. You're a woman on the brink of a major career. Yet you refuse to face the fact that somewhere along the line, you outgrew your husband. It's not a matter of laying blame. It happened before we became lovers. The truth is, he's holding you back and you damn well know it. There comes a time, Dasha, when hanging in there becomes self-destructive. It's not loyalty any more, it's martyrdom. You're funny." He kissed her swollen eyelids. "You can be so extraordinarily adventurous in business. In bed too, I may add. Ready to dispense with every convention. Yet when it comes to your domestic life . . . "

"Please, Frank!" And the subject was dropped for the moment.

"Speaking of careers," he said as they were getting dressed, "I'd like you to help me with some antitrust problems we have looming over at FBC. You can start in as soon as we get back to the office."

"I thought I was going to be working on the Kim appeal." Dasha was surprised.

"Since Tom Hatt picked the strategy," Frank said irritably, "since he managed to lose the fucking case, he can goddam well handle the appeal. I should think you'd be glad to have it off your back for a while. You've been awfully close, maybe too close to it all."

"You're the rabbi." She was disappointed, but she trusted Frank's judgment. He was usually right.

The antitrust assignment proved engrossing and, after the ignominies of the Kim case, was providing a chance to cover herself in glory.

At home, however, everything and everyone staggered along as before, neither better nor worse.

Except for Charlotte.

"What's the matter with my mother, do you think?" Jordan asked. "She's been down in the dumps since Christmas. I gather it has something to do with Ben McCabe."

"Could be," Dasha agreed. "I'll see if I can find out."

That Saturday, she took her mother-in-law to a matinee, followed up by tea at the Palm Court.

"I love the Plaza," Charlotte said approvingly. "Jordan's father and I used to come here all the time. They have marvelous pastries." She dithered for an eternity between the strawberry tart and the *mille-feuilles,* till Dasha settled the matter by ordering them both.

It wasn't until the last flaky crumb was demolished and the mood grown happy and relaxed that she tackled the matter at hand.

"We haven't seen Ben in ages, Charlie." Immediately, a wary expression clouded the older woman's face. "I don't mean to pry," Dasha pursued, "but Jordan and I are both concerned about you. Have you and Ben broken it off? Is there any way we can help?"

Charlotte averted her eyes and reached for the teapot. "If you must know"—her hands were trembling—"Ben proposed."

"Why that's wonderful!" Dasha exclaimed. "What's the problem? I thought you two cared so much about each other. Wouldn't you like to remarry after all these years? Have somebody for your very own? And Ben's such a sweetie."

Instead of replying, the tears began streaming down Charlotte's cheeks. "Excuse me." She tore to the ladies' room. Dasha waited a couple of minutes, then went after her. Charlotte was huddled in a lounge chair, weeping furiously, while the washroom attendant watched helplessly.

"Can you give us a few minutes?" Dasha slipped a bill into the attendant's hand. "This is a private conversation." Then she pulled up a stool next to Charlotte.

"It's no good," Charlotte sobbed. "I've already told him no."

"But *why?*" Dasha was astounded. "You obviously care for each other."

"I'm nearly sixty . . . "

"All the more reason."

" . . . and what will people think?" she burst out. "I am, after all, Martin Croy's widow. It's hard for you to understand but, well, I may not have had much over these last years, but I've had *that.* I've had the privilege of bearing a distinguished name . . . the memory of a great man. It's true, Dasha. You'll find that Martin Croy is still a name to conjure with, still written up in all the textbooks on broadcasting. I understand young film students pore over his scripts like they were the Bible. His whole life was a testament of courage. Dignity. It would have been so easy for him to name names. Other men did, but not Martin. Never! He kept faith and in a way, that's what I'm doing too. As for Ben, yes, it's true I'm fond of him, but—he's a nobody, a shopkeeper. He works with his hands. How can I give up the Croy name for that? And what . . . " She had come full circle. "What will people think?"

"*Which* people?" Dasha wanted to know. Incredible after all these years of hard work and penny-pinching that Charlotte should cling to outmoded notions of gentility. "Jordan, me, the children? We'd be delighted. We think Ben is a dear. Besides, why should you care about what other people think? You marry for yourself, not for others. Ah, Charlotte, Charlotte," she grieved, "Martin Croy was not a god. He was a human being like the rest of us."

"How can you say that! You never knew him."

"Please." Dasha took the other woman's hand. "I don't want to wound you, but there's something you should know. Something Amory First told me in confidence. I'm telling it to you in the same kind of confidence."

For six months, during the height of the witch hunt, Martin Croy had indeed kept the faith. Despite the terrors of life on the broadcasting blacklist, he stubbornly refused to name names. But as the vise tightened, as the money began to run out, the pressures proved more than he could bear. He was a man—not a god—a frightened human being with a wife and young child to support.

"He panicked. He talked. And who am I to sit in judgment, Charlotte? Who knows how any of us will behave when the squeeze is on?"

In a secret session of the House Un-American Activities Committee, Martin Croy finally testified. Among the names he volunteered were several of his closest colleagues.

Then he went to see Amory First.

In the past, Martin had turned down repeated offers to write for FBC. First himself had courted him assiduously, but he considered the network to be beneath contempt. Now, however, it seemed a good place to start anew.

"I come to you as a supplicant."

He had just made the hardest, most painful decision of his life, he told First, and now he pleaded to be given work. Anything. Kid shows, crime shows, soap operas. Anything!

He had expected mercy, understanding, compassion. Above all, he had expected a job.

"You're a goddam fool," First replied coldly. "A fool and a weakling. FBC wasn't good enough for you when you were on top. And now you expect me to take you in like a charity case. Do you think, when this gets around the business, that there'll be an actor, a producer who'll want to work with you? You're a leper in this business from now on, Croy. Here and everywhere else."

"Then I've done this all for nothing?" Martin was horrified. "I've betrayed my friends, sold my soul—all for nothing? How can I live with myself?"

"That," came Amory's answer, "is your problem, not mine."

That same afternoon, driving home from the interview, Martin died in a car crash.

"He killed himself." Dasha put her arms around Charlotte. "You knew it all along in your heart of hearts. You must have known it from the time the life insurance company refused to pay your claim. Otherwise you would have sued."

"What are you saying?" Charlotte wept. "That I was married to a monster?"

"I'm saying no such thing." Dasha fought back her own tears. "Only that Martin Croy was a mixture of qualities, like everyone else on earth. He had the strength of his love for you and Jordan, the weakness of his needs. Don't sacrifice your last chance of happiness for yesterday's myths. You've lived so long for your memories, Charlie. For your son, your grandchildren. Now live life for yourself!"

Charlotte said nothing. She opened her bag and began repairing her makeup. Fresh mascara applied over tear-stained eyes. Dasha made one last stab.

"Promise me you'll think seriously about what I've said."

"I promise," she whispered. "And now I'd like to go home, if you don't mind."

She dropped her mother-in-law off and spent the rest of the evening playing Scrabble with the children.

"How'd it go?" Jordan asked when they were alone.

"Basically"—Dasha saw no point in reopening the Martin Croy affair—"I suggested it's time she stopped living in the past."

"Absolutely!" Jordan nodded approval. "You're so wise."

Through the night, however, she was haunted by the very advice she had given Charlotte.

Bury the past, she had said. *Seize the moment.*

Yet she herself was helpless to shuffle free from the ties of memory. To trade old loyalties for new love.

She, too, would have to do some serious thinking.

One month later, FBC lost its appeal in the Kim case. It was a stunning defeat, especially for Tom Hatt, who had staked his reputation on the outcome.

Dasha was in Frank's office when the news came in. "Goddam!" Dasha exploded. "It should never have come to this. Tom botched the trial strategy, he botched the appeal. If he had any sense of decency, he'd resign."

She was still simmering when she got home a half-hour later, slamming into the house with such gusto that even Robin in the music room broke off from her practicing.

"What's up, Mom? You look like you could eat raw dinosaur for dinner. Have a bad day at the office?"

"I'll say!" Dasha slumped into a chair. "Although why should I bore *you* with it? On second thought"—Robin had always been intrigued by Dasha's career and she was intelligent enough to understand the issues—"today we lost the Kim case on appeal, honey." She summarized the day's events and their import, concluding, "So we're all wildly disappointed."

"But it's not all over, is it?" Robin asked. "Aren't you going to take it to the Supreme Court?"

"Easier said than done," Dasha answered. "You see, the Supreme Court only hears very special cases."

Before you went to the Supreme Court, she explained, while Robin sat at the piano frowning, you had to persuade the Court that you deserved a hearing, that your particular case raised a significant legal question that had never been resolved before. The first step, therefore, was to petition the Court to hear the case. About three thousand such petitions were filed each term, and maybe a hundred and fifty of them were accepted for review.

"The exciting thing is, Robin, I feel we really have such an issue —an important one." Her eyes glittered. "Because I believe this case goes far beyond the money involved. It deals with . . . well, I don't want to get all preachy on you, but such basic principles as freedom of speech, freedom of the press."

"And will you be the one who argues it, Mom?"

"Oh, I don't know." Dasha laughed. "I'm inclined to doubt it. I expect one of the partners will be assigned. Why, cookie? Would you like it to be me?"

"Oh wow!" Robin grinned. "Would I ever! I mean it's *gotta* be you. I've always told everyone—that's my mom, the lady behind the great big humongous Kim case. So it's only fair you should be the one who goes to the Supreme Court." Robin paused, then looked at her mother with a quizzical smile. "Besides which, that's a kind of acid test, isn't it? Like getting an Oscar or playing in the World Series . . . "

"Or winning a scholarship to Curtis," Dasha finished her daughter's sentence, and they exchanged affectionate glances. "I'm awfully proud of you, darling."

"And if you win," Robin said thoughtfully, "does that mean David will be coming home to Uncle Alex?"

"Who can say?" Dasha sighed. "In a way, it was because of David that I got involved with this in the first place. Still, it's quite possible he'll never forgive me for meddling."

"But isn't that exactly *why* you have to follow it through? To prove to him you were right?"

With that, Robin turned back to the piano and Dasha tiptoed out of the room.

God bless the child. She was absolutely right.

"Frank." She sought him out first thing next morning. "I'm here to make an official request, which is, I want to work up a petition for *cert* on the Kim case. I know I'm not terribly senior around here, I know there are attorneys with more experience. But no one in the firm, no one in the world cares about the case as passionately as I do. And I promise you there isn't a lawyer in the world who'll work any harder. I know I'm going over Tom Hatt's head on this but . . . "

"Tom Hatt just quit."

"You're kidding!"

"Nope. Thomas Christopher Hatt reluctantly resigned last night after informing the Management Committee that he has decided to pursue a career in politics. At least that's his story."

"Then *can* I . . . ?"

"You're awfully young."

"I'll lie about my age."

"And it's a huge case."

"What my daughter called humongous."

"And the decision won't be mine alone. However, I'll take it up with the committee and see what can be done."

Two weeks later, and two years ahead of schedule, Dasha Croy made partner.

"Congratulations!" Miranda said. "I knew you'd do it. And I understand you're back on the Kim case?"

"Yes, isn't it wonderful! I've already started on the petition."

"Wonderful, if bustin' your ass happens to be your idea of fun. How are you going to celebrate?"

"Would you believe a wedding?" Dasha laughed. "Yes, ma'am, a great big wedding, right in my apartment. And you know something, I feel like the mother of the bride."

CHAPTER NINETEEN

☐ "So what does that make me?" Andy McCabe wanted to know.

"My stepbrother-in-law once removed, I think," Dasha said.

"Country cousin would be more like it. Anyhow, it's a terrific wedding. And good to be in New York. That's the only time we seem to get together, Dasha. Weddings. Mine or my dad's."

"Has it been that long?" she marveled. "I guess so. How's Vermont treating you? You're looking well."

"I look like a walking goddam L. L. Bean catalogue, if you really want to be honest. They don't have tailors up there, you know." He grabbed a canapé from a passing waiter. "Nor *shitake* mushrooms, either. Cows! Cows they got. I defended one in court last month. A bull, actually, name of Oscar and literally the biggest client I've ever had. He had a way, as bulls do, of bustin' out and knocking up all the neighborhood Bessies, much to the distress of the local dairy farmers. You'll be happy to know I won the case for good old Oscar, saved him from a fate worse than death. My defense was Act of God. It was a landmark decision, Dasha. My noblest hour."

"Gee." She looked at him, disconcerted. "I thought country life was supposed to mellow a man. You sound so bitter."

"Not bitter, Dasha. Bored."

"Come on." She led him by the hand through the crush of guests. "Let's have a little sidebar in my study."

He grabbed a tray of canapés and followed her in.

"I want to come back," he pleaded. "I want to come back to Slater

Blaney in the worst way. I'm just not cut out for the rural life, Dasha. I miss the cut and thrust, the old adrenaline running. Josie says I'm just a crisis junkie at heart."

"How does she feel about it?" Dasha asked. "That was the whole point of your moving up to Vermont in the first place."

"She understands—she *says*—and she's willing to come back. Not ecstatic, but willing. I guess she'd rather see less of a happy me in New York than more of a miserable me in Vermont. You're a partner, Dasha. Take me on as your associate and let me help with the research on the Kim appeal. You know I'm good, and I'd give my soul to work on a case like that."

"If it were up to me," she said sincerely, "I'd welcome you with open arms. But I'm only a junior partner, Andy. I don't have that kind of clout . . ."

"Then ask Frank."

"What?"

"Ask Frank Hunicutt. He'll do it if you ask."

"I don't know what you mean," she said stiffly.

"Oh come on, Dasha. It's common knowledge about you two."

"In Rutland, Vermont?" She stared at him incredulous. "How does such 'common knowledge' get to Rutland?"

"Without getting into personalities, let me say that someone from the firm was up skiing in our neck of the woods and . . . well, I gather you two haven't been wildly discreet."

She sat down heavily. If Andy knew, then everyone in the office knew. Everyone in the world knew, with the possible exceptions of her own family and Clarisse Hunicutt.

"Very well," she said. "I'll speak to Frank, although if I thought for a moment this were blackmail . . . "

"Please, Dasha," he broke in, "you know me better than that."

"Yes, I do," she returned. "Otherwise I wouldn't even consider the matter. I'll talk to Frank and use such influence as I have. But don't for one minute think I can twist him round my finger. Frank Hunicutt makes up his own mind—on everything."

No, Frank was decidedly not twistable.

On the matter of Andy McCabe, there proved to be no problem.

"If you think he's really good and he can help you on the Kim case, then let's get him back in the fold. You know how much I rely on your business judgment, Dasha."

In fact, one associate more or less didn't make that much difference. But on other matters—matters more personal, farther reaching—Frank followed no counsel but his own. He chose his direction with scrupulous care and clarity, and once his course was set, pursued it with single-minded purpose.

Which was not to say he was close-minded. Indeed, Dasha found him the least doctrinaire of men, ever flexible, receptive to new ideas. He often took hair-raising chances. "When you're on a roll, Dasha, play it for everything it's worth." Yet for all his style, his freewheeling generosity, for all his uninhibited sexuality, he was curiously immune to emotional suasion. Moral arguments left him cold. He kept within him, even in the heat of physical passion, a small tight core of control.

It was the source of his strength, his power. The very power that rendered him so attractive.

"I heard on the news," she said one evening when they had rendezvoused at the loft, "that the Duchess of Windsor is dying. I always thought that was the great romantic story of the century."

"Did you?"

"Well, yes. 'All for love and the world well lost' . . . that sort of thing."

"The world is never well lost," was Frank's comment. "Personally, I always thought Edward was a damn fool. Will you pass me the corkscrew, darling?"

He opened a bottle of Beaujolais, endowing even such a simple act with physical grace. It was impossible not to watch him with pleasure. He would pour out two glasses, she knew, then leave his own untouched. No, she thought with a twinge of regret, Frank would never surrender a throne for the woman he loved. He'd probably never surrender the woman either. Frank, being Frank, would manage to hang on to it all.

In the twilight, the loft appeared stark and eerie: corners lost in shadow, uncurtained windows looking out onto empty streets.

"I can spend the night, darling," he said. "Do you think you could too?"

She shook her head. "I have to be home by midnight. And even if

I could, you know," she found herself saying, "this is sordid. This place is nothing but four walls, a bunch of paintings, and a bed."

"Would you rather go to a hotel?"

"Which one, Frank? The Plaza? The Helmsley Palace? A nice suite at the Carlyle?"

"No place so spectacularly public, but perhaps . . . "

"Perhaps"—she wet her lips—"perhaps it's time to end the charade. Make a commitment. I hate all this duplicity, this hole-and-corner stuff. An hour here, an afternoon there. It's just like . . . " She started to say, *Just like when I was a sophomore in college.* She had an odd sense of history repeating itself. "The thing is, Frank, I just don't get enough of you. I don't know that I ever will, certainly not this way. Let's do it, darling. Let's say goodbye to husbands, wives, mothers-in-law, dogs, cats, and move in together. I love you. You love me. Nothing else matters, am I right? You *do* love me, don't you?"

"What a question! I adore you, Dasha. I am crazy out of my mind about you. But this isn't the time to make a decision like that. To go through an emotional upheaval. Not now when you've just got your *cert* for the Kim case. You'll need to reserve all your energy and discipline for that. A few months more, dove, and all our problems should be resolved. And it's a bad time for me, too, you know. The situation with First is very delicate. All I can say is soon, very soon. But for now, darling . . . "

He pulled her gently down on the bed, spreading her hair out against the white of the pillow. Then he knelt atop her and studied her in the fading light. "Beautiful." He placed her hands above her head. "You look so vulnerable at this very moment. All I want for now is your touch, your taste . . . "

He slid her clothes off with deft seamless gestures, then soothed her thighs with strong warm hands.

"Is this sordid, darling?"

Instantly her body responded. "Or this?" One hand slid beneath her, cupping her buttocks, while the other hand traced a path through her pubic hair. She sucked in her breath while he massaged her with soft lapping motions till she felt her body melt between his hands, his questing satiny fingers.

"And is this sordid?"

He had drawn his hand from her vulva to her breast to her mouth, was rubbing it against her lips. "Taste—taste how beautiful you are. My delicious Dasha."

"Oh, Frank," she murmured. "God, what you do to me!"

"Nothing, my darling"—he climbed on top of her, thrusting deep inside her—"compared to what I'm going to do."

And in the act of love, the world beyond was once more forgotten. Later she got up to get dressed, her body sated and spent. Frank sat cross-legged on the bed amid the wreckage of the bed linen, watching her like a cat.

"Aren't you going home tonight, Frank?"

He shook his head. "I think I'll sleep here, on these sheets with your scent around me. Yes, Dasha"—he smiled at her contentedly—"we'll be together soon. Live together. It has to be. It's so right for us both. Just be patient, darling, and we'll work it out."

Riding home in the cab she felt strangely happy. The hiding, the lying was about to come to an end. She could scarcely believe it. She and Frank would live together. He was ready to make that commitment. And if he hadn't mentioned marriage, she really didn't care. That was one convention that was rapidly going by the boards. Besides, she and Frank had more than a marriage between them. They had an alliance, a superbly integrated point-by-point match of everything that mattered: of love and profession and interests and sexual chemistry. That dream that he had posed on the beach of Monterey—with Dasha the head of Slater Blaney, Frank the chairman of FBC—no longer seemed so fanciful. Indeed, it seemed their due. Some day. Some day soon.

It was all she could do when she arrived home to keep from bursting out and telling Jordan everything. He was sitting in the den, engrossed by an interview on "The David Letterman Show."

"Jordan?"

He put a finger to his lips. "Can it wait until the commercials?"

She pulled herself up short with a cold dose of reality. "It was nothing important," she said. "Enjoy your program. Goodnight."

And the moment passed.

The following week, Frank went out of town on business and Dasha arrived at the office on Monday to find a call from Clarisse Hunicutt waiting.

Was she free for lunch tomorrow, by any chance, the voice on the other end wanted to know.

Not tomorrow? Then how about Wednesday, or Thursday? Was that a possibility? Clearly, Dasha would run out of excuses before her inquisitor ran out of dates.

"I know!" Clarisse declared in a voice that preempted all refusals, "let's do it today. After all, you have those boring partners' luncheons on Monday and Frank always says it's one's duty to get out of them whenever possible. So come here instead. Twelve-thirty convenient? And of course you know the address."

At the precise time, Dasha found herself at the door of the huge apartment on Sutton Place in response to what she recognized as a command performance. It took all her courage to ring the bell.

A Filipino maid took her coat, then ushered her into a room, small but exquisite, furnished with antique bamboo chairs and hand-painted Chinese wallpaper. By the window, a lacquerware table had been set for two.

"This is my little sitting room." Clarisse cleared her lap of a silky blue-eyed Persian, brushed the cat hairs from a woolen dress the color of forest ferns, and extended a delicate hand. "Do you mind lunching in here? I thought it would be so much cozier than the dining room. You're looking well, Dasha. It's ages since we've seen each other."

"You're looking well, too, Clarisse," she replied with a sense of aching wonder. *Lovely and fragile and vulnerable, dammit. Can it be you don't know?* "And that's a stunning dress."

"Thank you." Clarisse gave her shy smile, then poured them both some sherry. "I had Adolfo make it up to match my earrings. They're pretty, aren't they?" She tossed her head lightly. "Antique jade. Jadeite, actually. Frank picked them up at Gumps in San Francisco. Marvelous store, especially for Orientalia. Have you ever been there?"

She knows. She knows, but she's too much the lady to say it straight out.

"No," Dasha answered. "I'm afraid I didn't get to do any shopping while I was out there."

"I don't blame you. It's hardly a pleasure any more."

While the butler served a cold sorrel soup, Clarisse began a technical dissertation on the new Japanese couture, working up to a detailed analysis of fabric and color and cut. "I like the outsize look as a whole, in the hands, say, of a Perry Ellis or Saint-Laurent. And I've always adored Hanae Mori, so you can't say I'm prejudiced against Japanese designers. But these new Miyakes—they're just plain *voluminous.*" Her distress was genuine. "Honestly, Dasha, it makes you despair. I mean, what's the purpose of keeping slim any more? And they're not even flattering. What do you think? Should I break down and buy one or two?"

Perhaps the topic was designed to promote a "between us girls" attitude, and she intended a natural progression from clothes to hair stylists to men. Or perhaps Clarisse really did care that passionately about clothes. In which case, poor Frank!

"I'm afraid, Clarisse, that I'm the worst person in the world to venture an opinion about avant-garde fashion. I don't know one Japanese designer from another." True, yet this once she half-wished she had some useful comment to make. Anything, *anything* to head off that terrible moment when Clarisse would say—however disguised—*"Please stop sleeping with my husband."*

The soup plates were removed to make way for a pale pink salmon mousse.

"Thank you, Barlow, that will be all." Clarisse dismissed the butler with a smile. "You don't realize how fortunate you are, Dasha, not having to worry about each little in and out of fashion. I wish I didn't have to either, but it goes with the job."

"The job?" Dasha was puzzled.

Oh definitely. Being married to a brilliantly successful man, Clarisse assured her, was one of the toughest jobs in the world. It takes two to make a major career, to provide the necessary environment. Not that much of it wasn't pleasurable, especially when the effort was on behalf of someone you dearly loved. Nonetheless, the larger part of her duties was sheer hard work. The entertaining, my God, the entertaining! Did Dasha have any notion how much drudgery was involved in providing the back-up for Frank's career? You had to know who should sit next to whom at dinner, who was still married, who was not, who was vegetarian, who was kosher, who wouldn't eat caviar for political reasons. She kept a master file of each dinner-party menu with every guest cross-indexed. Then there was the business of keeping track of birthdays, promotions, anniversaries . . .

She had a tendency to gush, a desire to explain herself over and over again which Dasha read as a mask to hide her essential timidity.

"Our Christmas card list!" Clarisse threw up her hands. "Would you believe, we sent out over a thousand last year? And I included a personalized hand-written note on each and every card."

"I know," Dasha said. "Thank you."

Please stop, Clarisse. I can't bear hearing this. I don't want to know the full measure of Frank's indebtedness to you.

Yet Clarisse, in her quiet way, was following a preordained course and now at last she was reaching her objective.

"One does what one can." She averted her eyes before taking the plunge. "Perhaps you'll think I'm telling tales out of school, Dasha, but I know how much trust Frank places in you. All this is in the strictest confidence, but—are you aware that my husband hopes to replace Amory First as the head of FBC?"

The change of tack confused Dasha, who answered with a noncommittal "Oh?"

"Yes, indeed," Clarisse continued, "I would say that's his goal in life. He wants that post more than anything else in the world, I dare say. He's dreamed about it for years, and now it looks as if Amory really can be pushed out. That's why Frank's on the road so much these days. He's making the rounds, politicking, maneuvering"—she rolled her eyes. "I think there's a rebellion brewing among the board of directors, although don't say you heard it from me. Frank himself isn't on the board of FBC, you know."

"Oh?" Dasha sat up in surprise. "I understood he was."

"Everyone thinks so, but he's not—technically speaking. I'm the one with the seat on the board. Frank attends those meetings as my proxy. He represents my interests and votes my stock. I expect you know I inherited a substantial stake in FBC when my father died."

In fact, Clarisse continued, she was the single largest shareholder in the company, except for Amory First himself. Naturally, she had no hesitation in lending Frank her clout and the use of her stock for his own purposes. Especially now, with the action hotting up. And when Frank *did* finally make his bid for power, she wouldn't be surprised if her personal holdings spelled the difference between success and failure.

"As I was saying, it takes two to make a career like his. Of course, I'm only too glad to back him to the hilt. If being head of FBC is what he wants, then I'll do everything I can to see he makes it. After all, it's the sort of thing one does for one's husband."

Provided he remains one's husband, her eyes implored. Dasha was the first to look away.

So there it was, the message, never stated yet perfectly clear. Frank could have Dasha or Frank could have his crack at the top. There was no way he could have both.

Clarisse smiled, her sad shy smile. Then she leaned over to pick up the blue-eyed Persian and feed it a spoonful of salmon from her plate.

"I love animals," she said softly. "They're so faithful. Shall I ring for coffee?"

Dasha made her excuses and fled.

Going back to the office was out of the question. There were too many things to think through. Instead, she took a cab down to the loft in SoHo and spent the remainder of the afternoon in a state of quiet despair.

If only Clarisse had screamed at her, cursed, harangued, shed tears . . . if only she had *attacked,* then Dasha's defensive instincts would have come into play. But Clarisse was neither a shrew nor a whiner; simply a shy, unambitious woman whose husband was the centerpiece of her life.

Granted that Clarisse was not, in theory at least, an object of pathos. She was still lovely, immensely chic and, given the size of her fortune, should have little difficulty in finding a highly suitable second husband. One, perhaps, less intellectually demanding than Frank and more determinedly faithful. One who shared her interests in clothes and pets and parties. With another man, Dasha rationalized, it was altogether possible that Clarisse would be considerably happier in the long run.

But that was in theory. In fact, it was patent she adored her husband, faults and all.

And the worst of it was—Dasha liked the woman. Clarisse was a lady. And she believed Dasha to be one, too, for she had pitched her appeal to Dasha's noblest instincts. *Don't make me fight for my husband. Don't stand in the way of his ambition. If you really love him, give him up.*

But Dasha couldn't give him up. She might as well give up eating, breathing. Every cell of her being was geared to him. Their lives, their careers were intertwined beyond extrication.

And if Clarisse loved him, so did she—just as deeply. No, far more deeply, for she loved him with a depth of understanding that his wife could never share. "We're suited, you and I"—how many times had he told her that?—"We're suited right down to the ground." Clarisse would find her compensations. So, in the end, would Jordan. But *Frank and Dasha:* that had to be. It was inevitable. Frank himself had said as much. And Clarisse's veiled threat was nothing less than moral blackmail. Well, Dasha, for one, would not submit. That decision was out of her hands.

Only Frank could determine his priorities. The choice must be his alone. And the sooner it was made, the better. The sooner the charade would end.

She spent an anguished hour trying to reach him, and after a couple of dozen abortive phone calls, tracked him down in the midst of a meeting at the FBC office in Cleveland.

"How are you, darling?" he asked. "I'd been trying to reach you at the office."

"I'm at the loft. Frank, I've got to see you about something urgent. Non-business . . . nonetheless it can't wait. Can you come back tonight? Please say yes."

"I wish I could, lamb, but I've got to be in Chicago tomorrow. Can you tell me about it on the phone? No? In that case, why don't you come out here tomorrow and I'll meet you for lunch. One-ish at the Palmer House. I'll reserve a room in your name and we can spend the afternoon together."

"The Palmer House," she echoed. She had a faint memory of a room in that very hotel, of lying in bed with the kiss of a red-headed lawyer fresh on her cheek, and being thoroughly outraged at the mere suggestion of infidelity. She'd come a long way, indeed!

"Yes, that'll be wonderful, Frank. I'll take an early plane out." She paused. "I love you very very much, you know."

"I miss you too, darling. Till tomorrow."

CHAPTER TWENTY

☐ It was nearly two by the time he arrived, bearing a bouquet of long-stemmed roses and trailed by a waiter with a serving cart.

"We'll help ourselves." He tipped the waiter and practically pushed him out the door. "I'm sorry I'm late, darling. Rupert Angel had me cornered and I couldn't get away earlier. My God"—he flung the roses on the bed and gathered her into his arms—"it's a treat to see you. You look marvelous. Pale, tired, but marvelous."

"And you look—glowing."

Today, for some reason, he seemed even more buoyant than usual, filling the room with his radiance, his eyes and cheeks bright from the wintry wind. A happy warrior, fresh from the battlefield.

Clearly, he could have no inkling of his wife's ultimatum, as he bustled about the room, stripping off his jacket, loosening his tie, poking his nose into each of the covered dishes. "Mmmmm." He scooped up a handful of French fries and began popping them into his mouth. "These are delicious. Do you mind, darling? I'm famished. First we'll eat and then we'll go to bed."

"That's not what I came to Chicago for, Frank."

"No?" He laughed, and stole another French fry. "I had so hoped. Well, whatever it is you want to discuss, could it wait fifteen minutes? I can't listen on an empty stomach."

She sat down and watched him as he sliced the chateaubriand and poured her a glass of Bordeaux. It would be a pity to spoil his mood.

"Who in heaven's name is Rupert Angel?" she asked out of politeness. "I gather that he's made your day."

272

"The first half of it, anyway.", Frank beamed. "Mr. Angel is Chicago's hottest investment banker. Also a director of FBC. And also—if indications can be believed—a charter member of my fan club. By all accounts, an aptly named man. I have his word he'll go down the wire with me should it come to a showdown with Amory First. It's looking good, darling. And the beauty of it is the old pirate doesn't have a clue about what's happening. Six months, I give Amory. Six months . . . at the outset a year, before I'm in the driver's seat at FBC and he's collecting his Social Security. God, it's wonderful"—he began wolfing down his steak—"what the prospect of victory does for the appetite." He spent the next ten minutes babbling away gleefully about developments in his subterranean campaign. "Of course, if we can get Amory to resign peacefully, that will be the best solution. But if not . . . "

The higher his spirits soared, the deeper her own sank. She had left New York that morning without even having booked a flight home, in the grip of some absurd notion that everything would be resolved today. That perhaps she would never come back to what she had left. It was all over with Jordan, all over with Clarisse. The lying, the deceit. All over.

And here was Frank, talking about six months, a year. She couldn't live another year on those terms. Perhaps not even another day.

"But you haven't touched your steak, darling." He paused in mid-flight. "Shall I order something else for you?"

"I'm not hungry." She passed the platter over to him. "You eat it, if you like."

"You're sure?" In fact, he was already slicing the meat. It was blood rare. "At least have a glass of wine."

A man of enormous appetites, he had once described himself. Also of enormous ambition. Yes, Frank would surrender his soul for the job at FBC. What else would he give up? she wondered. The time had come to find out.

"Tell me something, will you?" she asked. "If push came to shove, how much support could you rally from the other directors? Right now, I mean. If there were a showdown today."

He shrugged. "Hard to say, Dasha. Thus far everything has been done on the quiet, you know. I don't want to tip my hand prematurely. Why, what makes you ask?"

"I just wanted to know if you could take control of the network without the help of Clarisse's stock."

"Oh shit!"

He put down his fork, the joy draining from his face like air from a pricked balloon. "By that, am I to infer you've been in touch with my wife?"

She nodded.

"At your request or hers, Dasha?"

The question jangled. "I haven't blown the whistle on you, if that's what you're thinking." She nearly choked on the words. "I would never do a thing like that."

"Of course not, darling." He leaned over and handed her a glass of ice water. "Now take a swallow, calm down, and tell me exactly what happened."

She did, as simply and directly as she could, while her heart beat wildly against her ribs. Then she folded her hands in her lap and waited for the inevitable.

Waited for Frank to take her in his arms. Waited for him to bury her with kisses. Waited for him to say the magic words, "To hell with Clarisse. To hell with the network. To hell with everything except you and me, my love."

She sat and waited for that great and spontaneous outburst of passion that was never to come.

His face was a barometer of shifting emotions. Rage, pain, conflict, vexation—all were there for Dasha to read. But one was missing, the only message that mattered: that of unthinking, unqualified love.

"Damn it to hell," he said finally. "She should never have done that. It's not like her to make a scene. Of course, you must admit, darling, we haven't been awfully discreet thus far."

"What is that supposed to mean, Frank?" she cried.

"Just that we'll both have to be a bit more prudent in the future. That loft in SoHo—that's probably what did us in. I'm sure of it! All those damn art galleries down there. You never know who you're going to stumble into. Maybe if I took a place in Brooklyn Heights? It's convenient to the office, and no one ever goes there. At least no one Clarisse would know. Oh screw it, darling!" He reached for her hand. "It's not going to be solved today, in any event. So let's put it all aside for the interim."

"What interim, Frank?" She fought back a fresh round of tears.

"Spell it out. I want to know. The interim between now and tomorrow? Or the interim between now and when you've got FBC sewed up? Because I don't think I can tolerate being put on the back burner any more."

"Now, darling." He came over and drew her up out of her chair. "There's no question of back burner. Shhh . . . shhh," he crooned, cradling her in his arms, rocking her with a gentling to-and-fro motion. She shut her eyes for a moment, lost in the comfort of his strong protective arms. In the music of his words. "Sssshhh, my dove. My own sweet Dasha. It will be all right, soon, very soon, my darling, and then we'll be together for the world to see. Meanwhile just let me handle everything. My darling Dasha." He kissed the tears from her face and slowly led her toward the bed.

"Mmmm. You smell so good." He pulled her down beside him and placed a hand on her breast. "Ah . . . what's this? You're wearing the jade necklace for me." He smiled at her with unabashed delight, then slid his hand down over her nipple. Her body responded like the poor dumb animal it was. "Let's take a bath together, shall we?" He began unbuttoning her blouse. Her flesh turned liquid beneath his fingers.

"Please!" She broke loose from his embrace. "Please don't try to manipulate me."

"Manipulate you? Darling, I only want to make love."

"No," she cried. "You're manipulating me the same way you manipulated Blagden Geere. The way you manipulated your investment banker this morning, I have no doubt. The way you plan to manipulate your wife. Everything will be all right, you say. All right for whom? You know, Frank"—the realization suddenly overwhelmed her—"in all the hundreds of times we've made love, all the thousands of hours we've spent together, I don't think you've ever once told me that you loved me."

"Dasha!"

"No, hear me out. You never have! At least not in those exact words. You're crazy about me, wild about me, besotted with me . . . I've heard it all. But *love* . . . ?"

"It's just a word, Dasha." He sat up very straight. The erotic moment had vanished for them both. "Very well, you want to talk this out now, let's do it. Let's clear the air. I gather from this extraordinary outburst that you feel I should jeopardize everything, my only chance of making it at FBC for what you choose to call love. I'm not too sure what you mean by love, or why a token word is so important. Well, love is a lot of things, I suppose, but for God's sakes, let's not get bogged down in semantics. What is it I'm asking you that's so terrible, Dasha? To wait a little? To try to keep a low profile for a few more months? If you love me, is that such a sacrifice? We'll have the rest of our lives together!"

"In other words"—she could scarcely credit her ears—"you would string Clarisse along until you have what you want. Then what? Then you would dump her for me? Is that it?"

"What a dreadful way of putting it, Dasha. I'm not a total swine, simply a pragmatic man. There's a difference. What is it you really expect of me, Dasha? For the sake of argument"—his eyes narrowed—"let me turn the tables and you answer the very same question. What would *you* give up for *me?* And don't say your marriage because that's already on the rocks. Would you give up your career? Give up the Kim case? Slater Blaney? You didn't do it for your husband, when he asked. Am I to believe you would do it for me?"

"Yes!" she said passionately. "Up until one hour ago I would have. I would have scrapped everything if you had only said the word. I would have lived with you in a hut. Happily. At least we would have been honest. And I would have done it for *love,* Frank. For that awful word you can't quite bring yourself to utter." She was weeping now, something she knew he hated. Weeping just as Clarisse must have done how many many times. "You know, Geoff once asked me whether I would still love him if he committed some awful crime. And I said yes, of course. Even murder? he wanted to know. And I said yes. Because, I told him, when you really love someone, you don't stop to count the cost. You don't ask yourself, Is this a smart thing or a dumb thing? At least, I don't. But you do, Frank. You do it with everyone, on every occasion. Even the Kim case! For you it was always a business decision, nothing moral, nothing really intense about it. I remember your saying that once. 'Let the case drag on forever in court because the meter's running all the time.' I thought at the time you were joking. But you weren't. You were calculating. What? A ten-million-dollar legal fee? Because for all your style, your lavishness, all your sexual expertise, you can't make an uncalculated move. And that's the difference between us!"

He got up silently, crossed the room, and poured himself a glass of wine. Then he settled into an armchair.

"I love you—in my way, Dasha," he said slowly. "But you're right, my way isn't yours. I'll be honest. I had never expected our affair to become so . . . intense. I hadn't, as you put it, calculated on that. In fact, I was totally unprepared for your passion, the way everything was barreling out of control. All the other girls I've known have been so casual. By design, I may add. Before you, I'd always managed to keep my life in different compartments—work, sex, separate but equal so to speak. A place for everything—everything except raw emotion. I wanted no part of that. Then you happened, and all the boundaries began to vanish. From the first day we met, I always wondered how you would be in bed. I always wanted you. But I never made any move. It was too dicey. I didn't know if you fucked around. I rather thought not. Besides, I liked you too much as a colleague and a friend, and I have a pretty shrewd estimate about the life expectancy of love affairs. A few months, a year at the most. Then you phoned me from San Francisco . . . and there we were in a whole new ball game. Not just the sex, you know. The sex was marvelous—but why shouldn't it have been? Sex is a marvelous thing. I never tire of it and I don't think I ever shall. But it's fungible, if I may use the legal term. Fungible. Interchangeable. And one warm sweet body isn't that different from the next. When you've had other affairs, you'll know what I mean. And you will have other affairs, I have no doubt. But to talk of love . . .

"I look at my own family—my father fucking up half a dozen lives for some romantic escapade, my mother bitter till the day she died. For what? For love, that same kind of crazy out-of-control love you're talking about, the kind that never counts the costs. Well, *I* count them, Dasha, because I *paid* them when I was a boy. Six or seven, just about the age your Geoff was when he asked you whether you'd love him no matter what, even if he committed murder. Well, maybe Geoff got one message and I got another. Because it was somewhere way back then— I can't pinpoint the day but it was long before I met you—I made a vow to myself. I swore I would never turn over the reins of my life to anyone, never leave myself open to injury in that particular way. Yet it's been a near-run thing with you. So perhaps it's just as well all this has come to a head. You're like a fever in the blood, Dasha. But I don't know that I'm capable of living every day at fever pitch the way you do, of having my life slip out from beyond my control. Yes, I am manipulative, and I don't think I could manipulate you. But if it's any consolation, let me tell you this, Dasha. I care for you more than I've ever cared for any woman. I always shall."

He finished off the wine and placed his glass on the table, his face sadder than she had ever known it. The eyes bluer, perhaps with tears.

"Are you leaving me, Frank? Is that what you're saying?"

His voice floated to her over a vast distance.

"No, darling. You're leaving me."

He sent her off to the airport in a rented limousine, and mechanically, she managed to board the flight. In her mind, the afternoon's events assumed the mythic quality of a dream. They never happened. They couldn't have happened. Her ears were closing shut. Her brain grew numb.

The movie went on, but there was something wrong with her headphones. The sound was muffled, distorted. All she could hear was *"You're leaving me."* Over and over and over. Which was ridiculous, because it hadn't happened. She shut her ears tighter. For that too was a movie, a very bad one. Remote, unreal. Two strangers in a hotel room viewed through a long-distance lens. She didn't know who those people were in that picture. But certainly not her. Not Frank. She closed her ears against the sound, her eyes against the memory . . .

"We're here," the lady next to her mouthed, and nudged her gently.

Where? New York, Chicago, San Francisco?

She stumbled out into the terminal. An utterly disoriented woman, moving along with the crowd past counters reading AVIS, HERTZ. Should she rent a car, take a taxi, get on a bus going somewhere?

She couldn't think. Wouldn't want to if she could. Better to tune out, wrap herself in a cloak of silence. For a minute she stood teetering in the center of the terminal without a notion of where to go, what to do next.

A fair-haired boy in a candy-red jacket came over and slipped a carnation into her lapel. She ought, she supposed, to give him money. Then perhaps he would leave her in peace. In blessed silence. She opened her bag, reached for her wallet. Her credit cards trickled to the floor. The boy bent over to pick them up.

Then suddenly she was surrounded by a sea of red-coated children, chanting, pressing in on her. Who were they? What did they want of her? Why wouldn't they leave her alone in her deep protective silence? They were singing, jeering, and now she could just make out the words.

"Father Kim loves you. Father Kim loves you."

"That's her!" one of the redcoats screamed into her ear, piercing her inner hush. "That's Croy."

"Go away." She clapped her hands over her ears. "Go away and leave me in silence."

But the sound had returned, and with the sound had come memory. Feeling.

For the first time in her life, she fainted.

"Are you all right?" An anxious airline clerk had managed to drag her into a seat behind the ticket counter. Another was holding a tot of brandy to her lips. "Don't move. We have a doctor on the way."

"No, no." Dasha shook her head vehemently. "I'm not hurt." *At least not where it shows.* "Please . . . I don't need a doctor."

"You might have a concussion," her rescuer argued. "Loss of memory. Do you know who you are? Where you are?"

She nodded slowly. "My name is Dasha Croy. I'm at JFK. It's early Tuesday evening. And"—her eyes spilled over—"I would very much like you to call my husband and ask him to take me home."

CHAPTER TWENTY-ONE

☐ "Oyez oyez oyez. All persons having business before the honorable, the Supreme Court of the United States are admonished to draw near and give their attention, for the Court is now sitting. God save the United States and this honorable Court."

Dasha smoothed an invisible wrinkle on her skirt and walked briskly to a small wooden rostrum facing the bench where eight black-robed men and one woman were seated. On the lectern a small green light would tell her when it was time to begin.

She drew a deep breath and silently acknowledged that—win or lose—the very fact of her being here constituted a miracle. A miracle of Jordan's making. And if she won, then much of the victory was surely his.

He had found her sitting dazed and huddled behind the United Airlines counter, that calamitous day, and bundled her off into the car without an unnecessary word. She lay down in the back seat, too numb to cry, too devastated even to think about framing answers to the questions Jordan would inevitably ask: *Where have you been? What happened?*

Conceivably, she might have lied, as she had done so many times before. What difference would one lie more or less make to the grand total of falsehoods accumulated this past year?

But too many lies had already corrupted what was left of their marriage, and the least she owed him now was total honesty. He would ask. She would tell. *My lover has left me,* she would say. *And it hurts me more than I can bear.*

The car rounded a curve on the Parkway and suddenly the Manhattan skyline hove into view, glittering in the frozen air. She had a swift memory of another journey on this road. The drive in from Southampton, only that journey had been made in summer, with Dasha behind the wheel, and Jordan sick and troubled in the back.

Now it was she, being chauffeured home like a lost soul, being put to bed under some face-saving pretext.

"Overwork," Jordan said when he called her office the following morning to make her excuses. "Dasha may not be in for a few more days. She's absolutely exhausted."

Which was part of the truth, certainly. She had never been so utterly weary in her life. "I want to sleep," she told Jordan. "That's the only thing I want to do—sleep."

She spent the rest of the week in bed, sleeping ten, fifteen hours at a stretch, refusing to face anyone. Jordan disconnected the bedroom phone, and—except for bringing her in light meals on a tray—left her undisturbed. No questions. No reproaches. Not yet.

Sometimes she would hear his voice in the next room, low, protective, sheltering her from the assault of outsiders. Then she would bury her head once more in the pillows. The only other sound to intrude was the whirr of the vacuum cleaner as their housekeeper, a tiny birdlike Nicaraguan, went about her duties. Then that too stopped. Jordan must have shooshed her. Bless him. He was going to let her sleep forever.

Each time she shut her eyes it was in the hope that she would open them onto another world. That, through some miracle, time had raced past as she slept and it was no longer today but a month from now, a year from now. And with the passage of time, the ache had gone, the memory dulled. As soon as she woke to the reality, she would roll over and escape again into sleep.

It was a full week before she dragged herself out of bed and went into the kitchen to make tea. The housekeeper had gone for the day, Jordan was still at the office. The apartment was silent as a tomb. She put on a kettle and went to get a lemon.

Shocking. There was no other word for it. The inside of the refrigerator was in shocking condition. Not a fresh vegetable, not a celery stalk or a lettuce leaf in sight. A shriveled-up grapefruit, a half-eaten can of baked beans, packets of mystery meat wrapped in aluminum foil, and long-forgotten storage dishes of undefinable origin, liquefied into a foul-smelling green mold. All she could think was "What a godawful mess!"

The new housekeeper, for all her enthusiastic vacuuming, was a total dud in the kitchen. Chances were, Jordan hadn't had a proper dinner in a week. Longer. In fact, she couldn't remember the last time the two of them had had dinner home together, a decently cooked meal with two vegetables and a salad. Not since the children had gone off to school.

She was tempted to shut the door on the whole disaster area and write a cranky note to Maria. What was she paying the woman for? Except that Maria didn't read English. And, in all fairness, whose home was it anyhow? Whose mess was it anyhow?

"My mess," she admitted aloud. "My messy kitchen . . . my messy life." Both equal victims of neglect.

She called up Gristede's and had them send up fresh meat and fruits and vegetables, then fell to cleaning. There was a certain pleasure in physical action after all those supine days, in doing chores that entailed no thought, no moral choices, no difficult decisions. A simple therapy to be found in a Handi-Wipe and a tin of Ajax.

She scoured out the refrigerator, put together a beef stew, then sat down at the kitchen table for a cup of tea.

For the first time since she stepped off that flight from Chicago, she allowed herself to think openly of Frank.

It was over. Dasha understood that. She accepted his reasons. They had the ring of truth.

For all his generosity, she had demanded of Frank the one thing he was incapable of giving. She had asked that he be indistinguishable from those dinner-table companions whose foibles he took such glee in chronicling: men victimized by their passions, their weaknesses, their hungers. She had asked him to surrender to emotion. To relinquish control. To make a decision based solely on impulse.

Frank had to control—that was the given. He had to manipulate, to be the puppeteer who made the world dance to his motion. With Dasha, he had come perilously close to losing that control. And while for her, indeed for most people, to lose oneself in love was the supreme happiness—was it not what life was all about?—to Frank, it posed a dangerous precedent. She threatened him. Her ardor, her vitality, the qualities he so prized in her were precisely those he found most menacing. He *had* to drive her away, she now realized. His independence, his very survival depended on it, at least in his own mind. Conceivably, he himself had engineered that confrontation between her and Clarisse, not out of malice but out of an inner necessity.

And yet knowing all this changed nothing. She loved him still, wanted him still. It was impossible to believe her feeling for him would ever die, that her sense of loss would ever fully disappear. Frank had been more than a lover to her. He had been everything: her guide, mentor, teacher. Her religion. Yes, Frank had been her article of faith. As Father Kim, in a way, was David's. The analogy was uncomfortably apt.

And now, for her to picture life at Slater Blaney without his insights, his encouragement, above all without his support, was to picture herself stripped naked in a tough cold world. He had always been her first line of defense, her final court of appeal.

The Kim case, for example. She could never handle it without Frank's backing. Looking back over her long involvement with the case, it was hard to say how much of her work had been done not for the merits of the cause, not even for David's sake, but to win Frank's approval, to draw herself closer into his magic circle. Not all, but a great deal, certainly.

The more she thought of it, the grimmer the prospect of returning to the office and finishing the appeal without Frank's mantle around her appeared. She couldn't work with him again. It would be too agonizing. Nor could she work without him. In fact, there didn't seem much she was good for at this moment except maybe getting dinner on the table for Jordan.

Poor Jordan! He had been extraordinary this past week. Kind, restrained, never once asking for a word of explanation. Perhaps he would tonight, when he saw she was once more mobile. Then again, perhaps not. She couldn't decide whether his reticence thus far had been to spare her feelings or his own. Either way, she was grateful.

She was still sitting at the table in her bathrobe, brooding, when he came home well after seven.

"Well, isn't this nice to see you up and about. And what are you making? It smells delicious."

"Plain old beef stew." She rubbed her eyes wearily.

"Do me a favor while I set the table. Put on some proper clothes, at least a skirt and blouse. I think you'll feel better for it."

She did as he asked, then washed her face and put on makeup for the first time in days. When she finished, she saw that he had set their places in the dining room, with linen napkins and her mother's brass candlesticks.

"How was your day, Jordan?" She tried to make conversation. "You were working late, I gather?"

"Busy, busy." He picked at his food. "That Romero case, remember it? The Cuban boy facing a rape charge? We're going to trial next week, and I've been getting everything ship-shape."

"Oh yes," Dasha recalled. Jordan's first venture into criminal law. "Did he do it, your client?"

"Dasha!" Jordan shot her a reproving look. "Would I defend him if I thought he had?"

"Why not?" She shrugged. "Everyone's entitled to a defense."

"Well, as it happens, he didn't! If you're really interested," he began, and she realized she had never asked him about the case before. She put down her fork. "Yes, I'm interested."

The details were sparse, but compelling. The victim was a twenty-five-year-old teacher at St. Ignatius, who lived in a brownstone on the Upper West Side. Her story was that she had come home one night after a movie and surprised a burglar in her apartment. She screamed for help, whereupon the intruder assaulted her. "At knife-point, she claims. Rape, sodomy, you name it. In any event, she wound up with three broken ribs so there's no question *somebody* gave her a going over."

The next day, she picked Santos Romero out of a line-up. "The boy has no record. Just his rotten luck to have been in the area at the time plus he matches the physical description."

"What's your defense going to be—mistaken identity?"

"No." Jordan shook his head vigorously. "She's sticking to her story like it's a baby blanket. I personally think there never was any burglary, any unknown intruder . . . "

Jordan had an alternative theory to offer the jury. He had done some investigation at his own expense, and discovered that the girl had been a regular fixture at the downtown singles bars. She apparently led a double life. Teacher by day, swinger by night.

"And for all that these are liberated times, that's not the kind of thing sits awfully well with the hierarchy of a Catholic school. No, ma'am. What I think happened is, she picked up some guy in a bar, took him home, and he beat up on her. So there's Helene Ryan, third-grade teacher at St. Ignatius, looking like she's just gone ten rounds with Mister T, and what's she gonna tell 'em at school? That she's into rough trade? No way. Your sex-crazed intruder would be much more convenient."

"You've really been doing your homework, haven't you?" she said.

"Yes," he murmured. "That's one reason I was late tonight. The other is I was having a drink with Andy McCabe."

"Oh really?" She pushed her plate away. "He called you, I suppose."

"He's been calling *you,* every day about ten times. He's very concerned, Dasha, what with the Supreme Court date only a little ways off."

"Yes . . . well . . . " She wanted nothing so much as to go back to bed now, pull the covers over her head. But she couldn't hide forever.

"I've been thinking, Jordan, about taking a sabbatical from Slater Blaney. I've been working very hard, as you know. I'm very tired, and perhaps the best thing for me to do—the best thing all around, for me *and* the case, is to take a year off." She wet her lips. She would give Jordan the opening, for him to take or bypass as he chose. "I have had a falling out with Frank Hunicutt, you see." She paused, but he said nothing. His eyes were sad.

No. He was not going to wound her. Not going to savage her with I-told-you-so taunts about "Joe Sincere."

She waited in silence for a minute, then continued: "As I've said, Frank and I have had a . . . well, a disagreement, and I don't feel that I can continue working alongside him. Which means, you see, that I'll have to opt out of the Kim case. I can't cope with it on my own. It's too big. Not that it will make any difference in the outcome. As you've said on occasion, there are fifty lawyers up there who could handle it as well. Most of the research and preparation has already been done, so it's largely a question of who's going to make the final argument before the Court and"—she averted her eyes—"well, I don't kid myself that I'm indispensable. Nobody is. Anyhow, I just don't feel up to it."

"So you're going to cut and run, right?"

"If you want to put it that way. Although your choice of words surprises me. I should think, after all we've been through, you'd be delighted to hear the last of the wretched case. You were opposed to my involvement from the start, and I know you feel there's nothing much to choose from between the litigants. Pot and kettle, wasn't that how you sized up the two of 'em? In any event, wouldn't you prefer having me home for a while?"

"Doing what, Dasha? Sleeping your life away? Copping out? Or do you plan to go back to serious bread-baking?"

She had no answer for that. "If you don't mind, Jordan, I think I'll turn in."

"I do mind," he shouted. "I mind that you are only a few weeks away from the kind of opportunity we all dreamed of when we were young, and you're running away like a deserter. I mind because you have the rare good fortune to champion what may well be the most significant First Amendment case of the decade, and you're ready to jeopardize it on a whim. I mind because your associates have been knocking themselves out for you, working seventy, eighty hours a week, and you don't even want to know. Yes, I mind that you're abandoning your convictions. And above all"—his voice had a low dangerous throb—"I mind the fact that you are so damned emotionally dependent on Franklin Hunicutt that you can't conduct your career without him. Because that's really what it's all about, isn't it? You're scared shitless to make a move without Frank standing behind you to pick up the pieces. And since you and he have what it pleases you to call a 'disagreement,' that gives you the right to walk away from your basic obligations. Well, I'm not going to let you. I'm not going to permit you to waste all the effort I have put into your career. Yes, and Robin and Geoff. All the sacrifices we've made as a family . . ."

"I can't do it, Jordan"—she started to weep, but her tears only fueled his wrath.

"Why the hell not?" He reached across the table and seized her arm in an iron grip. "Don't you know, don't you realize you're probably ten times the lawyer, ten times the human being that Hunicutt is!"

"Please . . . you're hurting me."

He released her arm.

"No, Dasha, you're hurting me. Do you remember that weekend in Southampton? That fiasco and then the scene you and I had? At the time, you asked me if I were envious of Hunicutt. I've given that a lot of thought, and I don't think I was, really. You know who I envied?"

She shook her head, totally at sea.

"I envied *you*, Dasha. Of everyone in that house party, all those glitzy celebrities, smartass lawyers, the one I really envied was you. From the day you went back to law school right up until last Tuesday when I went to fetch you at the airport, I envied you—your drive, your courage, your tenacity. I'd watch you in action and for all my bitching, it was with a sense of wonder. Maybe mixed with a little bit of fear, because you can be pretty awesome at times. Still there it was. You had done it. You had realized the dreams I never could. And now, so close to the end, you want to walk away."

"You extraordinary man!" she said. "I thought you'd be so happy if I left the firm. Isn't that what you've wanted all these years?"

"What I want and what is possible are two different things. You couldn't go back to the old life as if none of this had happened. In theory, I'd like you home, waiting for me with the beef stew and the dry martinis. In fact, you'd probably drive both of us crazy. You'd never know if you'd have won the appeal or not. You'd probably spend the rest of your life second-guessing. I haven't a clue, Dasha, not the faintest notion whether we're going to emerge from all this with a viable marriage. But one thing I do know, if you cop out now, we have had it." He left the room abruptly, and returned a minute later lugging a heavy briefcase.

"This is some of the stuff Andy and Teddy Keller have been compiling last week. They've done a lot of research but are not too sure what's germane, so they both have plenty of questions for you. Andy'll be here tomorrow morning at eight, Keller can't make it till nine. I've also asked Fran to come, because you'll probably need secretarial help. They're all willing to work from the apartment, should you find that more convenient. If necessary, we can install a few more phones. Well, that's it. So if you're going to chicken out at this late date, at least have the decency to inform your associates face to face. If not"—he opened the briefcase and spilled its contents onto the table before her; the top page was a list of forty-five relevant law review articles which Andy had headlined MANDATORY READING—"if you're going to fight the case after all, then you better get cracking right now. Because you have a whole lot of all-nighters coming up."

Two days later she was back at Slater Blaney, plunged in a maelstrom of work.

Frank had returned to New York in her absence, and there were moments, illogical and instinctive as a reflex, when she looked up from her desk expecting to find him standing there. Even in the midst of a thousand details, one part of her mind remained detached, waiting, listening in a state that wavered between hope and fear, for a ring on their private telephone. For the command that would draw her back forever into his fold. *I want you. I want you now.*

The call never came.

The first time she set eyes on him was at the Monday partners' lunch and he was looking remarkably fit. Why not? He had extricated himself from a fate worse than death.

She wondered if he had kept the sublease to the loft in SoHo. If he had resumed the patterns of the past. The quick lay. The casual affair. Probably. He had told her once that he had never gone two consecutive days without a woman. "Sport-fucking," he called it, the way another man might acknowledge a fondness for jogging. "But of course, darling, that was before I met you." Did she believe him? What difference did it make?

He said nothing to her over the lunch table, but afterwards passed by her chair and clapped a friendly arm on her shoulder.

"How are you, Dasha?" He spoke, as always, with genuine warmth.

"Quite well," she managed to stammer.

"Splendid. Keep up the good work on the Kim case, will you?" He gave his glorious smile and left the room.

She returned to her office profoundly depressed. *Still,* she comforted herself, *it wasn't so bad. I survived. I didn't cry or have hysterics or fling myself at his feet. Looks like I'm going to make it after all. And the next time will be easier. I hope.*

That evening Jordan reminded her that the Romero case was on the calendar that week.

"See if you can sneak away for a couple of hours when I cross-examine Ryan, will you? Because that's the crux of our defense."

Accordingly, on Wednesday mid-morning she made her way into a small harshly lit courtroom on Centre Street and took a seat on the hard wooden bench. The girl was recounting the nature of her injuries. There were only half a dozen spectators. Romero's mother. A couple of nuns, presumably from the school. Not like the circus in San Francisco. For though it was a sordid case, in some ways even nastier than Kim, it was in no wise notable. Dasha might, at random, have dipped into any of the adjacent courtrooms and met with equally lurid tales: incest, drug dealing, muggings, murder. Jordan was right. The city was a swamp.

She caught his eye just as he got up to cross-examine, and he returned a complicitous wink before turning to the witness.

The woman on the stand seemed an unlikely candidate for the excesses Jordan hoped to reveal. She was a tall, bony girl with wiry hair and an unfortunate number of freckles.

Jordan started off nice and easy, the usual questions with his smile of quick ready sympathy. Dasha could see Helene Ryan unwinding. After all, they were both middle-class whites together, weren't they?

"So you came home from the movies and found the defendant there. Am I correct? By the way, what movie did you see?"

Helene Ryan looked startled. "I don't remember."

"You don't remember," Jordan echoed, then his voice took on an edge. "The most terrible night of your life. The night you were raped and sodomized by a total stranger. And you don't remember? Is it possible that you weren't at the movies at all that night, but at a singles bar in Greenwich Village called"—he paused for emphasis—"the Meat Rack?"

The girl looked as if she were about to vomit. Then she shook her head no.

"Speak up, Miss Ryan. The court can't hear you. So you would have us believe that you have never set foot in"—he shook his head in revulsion—"the Meat Rack, let alone picked up companions there?"

She swallowed hard. "I wasn't there that night."

For God's sakes. Dasha sat up. What the hell was the matter with the Assistant District Attorney? He should have been jumping up, objecting to Jordan's questions with every breath. She shot a glance at the prosecutor's table, but the ADA seemed to have lost his bearings. He was a kid, Dasha realized, probably fresh out of law school, a novice unprepared and overworked.

Now Jordan was upon Helene Ryan like a dog on a piece of raw meat, for she had given him the opening he sought.

"I see. You weren't at the Meat Rack that night, but you have been there other nights. Many other nights, am I right? It's where you hang out, isn't it? How would you describe the Meat Rack, can you tell me? What's the attraction?"

"You go there to . . . to meet friends," she answered in a tiny voice.

"To meet friends. New friends, I presume. Now tell me, would they be women friends or men friends?"

From that point on he began stripping her naked, flaying her alive. Each question laced with fury, each a direct assault on her modesty, her virtue, so that within five relentless minutes, Helene Ryan of St. Ignatius School appeared to the stunned jurors as wanton and depraved as the Whore of Babylon.

Dasha watched with breathless intensity. Jordan was degrading the woman. Destroying her with a ferocity, a savagery of which she had never deemed him capable. It was a virtuoso performance.

And in one shattering burst of insight, she knew what the source of Jordan's outrage was, recognized the true object of his attack. Not that pitiful creature up on the witness stand. Not Helene Ryan, whatever her faults, but herself. Dasha Croy. Dasha the whore. The adulteress. Insatiable, shameless Dasha who fucked in SoHo lofts and the back seats of limousines and overheated Chicago hotel rooms.

"You can't get enough of it, can you?" he now flung at the hysterical Ryan woman until at last—at last, the judge reined him in.

Jordan had channeled the anger he dared not show his wife and let it loose in an astonished courtroom. She didn't even think he realized what he was doing, but of one thing she was certain: She could take no more of it.

She scribbled him a note—*"You are a great trial lawyer. About the best I've ever seen"*—then reeled out of the courtroom.

"How'd Jordie do in court today?" Andy asked when she got back to the office.

"Jesus," she gasped. "He really missed his calling. He should have been a criminal lawyer or at the very least a U.S. attorney. My husband has got the stuff to be another Bomber Hazzard."

She worked late that night and didn't get home until nearly midnight. Jordan was sitting in the living room, nursing a brandy. His shoulders were slunk in despair.

"Don't tell me"—she darted across the room—"don't tell me you lost this afternoon? You *can't* have! You were superb!"

"I won," he said morosely. "Isn't that what it's all about—winning?"

Dasha poured herself a drink and curled up at his feet. Clearly he'd had second thoughts about the day. "I know it wasn't a pleasant experience, Jordan, dragging all that filth up in court . . . "

"I raped her," he broke in. "I raped Helene Ryan just as surely as anyone ever has, only I did it with words!"

The cross-examination had gone brilliantly. By the time it was over, Helene Ryan didn't have enough moral credit left to run a peanut stand. Jordan could hardly conceal his jubilation. He didn't even need to mount a defense. The Romero boy never took the stand.

The jury deliberated less than an hour before returning a not guilty verdict, and Jordan threw his arms around his client.

"That's it, Santos! Congratulations!"

But the boy still looked doubtful.

"They no try me again, huh?"

Well, these Cuban kids, after what they'd been through in Castro country, to say nothing of the sidewalks of New York, small wonder they were wary of official justice.

Jordan patiently explained to him about double jeopardy. "They can't. Once you're cleared, Santos, once a jury's found that you're not guilty, that's it. *Nada mas.* Never again. Understand?"

And as the import of Jordan's message sank in, Santos Romero broke into a smile.

("But such a smile, Dasha! Sly, gloating. The cat who swallowed the canary. The moment I saw that smile, I knew.")

"It was you!" Jordan trembled with shock. "My God! It *was* you, after all, who raped that girl."

"Fuckin' *puta,*" Romero burst out laughing. "You sure showed that bitch. Hey, you one fuckin' good lawyer. I'm gonna pass the word to my pals."

It was all Jordan could do to keep from killing him.

"I never knew I had so much anger in me, Dasha. I've never hated myself so much."

"It's not your fault!" She flung her arms around him. "You did what any good attorney does for a client. You presumed he was innocent and fought your hardest. You have nothing to reproach yourself for."

"Winning is all . . . isn't that what you guys say?" She could feel his tears hot against her cheek. "And you want to hear the ultimate irony?" He pulled back, swiped at his eyes. "You ready for the grand finale?" He made a strange honking sound that was a cross between a laugh and a sob. "You know what a sewer that courthouse is, the lobby always jammed with people. Anyhow, I get out on the street, just about ready to throw myself in front of a passing car—and I discover some son of a bitch has stolen my wallet. Jesus, everything. Credit cards, driver's license, everything. Come to New York and get robbed in the court-house, for Chrissakes. Pretty fuckin' funny, as my beloved client would put it."

Her heart went out to him. Her admiration as well.

For Dasha, the irony of the day's events lay not in the robbery but in the fact that today, for the first time in his career, he had demonstrated the full measure of his ability. Uncovered a talent she had never known him to possess. He had been magnificent in court. He had shown both the mastery and passion of a great trial lawyer.

For the first time. And the last.

"Never again," he said. "I'm never going to step into a criminal courtroom again!"

"They're not all Santos Romeros, you know," she said softly. "You could have a big career."

"Ah, Dasha, Dasha . . . What kind of career? As a paid assassin? You know, I think I've been in the wrong profession my whole life."

"Come on, darling." She took his hand and pulled him gently out of the chair. "Let's go to bed and comfort each other."

They slept in each other's arms that night, close as paint. Two survivors clinging to the wreckage.

Two days before she was to leave for Washington, Frank Hunicutt called an urgent meeting. The managing partners were there, the firm's top financial officer, their own outside counsel, and Dasha.

"First the good news," Frank announced. "FBC has thus far run up over eight million dollars in legal fees with our firm. Some but not all part of the Kim case. Now the bad news. Amory's refusing to pay. That is, unless the Kim case goes his way. We got him into it, he claims, and we can damn well get him out. If not, what it comes down to is this.

First has no intention of paying out millions for the privilege of losing millions more. Of course we can sue, but that's not a happy alternative. He is very very angry, and that's the sort of thing we certainly don't want other clients getting wind of. I had hoped that Amory would have 'retired' by now"—Dasha shot him a quick look; clearly, Frank's palace revolution had not met with success—"but he persists in hanging on. If worst comes to worst, Slater Blaney is going to be stiffed for a great deal of money. Our safest bet, obviously, is to win the goddam Kim case and cut the ground out from under him. Dasha, what's your prognosis?"

She began a detailed rundown—which justices would most likely favor the FBC plea, which she believed to be hostile on the basis of previous opinions—when Porter Collins cut her short.

"Can you put it into two words—We win? We lose?"

"Three words," she said. "I don't know."

"Well ain't that just dandy!"

"However," she concluded, "if there's any moral justice, we should win hands down."

For, everything else aside (research, precedent, and factual arguments), what the Kim case ultimately came down to was a moral issue.

Don't get hung up on abstract concepts, everyone had warned her, and she had done sufficient research to know precisely what an argument before the Supreme Court entailed.

For all its grandiosity—the massive bronze gates, the velvet hangings, the vast marble columns; for all the ritual pomp accumulated over nearly two hundred years—the robing room, the Court Crier's gavel, the entrance through parted crimson drapes; for all the monumental decisions —from *Marbury vs. Madison* to *Dred Scott* to *Miranda*—the Court remained a no-nonsense place at heart.

"Talk to 'em," Blagden Geere had impressed upon her, "as you would talk to me. Say what you've got to say right out, in good clean English. As a rule they give you half an hour. When the green light goes on, you talk; when the red light goes on, you thank them and step down. So keep it concise. And if the justices interrupt you along the way, don't take offense. Answer their questions as frankly as possible. At least it shows that they're awake and listening."

"But the difficulty is, sir, we're not really dealing with hard-and-fast issues. There are moral factors involved on both sides. Kim's right to control the property of his life. Our right to inform the public. We are treading in a very murky area."

"Then it's your business to make it clear."

But all the advice was academic now. And as she stepped onto the rostrum and faced the Chief Justice of the United States, she had never in her life felt so utterly alone.

What if she should freeze? What if she should open her mouth and nothing came out, like that ghastly night of moot court back in Seneca. Only then, Jordan had been by her side, she remembered, springing out of nowhere with a glass of water and words of encouragement. But Jordan wasn't here now. He had chosen not to come. "It's your day, Dasha," he had said. "Your case, and anyhow, I've got my own work." She could only conclude it would have pained him to watch his wife in the role that had been the apogee of his youthful dreams.

No, Jordan wasn't here. Bomber Hazzard was, of course, sitting a few feet behind her awaiting his turn. Her brother Alex was here, leaning forward in the press gallery, pale and tense. And the justices were here, which was what it was all about.

"Mrs. Croy," the Chief Justice gave the traditional opening.

"Mr. Chief Justice, may it please the Court . . . " she gave the traditional return.

Atop the rostrum, the green light clicked on.

CHAPTER TWENTY-TWO

☐ She was sailing.

Never before had her voice rung so confident; never before had her control of material been so secure. It was the most delicious, most extraordinary sensation she had ever encountered, this sense of mastery, of unbounded power. Like breathing pure oxygen. Bliss.

She began by reciting the basic facts of the case, then moved swiftly to an exposition of the conflict. It was simple, she stated. There were no peripheral issues.

The Reverend Kim's contention was that his life belonged to him alone. That no one could use it without his express permission. No one, not even the press, was allowed to present it to the general public. To do so would be to show him in false light.

But the life of a public figure is not merchandise. It cannot be copyrighted like a pop song. It is not "protectable" like a trademark or a patent. It is not a commodity for rent or sale. Were this to be the case, legitimate comment in this country would cease to exist.

For once you admitted the doctrine as valid, once you opened the floodgates to such suits as that of the Reverend Kim, where did you draw the line?

The cartoonist who exaggerated Ronald Reagan's dewlaps—was he showing the President in a false light? The nightclub satirist who poked fun at the Ku Klux Klan—could the Grand Dragon sue him for false light? Carry the premise one step further and there would no unauthorized biographies of public figures, no movies dealing with current events, no historian who dared speculate on a leader's state of mind, no timely docudramas on television.

Indeed, carry the premise to its logical extreme and there would be no reporting of any kind. "If all of us can repress every word that is said or written about ourselves, what would ensue would be the most dangerous kind of pre-censorship. Prior restraint. Writers too intimidated to touch upon any controversial person for fear of being hauled into court. Reporters, editors, publishers all being frightened into silence. The end result would be the death of history."

The questions began pouring in thick and fast, a veritable bombardment, and Dasha fielded them just as swiftly. What distinction did she make between news and entertainment? Where did fiction begin and fact end on this kind of show? With each reply, Dasha felt her assurance grow. Her answers shaped up with a beautiful logic, a brilliant clarity. Most of them, anyway. "What's your precedent for that statement?" she was asked at one point. She paused for a moment. "Mr. Justice, I have none." And a bout of laughter cleared the air.

She sneaked a look at her watch. She had been on her feet for well over the allotted half-hour and the light was still green! She could have stayed there forever, she felt, like an athlete in peak condition. And when she finally sat down after a full hour, she couldn't resist looking over to Hazzard.

Today, the Bomber wasn't winking at her snidely, giving that "Little Girlie" leer. On the contrary, he was looking at her with an expression in which respect was mingled with a certain amount of trepidation. Then he stepped up to the rostrum and Dasha leaned back.

Whatever the outcome of today's hearing, whatever the Court in its wisdom should determine, this day must mark the high point of her life. She had been put to the highest challenge. Had drawn upon her deepest strengths. She had done her best, and even if she lost, she knew her best was magnificent.

"Absolutely terrific!" Alex hugged her tight as soon as it was over. Yet even now, he felt called upon to qualify his praise with a touch of mockery. "You always were a smart kid, Dasha."

Nonetheless, she could read the admiration in his eyes.

"And you always were a patronizing bastard."

Alex's face fell. She had never lashed back before. "Not that it matters"—she returned the pressure of his hug—"because I love you anyway. Now, are you going to buy me a drink, yes or no?"

She didn't need that first martini; it couldn't possibly add to the euphoria she already felt.

And there was Alex—Alex of all people!—giving her the royal treatment.

"I was sitting next to Billy Halprin of Reuters," he said, "and he thought you were pretty hot copy. He loved that phrase of yours, what was it?—'death of history.' So don't be surprised if it goes out over the international wire services tonight." He called for a second round of drinks and then turned to her, mollified.

"Am I really a patronizing bastard, Dasha? On second thought, don't answer that. I don't know." He shrugged. "Maybe it was the age difference, maybe it was the way we were both brought up. Some habits take a long time to unlearn. Did I tell you I had a card from David last week? It was postmarked San Francisco, so he's still out there."

"What did he say?"

" 'Happy Birthday, Dad.' Some message. Well, after two years' silence, it's better than nothing." His eyes moistened. "What do you think, Dasha? Do you think the boy is coming around?"

"Are you, Alex? Are you coming around?"

"I'd give my soul to have him back. David could have a career selling Crackerjacks at the zoo, as far as I'm concerned, and I wouldn't love him any the less. It's been"—he managed a smile—"quite an education."

He urged her to come home and join the family for dinner, but she was too eager to get back to New York. If she left now, she could be there by six. In fact, she could scarcely wait to relive the day's events with everyone at Slater Blaney. Relish it even more the second time around with a blow-by-blow rehash . . . *He said, I said, the Chief Justice said* . . . What bliss!

"Nope, Alex. Just point me in the direction of the airport and I'll catch the next flight home."

"Okay." He laughed. "But are you sure you need a plane? You look like you're flying already."

A half-hour later she was boarding the Eastern shuttle as she had done a hundred times in the past. As always, it was packed.

She got one of the last seats on the flight, caught her breath, and looked about her. No one she knew, dammit. Too bad. There usually was.

"Hey you guys!" she wanted to shout. "Wake up. Smile. Today's a red-letter day. I just argued a case before the Supreme Court. And I was sensational. Even the great Alex Oborin said so."

The more she thought about it, the more remarkable it struck her. She, Darya Maximovna Oborin Croy, had knocked 'em dead in the highest court in the land. She wanted to jump or sing or order champagne all around. Except they didn't have champagne on the shuttle flights and you were lucky if you could cadge a cup of coffee.

At last she could contain herself no longer. If she didn't talk to someone, she'd explode.

"Excuse me"—she turned to the man sitting next to her, a nice-looking fellow in a polo neck sweater, and said in a barely controlled voice—"but I have just argued a major case before the Supreme Court."

"What? Sorry?"

Perhaps he was hard of hearing. Cabin pressure sometimes did that to people.

"The Supreme Court," she articulated every syllable. "I have just argued a case before the Supreme Court."

"Oh?" He gave a puzzled smile "Is that a good thing? Is that important?"

He had a Scandinavian accent an inch thick.

Dasha's jaw dropped. Of all the passengers in the whole damn plane, which probably included about fifty government officials and at least as many lawyers, she had to pick the one seat-mate who'd never even heard of the Supreme Court.

"Are you a tourist"—she was curious—"a diplomat?"

No, he replied. He was coming to New York to take up a teaching post at Columbia.

"My alma mater," Dasha said. "What's your field?"

Anthropology, he answered. His particular specialty was cargo cults of the South Pacific. In fact he had just returned from a three-year stay in Melanesia.

Dasha was intrigued. "What on earth are cargo cults?"

He blinked, an astonished where-on-earth-have-you-been blink, and proceeded to enlighten her about Melanesian culture.

She listened, fascinated. As he spoke, his gray eyes danced, his face lit up beneath the tropical tan, and Dasha could hardly could keep from smiling. She recognized the look, the excitement of the born enthusiast. The Melanesians were his Supreme Court.

"Ah, but I'm boring you," he said as the plane began its descent into New York.

"Not at all," Dasha said. "I've really enjoyed it. You've managed to put things in quite a different perspective."

The moment she got into the taxi, Dasha burst out laughing. "I feel," she told the cabbie, "as if I've just been on a trip to the Stone Age."

She arrived at the office to find Fran and Andy and half a dozen other colleagues waiting to greet her with buckets of Dom Perignon.

"I heard it went like gangbusters," Andy said. "The guy from the *Times* called me up. Congrats."

"Yes, well . . . we haven't won yet!" She gulped down a glass of champagne. "I shouldn't be doing this on top of a whole bunch of dry martinis, but—aw shit!" She threw her arms around Andy. "I feel on top of the world!"

"Your husband called." Fran refilled her glass. "He says he's having dinner with friends, he'll catch up with you later. And oh yes, Mr. Hunicutt would like to see you in his office."

The champagne suddenly lost its savor.

"When?" she asked. "Did he say what about?"

"As soon as you got back. I guess he wants to know how it went."

She hadn't seen Frank alone since that day at the Palmer House. In fact, she had scrupulously avoided any confrontation. The memory was still too fresh, too painful. Yet other memories were far more painful—the memory of all that shining love, that glorious sex. "You've spoiled me," she once had told him, "for every other man." He had certainly spoiled her for Jordan.

And yet, as ever, there was that old desire to confide in him. To share her triumphs with him, her anxieties, to earn his smile, to have the benediction of his approval.

She handed her glass back to Fran—"Finish the party without me"
—and made her way to his office.

He was stretched out on the butterscotch sofa, in his shirtsleeves,
collar loosened, hands clasped behind his head.

"Come in, darling." He made no move to get up. "Would you like
something to drink?"

"No thanks. I've had a few already."

"Then perhaps you'll get me one, a Chivas and soda please. On the
rocks. It's been quite a day all around."

She fetched his drink, then sat down opposite him on a pretty little
Sheraton cane chair. Behind them, dusk settled over the harbor.

"So," he said finally. "Tell me about your day. I understand you
had the old boys eating out of your hand."

"It went well," she began coolly. "In fact, it went very well," then
the words began spilling out. For all the tears he had cost her, all the
misery, this was still Frank—her greatest intimate, her closest confidant.
Frank, from whom she had no secrets.

"Would you care to place a bet on the outcome?" he asked when
she finished her recitation.

"Who can say? It's in the lap of the gods. And as you know, Bomber
Hazzard is no slouch either. He made one helluva case for the Reverend.
But all that aside, something interesting happened to me down in Wash-
ington today, something I can tell you and probably no one else."

"Oh?"

"Do you remember when we were on the beach at Monterey that
first weekend? Well, of course you do. Anyhow, you said something to
me about power. Why it was permissible to seek it. Why it was good
to achieve it. That it wasn't an exclusively masculine goal. As I recall,
I pooh-poohed you at the time. To tell the truth, I found the whole
conversation intimidating. But now I know. And you were right. I
realized that today when I stepped up on the rostrum and faced the
justices. I was all alone, Frank. You weren't there, Jordan wasn't there.
All I had was my own resources. And I was maybe five minutes into my
statement when it struck me that I was in total control, not only of the
case but of my life. Total! For the first time since I could remember, I
was dependent on no one, beholden to no one. I was absolutely on my
own."

"And were you frightened?"

She considered. "No . . . no I wasn't. It was a strange sensation, I admit. Rather like being in foreign country. But wonderful, too. Can I ask you something, Frank?"

"Anything, Dasha. Everything."

"No, not everything, my love. I already asked you for that. This time I'll settle for a simple answer to a simple question. When you dumped me in Chicago, weren't you afraid that I would quit the firm, walk out flat on the Kim case, leave everyone in the lurch?"

"No." He raised his head and smiled at her. "I wasn't worried."

"I almost did."

"Almost doesn't count. The point is you didn't. I knew, when it came to the crunch, you'd see it through. You could never walk away from a challenge like that. You see, Dasha, I know you better than you know yourself." He watched the sky for a few minutes. The room was almost in total darkness. Then he said, "I've missed you terribly, Dasha."

"Please, Frank."

"I'm not offering to change anything, just making a statement of fact. Now let me tell you what happened to me today."

The day had started for him with the arrival of a messenger at ten in the morning. "One of those pimply kids from the Swifty Nifty Services, or whatever. They scoot around the city on bikes, delivering salami sandwiches, advertising layouts, that kind of trivia. Not exactly the picture of dignity."

The boy handed Frank's secretary an envelope with a single sheet of paper enclosed. On the paper was the date and one hand-written sentence. It read:

> The services of Slater Blaney are no longer required by me or my corporation, effective today at the close of business hours.

It was signed by Amory First.

The old man had finally gone bananas. That at least was Frank's appraisal. Either that, or someone was playing a practical joke. You don't end a relationship that has lasted more than half a century with a one-line note sent over by messenger. "At least no civilized person does."

Frank tore over to the network and physically thrust his way into the black-and-white office. Amory First was there, sipping milk and watching television.

"I was sure I could reason with him, Dasha, or barring that, charm him into backing down. What the hell, I've known the man for over twenty years. He came to my wedding; we named our oldest boy after him."

"I can't believe you really wrote this, Amory."

"I should think you're familiar with my handwriting by now."

"In which case, you owe me an explanation."

"Indeed!" The old man faced him briefly. The eyes, always cold, were now arctic. "First you claim I owe you eight million dollars in legal fees. Now you claim I owe you an explanation as well." With that, he turned back to his milk.

Frank sat for a moment in stunned silence.

"I thought we were friends, Amory."

"I have no friends"—the answer was devoid of all emotion—"I have only paid personnel, and you are no longer among them."

The interview lasted less than two minutes.

The rest of the day passed in a frenzy of activity.

By noon, Frank had got in touch with investment bankers, major stockholders, with every member of the board he judged to be ripe for rebellion. "I've never worked so hard in my life, Dasha. I was chartering planes, limos, everything but carrier pigeons, pulling people out of meetings, out of men's rooms. The thing was, I was determined to get the powers that be all in one place before old Amory got the wind up. It would have to be a commando attack."

By mid-afternoon, the principals were assembled in secrecy at a conference room in a Queens hotel situated halfway between Wall Street and the airport. It was pandemonium. Not just the firing of Slater Blaney—Frank had no illusions that anyone but himself really cared about the firm—but Amory's behavior in general was proving that the time had come. The old man had outraged everyone from the executive vice-president of Morgan Guaranty to Frank's mother-in-law who had come up from Palm Beach. One after another, First's failures were trotted out for inspection: the crazy acquisitions, the rotten programming, the way the stock was falling through the floor. For Amory had wounded these people where it hurt the most: in the pocketbook. The air was thick with the smell of blood.

And now, at last, it was Frank's turn to call in his credits. "All the men I'd golfed with and gracefully lost to over the years, all the free advice I'd given, all the favor I've curried, all the dinners and social entrees Clarisse and I have provided—it was all for this moment."

Within two hours, Amory First was ousted and Frank Hunicutt invited to become the new chairman of the board of FBC.

"Congratulations!" Dasha was overjoyed. "I'm so happy for you, Frank, I can't tell you. I know how much you've always wanted it. And you'll be wonderful in the job. When do you start—when are you going to make the announcement?"

"I turned it down, Dasha."

"You what?" She couldn't believe her ears. "Are you out of your mind or am I?"

"Both of us, I suspect." He sighed. "I turned it down cold, at least for the present. And for a reason that will make sense only to you."

There it was within his grasp, the culmination of a lifetime's effort. And for the first time in his entire career, he had qualms. Scruples, if you will.

"For twenty years, I've dreamed of taking up this post," he had told the assembled stockholders. "For twenty years I've also been a part of Slater Blaney. My entire professional life has been spent there. I have ambitions, yes, but I also have loyalties."

The Kim broadcast, he went on to explain, had been mounted with his blessing. True, a relatively junior associate had made the initial recommendation, but he believed then—as he still did—that she had exercised proper judgment and her decision had been correct.

Nonetheless that course of action had embroiled the network in the most massive litigation ever launched. Many people, from Amory First to members of other law firms to rank outsiders, had questioned Slater Blaney's actions in the case, on both ethical and professional grounds. The charge had been raised that the million–dollar fees, rather than the welfare of the client, had motivated Slater Blaney's strategy. According to its critics, the firm had been at best reckless. At worst, venal.

As for the wisdom of their advice on the Kim program, the Supreme Court was hearing the matter even as they sat today in this conference room. They would be the final arbiters of Slater Blaney's judgment.

But as for the morality of the firm's behavior, Frank would stake his reputation on it. More than his reputation. He would stake his future at FBC.

"If the Supreme Court finds for us," he said, "I will take up the chairmanship of FBC with the greatest pleasure. If it does not, then I will regretfully have to decline. Nothing less would be honorable."

"You astonish me, Frank." Dasha was breathless.

"I astonished myself," he murmured. "Even as I was running on and on there, one part of me was shouting, 'Hey, this is nuts, professional suicide!' "

"But what on earth possessed you?"

"You did," he said. "Yes, some of you rubbed off on me this past year, some of your New England morality, I suppose. Just as I seem to have rubbed off on you. I won't be so self-serving as to say I've put my future on the line merely to win your respect. But you did figure, Dasha. Very heavily. And if I go to FBC, I want it to be with clean hands. And with your approval."

She got up and turned on a desk lamp. In the soft light, his hair was the color of burnished gold. She was tempted to lie down beside him on the sofa and place her cheek upon his. Instead, she returned to her chair.

"Then if I've lost today, Frank, I'll have lost more than a case. I'll have jeopardized everything you dreamed of, hoped for. I'll have let your future slip through my hands. I hadn't reckoned on that."

"Nor I."

"Have you really changed?" she wondered.

"In some ways, not in others."

"Have you"—she started to say, *Have you had many women since we parted?* but instead she asked, "Do you still have that loft in SoHo?"

The blue eyes flickered. "Yes," he whispered. "Would you like to go there with me now?"

More than anything in the world, Frank. I ache for you with every bone in my body.

She leaned over with a soft, supple motion and kissed him full on the lips.

"I have to go home," she said. "My husband's waiting."

Perhaps, the word hung in the air between them. *Perhaps some day when all this is over.*

PART THREE

CHAPTER TWENTY-THREE

☐ From that day to this, she had lived in a state of suspended animation. It was a time of breath held taut, of decisions deferred. A time of waiting for the other shoe to drop, as Jordan put it.

Not that life was devoid of external events—far from it. She was busy as ever, sometimes even more so now that the Kim case had released her for other duties.

The week following the Supreme Court appearance, she and Jordan took an overdue vacation at the dude ranch, this time with the children in tow. It was a pleasant break, relaxed and gregarious. Bernie Gross and his wife came up from Tucson to spend a weekend with them.

"The offer's still open, Jordie. You gonna come into the real-estate business with me?"

"I still have to clear it with the boss," Jordan laughed.

They all enjoyed the change of scenery, Geoff in particular, who had fallen in love with a chestnut colt in the Rio Verde stables. Geoff christened him Crusader.

When the time came to say goodbye, the boy was devastated.

"Can't we buy Crusader and take him with us?"

"Geoff, darling, we live in an apartment!"

"I could keep him at school. Please, some of the other kids have horses."

Jordan and Dasha exchanged glances.

"You'd have to look after him, feed him, train him," Dasha said. "We're talking about real responsibility."

"Oh, I would, Mom. I promise. Cross my heart."

"Besides which, the horse may not be for sale."

"Oh, Mother," Robin said crisply. "I know you. Even if he's not for sale, you'll manage to wangle Crusader out of 'em."

"Honestly, Robin, what you must think of me! Well, I'll give it a try."

Two hours later, Crusader was theirs, ready to be crated and flown to Connecticut.

"That was an awfully extravagant gift, Dasha," Jordan said, when the transaction was complete.

"My guilty conscience, I suppose. Still, I think he'll get a lot of pleasure from it. And it's a good learning experience."

Then it was back to the office and work.

She returned to find that a lunch date had been set up for her with Bomber Hazzard. "He was terribly insistent," Fran said. So after a minimum soul search, Dasha met her erstwhile tormentor at the Four Seasons. They had an amusing and bibulous lunch, to her surprise.

"What are you doing?" Dasha stared at a double portion of chocolate cake. "Trying to fatten me up for the kill?"

"Nope. I'm about to pop the question. How'd you like to come in with me as a full partner? You could make a fortune, Dasha, be up to your eyeballs in the green."

"You're kidding!" she replied, but clearly he was not. "That's very flattering, Bomber, but I don't think we practice the same kind of law."

"Nonsense, there's only one kind—the winning kind—and you're into it as much as I am."

"Thank you, I *think*." She smiled. "But if I do leave Slater Blaney, it won't be to join another firm."

She tried, subtly, to plumb him on the "dirty tricks" of the first Kim trial—the mistaken identities, vanishing witnesses—but he was too shrewd to be suckered into any admission. They parted on wary, if amicable, terms. "See you in court, counselor," had been his final shot.

Christmas came and went. The winter had turned reluctantly into a cold late spring.

Over recent months, Jordan had busied himself with the plight of political refugees in New York. Dasha judged it an idiomatic response to the Romero fiasco.

"They were a solid middle-class family in Cuba," Jordan kept saying. "Honest, law-abiding. What is it that our society does to immigrants? Why have all the social services failed?"

She welcomed his involvement. After the long years of apathy, he seemed to be shaking loose, seeking untried directions. Yet between them nothing essentially changed.

They continued to live together. They shared meals, visited the children, went to the theater, made love every now and then, more out of habit than desire. Yet there remained about their marriage an unsettled quality. Two people reluctant to face the issues that lay before them.

Can we go on forever like this, Dasha would sometimes ask herself, *living from day to day, biding time?* Marriages like theirs were, she suspected, a commonplace—the triumph of lethargy over passion.

As for Frank, his extraordinary act of self-denial had paved the way for a gradual resumption of their friendship. He never again asked her back to the loft. Presumably, any such overture would have to come from her. She never doubted he was seeing other women, and the thought always managed to wound her afresh. Nonetheless, they had managed to salvage some of their earlier intimacy.

He called her daily on their private line, to gossip or to mull a professional problem, sometimes just to say hello. He had called last Friday when she was about to leave the office.

"Hello, darling"—on the phone that was still how he addressed her. "I have what I hope is a pleasant surprise. It looks like you're going to get your Supreme Court decision on Monday."

"Oh Frank!" she countered. "You can't possibly know that." The Court's deliberations were always shrouded in mystery. Not a whisper, not a clue ever surfaced beforehand.

"Even Alex hasn't a notion," she told him, "and you know how well connected he is. Everyone who works there is sworn to secrecy, the clerks, the printers, the cleaning women . . . "

"But not the shoe-shine boys."

"The *what?*"

"If you let a word of this get out," he said laughing, "I'll probably be disbarred." Then he'd gone on to tell her of an "arrangement" made with the most invisible of the Supreme Court staffers. After all, who really notices shoe-shine boys?

"Well, my informant overheard that they'll be handing down their opinion this coming Monday."

"He didn't say"—Dasha hated herself for asking—"if we win or lose, did he?"

"Nope, but I can tell you which of our justices wears thermal underwear."

"Frank," she admonished. "You are behaving in a thoroughly improper manner."

"I think the world of you too, darling."

That had been late Friday afternoon. But it seemed forever ago. So much had happened in between.

On Saturday, there had been the Plaza ball with Jordan, the evening that ended in recriminations and tears. On Sunday, he had given his ultimatum. This very morning, Blagden Geere had come into her office and dangled the promise of a senior partnership before her dazzled eyes. This very evening, Jordan expected his answer of a simple yes or no.

She checked her watch. Almost quarter of two. She had been sitting on this wooden bench in Battery Park for well over an hour and was still no closer to reaching a decision.

The lunchtime crowds had thinned, the sky grown overcast. In Washington, the justices would be reassembling for the afternoon session.

She crumpled the paper from her hero sandwich, dropped it in a trash bin, and started heading back to the office.

"Any word yet, Fran?"

Her secretary shook her head. "Not from Washington, but some reporter's been trying to reach you like crazy. Katie Evans of the San Francisco *Chronicle*." Yes, Dasha remembered her. They'd had drinks together on occasion. "I've got her holding on your third extension, Mrs. Croy, and she says she won't hang up until she's spoken to you."

Dasha had a flight of premonition.

She went into her office to take the call.

"I hope you're sitting down," the reporter's throaty contralto came on the wire, "because I've got news that's gonna curl your hair."

It was now eleven o'clock in California. Some three hours earlier, at eight o'clock local time, the Solano County sheriff's office had staged a surprise raid on the headquarters of Reverend Elijah Kim. It appeared that one of the faithful had recently grown suspicious about goings-on within the estate. He'd snooped around, kept careful notes, and when his suspicions reached the stage of certainty, called in the police.

"The cops have cordoned off the entire estate," Katie said, "and nothing's been officially confirmed yet, but I've got a friend in the sheriff's office keeping me posted. They're digging up the flowerbeds, tearing the place apart. And listen"—Dasha began trembling—"they've dug up some bodies. Three at least, but could be more . . . "

"Oh my God!" she cried out. "David!"

"What?"

"David—David Oborin, is that who?"

"Yes, but how did you know?"

"Oh God," Dasha could only repeat through anguished tears, while Katie continued to babble on the other end.

"Yup, David Oborin. That's the one. I understand he's the columnist's kid. You know, Alex Oborin. Like father, like son, I guess. Anyhow, the boy's got quite a story to tell."

"*What?*" Dasha screamed into the phone. "What are you talking about?"

"Oborin. He's the kid who blew the whistle."

"Then he's alive!"

"You bet he's alive. In fact right now he's sitting in the District Attorney's office, layin' back their ears . . . "

Dasha jabbed at the intercom.

"Frannie—quick! Get my brother in Washington, put him on the conference phone. Urgent!" Then she went back to her phone call.

"Katie, you've just given me the scare of my life. Then whose bodies are they, do you know?"

"Well, one has been tentatively identified as an Ira Leitman. It seems he's been missing for quite some time . . . "

"I've got your brother on the other line," Fran broke in.

"Alex?"

"Listen, I can't talk to you, Dasha. I'm on my way to the airport."

"Then you heard!"

"I just spoke to him ten minutes ago. He called and I'm flying out to the coast to bring him home." Alex was crying, great heaving sobs he made no attempt to disguise. "I'm going to bring my boy home, Dasha. It's over."

"Oh, Alex." Dasha could scarcely control her tears. "Oh Katie, I don't know what to say—how to thank you . . . "

Suddenly every light on her phone system started flashing. Fran burst into the office and Dasha turned to her with streaming eyes. "It's over," Dasha wept. Then Miranda ran in and Teddy Keller and Porter and J.J. with a bottle of champagne and Billy Mae from the typing pool and Andy McCabe, who swooped down on her seat and lifted her straight up into the air.

"It's over, Dasha!" he was shouting. "We did it! Seven to two. Burger wrote the opinion, Rehnquist wrote the dissent, but you wouldn't have wanted it unanimous anyway. That's too boring."

The din was terrific. Champagne and caviar arrived on silver trays from the partners' dining room. One of the mailroom kids dragged in a stereo from out of nowhere and they were all treated to the unlikely sight of Blagden Geere attempting a stately waltz with a pretty paralegal to the music of the Police.

"There are half a dozen reporters out here." The front receptionist begged for help in a harried voice. "The *Times,* the *Washington Post.* It's a madhouse. And they all want a statement. Will you see them?"

"Nope"—Dasha put one arm around Andy, the other around Fran—"not today. This is strictly a family celebration."

More bodies kept pouring in.

"Christ!" Frank hollered from the threshold. "This is worse than Bloomingdale's at sale time. Do I have to fight my way in?"

And then they were each in other's arms, kissing, laughing, weeping.

"Congratulations, Dasha!"

"And you! Let me look at you!" She stepped back, holding him at arm's length, to savor the moment to the fullest. He was radiant, a Parsifal in possession of the Grail.

"I can only stay an hour"—he glowed—"I have to get over to FBC. They've just made an offer I can't refuse."

"Come on, Franklin." Carter Brice thrust a glass of champagne into his hand. "Break precedent. Get stinking drunk for once in your life."

But Frank was drunk on something much headier than alcohol. He managed a token sip, then set the glass down.

It seemed that everyone was vying for her attention.

"Hey, Dasha," Andy shouted at one point. "Get your ass over to the window, quick! Look. Look at the Kimfolk."

"Why, they're gone!" Dasha looked down in surprise. The Plaza was almost deserted. "What do you think happened to 'em, Andy?"

"I think, sweetie pie, the kids finally got the word about what happened in California and are having very heavy second thoughts. My bet is, they're probably heading for home right now. At least let's hope so."

Toward five, the party began thinning out, the noise subsided to what one of the associates described as "your basic New-Year's-Eve-Times-Square-at-midnight level."

"I have to go now, darling," Frank whispered in her ear, "but before I leave, there's something I want to show you."

With that he took her by the hand and steering through the crush led her down the corridor, through the oaken doors into his office.

This part of the building was blissfully quiet. "The hush of power," Andy McCabe once called it. In the silence, Dasha could hear her heart beat.

She headed for her usual spot on the butterscotch sofa, but Frank ushered her across the room.

"I want you to do something for me."

He stepped behind his desk and pulled out the black leather swivel chair. It was a massive piece, oversized, overstuffed, the only item of furniture in the office that was neither antique nor English. It had belonged, Frank once mentioned, to Ralph Slater.

"I want you to sit down here."

She sat down. The chair dwarfed her with its high back and broad arms. Ralph Slater must have been built along large powerful lines, rather like Frank. She leaned back, tentatively, timidly, feeling almost like a sneak thief. The pliant quilting shifted to accommodate the curve of her body. She settled in further, until the leather conformed to her spine, nestled against her shoulders, cradled her head. Then she placed her hands on the armrests. It was surprisingly comfortable. Welcoming.

Frank watched her, fascinated. Then he nodded.

"Yes," he said finally. "It suits you."

"I don't know"—she hesitated. "I don't know where I'm going from here."

"Don't you?" He smiled. Then he fetched his coat from the closet. Fished in the pockets for pigskin gloves. Found them, pulled them on slowly. "Don't you really? Sit here in this chair and think about it."

She sat motionless for a long time in the encroaching darkness, then swung around to watch the sunset. The day was ending in a burst of glory. Out in the harbor, the last rays of the sun were gilding the torch on the Statue of Liberty, illuminating the points of the crown in gold.

Was that how Liberty had appeared to her father decades earlier when he arrived in this country? No. Max would have glimpsed it from the crowded, noisy warrens of Ellis Island. His would have been a different perspective, looking up with the eyes of a newcomer. The freshness of an outsider.

Yet here she was, an immigrant's daughter, looking down upon that same symbol of promise from the vantage point of privilege. The *sanctum sanctorum*.

For in this office, at this desk, from this very chair, the fortunes of Slater Blaney had been directed for years. Decisions of weight and significance had been made within these walls. Multi-million-dollar deals had been concluded. New companies born. Vast mergers conceived and realized. Great battles had been won and lost.

From the day she first came to Slater Blaney, this office had been the pinnacle of her dreams. The ultimate symbol. How much of her work and hope and struggle had gone into this moment: to sit here in the gathering darkness at the very seat of power.

The celebration party must have long since broken up. The nocturnal army of cleaning women would be arriving soon to empty ashtrays, clear away champagne glasses, erase the visible evidence of what would, in a few hours, be yesterday's victory. But the more permanent proof of that victory would lie elsewhere: in law books, in hundreds of classrooms, in the heightened freedom of the press, in the continuing tradition of American jurisprudence.

She watched, breathless, until the last glimmer of daylight fled the sky.

Behind her a door opened.

She turned and switched on the lamp.

"Come in, Jordan."

"I thought I'd find you here."

He crossed the room and sat down opposite her. His face was grave.

"Congratulations, Dasha, although I don't know that I can add to what everyone else has already said. Still"—he spoke with a wealth of feeling—"it was a glorious victory, and a richly deserved one. You must be very proud."

She leaned across the desk and placed her hand atop his.

"A great deal of that credit is yours, Jordan. I'm not sure I could have made it through without your help, your encouragement . . . "

"Oh, you would have made it through, Dasha. You would have argued that case if you'd had to get off your deathbed to do it."

She stared at him. Essentially, that was what Frank had said.

"And now, I suppose," he continued, "they'll be offering you a senior partnership?"

She nodded.

"So!" Jordan got up and began circling the office with the measured gait of a museum-goer. "So this is it."

He studied the furniture, the Orientals, the antique porcelains.

"I must say, that's a truly beautiful Renoir. And what have we here?"—he peered at a small seascape—"a Dufy, *La mer à Deauville.* Charming. Tell me, do the paintings go with the office?"

She paused. "They're Frank's personal property."

He faced her with a bitter smile and she could read his mind.

She, too, was Frank's personal property. Or so Jordan believed.

Having completed the tour, he returned to his chair.

"And now, Dasha"—he folded his hands on the desk like a schoolboy—"I think we must dispense with the pleasantries. I asked you last night if we still had a marriage. I asked you for a yes or no answer, but before you give it to me, I'd like us to explore an alternative. I'm here in the spirit of compromise. Presumably, we've gone well beyond scenes and recriminations, and my hope is that we can reach some arrangement that's equitable to both of us. But first there are several things I want to say.

"If you feel life won't be worth living unless you take up the senior partnership, then we've gone about as far as we can. I should think the mere fact of your being offered the post might be satisfaction enough. I can't see that a senior partnership would add anything significant to what you've already achieved. You don't need it, Dasha. You set out to become a somebody, to prove yourself—I recognize that, and you've done it magnificently. If you were to quit the bar tomorrow—which I wouldn't for a moment dream of asking—but even if you did, you'd have accomplished more in these few years than most lawyers do in a lifetime.

"You and I have been together for twenty years. Almost all of them as husband and wife. That's our total lifetime as adults. And most of those years were happy ones, at least for me. Close ones. I don't know of any couple quite as close as we used to be."

She heard him out, tears streaming.

"Today," he said, "Bernie Gross called me up from Tucson. He's put on more business than he can handle, and he'd like me to come in with him as a full partner. Not as an attorney, essentially, though my knowledge of law would come in handy. But Bernie thinks . . . now, don't laugh, he thinks I'd make a fabulous real-estate man, especially in sales. According to him, I've got just the qualities it takes. I'm sociable, relatively easy to get along with, and—if it doesn't sound too immodest —I can be awfully persuasive. Bernie himself is not the most verbal guy in the world. It would suit me, Dasha, more than I think the practice of law ever did. I'd still like to do some work with immigrants, and lord knows there's plenty of it down there. But on a strictly volunteer basis. I just don't have an adversarial temperament. I don't have the stomach for combat."

"You don't," she agreed, "but I do. And . . . "

"And what would there be for you down there, right? Well, Dasha, you could have a terrific career and I'm not talking small-town law. I'm talking substantial corporate practice. That whole Sun Belt area is just booming with business these days. Electronics, banking, airlines, insurance—plenty of action for a hustling attorney. You could open your own firm, fix up an office, hire some associates. It's not Slater Blaney, I grant you, but it's not the boondocks either.

"I accept that you could never stay home and be one of the ladies who lunch. Whether I like it or not is another matter, but that's a compromise I'm willing to make. The thing is, it would be a fresh start for all of us. We could build ourselves a beautiful ranch house with a swimming pool. Maybe even a stable for Crusader. Geoff would love it. I imagine Robin would prefer to stay on in Philly during the school year, but that's okay. She's a big girl now." He stopped and caught his breath.

"If our absent host won't mind," he said, "I'll mix us both a couple of drinks and we can hash it out."

No need to tell him what she wanted. A Dewar's on the rocks with a splash.

"Well, Dasha." He returned with their drinks. "What do you think?"

She wiped her eyes and took a huge swallow of scotch.

"Would you really want me back, Jordan? After all this? We've never discussed it, but—I haven't been a faithful wife."

"I know that, Dasha." The pain was still in his eyes. "I could hardly live with you all these years and be unaware of what was happening. I can tell exactly when it started and when it ended. And it has ended, hasn't it?"

"In some ways. And yet at heart, I'm not certain. Everything you've said," she murmured, "about us, about our marriage is true. Yes, I've been happy with you and looking back, I agree. Those early years, when we were in college, when the kids were young—those may very well have been the happiest years of my life. Certainly the most contented. I could never, under any circumstance, wish them away.

"I loved you then, Jordan. I love you now. Not with the same intoxicated fervor as I did at eighteen, but just as deeply, only in a different way. I love you for being man enough to forgive, generous enough to search for a compromise. If it were in my power to turn the clock back, if we could only be twenty again, I still wouldn't live one minute of those early years the least bit differently. But"—she tried to swallow down a painful lump in her throat—"I was another person then. At the time, that was the only life I wanted. The only one I could conceive. Just as when you were young, all you dreamed of was being a great lawyer. Now you too want other things. We grow. We change. And who can predict what either of us will want fifteen years hence?"

"I would hope," he said, "that fifteen years hence you and I will still want to be husband and wife."

"Even six months ago," she continued, "even as recently as that I thought, 'If I could only win the Kim case—wow! That would be the culmination of everything.' My way of putting my mark on the world, if that doesn't sound too pretentious. What more could I possibly desire?"

She blinked back the tears. "But I've changed even these past few weeks. In a way I've come to terms with myself. What I am, what I want out of life. That day in the Supreme Court, it was as though I'd turned a corner and discovered a whole new horizon. Bigger challenges, broader vistas. If it were *only* a senior partnership, perhaps I might relinquish it. But I think it will be more. I want this firm some day to be Slater Blaney and Croy. Under my leadership, according to my values. I want it to be everything it can be. I want *me* to be everything I can be. And do you know, my darling Jordan, it was you who first instilled that vision in me.

"But you should know something else. I can't be certain I'll even be content to rest there. Conceivably, it may prove to be only a way station, a transition leading to something else. Politics, perhaps. Or a career in international diplomacy. Or a professorship at Harvard. Maybe a seat on the Supreme Court some day. I'm still shy of forty and I have all those years ahead of me. What I'm trying to explain, Jordan, is that I have no idea what the future will hold. I only know I have to explore it to the fullest."

"What are you saying, Dasha?" His voice broke with emotion. "That there is nothing permanent in life? Nothing immutable? That we're like snakes who shed their skins and slough them off every year or two?"

"They shed their skins because they must"—the tears coursed down her cheeks unchecked. "Because they've grown and they're going to keep on growing. The old skins don't fit them any more. They have no choice."

"But we, Dasha"—he seized her hand—"we have choices. And now that choice is yours. Make it, darling. Make the right choice. Please . . . please come home to me now."

It took all her courage to meet his gaze. All her strength to withdraw her hand from beneath his grasp and bring it to rest on the arm of the massive leather chair. All her will to utter the final words.

"I *am* home."

318

CHAPTER TWENTY-FOUR

☐ Dr. Davies of St. Andrews Wixton hardly looked the part of head-master at one of Connecticut's most prestigious prep schools. He was a comfortable man, balding, soft-spoken, with a generous pot belly half concealed beneath a commodious Shetland sweater. He offered Dasha the traditional tea and sympathy.

"I dread today," she told him, "more than I've ever dreaded any court appearance. Children are the harshest judges of all, I expect."

"If it's any consolation, Mrs. Croy, roughly half the boys here are children of divorce. There's certainly no stigma attached, not any more."

Despite herself, Dasha winced. Even now, with the final break but a few days off, she found it difficult to come to terms with the realities of the situation.

Divorce. The word stuck in her craw. It had an alien sound, at least when she applied it to herself. In her family, people got married and stayed married. Her father had said as much when she broke the news to him a few days earlier.

"I'm very sad to hear it, Dashenka."

"I'm very sad about it too, Daddy, but . . . "

"You know, you're the first Oborin ever to get divorced. Ever—here or in Russia. No one in your mother's family ever did, either. Divorced, imagine that! However," he continued, and there was a colora-tion to his voice she had never heard before, an undertone of respect and pride, "however, you're also the first one in our family ever to argue a case before the Supreme Court, and how many fathers can say that about

319

their daughters? Well, darling, you must do what you think best. Only be happy."

But she wasn't happy. The whole situation was too strange, too painful. For the fact was that despite her acceptance that the marriage was indisputably over, she couldn't adjust to her new status. Other people got separated, divorced. Other children grew up in broken homes. Divorce may now be commonplace, but her children were not percentage points in the census figures. They were her own flesh and blood.

"My hope is," Dasha said, "that he'll want to stay on here, spend weekends with me in New York and vacations in Arizona. But it has to be his choice, and I think he may prefer living with his father. The two of them are very close."

At her request, Jordan had not accompanied her today. It would be painful enough to ask Geoff to make such a choice, but she felt the responsiblity of breaking the news was hers. "I've broken up the marriage," she said, "so I feel I'm the one who should take the flak." She had promised Jordan not to be an advocate for either side. "You have my word I won't put any pressure on him. Whatever I feel, I'll be as honest as I can. For all I know, Geoff may never want to see me again."

Now, as she explained her predicament to the headmaster, she could hardly help trembling.

"Conceivably, he may not even want to finish out the term here. His father's moving to Tucson next month."

"I understand," Dr. Davies replied. "Although we'd be sorry to lose him. He's been doing very well lately, growing in confidence. In any event, he's waiting for you now in the common room. Good luck."

"Well, look at you!" Dasha said in wonder. Was it only a couple of weeks since she'd seen him last? Incredible! He was sprouting up like a weed after a rainstorm, the wrists protruding a good inch from the sleeves of his jacket. "Is that your new blazer? The one we just got you? What happened to it?"

"Outgrowing it, I guess."

"For heaven's sakes!" She went to rumple his hair, but he recoiled, embarrassed. "Shall we go for a walk?"

"Sure."

His voice was breaking, she realized with a shock. "Dear God, he's not quite fourteen and already his voice is starting to change."

He led the way, walking briskly across the sodden lawn, always keeping two steps ahead of her, with the awkward grace of adolescence. Then he picked out a lonely bench at the edge of a stream.

She kept her word to Jordan. Her account of what had happened was scrupulously fair. "It's not a matter of apportioning blame," she tried to make clear, "although the essential responsibility for our breaking up is mine. But these things happen. People grow in different ways. They grow apart."

He looked woebegone, but not surprised.

"We both love you very much, darling," she reiterated, "and we would each like to have you with us, but unfortunately there's only one of you to go around."

He chewed his lip for a couple of minutes, then asked her, "What about Robin? What did she say when you told her?"

Robin had cried. Smart, sure, self-possessed Robin had put her head on the kitchen table and cried like a baby.

"I can't believe it," she'd wept. "I always think of you and Daddy as one person. Like twins, almost. I guess . . . I guess nothing is really permanent in life?"

And Dasha had taken her hand. "Some things are, darling. You and I—we've always loved each other and we always will. That's permanent. You can count on it."

"Robin's going to stay put." Dasha turned to her son. "She'll finish up at Curtis and come home weekends same as always. Her life is here."

Geoff sighed softly.

"I want to live with Dad."

She had expected that, had been geared—or so she thought—for disappointment, for loss. She had expected it but never really believed it, for always in the depth of her heart, against all reason and logic, she had been convinced that when the moment came, he would throw himself into her arms and the pain of the last few years would vanish. This was Geoff—her baby, her darling. No one had ever loved him as much as she did. No one had ever been so close.

"You . . . you've only given it a few seconds thought," she found herself pleading. "It's too big a decision to make so quickly."

"Mother"—he refused to meet her eye—"believe me, I've been thinking about it for months."

And this time when his voice broke, it was with pain.

She burst into tears, and Geoff was as incapable of comforting her as she was of comforting him. He simply sat there, shifting his feet unhappily in the moist turf.

"I'm sorry," he said after an eternity, and she made an effort to control her tears.

They sat for a few minutes more in silence.

"Would you like me to pack for you?" Dasha managed to get out. "I mean all the stuff you have in your room? Your record albums, stamp collection. What about all your games?"

There followed a long, strained discussion covering the disposal of Geoff's worldly goods. "I'll want the Monopoly, the Scrabble but not the chemistry set. My old cowboy hat, just for fun, of course. And be sure and pack *all* of my albums."

She listened, one half of her taking note of his instructions, the other half numb and disbelieving. Only a few nights earlier she had gone through a similar session with Jordan. Furniture, books, records, even photographs—it had been agony. Did you divorce children as well as husbands? It would seem so.

Ultimately the conversation ran out of steam.

"I guess that covers the important items," Geoff said. "Would you . . . would you like to see Crusader before you go? We're just a few minutes' walk from the stables."

That was the last thing in the world she felt up to, but she knew how much the colt meant to him.

"Yes, I'd very much like to—to say goodbye to him."

Crusader was stabled in what struck Dasha as extremely close confines for such a young, spirited horse, but Geoff assured her it was regulation stable size. Like his owner, the colt had grown furiously over recent weeks and now—rambunctious as ever—he greeted his visitors with a display of temperament, pawing the ground, thrusting up divots of earth and hay. His coat glistened like hand-polished mahogany.

"It looks like you've been taking marvelous care of him, darling."

Geoff grinned with pride. "Come on, baby," he whispered as the horse nuzzled his neck. "Come on, we're going to let you stretch those long legs for a bit."

He led the colt out into the field, holding him cautiously, but Crusader must have deemed any restraint as intolerable, for once outside the stable, he suddenly reared back, eyes wild and head high.

"For God's sakes, Geoff!" Dasha screamed. "Be careful!" But before she could finish her warning, the beast had broken free of Geoff, pushing him to the ground with a punishing lurch.

"Are you all right?" Dasha ran over, but already he was picking himself up, brushing the mud off his blazer.

"I'm okay, Mom. Nothing's broken. Everything's okay."

She helped him to his feet, subconsciously taking note that he had called her "Mom" for the first time that afternoon.

"No bruises?" she asked. She was glad of the excuse to touch him, to be physically close one last time.

"I'm okay," he insisted. "Honestly."

In the meadow, Crusader was galloping in joyous circles, mane streaming in the wind. Then, in a single breathless second, the horse headed into the trees and was gone.

"That's a dangerous animal you've got there, Geoff. I never realized that before."

"No, not really," her son replied. "Just feeling his oats. Most colts are like that, and after all he's pretty young."

"Well, let's hope he settles down very soon." Dasha's heart was still pounding. "That is, presuming he ever comes back. He could be halfway to Greenwich by now."

"Oh, he'll come back, Mom. He'll always come back to me in the end."

Dasha choked.

"And you?" she started to say. "Will you come back?"

But she hadn't the heart to continue. She bit her lips to keep the words from spilling out, for it would be too unfair, too cruel to subject Geoff to the pressure of that question. He had made up his mind. And for all that she hungered for open reassurance—the loving touch, the word of promise—she would not resort to emotional blackmail. The day had been agony enough for them both.

Did she dare to take his hand? To kiss him goodbye? Or would he, too, bolt out of her range?

But Geoff must have sensed her anguish, for suddenly he put his arms around her and hugged her with unexpected warmth.

"Come on, Mom." He took her hand. "I'll walk you to the car."

They parted in awkward silence, yet they did kiss. And that—she recognized—was a distinct step forward.

A step, but far short of a milestone. *No, not enough,* she kept repeating to herself. *One kiss is not enough.*

She drove back to New York in a state of shock, mechanically staying in lane, observing the traffic lights, but throughout with a feeling of detachment. The day had never happened.

It was only when she turned the key on her own front door that the full import of what had taken place bore down.

The Mausoleum.

Jordan's term for the apartment came to mind, and for once it seemed an apt description. The place was empty. Forlorn. Haunted by yesterday's echoes. Too large for a woman alone.

"Is anybody home?" she called softly. The words reverberated down the tiled corridor. But who would be home? The maid had left for the day and there was nobody else.

She took off her coat and went into Geoff's room with a sense of unease. She would do the packing now, this very afternoon, while his directives were fresh in her mind. It wasn't a job she could entrust to anyone else.

When they moved in, the room had been painted a warm sandalwood, but very little of it was still visible. Little by little, Geoff had covered over every available surface with posters: The Police, James Bond, Belmont Park, Garfield the Cat, Conan the Barbarian, a tearsheet announcing a John McEnroe match. Her son's autobiography was taped on these walls—his hobbies, passions, fads, fantasies. What to do with them? Roll them up in cardboard cylinders so they might decorate a strange bedroom in Tucson?

Gently she pulled one corner of a yellowing Peanuts blow-up, only to have the paper rip and a triangle of paint come away with it.

"No," she said aloud. "No, I won't."

She wouldn't. She wouldn't dismantle his room beyond recognition. Not without Geoff's express consent. He hadn't mentioned the posters. Perhaps he had deliberately refrained from disposing of them as an oblique way of saying that he would be back. The more she thought about it, the more certain she became. The posters were too big a part of his life to be left behind forever.

Very good then. When he did return, he would find his room unchanged.

Yes. The posters would stay. And the American Eagle bedspread, inkstains and all. And those dumb *Star Wars* sheets he'd been so crazy about a few years back. And the little hooked rug that Charlotte had made for him when he was small. Because this room was Geoff's and would always be his. Always be waiting—the bed made, the posters on the wall, everything in readiness for the day when he would return.

She packed his stamp collection, his old report cards. In the bottom of his dresser, stashed away amid a pile of dead tennis balls, she came across a plaque he had made at summer camp when he was ten.

The camp had been a folksy place, unpretentious, with log cabins and a heavy emphasis on nature lore and crafts. Geoff had taken up wood-burning that summer, engraving messages with a heated pen in the fanciest script he could muster. She had done the same thing at his age. The words, usually, were some traditional homily, like "God Bless This Home," or recipes for maple syrup or a sentiment from a back issue of *Reader's Digest*.

At the end of the season, he had come home with a small irregular rectangle of pinewood, grubby and much worked over, and she had forgotten its existence until now. Was that something he would want or not, she wondered. Routinely, she looked at the message he had chosen. The words sprang from the wood:

> *If you love something, set it free.*
> *If it comes back, it's yours forever.*
> *If it doesn't, it never was.*

Now, she read the words and reread them until they were graven in her heart as well.

My boy . . . my girl . . . my children.

How many times had she said that with the proud thrill of possession in her voice? "These are my children," she had boasted, "my beautiful wonderful children," the way the mother of the Gracchi had—according to the histories of ancient Rome—paraded her young sons in lieu of other wealth and said, "These are my jewels."

But children couldn't be owned. At best they were on loan, a precious trust that you cared for and nurtured, protected until they asserted the freedom that was their birthright. After that, control passed from you and every tie became voluntary, an unasked-for gift of love.

Should she have fought for him this afternoon? Should she have gone after him with every emotional stop pulled out? With every weapon in the maternal arsenal from tears to guilt to nostalgia?

Had she done so, she might have won the day—and ultimately lost him forever. For winning on those terms would be a hollow victory, a victory that must exact its cost in years to come. She wanted Geoff to be part of her life—not as a prisoner, not as a victim of her emotional power, but out of the bounty of his love.

She didn't know when that day would come; but she knew that they would never pass out of each other's lives. And the only way she could finally hold him was to let him go now.

If it comes back, it's yours forever.

CHAPTER TWENTY-FIVE

☐ The Management Committee's newest member surveyed the graceful proportions of the partners' conference room with a sense of awe. It was a chamber worthy of a museum, with its Adam sidechairs, its oak wainscotting transported in its entirety from one of England's stately homes, the massive Hepplewhite breakfront polished to the gloss of satin.

"Priceless," Tom Hatt had once stated with his usual hyperbole. "Everything in that room is absolutely priceless."

But he was wrong.

The furnishings were expensive, to be sure. Wildly expensive, in fact, but not priceless. Each object here had been bought and paid for in hard currency. You could always hire an appraiser to put a dollar price tag on the breakfront or the Tabriz carpet.

The only item in this room that could not be purchased with coin of the realm, the one truly priceless item, was your ticket of admission. The struggle to arrive, the toll exacted en route, the cost of sitting down at this very moment in this delicate Adam chair—that alone was beyond reckoning. That alone was not, as Frank Hunicutt might have termed it, one of life's fungible items.

For how did you assess disappointment, heartbreak? What value did you place upon lost love or dreams found? How did you balance the empty household against the overcrowded desk diary?

Was it worth it? She still didn't know.

Dasha had prepared for today's meeting with consummate care.

"After the preliminaries," Porter Collins had advised her a week earlier, "you'll be expected to address the committee formally. We have a tradition here that the first-time member gets a chance to lay it on the line, make a full presentation of his or her views."

"I shall look forward to it, Porter."

She had dressed, too, with more than usual thought, and after a good deal of deliberation decided to replace the traditional dark narrow suit with a soft beige cashmere dress. On this particular occasion, she felt it proper to remind them that she was a person, not a cipher. A woman rather than one of the boys.

Eleven of the World's Greatest Experts on Everything, the group had been designated, plus a rainmaker. Well, from now on, it would be Eleven of the World's Greatest Experts on Everything—plus one eager generalist. Who also happened to be a sentient and, she hoped, compassionate woman.

She sat through the ritual opening: a reading of the financial statement, a review of major litigation, and some internal housekeeping. At last, Harrison Cobb nodded to Dasha.

"And now we'll turn the chair over to our newest member." With a courtly gesture he indicated the empty seat at the head of the table. "It's all yours, Dasha."

She wet her lips.

"I'd like to begin with an announcement. As you know, FBC has resumed its relationship with Slater Blaney, so there will be no difficulty in collecting outstanding fees. Indeed"—she smiled faintly—"I think we will soon be ready to represent the network in a major lawsuit. Only this time, it will be FBC filing the charges and seeking restitution, rather than the other way around. *FBC versus Kim.*"

She had, she told the assembled panel, long suspected that a fraud had been perpetrated upon the network. From the start, the researchers on the Kim documentary had been deliberately fed false information with an eye to bringing suit eventually and thereby extorting a fortune. The scheme, she believed, had been cooked up by Kim himself, with the collusion of Bomber Hazzard.

"Even though the Reverend has been indicted on other charges, he still has immense financial assets. As does Mr. Hazzard. We therefore plan to initiate a damage suit against both of them not only for fraud but also for malicious libel. Mr. Hunicutt has suggested that we seek two hundred million dollars . . . "

"Plus punitive damages, I hope," J. J. Osborne interjected.

"Of course." Dasha nodded.

"That will," Porter said, "be a protracted piece of litigation. It could take years."

A happy murmur ran through the room, the lip-smacking hum of lawyers busily totting up fees. God, they were a bunch of tough bastards.

She cleared her throat in a call for attention, then spoke up as the buzz subsided.

"I'm delighted to enter into my senior partnership by bringing such a substantial piece of business into the firm. However, I would like to contribute something more than added billing. I would like to contribute my views as to where Slater Blaney should be heading. I want to talk about the future—and also about the past. We are each of us the inheritors of a long and honorable tradition."

It was a tradition, she declared, that went beyond the mere making of money, the stroking of corporate clients. It was a tradition of working *pro bono publico*—for the public good. Of being in the vanguard of reform and enlightened social conscience.

Once those values had distinguished Slater Blaney above every other firm in Wall Street, but not in recent years. She would like to return to that great tradition, to those forgotten ideals. And to do so with more than lip service.

True, the firm had its philanthropic side. "I know we donate the excruciatingly correct amount of corporate dollars to this charity or that museum. But our greatest wealth isn't our bank account. It's the skills of our two hundred lawyers. That's really what we have to give."

You could get on the subway at Wall Street, she declared, ride a few stops, and step out into a world that was light-years away. The slums of Bedford Stuyvesant, the ghettos of Bensonhurst, the rat-infested tenements of Harlem. Some of the greatest legal injustices in the nation were to be found festering in those mean streets. The ousted tenant, the abandoned wife, the children of despair, the exploited immigrant. The helpless victim of the loanshark or the mugger or the bigot.

That was New York, too. That was a part of Slater Blaney's city, just as much as Wall Street and Park Avenue and Rockefeller Plaza. And that dark and despairing New York was therefore a part of Slater Blaney's obligation in moral, if not in legal, terms. It was truly ironic that this firm—so rich, so powerful, so laden with talent and wisdom—should reserve its counsel only for those of even greater wealth and power. And that the very people most desperately in need of top legal advice were the very ones who could least aspire to it.

Even as she spoke, the words had a familiar ring. Jordan's words. Yes, they were his words, encompassing his thoughts, his experiences. Embracing his ideals. And as she spoke, she knew those years together had not been wasted. She had learned from him, grown through him. And now she paused for a moment in silent homage.

It was her wish, she stated, that all new associates be assigned a minimum of six months *pro bono* work to be spread out over the first two years of their employment.

There was an audible groan from a nearby chair.

"And after that, I want them to continue to donate a fixed percentage of their time to public service, whether it's poor law or civil rights work or involvement with environmental issues. And I'm not just talking about the kids. I mean every single lawyer in this firm from the first-year associates right up through the senior partners. Yes . . . you, me. All of us four-hundred-dollar-an-hour attorneys."

She could feel the hostile vibrations all around her, the shock waves. You didn't ask a million-dollar lawyer to make common cause with welfare mothers and unemployed blacks. Or did you? To her surprise, here and there she thought she sensed a warm reaction.

"I look at the kids out of law school today and, sure, they talk hard-nose because that's what they think we want to hear. But they still have hopes of changing the world. Then they come here, these brand-new graduates, and we tether their dreams. We force them into professional straitjackets. We turn them into narrow specialists . . . "

"We turn them into lawyers, goddammit." Carter Brice was outraged.

"Only sometimes," she shot back. "But more often, we transform them into automatons. Into profit centers. Into billing sheets to be printed out on a computer. And the longer they're here, the narrower they grow."

"They come here for the big bucks," Porter reminded her. And there was an unexpected gentleness in his tone.

"They come for the challenge, too. I did. We all did. I don't believe you can be a first-rate attorney and a tenth-rate human being simultaneously."

She spoke for nearly an hour, and when she finally sat down amid an ambiguous silence, it was with the feeling of a job well done. Deep inside her a small voice said, *Thank you, Jordan.*

On her way out that evening, she noticed Blagden Geere's light was on.

"Hello." She popped her nose in. "You're working late, I see."

"Can you come in, Dasha?"

"Only for a minute."

He cleared some papers off a chair to make way. The entire room was littered with lined yellow sheets, hundreds of them, each written top to bottom in his careful old-fashioned hand.

"My magnum opus." He shuffled a stack of them into a pile. "That was an excellent talk you gave this afternoon at the meeting. You stated the case very powerfully, and to my own way of thinking it was long overdue. You can anticipate a good deal of resistance, especially from the old guard, when it comes to remaking the firm. But you'll win, Dasha. You'll outlast them, outsmart them. You might even—who knows?—someday convince them. The important thing is to fight the good fight. Funny, but in a way, you reminded me of myself when young."

"Thank you, Blagden. You couldn't pay me a higher compliment." She gave an embarrassed shrug and changed the subject. "How's the book coming, by the way. Your history of Slater Blaney?"

"Very well, my dear. In fact, it's practically up to date. Yes, except for today's meeting, it's comprehensive right through 1983."

1984, she corrected mentally.

"Yes," he murmured. "Completely up to date. All it wants is a final chapter—the firm as it will shape up over the next decade. Under new leadership. And that"—he looked her squarely in the eye—"will surely be the finest chapter of all."

She turned her face, ashamed that he might see her cry.

Yes. The prize was worth the price that she had paid.

"So this is it." Dasha entered the room cautiously. "I wouldn't recognize the place. You've changed the decor so completely. It's very handsome. And warm-looking, too."

Gone were the stark black-and-white furnishings, the steel, the chrome, the abacus, the sterile feel of a hospital lab.

Only the silver fireplace remained from the old regime. That and the four television screens. Most of the furniture was familiar to her from Slater Blaney—the butterscotch sofa reupholstered now in mossy green, the Sheraton desk, Dufy's exquisite *La mer à Deauville*.

The Renoir, she noticed, was gone. Frank must have finally taken it home for security reasons. A splendid painting, that Renoir, but undoubtedly far too valuable to leave unguarded in a place as overrun with outsiders as Schlock Rock.

For the rest, Frank had done himself proud. He himself looked well, too, although a trifle tired. His face was rather more drawn than it used to be. Worry had etched a few fine lines around his eyes. The price of power, she supposed. Of holding down one of the heaviest jobs in the country. He had also lost some weight. It became him.

"Very handsome indeed, Frank. A beautiful office." She put her briefcase down on the sofa, uneasy at their first private meeting in months. Their first meeting ever as lawyer and client.

They exchanged a round of formal greetings. He was sorry they hadn't got together sooner, but he'd been on the road a great deal lately. Pressure of business. Other matters. Yes, of course she understood. She would try not to waste his time. With that she opened her briefcase and began pulling out papers.

"May I offer you a drink, Dasha?" he asked politely. Then without waiting for her answer, he stepped over to the bar and mixed her a Dewar's on the rocks with a splash. How well he knew her tastes. How thoughtful of him to remember. Frank Hunicutt: the perfect host.

For a moment she was tempted to take a page from his handbook on How to Succeed, the one that said you must never mix booze with business, but in fact she was grateful for that first bracing sip of whiskey. It helped calm her nerves.

"And if you don't mind, Dasha, I've arranged for dinner to be sent in. Lamb chops, some of that white asparagus you like so much. I thought it would be pleasanter than going to a restaurant. And frankly, who has time to go out and eat these days?" He smiled. "Not me. Not you either, I shouldn't think. I hear you caused a bit of a brouhaha this afternoon at the committee meeting. You really shook the old boys up, my informant tells me."

Despite herself, Dasha rolled her eyes in wonder. "You're too much, Frank. You still know all the news before it happens."

He looked at her for a moment, then threw his head back and roared with laughter.

"I love it!" He laughed until the blue eyes watered with tears. "I *love* it! The mighty senior partners doing *pro bono* in the slums. I have this mental picture of Carter Brice with his five-hundred-dollar suits and his fifty-dollar manicures traipsing up to Harlem to make housecalls. In his Bentley, of course! He knocks on the door, lady answers. 'Excuse me,' says Carter, 'is this the residence of Leroy Hubert Esquire?' Lady looks at him. 'Hey, Leroy,' she yells, 'there's some jive-talkin' dude here to see you. He sure do look like a pusher to me.' Perfect! And J.J.! God, that man's such a pompous bastard. Picture this one, Dasha. It's J.J. Osborne in full sail, and he's down at Civil Court on behalf of some old lady who's about to have her television repossessed. Talk about federal cases . . . so there's J.J. accompanied by three associates, four Mark Cross briefcases, six truckloads of documents, and at least one secretary because J.J. doesn't believe in coming into court unprepared—Jesus, can you picture the judge's face?"

But Frank couldn't continue for he had collapsed, doubled up with laughter on the sofa, face flushed, eyes streaming.

"Hand me a handkerchief, will you, darling?" He wiped his eyes. "Really, Dasha, you do have to admit it makes for one helluva picture."

It did. She herself was giggling like an idiot. "Now I'm beginning to wonder if I should even have made that speech today."

"Oh, you should have." His answer was wreathed with affection. "You should have and I suppose I should have done something along those lines myself years ago."

He handed her back the handkerchief and the smile slowly faded.

"Sweet Christ, but I've missed you, Dasha. I've missed laughing with you, talking to you. And a lot more besides. These have been the longest, loneliest two months of my life."

"Please . . . "

"Please what, Dasha?"

Please don't open up old wounds, she wanted to say. *Don't hurt me any more than you already have. Please let the past be forgotten once and for all or I shall never be able to see you again.*

But before she could answer, the waiter bustled in trailing a serving cart full of covered dishes. Dasha almost kissed the man out of relief.

"Ah, dinner." She stood up. "I'm starved, Frank. Aren't you?"

The waiter smiled and began setting the table, identifying the contents of each dish, dressing the salad, happy in the exercise of his craft until Frank, who had been sitting on the sofa watching the proceedings with distaste, now tapped his foot with impatience.

"That will do," he said curtly. "Thank you."

"Mmmm, this looks delicious." Dasha peeked under a cover to find a dish of braised endive. "I haven't had endive in ages."

She had a swift sense of *déjà vu,* a memory of that lunch in the Palmer House—the fussing of the waiter, the toying with food as a prelude to a scene she could never recall without pain. Only this time, she was wiser. Tougher. This time she wouldn't let her emotions rampage like a runaway steamroller destroying everything in its path. This time she would sit and eat asparagus and braised endive.

It was over. There would be no replay, no repeat of that day in Chicago. She hadn't broken with Jordan, surrendered her son, torn her life into ribbons only to submit herself to another emotional onslaught. This time she would be in control. A lesson learned long ago from Frank.

With an effort she pulled herself erect.

"May I serve you some salad?" she asked.

"Stop monkeying with the food, Dasha, and come here and sit down. Please!" He indicated a seat next to him on the sofa but she chose an armchair a half-dozen feet away. She crossed her legs sedately, folded her hands in her lap, fingers laced. After all she was a lawyer, he was her client.

"I'm here to talk business," she said with a quiet authority.

"And so am I, Dasha. I'm here to talk about the most important business of all. The business of you and me. Please, darling"—he held up a hand to cut off her protest—"please hold your fire until you've heard me out. I have a number of things I want to say. Why I haven't called you these past two months . . . what's been going on in my life, my mind. It's important you know. To begin with, I've left Clarisse."

Her reaction was instinctive: an uncontrollable shudder. She clasped her hands more tightly.

"I thought," he went on, "that you'd guessed as much when you walked in here this evening. I saw you looking for the Renoir, but I've returned it. It belongs to Clarisse."

"Frank." She gritted her teeth. "This has nothing to do with me."

"You're right, Dasha. In a way, it doesn't. Whatever happens between us this evening, whether you will have me or throw me out on my ear, I won't go back to Clarisse. The marriage is over. Finally. Utterly. And nothing could induce me to go back. Oh God, to be free of it, the chatter, the emptiness, the boredom . . . "

Despite her intention of staying aloof, Dasha found herself springing to Clarisse's defense. "That's not fair, Frank. That's not fair to her. She's always treated you so magnanimously."

"Fair! Life isn't fair, Dasha!" he burst out. "Sure, it would be wonderful if we could go through all the years of marriage with blinkers, control our feelings, and only love where it was proper and practical. My God, what is more eminently practical than my staying married to Clarisse? What could be more fair? She's such a nice woman. She's done so much for me. And I'm grateful. But I can't spend my life being grateful. I have needs, I have wants. This past half-hour with you . . . being with you, yacking away without having to watch every word, explain every distinction. It was a renewal, like filling my lungs with ozone. You're crucial to me, Dasha, crucial to my happiness, and I'm not going to let you go without a fight. I called you here to do battle, Dasha, because I want you, I love you!"

"In your way!" She shook her head wildly. "You told me that once before in Chicago. You love me *in your way,* Frank. And then you went to some pains to explain what you meant. Well, your way isn't enough."

"Is that what's holding you back, wounded pride? What do you want me to do, lay myself bare? I've done that in my mind a hundred times over the last few months. I was an idiot that day in Chicago. It's funny." He gave a bitter laugh. "All my life, I've prided myself on behaving so rationally, on being such a smart self-serving bastard. I worked smart, I married smart. And I never got involved. Every woman I laid was pretty much like every other, which was certainly a smart attitude to hold. Frank Hunicutt—first guy at the starting post each morning. Number one in the Smartass Olympics. Or so I thought. But that day I acted like a goddam fool. I threw away something that mattered very greatly to me. A lot more than I believed possible. I came back to New York after that trip and I thought 'Whew! Narrow escape! Now let's get my life back on the track.' Sure, I was crazy about you but not *so* crazy I was about to self-destruct over it. What is it Goethe said? 'At night all cats are gray.' Right? And there were plenty of girls in New York, pretty young things who weren't going to make any demands. Well, I won't deny I've had the occasional roll in the hay since then. But it wasn't the same, Dasha. The zest has gone out of it. I still enjoy going to bed with them. Why should I lie? It's waking up with them that's the problem. The fact is, you spoiled me."

"Frank," she began. "I find this very painful."

"So do I, darling. So do I. When I told you just now that my leaving Clarisse had nothing to do with you, that wasn't quite true. Perhaps if I hadn't known you, my wife and I could have gone on forever. And you want to know something else? I could have won the chairmanship without the help of her stock. It was useful, nothing more. Conceivably our marriage might have staggered on had I never met you. To be honest, I don't know. But I do know that being with you, falling in love with you, changed my expectations, my whole idea about what constitutes happiness. I was never that close to anyone before. I miss it now. I want that intimacy, Dasha, that love we shared. Because you and I, we've had it all . . . the good sex, the good talk, the good life. And we could have it all again. I want it and I can't believe you don't want it too. I beg you, don't jeopardize the future—both our futures—out of foolish misguided pride. I already did that number."

Suddenly, he sprang over to where she sat, hands clasped, and forced her fingers open one by one. "Here!" He drew her up as though she were deadweight until she faced him, eyes level. "Here. Put your hands on my face, your body against mine, feel my arms around you and then, if you can tell me in all honesty that you no longer love me, no longer care, that it's irrevocably over in your heart of hearts—if you tell me that, then this day never happened. I'll leave you in peace." Beneath her fingers she could feel the muscles of his cheek flex and tense. "But don't lie," he murmured, "not to me, not to yourself."

"I love you, Frank." She laid her head on his shoulder and wept. "And I'll probably love you till the day I die, but it doesn't matter any more. Because it's no good. Nothing can come of it."

"How can you say such a thing!" His arms closed about her like a vise. "We have it all in front of us, darling. Everything—the whole goddam world."

336

"Please, Frank." She tried to struggle free of his embrace. "You're hurting me."

She walked past him to the window, then through the glass door that led onto a spacious brick-paved terrace.

Sixty stories below, Sixth Avenue hummed with the buzz of evening traffic. But at this height, the sound was muted, pleasant, and the air curiously balmy with the scent of flowers and herbs.

Astonishing!

Frank had turned this glass-and-granite enclave into a garden in the sky, transforming it out of all recognition. In the heart of Manhattan, high above the grime and scuffle of the city, he had created a country garden, with cozy alcoves, ivied nooks, even an old-fashioned glider where one could sit and swing. All about, there were banks of primroses, boxes of crayon-colored portulaca, stands of scented yellow azaleas. Here and there herbaceous borders gave out the fragrances of thyme and verbena and rosemary. Along one wall, young rose bushes, thick with the buds of early summer, rambled in and out of wooden trellises with sweet abandon.

Could they survive at this height? she wondered. Could they thrive in face of the gales that whipped through the skyscrapered canyons? For none of these plants, homey and tender, had any right to be flourishing in this wildly improbable site. Yet flourish they did.

Only Frank, she marveled. Only Frank would so defy the simple logic of the elements. Frank with his unstoppable hubris.

He followed her out, bearing the remains of her drink.

"How do you like my backyard, Dasha?"

"Breathtaking!" she replied. *Ah wonderful.* She had found her equilibrium. Her distance. If only she could keep to neutral ground.

"The roses won't be in full bloom for another week or two, but . . . " He looked around to see which was the most luxurious of the bushes, then pinched off a perfect golden bud.

"Dammit!"

"You pricked yourself."

"Yup." He licked a gout of blood off his thumb. "No roses without thorns. That's the first law of gardening. Anyhow, here's your booty."

She rolled the bud between her fingers. It was silk velvet to the touch.

He motioned her to a little iron bench. "So, Dasha." He folded his arms. "It's your day in court. I want to hear from you exactly why it's over. I think you owe me an explanation."

I owe you a great deal more than that, Frank.

She couldn't bear the thought that he might misinterpret her, that he might think her vengeful. Grudge-bearing. That would be the final injury.

"No roses without thorns," she echoed. "It sounds like a rule of law as well. No gains without losses. Frank Hunicutt's Fungibles. This afternoon"—she turned at last to face him, her eyes glistening with tears—"this afternoon when I was in that committee meeting, all I could think of was how much I sacrificed to get there. Well, that's fair enough, isn't it? I achieved certain advantages, I gave up others in their stead. Things cost. That's a fact of life. Somewhere along the line you strike a bargain with yourself, and once you've struck that bargain, you stick to it.

"Today, I tried to assess precisely what that chair in the partners' room cost me. A lot. Still, if it had been just me involved, if I had been the only one called upon to make trade-offs—that would have been perfectly okay. And if it meant the death of my marriage, conceivably even that was permissible. That was the price. The given.

"But it didn't stop there, Frank. Because when I sacrificed my marriage, I sacrificed Jordan's as well, and he was never a party to that bargain. Frank, my darling Frank . . . don't you see? I've broken up a home that belonged not just to me but to him, to the children. Three other people, who really didn't have any say about what was happening. And I don't believe I had the right to do that."

"Don't flagellate yourself, Dasha. It would have ended one time or another. Even if you'd never set foot in Slater Blaney, something else would have tipped the balance."

"Would it have? I'm not so certain. From the day I started there, long before I met you, I had a presentiment about what the big career was going to cost in personal terms. Yet for all my qualms, my fears, I barged straight ahead, slam bang! And every time I made a career decision, it turned out that other people wound up paying for it. Jordan sure did. And Geoff. Above all, Geoff. I can't write that off so easily. It never stops hurting. And the thing is, given those choices, I would probably do the same thing all over again. Except that next time, if there is a next time, I'm not going to ask other people to make sacrifices."

"Even people you love, Dasha?" He was incredulous.

"Especially people I love. Especially you, Frank. It would be too selfish, too indulgent. Too"—she held her breath for a moment—"too dangerous. So I don't want to get involved that way again. I don't have that right."

He studied her with narrowed eyes.

"Am I to understand, Dasha, that because you've had this great whopping measure of professional success, you feel you're not entitled to personal gratification as well? Is that your quid pro quo?"

"Oh Frank, please." She wiped her eyes with the back of her hand under the guise of finishing her drink. She was determined not to cry, She would not. Because there was no telling where her feelings might take her. "Please, don't put me through this. There was a time, Frank, when I really thought I could have it all. The big job and the devoted husband and the beautiful children *and* you, the wonderful lover. Certainly you. I was so reckless, so greedy. And I almost wound up with nothing. Well, I'm more of a realist now. I've struck a bargain and I'll settle for what I have. I want to go it alone for a while."

"For how long a while?"

She shook her head for an answer.

"In other words, because Jordan may be unhappy down in Tucson, you owe it to him to be unhappy, too. Am I right? And, anyhow, the element of risk is too great."

Those were not the words she would have chosen, but that was the substance. There was nothing she could add.

He exhaled softly.

"I need a drink, Dasha."

Without further ado, he went inside, and was gone for a good ten minutes. When he returned, it was with a tall stiff whiskey in hand.

"I've been thinking over what you said." He sat down quietly beside her. "I've been thinking it over very, very carefully . . . "

"And you understand . . . " Of course, Frank understood. There wasn't a more perceptive man in the world.

" . . . and I've come to the conclusion that I have never heard anything so dumb in all my life." He raised his voice. "No! I take that back. The last time I heard such a bunch of dumb talk was in Chicago

—and I was the idiot mouthing it. Ye Gods, Dasha!" He slammed his glass down on the brickwork. His hands were trembling. She had never seen Frank so incensed. And suddenly he was yelling at her, berating her like a recalcitrant schoolchild. For the first time in his life, Frank Hunicutt had lost his cool.

"First of all, you've got to get it into your skull that there is nothing to atone for. You've committed no crime. You destroyed no lives. You outgrew a marriage. That happens. And did it ever occur to you that maybe, in a way, so did Jordan? Does he want what he wanted at eighteen? The hell he does! His old career, his whole pattern of living —they clearly don't suit him any more, or else he never would have gone to Tucson. He would have stayed right here and practiced law. Remember this, Dasha, he *chose* to leave. And right now, Jordan is starting out on a whole new life, getting a second chance. As are we all. Is that so awful? And you can mourn all you want for the death of your marriage; that still isn't going to make him any happier. Jordan will find his own way.

"And as for Geoff—Dasha, I know it hurts. You hate to see him suffer. But I ask you: How many happy, well-adjusted adolescents do you know? Believe me, darling, I've survived three teenagers of my own, and the fact of the matter is—adolescence is a godawful time of life. And finally, as for this crap about life being too dangerous. Jesus!" He clenched his fist and pounded the bench out of sheer frustration. "That is nothing but a copout. You know who you sounded like saying that? Me—the old me! Play it smart. Be in control. Don't let anyone rock your boat.

"You see, I remember that day in Chicago too, Dasha. And I recall something you said at the time, because it affected me very deeply. You said that when you really love someone, you don't stop to count the cost. Well, I really love you, Dasha. Goddammit, I do. And I love you not 'in my way,' but all the way. On your terms, Dasha. By your definition. But you! What happened to that risk-taking glory I so adored? That recklessness? That go-for-broke passion? Did you lose it all in the climb to the top? I don't believe it, any more than I believe that you have to pay for your success by forgoing happiness.

"You didn't claw your way up. You didn't sleep your way up. You *worked* your way up—honestly. On your merits. With or without me, you'd still be where you are. I helped, that's all. So you don't have to

salve your New England conscience by wearing a hair shirt. You're
entitled to what you have. And you're certainly entitled to me, if that's
what you want. But no holds barred, Dasha."

He seized her hands with a grip of steel.

"Oh Dasha . . . darling. Fuck all the rational arguments! I'm sick
of them. We love each other. We've waited so long, gone through so
much. What is it you're afraid of? Happiness? Or are you afraid that I'll
leave you again?" He didn't wait for an answer, but in one broad
swooping motion, gathered her in his arms. Then his lips were in her hair,
on her cheeks, in a murmur of kisses, a feathered rain of caresses. "My
own sweet darling, I won't let you go! I won't let you run away from
life!"

And at his touch, she burst into tears. For all her resolve, her
convictions, it was still there—the magic, the trembling, the powerful call
of flesh to flesh.

"Not fair!" she cried. "This isn't fair. How can I come to a sensible
decision while you're making love to me?"

"Oh Dasha. . . . God! The hell with fair. The hell with caution!
Just love me, and be done with it. Because I'm not the man I was. I've
grown. And so have you. We were never more right than we are now."

"But what if it doesn't last?" She clung to him, anguished. "What
if we change yet again?"

"What if we do?" he said. "I'm willing to risk it. Are you?"

For one split second she wavered, and then a lifetime's yearning
swept through every cell of her body. The right to happiness was hers.
It was everyone's. And the chance for happiness was here and now.

"Yes, my darling Frank. Oh yes, I'm willing to risk life itself." Yes
yes yes yes *yes!*

They made love for a long delirious hour on the pretty chintz-
covered glider, their bodies lit by the stars, washed by summer breezes;
then afterwards lay close and content in each other's arms.

"Isn't this better," he said, "isn't this better than lonely?"

"It's better than anything else in the world."

He laughed softly, then nibbled her ear.

"You know something, darling? You'll hate me for saying this but
I'm ravenous."

"I know."

"I mean for food."

"I hate you for saying it," she laughed, "but I am too. Let's go in and have our dinner."

By now, however, the asparagus had wilted, the soufflé had collapsed, the lamb chops turned cold and gelatinous.

"Yechh!" Frank said. "This looks disgusting. We'll have to go out to dinner after all. Unless you're willing to take me home and feed me."

"With pleasure, if you'll settle for scrambled eggs and a salad. I never cook any more, so God knows what's in the refrigerator. What about you, darling? Where are you living these days? You haven't told me. At a hotel, or have you found a place of your own yet?"

"At the moment I'm staying at the Carlyle. I've just closed on a huge duplex over on Fifth. Beautiful apartment, but there's not a stick of furniture in it. So at the moment it's more like a mausoleum than a home. You could shoot moose in the living room."

Instinctively she shivered. "Then come home with me tonight, darling. Come and fill my own mausoleum with laughter. We can stay up late and do some catching up. All night, if you like. I haven't begun to talk myself out. And I want to hear everything that's been happening with you. I must admit, I haven't had a real confidant since the day we broke up. And I bet you haven't either."

"Well, I hope, Dasha, you won't find I'm one of those fungible young hulks who are great in the sack, but what do you say to 'em in the morning? I'd hate to think I'm just another pretty body."

"Frank Hunicutt"—she burst out laughing—"you are still the most thoroughly amoral person I know!"

It was past ten when they arrived at her apartment, and even through the closed door she could hear the phone ringing relentlessly.

"You and your office." Frank rolled his eyes while Dasha fumbled with the key. "Terrible the way those people call at all hours. No consideration. You go get it and I'll poke around and see what's to eat."

He was in the kitchen slicing bread and frying bacon when she entered a few minutes later, eyes brimming.

"Why darling! What's wrong?" He dropped the breadknife and came to put his arms around her. "You look as if you've been pole-axed."

"It's Geoff," she blubbered. "No no, there's nothing wrong. In fact, it's good news. I guess it's just my night for crying. I call him most every day, you know, but well"—even through the tears, her smile lit up the room—"tonight he called me. He rambled on for about five minutes, his horse, the new kids he's meeting. And then the topper! He wants to come and spend the Fourth of July weekend with me. The whole weekend! How about that!"

"How about that! Well, plan something nice and I'll join you if I can. Oh shit! The bacon's burning and the eggs are going to be like hippopotamus hide."

They dined handsomely on burnt bacon and eggs and peanut butter sandwiches and canned peaches, talking nonstop, catching up on the recent past. And it was only after his third cup of coffee that Frank finally asked her, "Well, Dasha, where do we go from here? Do we get married?"

"I don't know." She furrowed her brow.

"Do we move in together?"

"I don't know that, either. It's all too new, too soon. I expect it sounds funny, darling, but I have never in my life been truly on my own. And I think I owe myself this time to see what it's like. At least for a while. I want to see how I manage. From the day I was born I've been dependent on men. I've lived in their shadows. First my father, then Alex, then Jordan. Then after a while, Jordan began living in my shadow, which wasn't much good either. But then I became dependent on you.

"What I'm trying to say is, I'd like to reach some arrangement that's . . . oh, I don't know, more honest, more equitable than anything I've had before. Maybe I'm being naive, but I think something better is possible between men and women. At least I hope so. A real partnership, a genuine balance. I want your love. My God, I want your love! But I want my independence, too, if that's not a contradiction in terms. And as you say, who can tell how either of us will see ourselves a few years hence? What or who it is we'll want. I think for me it'll be you. I think it will always be you but—who can say? So there we are. . . . " She spread her palms out in an uncertain gesture. "The future's as treacherous as ever."

"Not treacherous, darling. Promising. Full of hope. Of different possibilities. And meanwhile, what does it matter"—he buried his lips in her open palm, then held it against his cheek—"as long as we have the present. And for the present," he asked, "do you promise to be my lover?"

"Absolutely!"

"And my confidante?"

"If you'll be mine."

"And my lawyer?"

"Good God yes!"

"Then come on, counselor. As your most valuable client, I instruct you to leave the dishes in the sink and go to bed."

"Yes sir!" She gave a mock salute. "Do you know it's almost four and I have a nine o'clock meeting downtown. Which reminds me . . ."

"What, darling?"

"I left my briefcase in your office."

"It'll be waiting for you in the morning." He followed her into the bedroom whistling the theme from *The Bridge on the River Kwai*.

"It'll be waiting . . . and so will I, Dasha. And so will I."

THE BEGINNING